About th

Sharon Kendrick once ~~won~~ competition by describing ~~her~~ an exotic island by a gorgeous and powerful man. Little did she realise that she'd just wandered into her dream job! Today she writes for Mills & Boon, featuring often stubborn but always *to die for* heroes and the women who bring them to their knees. She believes that the best books are those you never want to end. Just like life…

Michelle Smart's love affair with books started when she was a baby, when she would cuddle them in her cot. A voracious reader of all genres, she found her love of romance established when she stumbled across her first Mills & Boon book at the age of twelve. She's been reading (and writing) them ever since. Michelle lives in Northamptonshire with her husband and two young Smarties.

Tara Pammi can't remember a moment when she wasn't lost in a book—especially a romance, which was much more exciting than a mathematics textbook. Years later, Tara's wild imagination and love for the written word revealed what she really wanted to do. Now she pairs Alpha males who think they know everything with strong women who knock that theory *and* them off their feet!

The Greek Mavericks

COLLECTION

July 2019

August 2019

September 2019

October 2019

November 2019

December 2019

Greek Mavericks: Winning the Enigmatic Greek

SHARON KENDRICK

MICHELLE SMART

TARA PAMMI

MILLS & BOON

First Published in Great Britain 2019
By Mills & Boon, an imprint of HarperCollins *Publishers*
1 London Bridge Street, London, SE1 9GF

GREEK MAVERICKS: WINNING THE ENIGMATIC GREEK
© 2019 Harlequin Books S.A.

The Pregnant Kavakos Bride © Sharon Kendrick 2017
The Greek's Pregnant Bride © Harlequin Books S.A. 2015
Bought for Her Innocence © Tara Pammi 2015

Special thanks and acknowledgement are given to Michelle Smart for her contribution to the *Society Weddings* series.

ISBN: 978-0-26-327607-7

1119

MIX
Paper from
responsible sources
FSC® C007454

This book is produced from independently certified FSC™ paper to ensure responsible forest management.

For more information visit: www.harpercollins.co.uk/green

Printed and bound in Spain
by CPI, Barcelona

THE PREGNANT
KAVAKOS BRIDE

SHARON KENDRICK

For the ever-amusing Amelia Tuttiett, who is
a brilliant ceramicist and an inspirational teacher

CHAPTER ONE

SHE WAS EVERYTHING he hated about a woman and she was talking to his brother. Ariston Kavakos grew very still as he stared at her. At curves guaranteed to make a man desire her whether he wanted to or not. And he most definitely did not. Yet his body was stubbornly refusing to obey the dictates of his mind and a powerful shaft of lust arrowed straight to his groin.

Who the hell had invited Keeley Turner?

She was standing close to Pavlos, her blonde hair rippling beneath the overhead lights of the swish London art gallery. She lifted her hand as if to emphasise a point and Ariston found his gaze drawn to the most amazing breasts he had ever seen. He swallowed as he remembered her in a dripping wet bikini with rivulets of water trickling down over her belly as she emerged from the foamy blue waters of the Aegean. She was memory and fantasy all mixed up in one. Something started and never finished. Eight years on and Keeley Turner made him want to look at her and only her, despite the stunning photographs of his private Greek island which dominated the walls of the London gallery.

Was his brother similarly smitten? He hoped not, although it was hard to tell because their body language excluded the rest of the world as they stood deep in conversation. Ariston began to walk across the gallery but if they noticed him approach they chose not to acknowledge it. He felt a flicker of rage, which he quickly cast aside because rage could be counterproductive. He knew that now. Icy calm was far more effective in dealing with difficult situations and it had been the key to his success. The means by which he had dragged his family's ailing company out of the dust and built it anew and gained a reputation of being the man with the Midas touch. The dissolute reign of his father was over and his elder son was now firmly in charge. These days the Kavakos shipping business was the most profitable on the planet and he intended to keep it that way.

His mouth hardened. Which meant more than just dealing with shipbrokers and being up to speed with the state of world politics. It meant keeping an eye on the more gullible members of the family. Because there was a lot of money sloshing around the Kavakos empire and he knew how women acted around money. An early lesson in feminine greed had changed his life for ever and that was why he never took his eye off the ball. His attitude meant that some people considered him controlling, but Ariston preferred to think of himself as a guiding influence—like a captain steering a ship. And in a way, life *was* like being at sea. You steered clear of icebergs for obvious reasons and women were like icebergs. You only ever saw ten per cent of what they were *really* like—the rest was buried deep beneath the self-serving and grasping surface.

His eyes didn't leave the blonde as he walked towards them, knowing that if she was going to be a problem in his brother's life he would deal with it—and quickly. His lips curved into the briefest of smiles. He would have her dispatched before she even realised what was happening.

'Why, Pavlos,' Ariston said softly as he reached them and he noticed that the woman had instantly grown tense. 'This *is* a surprise. I wasn't expecting to see you here so soon after the opening night. Have you developed a late-onset love of photography or are you just homesick for the island on which you were born?'

Pavlos didn't look too happy to be interrupted—but Ariston didn't care. Right then he couldn't think about anything except what was happening inside him. Because, infuriatingly, he seemed to have developed no immunity against the green-eyed temptress he'd last seen when she was eighteen, when she'd thrown herself at him with a hunger which had blown his mind. Her submission had been instant and would have been total if he hadn't put a stop to it. Displaying the sexist double standards for which he had occasionally been accused, he had despised her availability at the same time as he'd been bewitched by it. It had taken all his legendary self-control to push her away and to adjust his clothing but he had done it, though it had left him hard and aching for what had seemed like months afterwards. His mouth tightened because she was nothing but a tramp. A cheap and grasping little tramp.

Like mother, like daughter, he thought grimly—and the last type of woman he wanted his brother getting mixed up with.

'Oh, hi, Ariston,' said Pavlos with the easy manner which made most people surprised when they learned they were brothers. 'That's right, here I am again. I decided to pay a second visit and meet up with an old friend at the same time. You remember Keeley, don't you?'

There was a moment of silence while a pair of bright green eyes were lifted to his and Ariston felt the loud hammer of his heart.

'Of course I remember Keeley,' he said roughly, aware of the irony of his words. Because for him most women *were* forgettable and nothing more than a means to an end. Oh, sometimes he might recall a pair of spectacular breasts or a pert bottom—or if a woman was especially talented with her lips or hands, she might occasionally merit a nostalgic smile. But Keeley Turner had been in a class of her own and he'd never been able to shift her from the corners of his mind. Because she'd been off-limits and forbidden? Or because she had given him a taste of unbelievable sweetness before he'd forced himself to reject her? Ariston didn't know. It was as inexplicable as it was powerful and he found himself studying her with the same intensity as the nearby people peering at the photos which adorned the gallery walls.

Petite yet impossibly curvy, her thick hair hung down her back in a curtain of pale and rippling waves. Her jeans were ordinary and her thin sweater unremarkable yet somehow that didn't seem to matter. With a body like hers she could have worn a piece of sackcloth and still looked like dynamite. The cheap, man-made fabric strained over the lushness of her breasts and the blue denim caressed the curves of her bottom. Her mouth was bare of lipstick and her eyes wore only a lick of mascara as they studied him warily. Hers was not a modern look—yet there was something about Keeley Turner... An indefinable something which touched a sensual core deep inside him and made him want to peel her clothes from her body and ride her until she was screaming his name. But he wanted her gone more than he wanted to bed her—and maybe he should set about accomplishing that right now.

Deliberately excluding her from the conversation, Ariston turned to his brother and summoned up a bland smile. 'I wasn't aware you two were friends.'

'We haven't actually seen each other for years,' said Pavlos. 'Not since that holiday.'

'I suspect that holiday is an event which none of us particularly care to revisit,' said Ariston smoothly, enjoying the sudden rush of colour which had made her cheeks turn a deep shade of pink. 'Yet you've stayed in touch with each other all this time?'

'We're friends on social media,' Pavlos elaborated, with a shrug. 'You know how it is.'

'Actually, I don't. You know my views on social media and none of them are positive.' Ariston made no attempt to hide his frosty disapproval. 'I need to talk to you, Pavlos. Alone,' he added.

Pavlos frowned. 'When?'

'Now.'

'But I've only just met up with Keeley. Can't it wait?'

'I'm afraid it can't.' He saw Pavlos shoot her an apologetic glance as if to apologise for his brother's bullish behaviour but social niceties didn't bother him. He'd worked hard for most of his life to ensure that Pavlos was kept away from the kind of scandals which had once engulfed their family. He'd been determined he wouldn't go the same sorry way as their father. He'd made sure that he'd attended a good boarding school in England and a university in Switzerland, and he had carefully influenced his choice of friends—and girlfriends. And this pretty little tramp in her cheap dress and come-to-bed eyes was about to learn that his baby brother was strictly off-limits. 'It's business,' he added firmly.

'Not more trouble in the Gulf?'

'Something like that,' Ariston agreed, irritated at his brother's attitude and wondering why he'd forgotten you didn't talk family business in front of strangers. 'We can use one of the offices here at the gallery—they're very accommodating,' he added smoothly. 'The owner is a friend of mine.'

'But Keeley—'

'Oh, don't worry about Keeley. I'm sure she has the imagination to take care of herself. There's plenty for her to look at.' Ariston turned to give her a hard version of a smile, noticing that her knuckles had suddenly whitened as she clutched her thin shawl. For the first time he spoke directly to her, dropping his voice to a silken murmur which his business rivals would have recognised as being a tone you didn't mess with. 'And plenty of men hanging around who would be all too happy to take my brother's place. In fact, I can see a couple watching you right now. I'm sure you could have a lot of fun with them, Keeley. You really mustn't let us keep you any longer.'

Keeley felt her face freeze as Ariston spoke to her, wishing she could come up with a suitably crushing response to throw at the powerful Greek who was looking at her as if she was a stain on the pale floorboards and talking to her as if she was some kind of hooker. But the truth was that she didn't *trust* herself to speak—afraid that her words would come out as meaningless babble. Because that was the effect he had on her. The effect he had on all women. Even when he was talking to them—or should she say *at* them?—with utter contempt in his eyes, he could reduce them to a level of longing which wasn't like the stuff you felt around most men. He could make you have fantasies about him, even though he exuded nothing but darkness.

She'd seen the way her own mother had looked at him. She could see the other women in the gallery watching him now—their gazes hungry but wary—as if they were observing a different type of species and weren't sure how to handle him. As if they realised they should stay well away but were itching to touch him all the same. And she could hardly judge them for that, could she? Because hadn't *she* flung herself at him? Pressed her body hard against his and longed for him to take away the aching deep inside her. Behaved like a cheap little fool by misinterpreting a simple gesture on his part and managing to make a bad situation even worse.

The last time she'd seen him her life had pretty much imploded and eight years later she was still dealing with the fallout. Keeley's mouth tightened. Because she'd come through far too much to let the arrogant billionaire make her feel bad about herself. She suspected that the mocking challenge sparking from his blue eyes was intended to make her excuse herself and disappear, but she wasn't going to do that. A quiet rebellion began to build inside her. Did he really think he had the power to kick her out of this public gallery, as once he had kicked her off his private island?

'I wasn't planning on going anywhere,' she said, seeing his eyes darken with anger. 'I'm quite happy looking at photographs of Lasia. I'd forgotten just what a beautiful island it was and I can certainly keep myself occupied until you get back.' She smiled. 'I'll wait here for you, Pavlos. Take as long as you like.'

It clearly wasn't the response Ariston wanted and she saw the irritation which hardened his beautiful features.

'As you wish,' he said tightly. 'Though I cannot guarantee how long we'll be.'

She met his cold blue stare with a careless smile. 'Don't worry about it. I'm not in any hurry.'

He shrugged. 'Very well. Come, Pavlos.'

He began to walk away with his brother by his side and, although she told herself to look away, Keeley could do nothing but stand and stare, just like everyone else in the gallery.

She'd forgotten how tall and rugged he was because she had *forced* herself to forget—to purge her memory of a sensuality which had affected her like no other. But now it was all coming back. The olive skin and tendrils of hair which brushed so blackly against his shirt collar. Yet she thought he seemed uncomfortable in the exquisite grey suit he wore. His muscular body looked constrained—as if he was more at home wearing the sawn-off denims he'd worn on Lasia. The ones which had emphasised his powerful thighs as he'd dived deep into the sapphire waters surrounding his island home. And it suddenly occurred to her that it didn't matter what he wore or what he said because nothing had changed. Not really. You saw him and you wanted him, it was as simple as that. She thought how cruel life could be—as if she needed any reminding—that the only man she'd ever desired was someone who made no secret about despising her.

With an effort, she tore her gaze away and forced herself to focus on a photograph which showed the island which had been in the Kavakos family for generations. Lasia was known as the paradise of the Cyclades with good reason and Keeley had felt as if she'd tumbled into paradise the moment she'd first set foot on its silvery sands. She had explored its surprisingly lush interior with delight until her mother's startling fall from grace had led to their visit being cut brutally short. She would never forget the hordes of press and the flash of cameras in their faces as they'd alighted from the boat which had taken them back to Piraeus. Or the screaming headlines when they'd arrived back in England—

and the cringe-making interviews her mother had given afterwards, which had only made matters worse. Keeley had been tainted by the scandal—an unwilling victim of circumstances beyond her control—and the knock-on effect had continued to this day.

Wasn't it that which had made her come here this afternoon—to meet up with Pavlos and remind herself of the beauty of the place? As if by doing that she could draw a line under the past and have some kind of closure? She'd hoped she might be able to eradicate some of the awful memories and replace them with better ones. She'd seen a picture of Ariston in the paper, attending the opening night, with some gorgeous redhead clinging like a vine to his arm. She certainly hadn't expected him to show up here today. Would she have come if she had known?

Of course she wouldn't. She wouldn't have set foot within a million miles of the place.

'Keeley?'

She turned around to find that Pavlos was back—with Ariston standing slightly behind him, not bothering to disguise the triumph curving his lips as his gaze clashed with hers.

'Hi,' she said, aware that the blue burn of his eyes was making her skin grow hot. 'You weren't long.'

A look of regret passed over Pavlos's face and somehow Keeley knew what was coming.

'No. I know I wasn't. Look, I'm afraid I'm going to have to bail out, Keeley,' he said. 'And take a rain check. Ariston needs me to fly out to the Middle East and take care of a ship.'

'What, now?' questioned Keeley, before she could stop herself.

'This very second,' put in Ariston silkily before adding, 'Should he have checked with you first?'

Pavlos bent to brush a brief kiss over each of her cheeks before giving her a quick smile. 'I'll message you later. Okay?'

'Sure.' She stood and watched him leave, aware that Ariston was still standing behind her but not trusting herself even to look at him. Instead, she tried very hard to concentrate on the photo she'd been studying—a sheltered bay where you could just make out shapes of giant turtles swimming in the crystal-clear waters. Perhaps he might just take the hint and go away. Leave her alone so that she could get to work on forgetting him all over again.

'I can't quite work out whether you are completely oblivious to my presence,' he said, in his dark, accented voice, 'or whether you just get a kick out of ignoring me.'

He had moved closer to stand beside her and Keeley lifted her gaze to find herself caught in that piercing sapphire stare and the resulting rush of blood went straight to her head. And her breasts. She could feel them become heavy and aching as the slow beat of her blood engorged them. Her mouth dried. How did he *do* that? Her fingers had grown numb and she was feeling almost dizzy but somehow she managed to compose a cool sentence. 'Why, do women always notice you whenever you walk into a room?'

'What do you think?'

And it was then that Keeley realised that she didn't have to play this game. Or *any* game. He was nothing to her. Nothing. *So stop acting like he's got some kind of power over you.* Yes, she'd once made a stupid mistake—but so what? It was a long time ago. She'd been young and stupid and she'd paid her dues—not to him, but to the universe—and *she didn't owe him anything.* Not even politeness.

'Honestly?' She gave a short laugh. 'I think you're unbelievably rude and arrogant, as well as having the most over-inflated ego of any man I've ever met.'

He raised his brows. 'And I imagine you must have met quite a few in your time.'

'Nowhere near the amount of women *you* must have notched up, if the papers are to be believed.'

'I don't deny it—but if you try to play the numbers game I'm afraid you'll never win.' His eyes glittered. 'Didn't anyone ever tell you that the rules for men and the rules for women are very different, *koukla mou*?'

'Only in the outdated universe you seem to occupy.'

He gave a careless shrug. 'It may not be fair but I'm afraid it's a fact of life. And men are allowed to behave in a way which would be disapproved of in a woman.'

His voice had dipped into a velvety caress and it was having precisely the wrong effect on her. Keeley could feel a hot flush of colour flooding into her cheeks as she made to move away.

'Let me pass, please,' she said, trying to keep her voice steady. 'I don't have to stand here and listen to this kind of Neanderthal…*rubbish*.'

'No, you're right. You don't.' He placed a restraining hand on her forearm. 'But before you go, maybe this is the ideal opportunity to get a few things straight between us.'

'What kind of things?'

'I think you know what I'm talking about, Keeley.'

'I'm afraid you've lost me.' She shrugged. 'Mind-reading was never one of my talents.'

His gaze hardened. 'Then let me give it to you in words of one syllable, just so there can be no misunderstanding.' There was a pause. 'Just stay away from my brother, okay?'

She stared at him in disbelief. 'Excuse me?'

'You heard. Leave him alone. Find someone else to dig your beautiful claws into—I'm sure there must be plenty of takers.'

His hand was still on her arm and to the outside world it must have looked like an affectionate gesture between two people who'd just bumped into one another, but to Keeley it felt nothing like that. She could feel the imprint of his fingers through her sweater and it was almost as if he were branding her with his touch—as if he were setting her skin on fire. Angrily, she shook herself free. 'I can't believe you have the nerve to come out and say something like that.'

'Why not? I have his best interests at heart.'

'You mean you regularly go around warning off Pavlos's friends?'

'Up until now I haven't felt the need to do more than keep a watchful eye on them but today I do. Funny that.' He gave a mirthless smile. 'I have no idea of your success rate with men, though I imagine it must be high.

But I feel I'd better crush any burgeoning hopes you may have by telling you that Pavlos already has a girlfriend. A beautiful, decent woman he cares for very much and wedding bells are in the air.' His eyes glittered. 'So I wouldn't bother wasting any more time on him if I were you.'

It struck Keeley again how *controlling* he was. Even now. As if all he had to do was to snap his fingers and everyone would just jump to attention. 'And does he have any say in the matter?' she demanded. 'Have you already chosen the engagement ring? Decided where the wedding is going to be and how many bridesmaids?'

'Just stay away from him, Keeley,' he snapped. 'Understand?'

The irony was that Keeley had absolutely no romantic leanings towards Pavlos Kavakos and never had done. They'd once been close, yes—but in a purely platonic way and she hadn't seen him in years. Their current friendship, if you could call it that, extended no further than her pressing the occasional 'like' button or smiley face whenever he posted a photo of himself with a crowd of beautiful young things revelling in the sunshine. Meeting him today had been comforting because she realised he didn't care what had happened in the past, but she was aware that they moved in completely different worlds which never collided. He was rich and she was not. She didn't know or care that he had a girlfriend, but hearing Ariston's imperious order was like a red rag to a bull.

'Nobody tells me what to do,' she said quietly. 'Not you. Not anyone. You can't move people around like pawns. I'll see who I want to see—and you can't do a thing to stop me. If Pavlos wants to get in touch, I'm not going to turn him away just because *you* say so. Understand?'

She saw the disbelief on his face which was quickly followed by anger, as if nobody ever dared defy him so openly, and she tried to ignore the sudden sense of foreboding which made her body grow even more tense. But she'd said her piece and now she needed to get away. Get away quickly before she started thinking about how it had felt to have him touch her.

She turned away and walked straight out of the gallery, not noticing that her cream shawl had slipped from her nerveless fingers. All she was aware of was the burn of Ariston's eyes on her back, which made each step feel like a slow walk to the gallows. The glass elevator arrived almost immediately but Keeley was shaking as it zoomed her down to ground level and her forehead was wet with sweat as she stepped out onto the busy London pavement.

CHAPTER TWO

THE JOURNEY BACK to her home in New Malden passed in a blur as Keeley kept remembering the way Ariston had spoken to her—with a contempt he'd made no attempt to disguise. But that hadn't stopped her breasts from tightening beneath his arrogant scrutiny, had it? Nor that stupid yearning from whispering over her skin every time she'd looked into the blue blaze of his eyes. And now she was going to have to start forgetting him all over again.

A sudden spring shower emptied itself on her head as she emerged from the train station. The April weather was notoriously unpredictable but she was ill-prepared for the rain and hadn't packed an umbrella. By the time she let herself into her tiny bedsit she was dripping wet and cold and her fingers were trembling as she shut the door. But instead of doing the sensible thing of stripping off her clothes and boiling the kettle to make tea, she sank into the nearest chair, not caring that her clothes were damp and getting all crumpled. She stared out of the window but the rods of rain spattering onto the rooftops barely registered. Suddenly she was no longer sitting shivering in a small and unremarkable corner of London. Her mind was playing tricks on her and all she could see was a wide silver beach with beautiful mountains rising up in the distance. A paradise of a place. Lasia.

Keeley swallowed, unprepared for the sudden rush of memory which made the past seem so vivid. She remembered her surprise at finding herself on Lasia—a private island owned by the powerful Kavakos family, with whom she'd had no connection. She'd been staying on nearby Andros with her mother who had spent the holiday complaining about her recent divorce from Keeley's father and washing her woes away with too many glasses of *retsina*.

But Ariston's own father had been one of those men who were dazzled by celebrity—even B-list celebrity—and when he'd heard that the actress and her teenage daughter were so close, had insisted they join him on his exclusive island home to continue their holiday. Keeley had been reluctant to gatecrash someone else's house party but her mother had been overjoyed at the free upgrade, her social antennae quivering in the presence of so many rich and powerful men. She had layered on extra layers of 'war paint' and crammed her body into a bikini which was much too brief for a woman her age.

But Keeley had wanted none of the party scene because it bored her. Despite her relatively tender years, she'd had her fill of the decadent parties her mother had dragged her to since she'd been old enough to walk. At eighteen, she just tried to stay in the background because that was where she felt safest. Over the years her

mother's sustained girlishness had contributed to her becoming an out and out tomboy, despite her very bother-
some and very feminine curves. She remembered being
overjoyed to meet the sporty Pavlos, with whom she'd
hit it off immediately. The Greek teenager had taught
her how to snorkel in the crystal bays and taken her
hiking in the blue-green mountains. Physical attraction
hadn't come into it because, like many children brought
up by a licentious parent, Keeley had been something
of a prude. She'd never felt a single whisper of desire
and the thought of sex had been mildly disgusting. She
and Pavlos had been like brother and sister—growing
brown as berries as they explored the island paradise
which had felt like their own miniature kingdom.

But then one morning his older brother Ariston had
arrived in a silvery-white boat, looking like some kind
of god at its helm, with his tousled black hair, tawny
skin and eyes which matched the colour of the dark sea.
Keeley remembered watching him from the beach, her
heart crashing in an unfamiliar way. She remembered
her mouth growing dry as he jumped onto the sand, the
fine silver grains spraying up around his bronzed calves
like Christmas glitter. Later, she'd been introduced to
him but had remained so self-conscious in his presence that she'd barely been able to look him in the eye.
Not so all the other women at the house party. She'd
cringed at the way her mother had flirted with him—
even asking him to rub suncream into her shoulders.
Keeley remembered his barely perceptible shudder as
he delegated the task to a female member of staff, and
her mother's pout when he did so.

And then had come the night of the party—the impressive party to which the Greek Defence Minister had been invited. Keeley remembered the febrile atmosphere and Ariston's disapproving face as people started getting more and more drunk. Remembered wondering where her mother had disappeared to—only to discover that she'd been caught making out with the minister's driver, her blonde head bobbing up and down on the back seat of the official car as she administered oral sex to a man half her age. Someone had even filmed them doing it. And that was when all hell had broken loose.

Keeley had fled down to the beach, too choked with shame to be able to face anyone, too scared to read the disgust in their expressions and wanting nothing but to be left alone. But Ariston had come after her and had found her crying. His words had been surprisingly soft. Almost gentle. He'd put his arms around her, and it had felt like heaven. Was it because her mother never showed physical affection and her father had been too old to pick her up when she was little which had caused Keeley to misconstrue what was happening, so she mistook comfort for something else? Was that why the desire which had been absent from her life now shot through her like a flame, making her behave in a way she'd never behaved before?

It had been so powerful, that feeling. Like a primitive hunger which *had* to be fed. Pressing her body against Ariston's, she'd risen up on tiptoe as her trembling mouth sought his. After a moment he had responded and that response had been everything she could have dreamed of. For a few minutes the feeling had intensified as his lips had pressed down urgently against hers. She'd felt his tongue nudging against her mouth and she'd opened her mouth in silent invitation. And then his fingers had been on her quivering breasts, impatiently fingering her nipples into peaking points before guiding her hand towards his trousers. There had been no shyness on her part, just a glorious realisation of the power of her own sexuality—and his. She remembered the ragged groan he'd made as she'd touched him there. The way she'd marvelled at the hard ridge pushing against his trousers as, greedily, she had run her fingertips over it. Passion had swamped shyness and she'd been so consumed by it that she suspected she would have let him do whatever he wanted, right there and then on the silvery sand—until suddenly he had thrust her away from him with a look on his shadowed face which she would remember as long as she lived.

'You little...*tramp*,' he'd said, his voice shaking with rage and disgust. 'Like mother, like daughter. Two filthy little tramps.'

She'd never realised until that moment how badly rejection could hurt. Just like she hadn't realised how someone could make you feel so *cheap*. She remembered the shame which flooded through her as she vowed never to put herself in that position again. She would never allow herself to be rejected again. But her own pain had been quickly superseded by what had happened when they'd returned to England and her mother's lifestyle had finally caught up with her—and in one way and another they'd been paying the price ever since.

She pushed the bitter memories away because her

hair was still damp and she had now started to shiver so Keeley forced herself to get up and to go into the cramped bathroom, where the miserable jet of tepid water trickling from the shower did little to warm her chilled skin. But the brisk rub of a rough towel helped and so did the big mug of tea she made herself afterwards. She'd just put on her uniform when there was a knock on the door and she frowned. Her social circle was tiny because of the hours she worked, but even so she didn't often invite people here. She didn't want people coming in and judging her. Wondering how the only daughter of a wealthy man and an actress whose face had graced cinema screens in a series of low-budget vampire movies should have ended up living in such drastically reduced circumstances.

A louder knock sounded and she pulled open the door, her curiosity dying on her lips when she saw who was standing there. Her heart pounded in her chest as she looked into the blaze of Ariston's eyes and she gripped the door handle, hard. His black hair was wet and plastered to his head and his coat was spattered with raindrops. She knew she should tell him to get lost before slamming the door shut in his face but the powerful impact of his presence made her hesitate just as the siren tug of her body betrayed her yet again. Because he was just so damned *gorgeous*…with his muscular physique and that classical Greek face with the tiny bump midway down his nose.

'What are you doing here?' she said coldly. 'Did you think of a few more insults you'd forgotten to ram home?'

His lips curved into an odd kind of smile. 'I think you left…this.'

She stared down at the cream shawl he was holding, her heart automatically contracting. It was an old wrap which had belonged to her mother—a soft, cashmere drift of a thing embroidered with tiny pink flowers and green leaves. These days it was faded and worn, but it reminded her of the woman her mother used to be and a lump rose in her throat as she lifted her gaze to his.

'How did you find out where I live?' she questioned gruffly.

'It wasn't difficult. You signed the visitors' book at the gallery, remember?'

'But you didn't have to bring it yourself. Couldn't you have asked one of your minions to do it?'

'I could. But there are some things I prefer not to delegate.' He met her eyes. 'And besides, I don't think we've quite finished our conversation, do you?'

She supposed they hadn't and that somehow there seemed to be a lot which had been left unsaid. And maybe it was better that way. Yet something was stopping her from closing the door on him. She told herself he had gone out of his way to bring her mum's shawl back to her and he *was* very wet. Did he sense her hesitation? Was that why he took a step forward?

'So aren't you going to ask me inside?' he persisted softly.

'Suit yourself,' she said carelessly, but her heart was thumping like a crazy thing as she walked back into the little bedsit and heard him shut the door to follow her. And when she turned round and saw him standing there—so powerful and masculine—her breasts grew hot and heavy with desire. Why him? she thought despairingly. Why should Ariston Kavakos be the only man who should make her feel so insanely *alive*? Her smile was tight. 'Though if you're going to try to justify your ridiculously controlling behaviour, I wouldn't bother.'

'And what's that supposed to mean?' he questioned silkily.

'It means that you turn up and suddenly send your brother away to sea—just to get him away from me. Isn't that a little desperate?'

His lips hardened. 'Like I told you. He already has a girlfriend. A young woman of Greek origin who has just qualified as a doctor and is light years away from someone like you. And if you must know, the business in the Gulf is both urgent and legitimate—you flatter yourself if you think I'd manufacture some kind of catastrophe just to remove him from your company. But I'm not going to lie. I can't deny I'm happy he's gone.'

She felt the sting of his words yet she could almost understand his concern—even though it was misplaced—because the contrast between her and Pavlos's girlfriend couldn't have been greater. She could imagine how Ariston must see it, in that simplistic and chauvinistic way of his. The qualified professional doctor versus someone with barely an exam to her name. If he'd gone about it differently—if he'd asked her nicely—then Keeley might have done what he wanted her to do. She might have given him her word that she'd never see Pavlos again—which was probably true in any case. But he wasn't asking, was he? He was *telling*. And it wasn't so much the contempt in his eyes which was making her angry—it was the total lack of respect. As if she meant nothing. As if her feelings counted for nothing. As if she was to spend the rest of her life paying for one youthful mistake. She tilted her chin upwards. 'If you think you can tell me what to do, then you're wrong,' she said. 'Very, very wrong.'

Ariston stiffened because her defiance was turning him on and that was the last thing he wanted. He'd come here ostensibly to return the shawl she'd left behind and yet part of him had *wanted* to see her again, even though he'd convinced himself he was only looking out for his brother's welfare. In the car he had briefly buried his nose in the soft cashmere and smelt Keeley's faint and flowery perfume. He'd wondered whether she had deliberately left it behind to get his brother to come running after her when he arrived back in England. Had that been her not so subtle plan? Did she sense a softness in his younger sibling and a susceptibility to her blonde sexiness which could override what seemed to be a perfect relationship with his long-term girlfriend?

He remembered how close she and Pavlos had been on that holiday, how they used to run around together all the time. People said the past had powerful and sentimental tentacles and she'd known his brother when he was young and impressionable. Long before he'd reached the age of twenty-five and come into the massive trust fund which had changed people's attitude towards him, because wealth always did. Mightn't Pavlos read more into his date with the sexy blonde than there really was and forget the safe and settled future which was carefully laid out for him? What if Keeley Turner realised that a fortune was there for the taking if she just went about it the right way?

He glanced around her home, more surprised by her environment than he could remember being surprised by anything in a long time. Because this wasn't just a low standard of living—this was *breadline* living. He'd imagined peacock feathers and glittery necklaces draped over mirrors. Walls dripping with old photos depicting her mother's rather tawdry fame, but there was nothing other than neatness and an almost bland utilitarianism. The most overriding feature was one of *cleanliness*. His mouth hardened. Was that simply a clever ploy to illustrate what a good little homemaker she could be, if only some big and powerful man would take her away from all this and give her the opportunity?

He'd been doing his best not to stare at her because staring only increased his desire and a man could think more clearly when his blood wasn't heated by lust. But now he looked at her dispassionately and for the first time he registered that she was wearing some kind of *uniform*. He frowned. Surely she wasn't a nurse? He took in a shapeless navy dress edged by a paler blue piping and then noticed a small badge depicting a bright, cartoon sun and what looked like a chicken drumstick underneath the words 'Super Save'. No. His mouth twisted. Definitely not a nurse.

'You work in a shop?' he demanded.

He could see the indecision which fretworked her

brow, before she gave him another defiant tilt of her chin which made her lips look utterly kissable.

'Yes, I work in a shop,' she said.

'Why?'

'Why not?' she questioned angrily. 'Somebody has to. How else do you think all the shelves get stacked with new produce? Or, let me guess—you never actually *do* your own shopping?'

'You're a shelf-stacker?' he asked incredulously.

Keeley drew in a deep breath. If it had been anyone else she might have blurted out the truth about her mother and all the other dark stuff which had led her to having to leave so many jobs that, in the end, Super Save supermarket had been her unlikely saviour. She might have explained that she was doing her best to make up for all those lost, gypsy-like years by studying hard whenever she had a spare moment and was doing an online course in bookkeeping and business studies. She might even have plunged the very depths of her own despair and conveyed the sense of hopelessness she felt when she visited her mother every week. When she saw how the once vibrant features had become an unmoving mask while those china-blue eyes stared unseeingly into the distance. When, no matter how many times she prayed for a different outcome, her mother failed to recognise the young woman she had given birth to.

Briefly Keeley closed her eyes as she remembered the awkward conversation she'd had last week with the care-home manager. How she'd been informed that costs were spiralling and they were going to have to put the fees up and that there was only so much that the welfare state could do. And when she'd tried to protest about her mum being moved to that horrible great cavern of a place which was not only cheaper but miles away, she had been met with a shrugging response and been told that nobody could argue with economics.

But why imagine that Ariston Kavakos would have anything other than a cold and unfeeling heart? As if he would even *care* about her problems. The controlling billionaire clearly wanted to think the worst about her and she doubted whether coming out with her own particular sob story would change his mind. Suddenly she felt sorry for Pavlos. How awful to have a brother who was so determined to orchestrate your life that you weren't allowed the personal freedom to make your own friends. Why, the sexy Greek billionaire standing in front of her was nothing more than a raging megalomaniac!

'Yes, I'm a shelf-stacker,' she said quietly. 'Do you have a problem with that?'

Ariston wanted to say that the only problem he had was with *her*. With her inherent sensuality, which managed to transcend even the ugly outfit she was wearing. Or maybe it was because he'd seen her in a swimsuit, with the sopping wet fabric clinging to every feminine curve. Maybe it was because he knew what a killer body lay beneath the oversized uniform which was making him aroused. Yet it was a shock to discover just how humble her circumstances were. As a gold-digger she clearly wasn't as effective as her mother had been or she wouldn't have ended up in a crummy apartment, working unsociable hours in a supermarket.

In his mind he began to do rapid calculations. She was obviously broke and therefore easy to manipulate, but he also sensed that she presented an unknown kind of danger. If it hadn't been for Pavlos he would have fought the infuriating desire to kiss her and just walked away, consigning her to history. He would have phoned the sizzling supermodel he'd taken to the photographic exhibition and demanded she drop everything. Especially her panties. He swallowed, because the equally infuriating reality was that the model seemed instantly forgettable when he compared her to Keeley Turner in her unflattering uniform. Was it the fire spitting from her green eyes and the indignant tremble of those lips which made him want to dominate and subdue her? Or because he wanted to protect his brother from someone like her? He'd sent Pavlos off to sea to deal with a crew in revolt—but as soon as the situation was resolved he would return. And who was to say what the two of them might get up to if his back was turned? He couldn't keep them apart—no matter how powerful he was. Mightn't her ethereal blonde beauty tempt his brother into straying, despite the lovely young woman waiting for him in Melbourne?

Suddenly his thoughts took on a completely different direction as a solution came out of nowhere. A solution of such satisfying simplicity that it almost took his breath away. Because weren't men territorial above all else—especially Kavakos men? He and Pavlos hadn't been brought up to share—not their toys, nor their thoughts, and certainly not their women. The age difference between them had guaranteed that just as much as the bleak and unsettled circumstances of their child-hood. So what if *he* seduced her before his brother got a chance? Pavlos certainly wouldn't be interested in one of *his* cast-offs—so wouldn't that effectively remove her from his brother's life for good?

Ariston swallowed. And sex might succeed in erad-icating her from *his* mind, once and for all. Because hadn't she been like a low-grade fever all these years—a fever which still flared up from time to time? She was the only woman he'd ever kissed and not had sex with and perhaps it was his need for perfection and comple-tion which demanded he remedy that aching omission.

He looked around her shabby home. At the thin cur-tains at the window which looked out over a rainy street and the threadbare rug on the floor. And suddenly he realised it could be easy. It always was with women, when you brought up the subject of cash. His mouth hardened with bitter recall as he remembered the mon-etary transaction which had defined and condemned him when he had been nothing more than a boy. 'Do you need money?' he questioned softly. 'I rather think you do, *koukla mou.*'

'You're offering me money to stay away from your brother? Seriously?' She stared at him. 'Isn't that what's known as blackmail?'

'Actually, I'm offering you money to come and work for me. More money than you could have ever dreamed of.'

'You mean you have your own supermarket?' she questioned sarcastically. 'And need your very own shelf-stacker?'

He very nearly smiled but forced himself to clamp his lips together before returning her gaze. 'I haven't been tempted into retail as of yet,' he said drily. 'But I have my own island, on which I occasionally entertain. In fact, I'm flying back there tomorrow to prepare for a house party.'

'How nice for you. But I don't see what that has to do with me. Am I supposed to congratulate you on having so many friends—even though it's difficult to believe you actually have *any*?'

A pulse began to beat insistently at his temple because Ariston wasn't used to such a feisty and insolent reaction—and never from a woman. Yet it made him want to pull her into his arms and crush his lips down hard against hers. It made him want to push her up against the wall and have her moaning with pleasure as he slid his fingers inside her panties. He swallowed. 'I'm telling you because during busy times on the island, there is always work available for the right person.'

'And you think I'm the right person?'

'Well, let's not push credibility too far.' His lips twisted as he looked around. 'But you're clearly short of money.'

'I'm sure most people are compared to you.'

'We're talking about your circumstances, Keeley, not mine. And this apartment of yours is surprisingly *humble*.'

Keeley didn't deny it. How could she? 'And?'

'And I'm curious. How did that happen? How did you get from being flown around Europe on private jets to… this? Your mother must have made a stack of money from her various *liaisons* with wealthy men and her habit of giving tell-all interviews to the press. Doesn't she help fund her daughter's lifestyle?'

Keeley stared him out, thinking how very wrong he'd got it but she wasn't going to tell him. Why should she? Some things were just too painful to recount, especially to a cold and uncaring man like him. 'That's none of your business,' she snapped.

A calculating look entered his eyes. 'Well, whatever it is you're doing—it clearly isn't working. So how about earning yourself a bonus?' he continued softly. 'A big, fat bonus which could catapult you out of the poverty trap?'

She looked at him suspiciously, trying to dampen down the automatic spring of hope in her heart. 'Doing what?'

He shrugged. 'Your home is surprisingly clean and tidy, so I assume you're capable of doing housework. Just as I assume you're able to follow simple instructions and help around the kitchen.'

'And you trust me enough to employ me?'

'I don't know. Can I?' His gaze seared into her. 'I imagine the reason for your relative poverty is probably because you're unreliable and easily bored by the mundane—and that maybe things didn't fall into your lap as effortlessly as you thought they might. Am I right, Keeley? Did you discover that you weren't as successful a freeloader as your mother?'

'Go to hell,' she snapped.

'But I suspect that if the price was right you would be prepared to knuckle down,' he added thoughtfully.

'So how about if I offered you a month as a temporary domestic on my Greek estate—and the opportunity to earn yourself the kind of money which could transform your life?'

Her heart was beating very hard. 'And why would you do that?' she croaked.

'You know why.' His voice grew harsh. 'I don't want you in London when Pavlos returns. He's due to fly to Melbourne in two weeks' time, hopefully with a diamond ring tucked inside his pocket—and after that, I don't care what you do. Let's just call it an insurance policy, shall we? I'm prepared to pay a big premium to keep you out of my brother's life.'

His disapproval washed over her like dirty water and Keeley wanted to tell him exactly what he could do with his offer, yet she couldn't ignore the nagging voice in her head which was urging her to be realistic. Could she really afford to turn down the kind of opportunity which would probably never come her way again, just because she loathed the man who was making it?

'Tempted?' he questioned softly.

Oh, she was tempted, all right. Tempted to tell him that she'd never met anyone so charmless and insulting. Keeley felt her skin grow hot as she realised he was offering her a job as some kind of *skivvy*. Someone to get her hands dirty by tidying up after him and his fancy guests. To chop vegetables and change his bed while he cavorted on the silvery beach with whoever his current squeeze was—probably the stunning redhead he'd taken to the gallery opening with him. He was looking down his proud and patrician nose at her and she opened her mouth to say she'd rather starve than accept his offer until she reminded herself of the significant fact she'd been in danger of forgetting. Because it wasn't just herself she had to consider, was it?

She stared down at one of the holes in the carpet as she thought of her mother and the little treats which added to her life, even though she was completely oblivious to them. The weekly manicure and occasional hairdo to primp those thinning curls into some sort of shape, so that in some ways she resembled the woman she had once been. Vivienne Turner didn't *know* that these things were being done for her, but Keeley did. Sometimes she shuddered to imagine what her mother's reaction would have been if she'd been able to look into a crystal ball and see the life she'd been condemned to live. But nobody had a crystal ball, thank goodness. Nobody could see what lay ahead. And when occasionally other patients' relatives or members of staff recognised the shell of the woman who had once been Vivienne Turner, Keeley was proud that her mother looked as good as she possibly could. Because that would have mattered. To her.

So test him, she thought. See what the mighty Ariston Kavakos is putting on the table. See if it's big enough to enable you to endure his company for longer than a minute. 'How much,' she said baldly, 'are you offering me?'

Ariston swallowed down his distaste as he heard the shrewd note which had entered her voice and he realised that Keeley's greed was as transparent as her mother's. His mouth twisted. How he despised her and everything she stood for. Yet his natural revulsion was not enough to destroy his desire for her and his mouth grew dry as he thought about having sex with Keeley Turner. Because it was inconceivable that she would return to Lasia and *not* sleep with him. It would bring about satisfaction and closure—for both of them. The fever in his blood would be removed and afterwards she could be quietly airbrushed from all their lives. She would be rewarded with enough money to satisfy her. She would disappear into the sunset. Most important of all—Pavlos would never see her again.

He smiled as he mentioned a sum of money, expecting her simpering gratitude and instant acceptance, but instead he was met with a look from her green eyes which was almost glacial.

'Double it,' she said coolly.

Ariston's smile died but he could feel the insistent beat of lust intensifying because her attitude made his callous plan a whole lot easier to execute. Every woman could be bought, he remembered bitterly. You just had to negotiate the right price.

'You have a deal,' he said softly.

CHAPTER THREE

LASIA WAS AS beautiful as Keeley remembered it. No. Maybe even more so. Because when you were eighteen you thought that sunny days would never end and beauty would last for ever. You never imagined that life could turn out so different from how you'd imagined. She'd thought the money would last. She'd thought...

No. She gazed out of the car window at the cloudless blue sky. She wasn't going to do that thing. She wasn't going to *look back*. She was here, on this stunning private island, to work for Ariston Kavakos and earn herself a nest egg for her poor, broken mother. Fixing her gaze on the dark blue line of the horizon, she reminded herself to start looking for the positives, not the negatives.

A fancy car had been waiting for her on Lasia's only airstrip—its air-conditioned interior deliciously welcoming because, even though it was still only springtime, the midday sun was intense. During the flight over she'd wondered if any of Ariston's staff might remember her and she was dreading any such recognition. But thankfully the driver was new—well, new to her—and his name was Stelios.

He seemed content to remain silent and Keeley said nothing as the powerful car snaked its way through the mountain roads towards the Kavakos complex on the other side of the island. But although outwardly calm, inside she was quaking for all kinds of reasons. For a start, she'd lost her job at the supermarket. Her manager had reacted with incredulity when she'd asked for a month's unpaid holiday, telling her that she must have taken leave of her senses if she expected *those* kinds of perks. He'd added rather triumphantly that she was in the wrong job, but deep down Keeley had already known that. Because no matter how hard she'd tried, she'd never fitted in. Not there. Not anywhere if she stopped to think about it—and certainly not here, on this private paradise which exuded untold wealth and privilege. Where costly yachts bobbed on the azure sea as carelessly as a baby floated toys in the bathtub. She leaned forward to get a better look as the car rounded the bend and made its slow descent towards the complex she'd last seen when she was eighteen, blinking her eyes in surprise because everything looked so different.

Oh, not Assimenos Bay—that hadn't changed. The natural cove with its silvery sand was as stunning as ever, but the vast house which had once dominated it had gone. The beachside mansion was no more and in its place stood an imposing building which seemed composed mainly of glass. Modern and magnificent, the transparent walls and curved windows reflected back the different hues of sea and sky so that Keeley's first impression was that everything looked so *blue*. As blue as Ariston's eyes, she found herself thinking, before reminding herself furiously that she wasn't here to fantasise about him.

And then, as if she had conjured him up from her restless imagination, she saw the Greek tycoon standing at one of the vast windows on the first floor of the house. Standing watching her—his stance as unmoving as a statue. A ripple of unwilling awareness ran through her body as she stared up at him because even at a distance he dominated everything. Even though she was surrounded by so much natural beauty and the kind of scenery she hadn't seen in a long time it still took a huge effort to drag her gaze away from him. And she mustn't be seen ogling him like some helpless fan-girl. Hadn't she made that mistake once before? And look where that had got her. This was her chance to redeem herself and the only way she could achieve that was by remaining immune to him and his effortless charisma. To show him she no longer wanted him—that ship had sailed—because she wasn't into cruel billionaires who treated you with zero respect.

The car stopped and Stelios opened the door and Keeley could smell lemons and pine and the salty tang of the nearby sea as she stepped onto the sun-baked courtyard.

'Here's Demetra,' said Stelios as a middle-aged woman in a crisp white uniform began walking through the shimmering heat towards them. 'She's the cook—but basically she's in charge! Even Ariston listens when Demetra speaks. She'll show you to your accommodation. You're pretty lucky to be staying here,' he observed. 'All the other staff live in the village.'

'Thank you.' Keeley turned to him in surprise. 'You speak perfect English!'

'Pretty much. I lived in London for a while. Used to drive taxis for a living.' Stelios gave an inscrutable smile. 'Though the boss doesn't like me to publicise it too much.'

No, she'd bet he didn't. A silent but understanding driver would be an asset for a control freak like Ariston, thought Keeley wryly. Someone able to eavesdrop on the conversation of his English-speaking guests should the need arise. Yet she heard the obvious affection in the driver's voice as he referred to his boss and wondered what the autocratic ship-owner had ever done to deserve it, apart from be born with a silver spoon in his mouth. But everyone liked you when you had money, she reminded herself. The world was full of hangers-on who were mesmerised by the lure of wealth. The same hangers-on who would drop you like a hot potato when all that wealth had gone.

She smiled as the cook approached, reminding herself it was important to be accepted by the people she was going to be working with and to show them she wasn't afraid of hard work.

'*Kalispera*, Demetra,' she said, holding out her hand. 'I'm Keeley. Keeley Turner.'

'*Kalispera*,' said the cook, looking pleased. 'You speak Greek?'

'Not really. Only a couple of phrases.' Keeley pulled a face. 'But I'd love to learn more. Do you speak English?'

'*Neh*. Kyrios Kavakos likes all his staff to speak English.' She smiled. 'We help each other. Come. I show you your house.'

Keeley followed the cook down a narrow sandy path leading directly to the beach, until they reached a small whitewashed cottage. She could hear the waves lapping against the shore and could see the moving glimmer of sunlight on the water, but, although she was surrounded by so much beauty, all she could remember was the uproar and the chaos. Because wasn't it over there beside that crop of rocks that Ariston pulled her into his arms for that tantalisingly sweet taste of pleasure, before thrusting her away again? She closed her eyes as goosebumps shivered over her bare arms, despite the heat of the day. How could the memory of something which had happened so long ago still be so vivid?

'You like it?' questioned Demetra, obviously misinterpreting her silence.

'Oh, gosh, yes. It's…beautiful,' said Keeley quickly.

Demetra smiled. '*Oreos*. All Lasia is *oreos*. Come to the house when you are ready and I show you everything.'

After Demetra had gone, Keeley went inside the cottage—leaving the door open so she could hear the waves as she set about exploring her temporary home. It didn't take long to get her bearings because, although it was small and compact, it was still bigger than her home in London. There was a sitting room and a small kitchen, while upstairs was a bedroom with space for little more than a large bed. The bathroom was surprisingly sophisticated and the whole place was simple and clean, with walls painted white and completely bare of decoration. But the light which flooded into every room was incredible—bright and clear and shot with the dancing reflection of the waves. Who needed pictures on the walls when you had that?

Keeley unpacked, showered and changed into shorts and a T-shirt—and was just making her way downstairs when she saw Ariston walking towards her cottage. And try as she might, she could do nothing to prevent the powerful squeeze of her heart and the molten tug deep inside her.

She wanted to turn away. To close her eyes and shut him out…yet she wanted to watch him like the rerun of a favourite TV show. The powerful thrust of his thighs as he walked. The broadness of his shoulders and the bunched muscle of his arms. The way his white T-shirt contrasted with the darkness of his olive skin. Her mouth dried as she noticed the narrow band of skin showing above the low-slung waistband of his faded jeans. Because this was Ariston as she remembered him—not wearing a sophisticated suit which seemed to constrain him, but looking as if he could have just finished work on one of the fishing boats.

He was the most alpha male she'd ever seen but it was vital he didn't guess she thought that way. She was going to have to respond to him indifferently— betraying none of her uneasy emotions whenever he came close. She needed to pretend he was just like any other man—even though he wasn't. Because no other man had ever made her feel this way. She sucked in an unsteady breath as he approached, because the most important thing she needed to remember was that she didn't actually *like* him.

'So. Here you are,' he observed, his blue eyes moving over her with their strange, cold fire.

'Here I am.' Feeling curiously insubstantial, she tugged at the hem of her T-shirt. 'You sound surprised.'

'Maybe I am. Part of me wondered whether you might change your mind at the last minute and not bother coming.'

'Should I have done?' She fixed him with a questioning gaze. 'Would it have been wiser to have dismissed your generous job offer and carried on with my life the way it was, Kyrios Kavakos?'

As she stared at him so fearlessly, her bright green eyes so cat-like and entrancing, Ariston thought about the answers he *could* have given her. If she was someone he cared about he would have told her that, yes, she should have stayed well away from his island and the doomed orbit of a man like him. But the point was that he didn't care. She was a commodity. A woman he intended to seduce and finish what she had started all those years ago. Why warn her to be on her guard against something which was going to bring them both a great deal of pleasure?

And closure, he reminded himself grimly. Because wasn't closure equally important?

He stared at the thick pale hair which hung in a twisted rope over one shoulder, wondering why he found it so difficult to tear his eyes away from her. He'd known women more beautiful. He'd certainly known women more *suitable* than some washed-up ex-party-girl with dollar signs in her eyes. Yet knowing that did nothing to diminish her impact on him. Her lush breasts were pushing against a T-shirt the colour of the lemons which grew in the hills behind the house and a pair of cotton shorts skimmed her shapely hips and legs. She'd slipped her bare feet into a pair of sparkly flip-flops so that she looked unexpectedly carefree—and young—as if she hadn't made the slightest effort to impress him with her appearance and the unexpectedness of this made desire spiral up inside him even more.

'No, I think you're in exactly the right place,' he said evenly. 'So let's go into the house and I'll show you around. I think you'll find things have changed quite a lot since last time you were here.'

'No, honestly. You don't have to do that,' she said. 'Demetra has already offered.'

'But I'm offering now.'

She tilted her head to one side. 'Surely it would be more appropriate if another member of staff took me round? You must have plenty of other things you'd rather be doing—a busy man like you, with a great empire to control.'

'I don't care whether or not it's *appropriate*, Keeley. I happen to be a very hands-on employer.'

'And what you say goes, right?'

'Exactly. So why don't you just accept that, and do what I say?'

He was so ridiculously *masterful*, Keeley thought resentfully. Didn't he realise how out of touch and *outdated* he sounded when he spoke like that? But even though she objected to his overbearing attitude, she couldn't deny its effect on her. It was as if her body had been programmed to respond to his masculine dominance and there was nothing she could do to stop it. Her face was hot as she shut the cottage door and followed him across the beach towards his home, her flip-flops sinking into the soft sand as she scurried to match his pace.

'Any questions you want to ask?' he said, glancing down at her.

There were a million. She wanted to know why—at thirty-five and surely one of the world's most eligible bachelors—he still wasn't married. She wanted to know what made him so hard and cold and proud. She wanted to know if he ever laughed and if so, what made those sensual lips curve with humour. But she bit all those questions back because she had no right to ask them. 'Yes,' she said. 'What made you knock the old house down?'

Ariston felt a pulse flicker at his temple as he lessened his stride so she could keep up with him. How ironic that she should choose a subject which still had the power to make him feel uncomfortable. He remembered the disbelief he'd faced when he'd proposed demolition of the old house, which had been rich in history. How people had thought he was acting out of a sense of misplaced grief after the death of his father. But it had been nothing to do with that. For him it had been a necessary rebirth. Should he tell her that he'd wanted to raze away the past along with those impressive walls? As if believing that those dark memories could be reduced to rubble, just like the bricks. That he'd wanted to forget the house where his mother had played with him until the day she'd walked away—leaving him and Pavlos in the care of their father. Just as he wanted to forget the parties and sickly-sweet stench of marijuana and the women flown in from destinations all over Europe—their given brief to 'entertain' his father and his jaded friends. Why would he tell Keeley Turner something like that—when she and her mother had been exactly those kind of women?

'New broom, new era,' he said, with a hard smile. 'When my father died I decided I needed to make a few changes. To put my own stamp on the place.'

She was staring up at the wide glass structure. 'Well, you've certainly done that.'

Her cooing words sounded speculative—the instinctive reaction of an avaricious woman confronted by affluence—but that didn't quite cancel out the pleasure Ariston got from her praise. Or stop him thinking how much he'd like to hear that soft English voice whispering some very different things in his ear. Was she one of those women who talked during sex? he wondered. Or did she keep quiet until she started to come, gasping out her joyful pleasure into the man's ear? His lips curved into a speculative smile. He couldn't wait to find out.

He gestured for her to precede him though her wiggling bottom made it difficult for him to concentrate on the tour. He showed her the tennis court, the gym, his office and two of the smaller reception rooms—but decided against taking her upstairs to each of the seven en-suite bedrooms or, indeed, his own master suite. His throat tightened. Demetra could do that later.

At last he led her into the main sitting room, which was the focal point of the house, carefully watching her reaction as she was confronted by the sea view which dominated three of the massive glass walls. For a moment she stood there motionless—not appearing to notice the priceless Fabergé eggs which lay on one of the low tables, nor the rare Lysippos statue which he'd bought from under the noses of international dealers in an auction house in New York and which had sealed his reputation as a connoisseur of fine art.

'Wow,' she said indistinctly. 'Who came up with this?'

'I asked the architect to design me something to maximise the views and for each room to flow into the next,' he said. 'I wanted light and space everywhere—so that when I'm working it doesn't seem like being in the office.'

'I can't imagine any office looking like this. It looks...well, it's the most stunning place I've ever seen.' She turned to face him. 'The family business must be doing well.'

'Reassuringly well,' he said blandly.

'You're still building ships?'

He raised his eyebrows. 'My brother didn't tell you?'

'No, Ariston. He didn't tell me. We barely had time to reacquaint ourselves before you dragged him away.'

'Yes, we're still building ships,' he affirmed. 'But we're also making wines and olive oil on the other side of the island, which have become a surprising hit in all kinds of places. These days people seem to value organic goods and Kavakos products are on the shopping list of most of the world's big chefs.' He raised his eyebrows. 'Anything else you want to know?'

She brushed the palms of her hands down over her shorts. 'In England you said you were expecting guests this weekend.'

'That's right. Two of my lawyers are flying in from Athens for lunch tomorrow and there are five people arriving at the weekend for a house party.'

'And are they Greek?'

'International,' he drawled. 'You want to know who they are?'

'Isn't it always polite to know people's names in advance?'

'And handy when you're trying to research how much each is worth?' he offered drily. 'There's Santino Di Piero, the Italian property tycoon who is coming with his English girlfriend, Rachel. There's also a friend of mine from way back—Xenon Diakos who for some reason has decided to bring his secretary. I think her name is Megan.'

'That's four,' she said, determined not to rise to the nasty digs he was making.

'So it is. And Bailey Saunders is the other guest,' he said, as if he'd only just remembered.

'Her name seems familiar.' She hesitated. 'She's the woman you took to the opening night of the photographic exhibition, isn't she?'

'Is that relevant, Keeley?' he questioned silkily. 'Or, indeed, any of your business?'

She shook her head, not knowing why she'd mentioned it, and now she felt stupid—and vulnerable.

Embarrassed by her own curiosity and angry at the unwanted jealousy which was making her skin grow heated, Keeley walked over to the window and stared out unseeingly. Was she going to have to spend days witnessing Ariston making out with a beautiful woman? See them frolicking together in that amazing infinity pool or kissing on the beach in the moonlight? Would she have to change their bedsheets in the morning and see for herself the evidence of their shared passion? A shiver of revulsion shot through her and she prayed it didn't show. Because even if she had to contend with those things—so what? Ariston was nothing to her and she was nothing to him and unless she remembered that, she was going to have a very difficult month ahead of her.

'Of course it's none of my business,' she said stiffly. 'I didn't mean to—'

'Didn't mean to what?' He had walked across the room to stand beside her at the window and she found herself inhaling his subtle citrusy scent. 'Check out whether or not I had a girlfriend? Find out whether or not I was available? Don't worry, Keeley—I'm used to women doing that.'

She struggled to say something conventional. To make some witty remark which might dissolve the sudden tension which had suddenly sprung up between them. To act as if she didn't care or take him to task for his spectacular arrogance. But he was standing so close that she couldn't think of a single word, and even if she could she didn't think she'd be capable of saying it with any degree of conviction. Just like she didn't seem capable of preventing the way he was making her feel—as if her body were no longer her own. As if it was silently responding to things she'd only ever dreamed of.

She looked up into his face to discover that his eyes had become smoky and it was as if he'd read her thoughts because suddenly he lifted his hand to frame her face with his fingers, and he smiled. It wasn't a particularly nice smile and it didn't even reach his eyes but the sensation of his touch sent Keeley's already heightened senses into overdrive. His thumb stroked its way over her bottom lip so that it began to tremble uncontrollably. That was the only thing he was doing and yet it was making her want to melt. He was making her more aroused by the second and surely that must show. Her nipples had hardened into two painful little points and somewhere low in her belly she could feel a distracting and molten ache.

Did he realise that? Was that why his hold on her changed so that instead of cupping her face with his fingers, he was pulling her towards him? Pulling her into his arms as if it were his right to do so. His eyes were blazing as they stared into hers and she could feel the softness of her body moulding perfectly into the hardness of his, as he brought his mouth down on hers.

And Keeley shuddered because this was like no other kiss. It was like every fantasy she'd ever had—and wasn't the truth of it that those fantasies had always involved *him*? He kissed her slow and then he kissed her hard. He kissed her until she was squirming, until she thought she would cry out with pleasure. She could feel the rush of heat and the clamour of frustration and all she wanted was to give into that feeling. To wrap her arms around his neck and let desire take over. Whisper in his ear to have him do whatever he wanted. What she wanted. Have him ease this terrible ache inside her as she suspected only he could.

And then what? Let him take you to his bed even though you know how much he despises you? Even though Bailey Saunders is arriving in a couple of days? Because that was how these people operated. She'd seen for herself the world in which he lived. Easy come, easy go.

It didn't mean anything. *She* didn't mean anything—hadn't he already made that abundantly clear? And for someone with an already shaky sense of self-worth, such an action would be completely insane.

'No!' Keeley jerked away from him, taking a couple of steps back and trying to ignore the silent protest of her body. 'What the *hell* do you think you're doing, Ariston?' she demanded. 'Jumping on me like that!'

His short laugh was tinged with frustration. 'Oh, please,' he drawled. 'Please don't insult my intelligence, *koukla mou*—or your own for that matter. You were—*are*—hot and horny. You wanted me to kiss you and I was more than happy to oblige.'

'I did *not*,' she snapped back.

'Oh, Keeley—why deny the truth? Not the best start, in the circumstances—not when I consider honesty an invaluable asset for all my employees.'

'And surely crossing physical boundaries with your staff is unacceptable behaviour for any employer—have you stopped to consider *that*?'

'Maybe if you stopped looking at me with such blatant invitation,' he said silkily, 'then I might be able to stop responding to you as a man, rather than as a boss.'

'I was not!' she said indignantly.

'Weren't you? Ask yourself that question again, only this time don't lie to yourself.'

Keeley bit her lip. *Had* she been looking at him in invitation? Her heart pounded. Of course she had. And if she was being brutally honest, hadn't she wanted him to kiss her since she'd seen him standing at the windows of his glass mansion, his powerful physique dominating everything around him? Maybe even before that—when he'd come striding across the London gallery towards her and Pavlos with a face like thunder and a body which was tensed and powerful. And she mustn't let herself feel that way. She was here to earn money to help care for her stricken mother—not tangle with a self-confessed chauvinist like Ariston and get her heart broken in the process.

Drawing in a deep breath, she willed herself to at least *look* as if she were in control of her own emotions. 'I can't deny that there's an attraction between us,' she said. 'But that doesn't mean we're going to act on it. Not just because you're my boss and it's inappropriate, but because we don't even like each other.'

'What does liking have to do with it?'

'Are you serious?'

'Totally serious.' He shrugged. 'In my experience, a little hostility always adds a touch of spice. Surely your mama taught you that, Keeley?'

The implied slur piled on yet another layer of hurt

and Keeley wanted to hurl herself at him. To slam her fists angrily against that powerful chest and tell him to keep his opinions to himself because he didn't know what he was talking about. But she didn't trust herself to go near him because to touch him was to want him and she couldn't afford to put herself in that position again. He had asked for honesty, hadn't he? So why not just give it to him, even if it meant swallowing her pride in the process? Why pretend there was no elephant in the room when a whole herd of them were threatening to trample over her?

'I have no intention of getting close to you, Ariston, mainly because you're not the kind of man I like,' she said slowly. 'I came here to earn good money and that's what I intend to do. Actually, it's *all* I intend to do. I am going to work hard and to stay away from you as much as possible. I don't intend putting myself in a position of vulnerability again.' She forced a smile, injecting the requisite note of subservience into her voice, reminding herself to behave like the humble employee she was supposed to be. 'So if you'll excuse me—I'd better go and find out if there's anything Demetra wants me to do in the kitchen.'

CHAPTER FOUR

She was driving him crazy.

Crazy.

Sucking in a lungful of air, Ariston dived beneath the inky waters of a sea just starting to be gilded by the sun coming up over the horizon. It was early. Too early for anyone else to be around. Not even the staff were awake yet and the shutters remained tightly closed in the bedroom windows of Keeley's cottage. And that was a pretty accurate metaphor for the current state of affairs between them, he thought grimly. For a man so utterly confident about his sexual power over women—and with good reason—things with Keeley Turner hadn't quite gone according to plan.

For a while he swam strongly beneath the shadowed surface of the water, trying to rid his body of some of the restless energy which had been building up inside him, but that was easier said than done. He had been sleeping badly, with images of Keeley in various imagined stages of undress haunting his erotic and frustrating dreams. Because she'd meant what she'd said, he was discovering with growing incredulity—and despite the sexual chemistry which sizzled so powerfully between them, she had stubbornly kept him at arm's length. He'd thought at first that her behaviour had been part of some contrived act intended to keep him on his toes. But there had been no relaxing of her attitude towards him. No sudden softening which might have indicated she was weakening. All interaction between them had followed a formal yet highly unsatisfactory path.

She politely enquired whether he would like coffee or bread, or water. She kept her eyes demurely lowered whenever their paths crossed. And no matter how many times he told her it was perfectly acceptable for her to use his Christian name in public, it fell on deaf ears. She was a conundrum, he thought. Was she really immune to the admiring glances she had attracted from his Athens-based lawyers when they had arrived on Lasia for lunch—or was she simply a very clever actress who knew the power of her own beauty? She acted as if she were made of marble, when he knew for a fact that beneath that cool and curvy exterior beat the heart of a passionate woman.

Had he thought that she would have succumbed to him by now? That the memory of the kiss they'd shared on her first day would have her sneaking in his arms to finish off what they'd started?

Of course he had.

That brief kiss had been the most erotic thing to happen to him in a long time but it had led precisely nowhere and although he wasn't a man used to being denied what he really wanted—he was now being forced to experience exactly that. So he'd been a little *distant* with her, intending to indicate his disapproval of women who teased, thinking his impatience would make her realise his patience was wearing thin. He'd anticipated her finding him alone in some quiet moment. He'd imagined her sliding down the zipper of his trousers and touching him where he ached to be touched. He swallowed. Any other woman would have done—and Keeley certainly had history on that score. If things had gone according to plan, by now he should have bedded her and enjoyed several sessions of mind-blowing sex. In fact, by now he probably would have been growing bored with her inevitable adoration and his only dilemma would be working out the best way to tell her it was over.

But it hadn't turned out like that.

She had thrown herself into her work with an enthusiasm which had taken him by surprise. Had she stacked supermarket shelves with such passion? he wondered wryly. Demetra had informed him that the Englishwoman was a joy to have around the kitchen and around the house. A joy? he wondered grimly. He had seen little evidence of it so far.

Was her frosty attitude intended to stoke up his sexual appetite? Because if that was the case then it was working. His blood pressure soared every time she walked onto the terrace in her crisp white uniform. The white cotton dress gave her a look of purity and her blonde hair was scraped neatly back into a no-nonsense chignon, which made her appear the perfect servant. Yet the glitter of fire in her green eyes whenever she was forced to meet his gaze was unmistakable—as if she was daring him to come near her again.

He resurfaced into the bright, golden morning, shaking droplets of water from his head before beginning to swim powerfully towards the shore. It was time to face the day ahead and to play at being host. Four of his guests had arrived but Bailey Saunders was no longer on the guest list. He'd phoned her a couple of days ago and asked for a rain check, and she had agreed. Of course she had. Women always did. He felt a beat of anticipation as he walked across the sand.

Maybe it was time for Keeley Turner to realise that it was pointless resisting the inevitable.

'Will you take the coffee out, Keeley?' Demetra pointed to the loaded tray.

'Of course.' Keeley smoothed down her white uniform dress. 'Shall I put some of those little lemon biscuits on a plate?'

'Efharisto.'

'Parakalo.' Automatically checking that she had everything she needed, Keeley carried it out onto the terrace with a heavy heart. Another trip to the table which had been set up next to the infinity pool, where Ariston was finishing a long lunch with his glamorous guests, and she was dreading it. Dreading seeing his rugged face watching her, his expression hidden behind his dark glasses as she tried to walk along the edge of the pool without appearing too self-conscious, but it was difficult. Just as it was difficult to forget that kiss they'd shared, when he'd made her usually non-responsive body spring to life—and left her in a state of frustrated

arousal ever since. It was as if he'd lit the touchpaper of her repressed sexuality and set it on fire.

And she had only herself to blame.

Why hadn't she stopped him from pulling her into his arms like that? Because she'd been powerless to stop him. She had wanted him to do it. She still wanted him to do it.

She bit her lip. She'd done her best to push him to the back of her mind—avoiding him whenever possible and concentrating on her work, determined to do a job she could be proud of. She wanted to wipe out his negative impressions of her and show him she could be honest and hard-working and *decent*. Just like she was determined not to raise the suspicions of the people she worked with. She *liked* Demetra and Stelios, just as she liked the extra staff who'd been drafted in from the nearby village to help with the house party. She didn't want them to think she had some kind of *thing* with the boss. All she wanted was to be seen as the helpful Englishwoman who was eager to take on her fair share.

The sun was warm on her head as she took the coffee outside to where the five of them were sitting around the remains of the meal she'd served them—Xenon, Megan, Santino, Rachel and Ariston. She'd been introduced to them yesterday and they all seemed the jet-setting type of people she no longer associated with. She'd forgotten that life where women changed their outfits four times a day and spent more on a straw hat than Keeley spent on her entire summer wardrobe. She'd been as polite and as friendly as her position required but she was also aware that as a member of staff she was mostly invisible. Only the friendly Rachel had treated her as if she was a real person—and always made a point of chatting whenever she saw her.

Rachel's long, bronzed legs were stretched out in front of her and she brightened when she saw Keeley approaching with the silver coffee pot glinting in the sunshine.

'Oh, yum. I love this Greek coffee!' she said. 'It's so thick and sweet.'

'I won't make the obvious comparison,' commented Santino drily, easily catching the hastily balled napkin which his girlfriend hurled at him in mock rage.

Rachel took a small cup from the tray. 'Thanks, Keeley. Is it possible to have some more sparkling water? It's so hot today. You must be baking in that uniform,' she observed, with a frown. 'Does Ariston allow you to cool off in the pool or does he constantly keep your nose to the grindstone?'

'Oh, Keeley knows she has the run of the place when she isn't working,' murmured Ariston. 'She just chooses not to take advantage of it, don't you, Keeley?'

They were all looking at her and Keeley was acutely aware of the fact that Rachel and Megan were both wearing gauzy kaftans over tiny bikinis, while she was wearing a uniform which made her feel completely overdressed as well as overheated. All Ariston's staff wore uniforms—but somehow on her it looked all wrong. It was the right size and everything but it did unwanted things to her figure. It was the one thing she'd inherited from her mother which she could do nothing about. Because no matter how much she tried to disguise her shape with loose-fitting clothes, her bust always seemed too big and the curve of her hips that fraction too wide, so everything clung precisely where she didn't want it to cling.

'I have a great big ocean on my doorstep if ever I feel the need to swim, but when I'm not working I mostly spend time doing stuff on my computer,' she said and then, because they were still looking at her questioningly, she felt obliged to offer some kind of explanation. 'I'm studying for a diploma in business studies,' she added.

'Well, that's all very admirable but you need to take time off occasionally. What's it they say about all work and no play?' questioned Rachel, raking her fingers back through her dark hair and shooting Ariston a quizzical glance. 'Didn't you say that Bailey has bailed this weekend, if you'll excuse the pun?'

'Bailey is no longer coming, no,' Ariston said smoothly.

'So we'll be a woman short at dinner?' persisted Rachel.

'Oh, I'm sure you'll be able to cope with that,' said Santino. 'Since when did you ever worry about odd numbers, *cara*? You always seem to have enough conversation to compensate for any absent guests.'

'That much is true.' Rachel smiled. 'But why doesn't Keeley join us instead, to make the numbers up?'

Ariston removed his dark glasses and glimmered Keeley an unfathomable look. 'Yes,' he said, his velvety accent seeming to whisper like velvet across her skin. 'Why don't you join us for dinner later?'

She shook her head. 'No, honestly. I can't.'

'Why not? I'm giving you permission to take the evening off. In fact, look on it as an order.' His smile was hard and determined. 'I'm sure we have enough staff for you not to be missed waiting at table.'

'It's very…kind of you, but…' Keeley put the last of the coffee cups down with trembling fingers before straightening up. 'I don't have anything suitable to wear.'

It was the wrong thing to say. Why hadn't she just come out with an emphatic *no*?

'No worries. You're about the same size and height as me,' said Megan, looking her up and down. 'You can borrow something from me. Say yes, Keeley. You've been working so hard that you deserve a little downtime. And it would be my pleasure to lend you something.'

The two female guests were clearly on a mission to get her to change her mind and inwardly Keeley began to fume. She knew they were just trying to be kind, but she didn't want their kindness. It made her feel patronised but, even worse, it made her feel vulnerable. They thought they were giving her a treat but in reality they were pushing her closer to Ariston and that was a place she didn't want to be. But she could hardly give them the reason for her resistance, could she? She couldn't really tell them she was worried she would end up in bed with her boss! And in the end, opposition was pointless because it was five against one and there was no way she could get out of it.

You're having dinner with them, that's all, she reminded herself as she stood beneath the cool jets of the shower later that afternoon. All she had to do was put on a borrowed dress and try to be pleasant. She could leave whenever she wanted. *She didn't have to do anything she didn't want to do.*

Which was how she found herself walking towards the starlit terrace that evening, wearing the only dress of Megan's which fitted her and which was the last type of outfit she would normally have worn. It was too delicate. Too feminine. Too...*revealing.* In soft, blush pink, the low-cut bodice showcased her breasts and the silky fabric clung to her hips in precisely the way she didn't want it to. And she wasn't blind. Or stupid. She saw the way Ariston looked at her when she walked out onto the candlelit terrace. Saw the instinctive narrowing of his eyes, which set off an answering tightening in her breasts.

Her throat was so dry that she knocked back half a glass of champagne too quickly and it went straight to her head. It soothed her frazzled nerves but it also had the unwanted side effect of softening her reaction to her Greek boss, because naturally she found herself seated next to him. She told herself she wasn't going to be affected by him. That he was a callous manipulator who had no regard for her feelings. But somehow her thoughts weren't making it to her body. Her body didn't seem to be behaving itself at all.

She could feel it in the heavy rush of blood to her breasts and in her restlessness whenever Ariston subjected her to that cool stare, which he seemed to do far more than was necessary. And if that weren't bad enough, she was having difficulty adjusting to this un-expected social outing. She hadn't been to a dinner party this fancy for a long time and she'd never really done so on her own terms before. She'd only ever been invited because of her mother, and this was different. She was no longer watching out of the corner of her eye in case her mum did something outrageous, anxiously wondering if she could get her home without making a fool of herself. This time people seemed to be interested in *her* and she didn't want them to be. What could she say about herself—other than that she'd done a series of menial jobs, because they were the only ones she could get after a fractured education which had led to zero qualifications?

She spent the evening blocking questions—some-thing she'd learnt to do over the years—so that when-ever she was asked something personal, she turned it around and moved the subject swiftly onto something else. She had become highly accomplished in the art of evasion but tonight it seemed to be having entirely the wrong effect. Was her elusiveness the reason why Santino began to monopolise her for the second part of the evening, while Rachel's pinched face seemed to indicate she was regretting her impetuous decision to have her join them? Keeley felt like standing up and an-nouncing that she wasn't remotely interested in the Ital-ian businessman—that there was only one man around the table who had her attention and she was having to fight very hard not to be mesmerised by him. Because tonight Ariston looked amazing—very traditional and heart-stoppingly masculine. His white shirt was unbuttoned at the neck revealing a silky triangle of olive skin, and his tapered dark trousers emphasised his long legs and the powerful shafts of his thighs.

And all the while he was watching her, his blue gaze burning into her so intently that the breath caught in her throat and she was barely able to eat. Course after course of delicious food was placed in front of her, but Keeley could do little more than push it around her plate. Were the other guests amused by her lack of appetite—not realising the cause of it—especially as she seemed almost to be bursting out of Megan's dress? Did they think she was one of those women who never ate in public but enjoyed secret binges with the biscuit packet whenever she was alone?

'Enjoying yourself, Keeley?' asked Ariston softly.

'Very much,' she said, not caring if he heard the lie in her voice. Because what else could she say? That she could feel ripples of awareness whispering over her skin whenever he looked at her? That she found his hard and rugged profile the most beautiful thing she'd ever seen and she wanted nothing more than to just sit and stare at it?

She broke the mould of her Cinderella evening by excusing herself long before midnight. As soon as the clock struck eleven she stood up and politely thanked them for a lovely dinner. Somehow she maintained her high-headed posture as she walked away from the terrace but as soon as she was out of sight, she began to run. Along the path leading to the beach she ran, straight past her cottage and down to the shoreline, glad she was wearing her practical sandals underneath the long dress. And glad too that the waves were pounding against the sand so that the heavy sound drummed out the beating of her thudding heart. Picking up the hem of her dress, she stood back, careful not to let the sea-water touch the delicate fabric as she stared out at the moon-dappled water.

She remembered how she'd felt when the supermarket had sacked her just before she'd flown to Lasia, when she'd been swamped by the sense of having no real place in the world. She could feel it now—because she hadn't really been part of that glamorous table, had she? She'd been the outsider who had been dressed up for the occasion in a stranger's dress. Had Ariston known how alienated she'd felt—or was he too busy reeling her in with his potent sexuality to care? Didn't he realise that what was probably just a game to him meant so much more to someone like her who didn't have his tight circle of friends, or wealth, to fall back on?

She felt stupid tears stinging her eyes and wondered if they had been caused by self-pity. Because if they were she was going to have to lose them—and quickly. Count your blessings, she told herself fiercely as she rubbed her eyes with the back of her hand. Just be glad you've been strong enough to resist someone who could never be anything more than a one-night stand.

But as she turned to walk back towards her cottage she saw a figure walking towards her—a man she recognised in a heartbeat, even from this distance. How could she fail to recognise him when his image was burned so powerfully onto her mind that she could picture him at the slightest provocation? His shadowy figure was powerful as he moved and the glint of moonlight in his eyes and the paleness of his silk shirt captured her imagination. She felt her skin prickle with instinctive excitement, which was quickly followed by a cold wash of dismay as he approached, because she'd tried to do the right thing. She'd done everything in her power to stay away from him. *So why the hell was he here?*

'Ariston,' she said steadily. 'What are you doing here?'

'I was worried about you. You left dinner so abruptly and I watched as you took the path to your cottage.' His eyes narrowed as they swept over her. 'Only no light came on.'

'You were spying on me?'

'Not really. I'm your employer.' His voice sounded deep above the soft lapping of the waves. 'I was merely concerned for your welfare.'

Her eyes met his. 'Is that so?'

There was a pause. 'Yes. No,' he negated and suddenly his voice had grown harsh. 'Actually, I don't know. I don't know what the hell it is. All I know is that I can't seem to stop thinking about you.'

Keeley saw the sudden change in him. The tension which stiffened his body, which she suspected mirrored the tension in her own. Just as she knew what was about to happen from the look on his face—a raw look of hunger which set off an answering need somewhere deep inside her.

'Ariston,' she whispered, but it sounded more like a prayer than a protest as he pulled her into his arms, into the warmth of his embrace, and she let him—ignoring the objections which were crowding her mind. And the moment he touched her, she was lost.

He drove his mouth down on hers and she heard his little moan of triumph as she kissed him back. Her lips opened and he slid his tongue inside her mouth to deepen the kiss. She swayed against him, her finger-nails digging into his chest through the fine silk of his shirt, and he circled his hips against hers in a move-ment which was unashamedly urgent. And now his hand was slipping inside the bodice of her dress so he could cup her braless breast with his fingers and she let him do that, too. How could she stop him when she wanted it so much?

His groan was muffled as he explored each diamond-tipped nipple and she could feel her panties growing moist. Was he going to do it to her now? Here? Push her down onto the soft sand without giving her time to object? Yes. She would welcome that. She didn't want anything to destroy the mood or the moment, because this had been a long time coming. Eight years, to be precise. Eight long and arid years when her body had felt as if it were made of cardboard, rather than respon-sive flesh and blood. Keeley swallowed. She didn't want time to have second thoughts about what was about to happen—she wanted to just go with the flow and be spontaneous. A rush of excitement flooded through her until she remembered what she was wearing and, un-locking her lips from his, she pulled away from him. 'The dress!' she stumbled.

He stared down at her uncomprehendingly. 'The dress?' he echoed dazedly.

'It's not mine, remember? I don't want to…to mark it.'

'Of course. You borrowed the dress.' Something hardened in his eyes as his gaze swept over her and his smile was tinged with a flicker of triumph as he picked her up and walked across the sand towards the cottage, before kicking open the door.

CHAPTER FIVE

ONCE INSIDE, ARISTON carried Keeley straight upstairs in a display of masculine dominance she found intoxicating. As he brushed hungry kisses over her neck and lips she was on such a delirious high of pleasure that she was barely aware of him lifting her arms above her head and peeling off her borrowed dress. Until suddenly she was standing in front of him wearing nothing but a pair of tiny thong panties. Half naked in the silver moonlight, she should have felt shy, but the look blazing from Ariston's eyes made her feel anything *but* shy. Tilting her chin, she felt the silky movement of her hair as it swayed against her bare back and a sudden sense of liberation rippled through her as she met his slow and appreciative smile.

'*Theos mou*, but you are magnificent,' he said, his body tensing as he cupped one of her breasts like a market trader calculating the weight of a watermelon.

And even that rather brutal gesture excited her. Every single thing about him was exciting right now—each nerve ending in her body feeling as if a layer of skin had been peeled away, leaving her raw and aching. His voice dipped approvingly as his gaze focussed on her tiny panties. 'It seems that beneath the often unexceptional clothes you favour, you dress in order to please your man.' He glittered her a smile. 'And I approve.'

His arrogance was breathtaking and Keeley wanted to tell him that his words were inaccurate on so many counts. That the tiny briefs were the only thing she *could* have worn under such a flimsy gown without getting a visible panty line and usually she wore a heavy-duty bra to contain her overripe breasts. But he was playing with her nipples again and it was such an unbearably sweet sensation that she didn't have the desire—or the strength—to break the fragile mood with stumbled words of explanation. Because during that short journey from beach to bedroom she'd known there was to be no turning back. It didn't seem to matter if it was right or wrong, it just seemed inevitable. She was going to let Ariston Kavakos make love to her tonight and nothing was going to stop her.

She lifted her gaze to his, watching as he began to unbutton his shirt, his eyes not leaving her face as he bared his hair-roughened chest.

'Play with your breasts,' he ordered softly. 'Touch yourself.'

The words should have shocked her but they didn't— maybe because he'd managed to turn them into an irresistible and silky command. Should she tell him that her sexual experience was laughably lacking and she wasn't sure how good she would be? But if she was going to do this, she needed to do it without any hang-ups. Tentatively, she spread her palms over the aching mounds and began to circle them as he'd demanded, and the weird thing was that once she'd banished her inhibitions, she started to *feel* sexy. She imagined it was Ariston's hands tracing erotic movements over her aroused flesh. She wriggled impatiently and her heavy eyelids fluttered to a close.

'No.' Another soft order rang out in the moonlit bedroom. 'Don't close your eyes. I want you to look at me, Keeley. I want to see your expression when I make you come. And believe me, I am going to make you come, *koukla mou*. Over and over and over again.'

Keeley's eyes widened because his words were so graphic. So *explicit*. She got the distinct impression he was deliberately demonstrating control over her. Was that the way he liked it? To be totally in charge? To tell her what to do and *show her who was boss*? Her heart started to race because he was naked now, his erection so pale and proud amid the dark curls—and even the daunting dimensions of *that* weren't enough to intimidate her. He walked over to where she stood, removing her hands from her breasts and replacing them with his lips, bending his head to kiss each nipple in turn, the tip of his tongue working expertly on the puckered flesh until she let out a small moan of pleasure.

'I like to hear you moan,' he said unsteadily. 'I promise I'm going to make you moan all night.'

'Are you?'

'Neh.' He tangled his fingers in the spill of her hair, anchoring her head so that she couldn't look anywhere except at him. 'Do you know how many times I have

imagined you like this, Keeley? Standing naked in the moonlight like some kind of goddess?'

Goddess? Was he crazy? A shelf-stacker from Super Save who was carrying too much weight? A wave of hysteria bubbled up inside her. She wanted to tell him not to say things like that but the truth was she liked it. She liked the way it made her feel. And why *shouldn't* she feel like a goddess for once when his words were painting pictures in her imagination which were increasing her desire? Because this was probably the way he did it. His method. Sweet-talking her into submission with his practised lines. Telling her the things she longed to hear, even if they weren't true. Presumably this was what men and women did all the time and it didn't mean a thing. Sex didn't mean a thing. That had been one thing her mother *had* taught her.

'Ariston,' she managed, through bone-dry lips.

'Have you dreamed about me too?' he murmured.

She supposed it would destroy the mood if she admitted that all the dreams she'd had about him were deeply unsettling. But why destroy the mood with an admission which no longer seemed relevant?

'Maybe,' she admitted.

He let out a low laugh of pleasure as he skimmed his hand over her tiny thong. 'I love that you blow so hot and cold,' he said. 'Did you learn long ago how to keep a man guessing?

Keeley bit her lip. His impression of her was a million miles away from the reality, but why puncture the bubble now? He obviously thought she was some kind of man-magnet and surely it would be a waste of time to try to convince him otherwise. Because she wasn't expecting any future in this. She knew that only a fool would expect a relationship with a man like Ariston, but her heart still clenched as she acknowledged just how fleeting it was going to be. And if his fantasies about her were turning him on, why not play the game? Why not scrabble up what little knowledge she had and work with it?

'Do you always waste so much time talking?' she purred.

Her softly spoken tease made the atmosphere change. She could sense a new tension in him as he picked her up and carried her over to the bed, not bothering to pull back the bedsheet as he laid her on it. His eyes were unfathomable as he stared down at her.

'Forgive me for not recognising your…' he slid his hand between her legs, pushing aside the panel of her panties with a murmur of acknowledgment as he flicked his finger over her slick, wet heat '…impatience.'

Keeley swallowed because now his finger was working with a purpose and she could feel the heat inside her building. She wanted him to kiss her again but the only area he seemed interested in kissing was her torso and then her belly and then…then… She sucked in a shocked breath as he pulled down her panties and moved his head between her legs so that she could feel the tickle of his thick hair brushing against her thighs. Her body was tensed for what was going to happen next but nothing on earth could have prepared her for that first sweet lick. She jerked on the bed and tried to wriggle away from the almost unendurable pleasure

which was spiralling up inside her, but he was holding
her hips so she couldn't move. And so she lay there help-
lessly—a willing prisoner of the Greek tycoon as layer
upon layer of pleasure built to such a level of intensity
that when it broke it felt like a swollen river bursting
its banks and she screamed out his name.

As the spasms slowly ebbed away she felt a delicious
warmth seeping through her body and opened her eyes
to find him leaning over her, a trace of amusement curving the edges of his lips.

'Mmm...' he said softly. 'For a woman who blows
so hot and cold, I didn't expect you to be quite so vocal.
Are you always so sweetly *enthusiastic* when you come,
Keeley—or are you trying to massage my ego by acting
like that was the first orgasm you've ever had?'

Keeley wasn't sure how to answer. She wondered if
it would be shameful to admit she'd never experienced
pleasure like that before and wondered how he would
react if he realised just how sketchy her sexual experience was. She licked her lips. Don't frighten him away,
she told herself. Why shatter this deliciously dreamy
mood with reality? Tell him what he expects to hear.
Be the woman you've never dared be before.

'You shouldn't be so good,' she said lazily. 'And then
I wouldn't be quite so...*vocal*.'

'Good? Are you kidding? I haven't even started yet,'
he murmured.

She swallowed, and suddenly she felt out of her
depth. 'I'm not...'

His gaze lasered into her. 'Not what, Keeley?'

She licked her lips again. 'I'm not on the pill or anything.'

'Even if you were, I always like to be doubly sure,' he said, his voice hardening as he groped around in the pocket of his trousers until he'd found what he was looking for.

Keeley watched as he slid the condom on and thought how *anatomical* this all seemed—as if emotion played no part in what was about to happen. She swallowed. Had she really thought it might be otherwise—that Ariston Kavakos might show her tenderness or affection?

'Kiss me,' she said suddenly. 'Please. Just kiss me.'

Ariston frowned as she made her breathless appeal and as he gave himself up to the kiss she'd demanded, his heart clenched. *Hell...* She was so...*surprising.* One minute the cool seductress and the next—why, she was almost *shy.* After making him wait longer than he'd ever had to wait for anyone, she was so sweet in her response. Had she learned at the knee of her mother how best to captivate a man? Had she discovered that keeping them guessing was the ultimate turn-on for men who'd seen everything, done everything and sometimes been bored along the way?

He felt as if he wanted to explode as he stroked her and kissed her and his heart was pounding as he moved over her, sucking in a deep breath of anticipation as, slowly, he entered her. And wasn't the most insane thing that he was almost *disappointed* at the ease with which he thrust into her slick, wet heat? Hadn't he been fantasising about her for so long that he'd allowed himself the ultimate illusion—and hadn't her wild reaction to her orgasm only reinforced that crazy notion? That maybe she was a virgin and maybe he was the first...

But his insanity lasted no longer than a second before he began to relax and to feast himself on all the soft and curvy flesh which was just there for the taking. She was so hot. So tight. He caught his hands under her thighs and hooked her legs around his back, enjoying her little squeals of pleasure as he increased his penetration. He drove into her hard and harder still, deliberately holding back until she could bear it no longer and called out his name again. And then she just went under, her body arching into a tight bow until she let it go with one long and shuddering cry. And wasn't *this* his fantasy? Not some woman she could never be, but Keeley Turner underneath him while he rode her, with those soft thighs tensing as she came all over again. He waited until her soft moans had died away and only then did he allow himself his own release, his heart clenching as the seed pumped hotly from his body and he reminded himself that *this* was what it was all about. The ultimate conquest of a woman who had been haunting him for years. A farewell to something which should have been finished eight years ago.

He fell asleep afterwards and when he awoke it was to find his lips touching one pouting breast. Barely any movement was needed to take the puckered nipple deep into his mouth and to graze it with his teeth and lick it, until she was squirming beneath him and before he knew what was happening he was inside her again. This time it was longer. Slower. As if it were all happening in some kind of dream. But his orgasm just went on and on and on. Afterwards he rolled onto his back, careful to allow her head to rest on his shoulder because women were very susceptible to rejection at times like this—and although he planned to wave her goodbye in the very near future, it certainly wouldn't be tonight. But he needed to think about what happened next because this was a situation which would need unusual levels of diplomacy. His fingertip skated a light survey over her belly and he felt her shiver in response.

'Well,' he whispered. 'I can't think of a more satisfactory end to the evening.'

Keeley nodded, trying not to show her disappointment. Of all the things he *could* have said and he came out with something like that. Why, he made her feel like an after-dinner brandy he'd consumed! She licked her swollen lips. But what did she expect? Words of admiration and affection? Ariston telling her she was the only woman for him and that he wanted a relationship with her? Of course not. It was what it was, she told herself fiercely. A one-night stand which wasn't supposed to mean anything. So she rolled away from him, shaking her tangled hair free as she attempted to find the level of sophistication which this kind of situation no doubt called for.

'Indeed it was,' she agreed coolly.

There was a short silence for a moment, during which he seemed to be mulling over his words.

'I'm surprised Santino didn't try to follow you down here to get to you before I did,' he said eventually.

It was such a random remark that Keeley frowned

as she turned her head to look at him, pushing back a handful of untidy hair. 'Why on earth would he have done that?'

He shrugged. 'I noticed how much attention he was paying you throughout dinner.'

'Did you?' she said, without missing a beat.

'I certainly did. And after you'd gone Santino and Rachel left pretty abruptly too. We could hear them arguing all the way back to their room.'

'And you thought…what?' she questioned softly as some inner warning system began to sound inside her head. 'Did you think it was about me?'

'I suspect it was. Your name was mentioned more than once.'

'And…what?' she demanded. 'Did you think I was hungry for a man, Ariston? Any man? That if Santino *had* arrived before you that I would be in bed with him?'

'I don't know.' There was a heartbeat of a pause as he lifted his eyes to hers. 'Would you?'

Keeley froze just before instinct kicked in and she longed to flex her fingernails over his skin and tear at his silken flesh. To inflict some kind of hurt on him—something which might mimic the searing pain which was clamping around her heart. She expelled the breath she'd been holding, bitterly aware of how little he thought of her. But she'd known that from the start, hadn't she? And had thought, what? That the growing sexual attraction between them would somehow cancel out his obvious lack of respect? That admitting him to her bed so quickly might make him admire her? What a stupid little fool she'd been.

'Get out,' she said, in a low voice.

'Oh, Keeley,' he said softly. 'There's no need to over-react. You asked me a question and I answered it truthfully. Would you rather I told you a lie?'

'I mean it!' she snapped. He made to pull her back into his arms but she jumped out of bed before he could touch her. 'Get out of here,' she repeated.

He shrugged as he swung his legs over the bed and reached for his trousers. 'I wasn't intending to insult you.'

'Really? In that case, I think you ought to take a good, long look at the things you just said. You think I'm sexually indiscriminate, do you, Ariston? That one attractive man is pretty much the same as any other?'

'How should I know? You are your mother's daughter, after all. And I've had enough experience of women to know what they are capable of,' he said rawly. 'I know just how unscrupulous they can be.'

Keeley reached for the cotton dressing gown which was hanging on a hook on the door and pulled it on, not daring to speak until she had tied the belt around her waist and her naked body was hidden from his gaze.

'Why *did* you seduce me, Ariston?' she questioned in a low voice. 'When you obviously think so little of me?'

He paused in the act of sliding on his shirt, the movement making his powerful muscles ripple beneath the silk fabric. 'Because I find you intensely attractive. Because you lit a longing in me all those years ago which never really went away. Maybe now it will.'

'And that's all?'

His eyes narrowed. 'Isn't that enough?'

But instinct told her there was something more. Something he was holding back. And suddenly she needed to know, even though she suspected it was going to shatter her. 'Tell me the truth like you did before,' she said. 'Just…tell me.'

His eyes gleamed like silver in the moonlight, before he shrugged. 'It started out with wanting to have you for myself, for all the reasons I've just stated,' he said in a low voice. 'But also because…'

'Because what, Ariston? Please don't stop now. Not when this is just getting fascinating.'

He zipped up his trousers before looking up. 'Because I knew that my brother wouldn't be tempted by you, if he knew I'd had sex with you first.'

'Which naturally you would have made sure he knew?'

He shrugged. 'If I'd needed to, then yes. Yes, I would.'

There was a disbelieving silence before she could bring herself to respond. 'So it was…it was some kind of territorial thing? The ultimate deterrent to ensure that your brother wasn't tempted, even though there is no spark between me and Pavlos and there never has been?'

He met her gaze unflinchingly. 'I guess so.'

Keeley felt faint. It was even worse than she'd thought. Briefly, she closed her eyes before going into damage-limitation mode and that was something which came as naturally to her as breathing. The thing she was best at. She sucked in an unsteady breath. 'You do realise I'm going to have to leave the island? That I can't work for you any more. Not after this.'

He shook his head. 'You don't have to do that.'

'Really?' She gave a bitter laugh. 'Then how do you see this playing out? Me carrying on with my domestic work while you occasionally sneak down here to have sex with me? Or am I now supposed to abandon my uniform as if this was some bizarre kind of promotion and join you and your guests for dinner every night?'

'There's no need to overreact, Keeley,' he gritted. 'We can work something out.'

'That's where you're wrong, Ariston. We can't. There's no working out something like this. I won't be treated in this way and I won't spend any more time in the company of a man who is capable of such treatment. Tonight was a mistake—but we can't do anything about it now. But I'm not staying here a second longer than I have to. I want to leave tomorrow, first thing. Before anyone is awake.'

He'd finished buttoning up his shirt and the expression on his rugged face was hidden by a series of shifting shadows. 'You're aware that you need my co-operation to do that? That I own the airstrip as well as the planes—and no other aircraft is allowed to land or take off from here without my permission. I might not be willing to let you go so easily, Keeley—have you thought about that?'

'I don't care what *you* want, you'd just better let me go,' she said, her voice shaking now. 'Because I'm a strong swimmer—and if I have to make my own way to the nearest island, then believe me I will. Or I'll contact one of the international newspapers and tell them I'm being kept prisoner on the Greek tycoon's island—I imagine the press could have a lot of fun with that. Unless you're planning to confiscate my computer while you're at it—which, I have to inform you, is a criminal offence. No? So get out of here, Ariston—and prepare one of your planes to take me back to England. Do you understand?'

CHAPTER SIX

ARISTON STARED OUT of the vast windows, but for once the travel-brochure views of his island home failed to impress him. He might as well have been in a darkened cave for all the notice he took of the sapphire sea and silver sand, or the neglected cup of coffee which had been cooling on his desk for the last half-hour. All he could see was a pair of bright green eyes and a pair of soft, rosy lips—and pale hair which had trickled through his fingers like moonlight.

What was his problem? he wondered impatiently as he stood up with a sudden jerking movement which made the cup rattle. Why did he persist in feeling so *unsettled* when all should have been well in his world? Weeks had passed since Keeley Turner had fallen eagerly into his arms during a sexual encounter which had blown his mind but ended badly. She had flown back to London the next morning, refusing to meet his eye and saying nothing other than a tight-lipped good-bye before turning her back on him. But she had taken the money he'd given her, hadn't she? Had shown no qualms about accepting the additional sum he had included. He'd thought he might receive an angry email telling him what he could do with his money—wasn't that what he'd *hoped* might happen?—along with some furious tirade suggesting he might be offering payment *for services rendered*. But no. She was a woman, wasn't she—and what woman would ever turn down the offer of easy money?

And that had been that. He hadn't heard from her since. He told himself that was a good thing—that he had achieved what he had set out to achieve and bedded a woman whose memory had been haunting him for years. But infuriatingly, little had changed. In fact, it seemed a whole lot worse. Surely by now he shouldn't still be thinking about her, or the way it had felt to press his lips to her pulsating heat as she had orgasmed right into his mouth. Was it because he wasn't used to a woman walking away from him, or because he couldn't help admiring the tempestuous show of spirit she had displayed when she had stormed away? Or just because she'd been the hottest lover he'd ever had?

But after yet another disturbed night he found himself wondering where was the closure he'd been chasing and why he hadn't tried a little harder to keep her here a bit longer, so he could have got her out of his system. Should he have softened his answers to her questions with a little diplomacy and told her what she wanted to hear, instead of giving it to her straight? His mouth hardened. It didn't matter. He didn't like lies and it was too late to go back over that now. What was done was done.

At least Pavlos had announced his engagement to

the beautiful Marina, with a wedding planned for early next year. His brother was happy—he'd called him just last night from Melbourne and told him so, and Ariston felt as if his work was done. That all was well within the Kavakos dynasty—its future now ensured…if only this damned disquiet would leave him.

But it didn't leave him, despite a schedule spent travelling across much of Southeast Asia—and although he threw himself into his work even more single-mindedly than usual, he remained as unsettled as ever. Which was why he found himself making an unplanned trip to England on his private jet, telling himself it was always useful to pay an unexpected visit to his London office because it kept his staff on their toes. And besides, he liked London. He kept a fully staffed apartment there which he used at different times during the year—often when the summer heat of Lasia was at its most intense. But even in London he found himself struggling to concentrate on his latest shipbuilding project or enjoy the fact that the company had been featured in the prestigious *Forbes* magazine in a flattering article praising his business acumen.

He told himself it was curiosity—or maybe courtesy—which made him decide to call on Keeley, to see how she was doing. Maybe she'd calmed down enough to be civil to him. He felt the beat of anticipation. Maybe even more.

He had his car drop him down the road from her bedsit and when he knocked on the door, the long silence which followed made him think nobody was home. A ragged sigh escaped from his lungs. So that was that.

He could leave a note, which he suspected would find its way straight into the bin. He could try calling but something told him that if she saw his name on the screen, she wouldn't pick up. And that had never happened to him before either.

But then the door opened a little and there was Keeley's face peering out at him through the narrow crack—her expression telling him he was the last person she had expected to see. Or wanted to see. His eyes narrowed because she looked terrible. Her blonde hair hung in limp strands as if it hadn't been washed in days, her face was waxy white and she had deep shadows beneath her eyes. He'd never seen a woman who had paid such scant attention to her appearance—but then he'd never made an impromptu call like this before. 'Hello, Keeley,' he said quietly.

Keeley stiffened, her knuckles tightening over the doorknob as she stared into Ariston's searing blue eyes and a wave of horror washed over her. What in heavens name was he doing here—and how was she going to deal with it? Her instinct was to slam the door in his face but she'd tried that once before without success and, besides, she couldn't do that, could she? Not in the circumstances. She might despise him but she needed to talk to him and it just so happened that fate had scheduled that unwanted prospect without her having to arrange it herself. She found herself wishing she'd had time to brush her hair or put on clothes she hadn't fallen asleep in, but maybe it was better this way. At least she wouldn't have to worry about him making a pass at her when she looked like this. Why, he must be wondering what had possessed him to take someone like her to his bed.

'You'd better come in,' she said.

He looked surprised at the invitation and she understood why. After the way they'd parted he must have thought she'd never want to see him again. But no matter how much she wished that could be true, she couldn't turn him away—just as she couldn't turn the clock back. She had to tell him. It was her duty to tell him.

Before he worked it out for himself.

'So what brings you here today, Ariston?' she said, once they were standing facing each other in the claustrophobically small sitting room. 'Let me guess... Pavlos is back in London and you've decided to check whether or not I've got my greedy hooks in him. Well, as you can see—I'm here on my own.'

He gave a short shake of his head. 'Pavlos is engaged to be married.'

'Wow,' she said, feeling winded though she wasn't sure why. 'Congratulations. So you got what you wanted.'

He shrugged. 'My wish to see my brother happily settled with a suitable partner has been fulfilled, yes.'

'But if Pavlos is safe from my supposed clutches, then what brings you to New Malden?' She frowned. 'An area like this isn't exactly a billionaire's stomping ground, is it? And I don't recall leaving anything behind on your island which might need "returning".'

'I was in London and I thought I'd drop by to see how you are.'

'How very touching. Do you do that with all your ex-lovers?'

His mouth hardened. 'Not really. But then, none of my lovers have ever walked out on me like that.'

'Oh, dear. Is your ego feeling battered?'

'I wouldn't go quite that far,' he said drily.

'So now you've seen how I am.'

'Yes. And I don't like what I see. What's the matter, Keeley?' His frowning blue gaze stayed fixed on her face. 'You look sick.'

Keeley swallowed. So here it was. He'd given her the perfect opportunity to tell him her life-changing news. She was surprised he hadn't worked it out for himself and if he'd bothered to look harder at her baggy shirt, he might have noticed the faint curve of her belly beneath. She opened her mouth to tell him but something made her hesitate. Was it self-preservation? The sense that once she told him nothing was ever going to be the same?

'I have been sick,' she admitted, before the words came out in a bald rush. 'Actually, I'm pregnant.'

He didn't catch on, not straight away—or if he did, he didn't show it.

'Congratulations,' he said evenly. 'Who's the father?'

It was a reaction she should have anticipated but stupidly she hadn't and Keeley felt hurt. She wanted to tell him that only one man could possibly be the father but he probably wouldn't believe her and why should he? She hadn't exactly acted with any restraint where he was concerned, had she? She'd fallen into his arms— not once, but twice and made it clear she'd wanted sex with him. Why wouldn't a chauvinist like Ariston Kavakos imagine she behaved like that all the time? She licked her lips.

'You are,' she said baldly. 'You're the father.'

His face showed no reaction other than a sudden coldness which turned his eyes into sapphire ice. 'Excuse me?'

Was he expecting his cool question to prompt her into admitting that she'd made a mistake, and he wasn't going to be a daddy after all? That she was trying it on because he was so wealthy? The temptation to do just that and make him go away was powerful, but her conscience was more powerful still. Because he *was* the father—there was no getting away from that and the important thing was how she dealt with it. Suddenly, Keeley knew that, despite her morning sickness and ever-present sensation of feeling like a cloth which had been wrung out to dry, she now needed to be strong. Because Ariston was strong. And he was a dominant male who would ride roughshod over her to get what it was he wanted, if she let him.

'You heard me,' she said quietly. 'You're the father.'

His face darkened as he studied her and suddenly she got an idea of just how formidable an opponent he might be in the boardroom.

'How do you know it's mine?'

She flinched. 'Because you're the only one it could be.'

'I only have your word for that, Keeley. You were no virgin.'

'Neither were you.'

He gave a cruel smile. 'Like I told you—it's different for men.'

'You think I would lie about something like this?'

'I don't know—that's the thing. I know very little about you. But I'm a wealthy man. There are undoubted benefits to getting pregnant by someone like me. So was it an accident, or did you plan it?'

'*Plan* it? You think I deliberately got myself pregnant, just to get my hands on your money?'

'Don't look so outraged, Keeley. You wouldn't believe the things people would do for money,' he said, his gaze flicking over her coldly. 'Or maybe you would.'

'You seem to be very good at dishing out blame, but I'm not going to carry the entire burden.' She sucked in a deep breath as she walked over to the window sill. 'I always thought contraception was the joint responsibility of both parties.'

Ariston met her shadowed eyes and was surprised by a sudden wave of compassion—and guilt. How many times had he made love to her that night? His brow furrowed. Just twice, before she'd kicked him out of her bed and announced that she was leaving the island. Had he been careful that second time, or had he…? His heart missed a beat. No. He hadn't. He'd been so aroused that in his sleepy and already sated state he had slipped inside her without bothering to put on a condom. How the hell had that happened, when he was traditionally always the most exacting of men?

And hadn't it felt beyond blissful to feel her bare skin against his? Her slick wet heat against his hardness. Had some protective instinct made his mind shut down so that only just now was he remembering it?

His heart was thundering as he watched her, noting the way she had slumped against the window sill. When she leaned back like that he could see the curve of her belly and for the first time noticed that her already generous breasts were even bigger than usual. She was undeniably pregnant—so should he simply take her word that he was the father?

But memories of his mother—and many of the women in between—made him wary. He knew all about lies and subterfuge because they'd been woven into the fabric of his life. He knew what people would do for money. He had learnt caution at an early age because he'd needed to. It had protected him from some of the darker things which life had thrown at him and Pavlos, so why shouldn't he seek its protection now?

'You're right, of course. Contraception is the responsibility of the man and the woman,' he said. 'But that still doesn't answer my question with any degree of satisfaction. How do I know—or *you* know—that I'm the father of your baby?'

'Because…'

He saw her bite her lip as if she was trying to hold the words back but then they came tumbling out in a passionate torrent.

'Because I've only ever had sex once before!' she declared. 'One man, one time, years ago—and it was a disaster, okay? Does that tell you everything you need to know, Ariston?'

He felt a dark and primitive rush of pleasure. It all added up now. Her soft sense of wonder when he'd made love to her. Her disbelieving cries as she had come. These all spoke of a woman achieving satisfaction for the first time, not someone who'd been around the sexual block a few times. But what if she was lying? What if she was simply using the skills of an actress, learnt at the knee of her mother? His mouth hardened. Surely he owed it to himself to demand a DNA test—if not now, then at least when the child was born.

But her waxy complexion and tired eyes were making him stall and he was surprised by another wave of compassion. He forced himself to sift through the available facts and the possible solutions. Despite her lack of qualifications, she wasn't stupid. She must realise that he'd come at her with all guns blazing if he discovered he'd been bamboozled by a false paternity claim.

He glanced around the shabby little room, trying to impose some order on his whirling thoughts. Fatherhood had never been on his agenda. He accepted that he was a difficult man who didn't believe in love, who didn't trust women and who fiercely guarded his personal space—and those factors had ruled out the forced intimacy of marriage. The desire to carry on his own bloodline had always been noticeable by its absence and he'd always supposed that Pavlos would be the one to provide the necessary heirs to take the Kavakos empire forward.

But this disclosure altered everything. In a few short minutes he could feel something changing inside him, because if this was *his* child then he wanted a part of it. A big part of it. His heart clenched. For how could it be any other way? Why would he not want to stake a claim on his own flesh and blood? He looked into Keeley's wary eyes and thought this must be the last thing she wanted—an unplanned baby with a man she loathed. And no money, he reminded himself grimly. Her circumstances were more impecunious than most. So why not offer her the kind of inducement which would suit them both?

'So when were you going to tell me?' he demanded. 'Or weren't you going to bother?'

'Of course I was. I was just…waiting for the right time,' she said, with the voice of someone who had been putting off the inevitable. 'Only it never seemed to come.'

He frowned. 'Why don't you sit down in that chair? You don't look very comfortable standing there and you really should be comfortable, because we need to talk.'

Her chin jutted forward but she didn't defy him, though he noticed that she stared straight ahead as she made her way towards a battered armchair. Yet despite her unwashed hair and sloppy grey sweat-pants, Ariston couldn't help his body from reacting as she walked past him. He could feel the tautness and the tension hardening his muscles and the instinctive tightening low in his abdomen. What was it about her which made him want to impale her whenever she came near?

She sank down onto the chair and lifted up her face to his. 'So talk,' she said.

He nodded, sliding his hands into the pockets of his trousers as he looked at her. 'I don't imagine you wanted to be a mother,' he began.

She shrugged. 'Not yet, no.'

'So how about I free you of that burden?'

She must have misunderstood him because her arms

instantly clamped themselves around her belly as if she was shielding her unborn child and suddenly she was yelling at him. 'If you're suggesting—'

'What I'm *suggesting*,' he interrupted, 'is that I have you moved from this miniature hell-hole into a luxury apartment of your choice. That you are attended by the finest physicians in the land, who will monitor your pregnancy and make sure that you both maintain tip-top health. And after the birth…'

'After the birth…*what*?' she said, her voice dropping to a whisper, as if she'd suddenly got an inkling of what he was about to say.

'You give up your baby.' He gave a cold smile. 'Or rather, you give it to me.'

There was a pause. 'Could you…could you repeat that?' she said faintly. 'Just so I can be sure I haven't misunderstood your meaning.'

'I will raise the child,' he said. 'And you can name your price.'

She didn't speak for a moment and he was taken aback by the naked fury which blazed from her green eyes as she scrambled to her feet. For a minute he thought she was about to hurl herself across the room and attack him and wasn't there a part of him which wanted her to go right ahead? Because a fighting woman was a woman who could be subdued in all kinds of ways and suddenly he found himself wanting to kiss her again. But she didn't. She stood there, her hands on her hips, her breath coming quick and fast.

'You're offering to *buy* my baby?'

'That's a rather melodramatic way of putting it,

Keeley. Think of it as a transaction—the most reason-able course of action in the circumstances.'

'Are you out of your mind?'

'I'm giving you the opportunity to make a fresh start.'

'Without my *baby*?'

'A baby will tie you down. I can give this child ev-erything it needs,' he said, deliberately allowing his gaze to drift around the dingy little room. 'You cannot.'

'Oh, but that's where you're wrong, Ariston,' she said, her hands clenching. 'You might have all the houses and yachts and servants in the world, but you have a great big hole where your heart should be. You're a cold and unfeeling brute who would deny your baby his mother—and therefore you're incapable of giving this child the thing it needs more than anything else!'

'Which is?'

'Love!'

Ariston felt his body stiffen. He loved his brother and once he'd loved his mother, but he was aware of his limitations. No, he didn't do the big showy emotion he suspected she was talking about and why should he, when he knew the brutal heartache it could cause? Yet something told him that trying to defend his own po-sition was pointless. She would fight for this child, he realised. She would fight with all the strength she pos-sessed, and that was going to complicate things. Did she imagine he was going to accept what she'd just told him and play no part in it? Politely dole out payments and have sporadic weekend meetings with his own flesh and blood? Or worse, no meetings at all. He met the green blaze of her eyes.

'So you won't give this baby up and neither will I,' he said softly. 'Which means that the only solution is for me to marry you.'

He saw the shock and horror on her face.

'But I don't want to marry you! It wouldn't work, Ariston—on so many levels. You must realise that. Me, as the wife of an autocratic control freak who doesn't even like me? I don't think so.'

'It wasn't a question,' he said silkily. 'It was a statement. It's not a case of *if* you will marry me, Keeley— just when.'

'You're mad,' she breathed.

He shook his head. 'Just determined to get what is rightfully mine. So why not consider what I've said, and sleep on it and I'll return tomorrow at noon for your answer—when you've calmed down. But I'm warning you now, Keeley—that if you are wilful enough to try to refuse me, or if you make some foolish attempt to run away and escape...' he paused and looked straight into her eyes '...I will find you and drag you through every court in the land to get what is rightfully mine.'

CHAPTER SEVEN

As she prepared for Ariston's visit next morning, Keeley stared at her white-faced reflection in the mirror and gritted her teeth. This time she wouldn't lose her temper. She would be calm and clear and focussed. She would tell him she couldn't possibly marry him but that she was willing to be reasonable.

She washed her hair and put on a loose cotton dress and a sudden desire to impose some order made her give her bedsit an extra-special clean—busying herself with mop and duster. She even went down to the local market and bought a cheap bunch of flowers from the friendly stallholder who implored her to, 'Cheer up, love! It might never happen!'

It already had, she thought gloomily as she crammed the spindly pink tulips into a vase as she waited for the Greek tycoon to arrive.

He was bang on time and she hated her instinctive reaction when she opened the door to see him in an exquisite pale grey suit, which today didn't make him look remotely uncomfortable. In fact, he came over as supremely relaxed as well as looking expensive and hopelessly out of place in her crummy little home. She didn't *want* to shiver with awareness whenever she looked at him, nor remember how it had felt to be naked in his arms, yet the erotic images just kept flooding back. Was she imagining the faint triumph which curved those cruel lips of his—as if he was perfectly aware of the way he made her feel? *He can't make you do anything you don't want him to*, she reminded herself fiercely. You might be carrying his baby but you are still a free agent. This is modern England, not the Middle Ages. He can hardly drag you up the aisle against your will.

'I'm hoping you've had time to come to your senses, Keeley,' he said, without preamble. 'Have you?'

'I've given it a lot of thought, yes—but I'm afraid I haven't changed my mind. I won't marry you, Ariston.'

He said something soft in his native tongue and when he looked at her, he seemed almost regretful as he sighed. 'I was hoping it wouldn't come to this.'

'Come to what?' she questioned in confusion.

'Why didn't you tell me about your mother?'

She felt the blood drain from her face. 'Wh-what about my mother?'

His gaze slid over her. 'That she's living in a care home and has been for the last seven years.'

Keeley's lips folded in on themselves because she was afraid she might cry, until she reminded herself that she couldn't afford the luxury of tears—or to show any kind of vulnerability to a man she suspected would seize on it, as a starving dog might seize on a bone. 'How did you find out?'

He shrugged. 'The gathering of information is simple if you know who to ask.'

'But why? Why would you go to the trouble of having me investigated?'

'Don't be naïve, Keeley. Because you are the mother of my child and you have something I want. And knowledge is power,' he added as his sapphire eyes bored into her. 'So what happened? How come a middle-aged woman has ended up living in an institution where the average age is eighty, unable to recognise her only daughter when she visits?'

Without thinking, Keeley grabbed the arm of the nearest chair before sinking into it before her legs gave way, as they were threatening to. 'Didn't your investigators tell you?' she questioned hoarsely. 'Didn't they gain access to her medical records and tell you everything you needed to know?'

'No—they didn't. I don't think it's morally right to do something like that.'

'How dare you talk to me about *morals*?' she bit back. 'I'm surprised you even know the definition of the word.'

'So what happened, Keeley?' he questioned again, more softly this time.

She wanted to tell him it was none of his business but she suspected that wouldn't deter him. And maybe it *was* his business now, she realised, with a wrench to her heart. Because her mother was the grandmother of *his* child, wasn't she? Even if she would never realise that fact for herself. A sudden wave of sadness engulfed her and she blinked away another hint of tears before he could see them. 'So what do you want to know?' she questioned.

'Everything.'

Everything. That was a tall order. Keeley leant her head back against the chair but it took a couple of moments before she had composed herself enough to speak. 'I'm sure you don't need me to tell you my mother's fleeting fame as an actress was quickly replaced by the notorious reputation she gained after that...' she stumbled on the words '...that summer at your house.'

His mouth hardened, but he didn't comment. 'Go on.'

'When we arrived back in England she was approached by lots of tabloid newspapers and the tackier end of the magazine market. They wanted her to be a torch-bearer for the older woman who was determined to have a good sex life, but in reality they just wanted a gullible fool who could shift a few extra copies in a dwindling retail market.' She drew in a deep breath. 'She talked at length about her different lovers—most of whom were considerably younger. Well, you already know that. She thought she was striking a blow for women's liberation but, in reality, everyone was laughing at her behind her back. But she didn't notice and she certainly didn't let it deter her. And then her looks began to fade...quite dramatically. Too much wine and sun. One crash diet too many.'

She stopped.

'Don't stop now,' he said.

His voice was almost gentle and Keeley wanted to tell him not to talk that way. She'd misinterpreted his kindness once before and she wasn't going to make the same mistake again. She wanted to tell him that she could deal with him better when he was being harsh and brutal.

She shrugged. 'She started having surgery. A nip here and a tuck there. One minute it was an eyebrow job and the next she was having goodness knows what pumped into her lips. She started to look…' She closed her eyes as she remembered the cruelty of the newspapers which had once courted her mother so assiduously. The snatched photos which had been only marginally less flattering than the awful ones she'd still insisted on posing for, usually dressed in something cringe-makingly unsuitable—like leather hot pants and a see-through blouse. How quickly she had become a national laughing stock—her face resembling a cruel parody of youth.

And how ultimately frustrating that she had been too blind to see what was happening to her.

'She started to look bizarre,' she continued, not wanting to appear disloyal but now the words seemed to be rushing to get out because she'd never talked about it before. She'd kept it buttoned up inside her, as if it was *her* shame and *her* secret. 'She met this surgeon and he offered to give her a complete facelift, only she didn't bother to check out his credentials or to wonder why he was offering her all that work at such an advantageous price. Nobody was quite sure of what happened during the operation—only that my mother was left brain-damaged afterwards. And that she never recognised me—or anyone else again. Her capacity for normal living is "severely compromised" is how they described it.' She swallowed. 'And she's been living in that care home ever since.'

He frowned. 'But you visit her regularly?'

'I do. Every week, come rain or shine.'

'Even though she doesn't recognise you?'

'Of course,' she said quietly. 'She's still my mother.'

Ariston flinched at the quiet sense of dignity and grief underpinning her words. Maybe it was inevitable that they made him think about his own mother, but there was no such softening in *his* heart. Bitterness rose in his throat but he pushed it away as he studied the woman in front of him. She looked very different today, with her newly washed hair shining over her shoulders in a pale fall of waves. The shapeless sweatpants and baggy top were gone and in their place was a loose cotton dress. She looked soft and feminine and strangely vulnerable.

'Why don't you tell me what it is *you* want?' he said suddenly.

She met his gaze warily, as if suspecting him of setting up some kind of trap. 'I want my baby to have the best,' she said cautiously. 'Just like every mother does.'

'And you think that living here...' he looked around, unable to hide the contemptuous twist of his mouth '...can provide that?'

'People have babies in all kinds of environments, Ariston.'

'Not a baby carrying the Kavakos name,' he corrected repressively. 'How are you managing for money? Are you still working?'

She shook her head. 'Not at the moment, no.'

'Oh?' His gaze bored into her.

She shrugged. 'I found another supermarket job when I got back from Lasia and then I started getting sick. I eked out the money you paid me but...'

'Then how the *hell*,' he persisted savagely as her words tailed off, 'do you think you're going to manage?'

Keeley swallowed in a vain attempt to stop her lips from wobbling, before drawing on her residual reserves. She'd overcome stuff before and she could do it again. 'Once the sickness has improved, then I can start working more hours. If I need to I might have to move to a cheaper area somewhere.'

'But that would take you further away from your mother,' he pointed out.

She glared at him for daring to point out the obvious but suddenly she couldn't avoid the enormity of her situation. She hadn't even got a buggy or a crib—and even if she had, there was barely any space to put them. And meanwhile Ariston was offering what most women in her situation would snatch at. He wasn't trying to deny responsibility. On the contrary, he seemed more than willing to embrace it. He was offering to *marry* her, for heaven's sake. Whoever would have thought it?

But yesterday he'd wanted her to give him the baby, she reminded herself. *To take her child away from her.* Because he could. Because he was powerful and rich and she was weak and poor. He'd wanted to remove her from the equation—to treat her like a surrogate— and *that* was a measure of his ruthlessness. At least if she was married to him she would have some legal rights—and wouldn't that be the safest place to start from? Staring into the watchful brilliance of his eyes, she repressed a shiver as she realised what she must do. Because what choice did she have? *She didn't. She didn't have a choice.*

'If I did agree to marry you,' she said slowly, 'then I would want some kind of equality.'

'Equality?' he echoed, as if it was a word he'd never used before.

She nodded. 'That's right. I'm not prepared to do anything until you agree to my terms.'

'And what *terms* might they be, Keeley?'

'I would like some say in where we live—'

'Accommodation is the last thing you need concern yourself with,' he said carelessly. 'Don't forget, I have a whole island at my disposal.'

'No!' Her response came out more vehemently than she'd planned but Keeley knew what she could and couldn't tolerate. And the thought of the isolation of his island home and of being at Ariston's total mercy made her blood run cold. 'Lasia isn't a suitable place to bring up a baby.'

'I grew up there.'

'Exactly.'

There was a flicker of amusement in his brilliantine eyes before it was replaced by the more familiar glint of hardness. 'Let me guess, you have somewhere else in mind—somewhere you've always longed to live? A town house in the centre of Mayfair perhaps, or an apartment overlooking the river? Aren't these the places women dream about if money were no option?'

'I haven't spent my whole life plotting my rise up the property ladder!' she snapped.

'Then you are rare among your sex.' His gaze bored into her. 'Lasia is my home, Keeley.'

'And this is mine.'

'This?'

She heard the condescension in his voice and suddenly she was fighting for her reputation and what she'd made of her life. It wasn't much, but in the circumstances hadn't it been the best she could manage? Hadn't she struggled to get even this far? But what would Ariston Kavakos know of hardship and making do, with his island and his ships and the ability to click his fingers to get whatever he wanted? Even her. 'I want to stay in London,' she said stubbornly. 'My mother is here, as you yourself just pointed out, remember? I can't just up sticks and move away.'

He rubbed his forefinger along the bridge of his nose and Keeley watched as he closed his eyes, the thick lashes feathering blackly against his olive skin. Was he wondering how he was going to tolerate a life saddled with a woman he didn't really want, with a mother whose incapacity had been brought about by her own vanity? Was he now working out how to back-pedal on his hastily offered proposal of marriage?

His eyes flickered open. 'Very well. London it shall be. I have an apartment here,' he said, rising to his feet. 'A penthouse in the City.'

Keeley nodded. Of course he did. He probably had a penthouse in every major city in the world. 'Just out of interest, how long do you think this marriage of ours is going to last?'

'The tone of your voice indicates that you think a long-standing union unlikely?'

'I think the odds are stacked against it,' she said. 'Don't you?'

'Actually, no, I don't. Put it this way,' he added softly. 'I don't intend for my child to be brought up by any other man than me. So if you want to maintain your role as the mother, then we stay married.'

'But—'

'But what, Keeley? What makes you look so horrified? The realisation that I am determined to make this work? Surely that is only a good thing.'

'But how can it work when it isn't going to be a *true* marriage?' she demanded desperately.

'Says who? Perhaps we could learn to get along together. Something which might work if we put our minds to it. I have no illusions about marriage and my expectations are fairly low. But I think we could learn how to be civil to one another, don't you?'

'That isn't what I meant and you know it,' she said, her voice low.

'Are you talking about sex?' A trace of sardonic amusement crept into his tone. 'Ah, yes. I can see from your enchanting little blush that you are. So what's the problem? When two people have a chemistry like ours it seems a pity not to capitalise on it. I find that good sex makes a woman very agreeable. Who knows? It might even bring a smile to your face.'

Keeley felt both faint and excited at the way he was

expressing himself—and didn't she despise herself for feeling that way? 'And if I...refuse?'

'Why would you?' His gaze flicked over her body. 'Why fight it when submission is much more satisfactory? You're thinking about it now, aren't you, Keeley? Remembering how good it felt to have me inside you, kissing you and touching you, until you cried out with pleasure?'

The awful thing was that not only was he speaking the truth—but she *was* reacting to his words and there didn't seem to be a thing she could do about it. It was as if her body were no longer her own—as if he was controlling her reaction with just one sizzling glance. Keeley's nipples were pushing against her cotton dress and she could feel a newfound but instantly familiar tug of desire. She wanted him, yes—but surely it was wrong to want a man who treated her the way Ariston did. He had used her as a sexual object rather than someone he respected and something told her he would continue to do so. And wouldn't that leave her open to emotional wounding? Because something told her Ariston was the kind of man who could hurt. Who could hurt without even trying.

'But what,' she continued determinedly, 'what if I decided I couldn't stomach the idea of cold-blooded sex with a man like you?'

'Sex with me is never cold-blooded, *koukla mou*— we both know that. But if you were to persist in such stubbornness, then I would be forced to find myself a mistress.' His face darkened. 'I believe that's what usually happens in these circumstances.'

'In that parallel universe of yours, you mean?' she spat back.

'It's a universe I was born into,' he snapped back. 'It's what I know. I won't consign myself to a sexless future because you refuse to face up to the fact that we are having difficulty keeping our hands off each other,' he said. 'But I will not insult you, nor feel the need to take another woman to my bed if you behave as a wife should, Keeley. If you give me your body then I will promise you my fidelity.'

And then he smiled, a hard, cold smile which suggested he was almost *enjoying* her resistance. As if he were savouring the moment until he was able to conquer her. Or defeat her.

'It's up to you,' he finished. 'It's your call.'

Keeley's heart pounded. The way he spoke about marriage and sex was so *primitive*. He was autocratic and proud and he stirred her up so she couldn't think straight, but deep down she realised she had no other place to go. She remembered his warning about taking her to court to fight for the baby if she tried to oppose him. Some men might have made such a threat lightly, but she suspected Ariston wasn't one of them. But women had rights too, didn't they? He couldn't force her to remain in a marriage if it wasn't working. And he couldn't demand sex from her because it was his marital right to do so. Surely even he couldn't be *that* primitive.

'Very well, I will marry you. Just so long as you understand I'm only doing it to give my baby security.' She tilted her chin to meet the triumphant fire blazing from his eyes. 'But if you think I'm going to be some kind of sexual pushover just to satisfy your raging libido, then you're mistaken, Ariston.'

'You think so?' The smile which flickered at the edges of his lips was arrogant and certain. 'I am rarely mistaken, *koukla mou*.'

CHAPTER EIGHT

'Wow! I've never seen a bride wearing red before!' exclaimed Megan. 'Is this some new kind of fashion?'

But before Keeley had a chance to answer the woman who'd lent her the ill-fated dress on Lasia, her brand-new husband leaned forward and spoke for her.

'It's an ancient Greek custom,' said Ariston smoothly, his words curling over her skin like dark smoke. 'Traditionally, the bride wore a red veil in order to ward off evil spirits. But I suspect Keeley has deliberately adapted the look and given it a modern twist by wearing a crown of scarlet roses to match her dress. Isn't that right, Keeley?'

Resenting his perception even more than the way he'd just butted in, Keeley looked up into the blue blaze of Ariston's eyes, trying not to react as he slipped his arm around her waist and pulled her closer, looking for all the world like a loving and attentive groom. How appearances could deceive, she thought bitterly. Because he was not a loving groom—he was a cold-hearted control freak who was positively *glowing* with satisfaction because an hour earlier he had slipped an embellished golden wedding ring onto her rigid finger. He'd got exactly what he wanted and she was now his wife, stuck in an unwanted marriage he was determined would last.

He dipped his mouth to her ear and she hated the involuntary shiver which trickled down her spine as his breath fanned her skin.

'Clever you for researching Greek customs so thoroughly,' he murmured. 'Am I the evil spirit you're trying to ward off, Keeley?'

'Of course!' she said, curving her mouth into a big smile, because she'd discovered she could do the appearance thing just as well as Ariston. She could play the part of the blushing bride to perfection—all it took was a little practice. And why spoil a day with something as disappointing as the truth? Why not let people believe what they wanted to believe—the fairy-tale version of their story—that the struggling daughter of a notorious actress had bagged one of the world's most eligible men?

In the back of her mind she'd wondered if her past might catch up with her and if Ariston would have second thoughts about marrying a woman with a history like hers. Yet when a newspaper had regurgitated the old story of Keeley's mother cavorting on the back seat of the ministerial limo and asked Ariston whether the tawdry behaviour of his new mother-in-law gave him any cause for concern, he had broken the habit of a lifetime and given them a quote: 'Old news,' he'd commented, in a bored and velvety drawl. 'And old news is so dull, don't you think?'

Which was kind of ironic when Keeley thought about

how much fuss he'd made about what had happened in the past. But she supposed her pregnancy changed everything. It made him overlook her mother's transgressions. It made him act proprietorially towards her, something which he made no attempt to hide. She could feel him stroking his finger across the front of her scarlet dress, lingering lightly over the curve of her belly as if it was his right to do so. And she guessed it was. Because he was pulling the strings now, wasn't he? Certainly the purse strings. He had given her a brand-new credit card and told herself to buy what she liked—to transform herself into the woman who would soon become his wife. 'Because I want you to *look* like my wife from now on.' His eyes had glittered like blue ice as he had spoken. 'Not some little supermarket stacker who just happens to be wearing my ring.'

His remark had riled her and she'd been tempted to wear her oldest clothes all the time and see how he liked *that*. Would such defiance make him eager to be rid of her and thus grant her the freedom she craved? But then she thought about her baby…and the fact that she was soon going to be a mother. Did she really want to be seen pushing her buggy around the fancy places which Ariston frequented, wearing clothes which had come from the thrift shop? Wouldn't that whittle away at her confidence even more?

But the disturbing thing was that once she'd started, she'd found it surprisingly easy to spend her billionaire fiancé's money. Perhaps there was more of her mother in her than she'd thought. Or maybe she'd just forgotten the lure of wealth and how it could make people do unpredictable things. During her childhood when they'd been flush, money had trickled through her mother's fingers like sand and sometimes, if she'd been feeling especially benevolent, she had spent some of it on her only child. But her gifts had always failed spectacularly. Keeley had been given impractical frilly dresses which had made her stand out from the other little girls in their dungarees. There had been those frivolous suede shoes, ruined by their first meeting with a puddle—and ribbons which had made her look like some throwback to an earlier age. No wonder she'd grown up to be such a tomboy.

But she took to her new credit card like a duck to water, shopping for her imminent role as Ariston's wife with enthusiasm and allowing herself to be influenced by the friendly stylist who had been assigned to her by the fancy department store. She bought new clothes chosen specially to accommodate her growing frame, as well as new underwear, shoes and handbags. And didn't she enjoy the feeling of silk and cashmere brushing against her skin instead of the scratchy qualities of the man-made fabrics she'd worn up till then? She told herself she was only doing what she'd been instructed to do, but the speculative rise of Ariston's dark eyebrows when his driver had staggered into the City apartment under the weight of all those shiny shopping bags had left her feeling…uncomfortable. As if she'd just affirmed some of his deeply held prejudices about women.

But money was liberating, she realised. It gave her choices which had previously been lacking in her life and that newfound sense of liberation encouraged her to buy the scarlet silk dress and matching shoes, secretly enjoying the stylist's shocked reaction when she explained it was for her wedding day.

'You're some kind of scarlet woman, are you?' the woman had joked drily.

And now, at the small but glittering reception, Keeley realised that Ariston's hold on her had changed and he was pushing her away by a fraction so his gaze could rake over her, those smouldering blue eyes taking in every centimetre of the scarlet silk which was clinging to her curves.

'Spectacular,' he murmured. 'Quite…spectacular.'

She felt exposed—almost naked—which hadn't been her intention at all. She felt aroused, too—and surely that was even more dangerous. She tilted her chin defiantly, trying to swamp the sudden rush of desire which was making her skin grow heated and her nipples hard. 'So you approve of my wedding dress?'

'How could I not approve? It would have been entirely inappropriate for such an obviously pregnant wife to wear virginal white.' He gave a slow smile. 'Yet despite your unconventional colour choice and what I suspect was your intention to rile me, let me tell you that you really do make a ravishing bride, Keeley. Glowing, young and intensely fecund.'

'I'll… I'll take that as a compliment,' she stumbled, the tone of his voice making her momentarily breathless.

'That's what it was intended to be.' His eyes narrowed. 'So how are you feeling, *wife*?'

Keeley wasn't quite sure how to answer, because

the truth was complex—and strange. For the first time in her life she actually felt *safe*—and cosseted. She realised that Ariston would never let anyone harm her. That he would use his strength to protect her, no matter what. But he wasn't doing it for *her*, she reminded herself. He was doing it because she was carrying the most precious of cargoes, and as custodian of his unborn child she merited his care and attention. *That* was why he was suddenly being so considerate—and if she read anything more into it than that, then she would be embarking down a very perilous road.

'I'm a little tired,' she admitted. 'It's been a long day and I wasn't expecting it to be such…such an occasion.'

He frowned. 'You want to skip the meal and go home?'

'How can I? It wouldn't look very good if the bride didn't turn up for her own wedding breakfast.'

'You think I care?' He reached out to stroke his fingertips beneath her eyes. 'Your welfare supersedes everything.'

'No, honestly. I'm fine.' The touch of his fingers was doing crazy things to her heart and as she noticed Megan hovering close by with a camera phone pointed in their direction, something made her want to maintain the whole myth of this marriage. Was it pride? She forced a smile as the phone flashed. 'Let's join the others,' she said. 'Besides, I'm hungry.'

But Keeley's reluctance to leave the reception wasn't just about hunger. She was dreading returning to Ariston's gleaming apartment as man and wife and not just because she'd found its vast and very masculine interior intimidating. She had been staying at the famous Granchester Hotel while all the necessary pre-wedding paperwork was completed, because Ariston had insisted that they would only share a home as man and wife. Which seemed slightly bizarre since her rapidly increasing girth made a mockery of such old-fashioned sensibilities. But at least it had given her some breathing space and the chance to get used to her new life without Ariston's distracting presence. She knew she couldn't keep putting off living with him but now the moment of reckoning was approaching, she was terrified. Terrified about sharing an apartment with him and unsure how she would cope. At times she felt more like a child than a grown woman who would soon have a child of her own. Was that normal? she wondered.

But she pushed her reservations aside as she sat down to the Greek feast which had been provided by the hotel and it was a relief to be able to eat after what seemed like weeks of sickness. She could feel her strength returning as she worked her way through the delicious salads, though she could manage only half of one of the rich baklava cakes which were produced at the end of the meal. Despite the relatively small guest list, it somehow managed to feel like a real wedding and Ariston had even asked if she wanted her mother there. Keeley had been torn by his unexpected suggestion. She had felt a wave of something symbolic at the thought of her mother witnessing her marriage, until a last-minute chest infection had put paid to the idea. And maybe that was best. Even if she *had* been aware of what was going on around her, what would her mum have cared about seeing her married, when she'd made such a mockery of marriage herself?

Keeley had wondered why Ariston hadn't suggested a short trip to the register office with the minimum fuss and no guests other than a couple of anonymous witnesses gathered from the street. Wouldn't that have been more appropriate in the circumstances? But his reply had been quietly emphatic.

'Maybe I want to make a statement.'

'A statement?'

'That's right. Shout it from the rooftops. What is it they say? Fake it to make it.'

'By putting your stamp on me, you mean?' she questioned acidly. 'Branding me as a Kavakos possession—just like you did the night you had sex with me?'

His eyes had glittered like sunlight on a dark Greek sea. 'Humour me, Keeley, won't you? Just this once.'

And somehow she had done exactly that. She'd even managed to smile when he stood to make a speech, his fleeting reference to shotguns getting an affectionate laugh, especially from his brother.

'It's funny,' Pavlos said afterwards, with a bemused shake of his head. 'Ariston always vowed he would never marry and he said it like he really meant it. I'd never have guessed there was anything going on between you two. Not after that day at the art gallery when you could have cut the atmosphere with a knife.'

And Keeley didn't have the heart to disillusion him. She wondered what he'd say if he realised that Ariston had bedded her simply to ensure that Pavlos would never want her for himself, and that she had been too stupid and weak to resist him. Yet his need to control had backfired on him because he was now saddled to a woman he didn't really want, though he hid it well. As he raised his glass to toast his new bride, Keeley should have resented his ability to put on such a convincing show of unity—but the reality was a stupid, empty ache in her heart as she found herself yearning for something which could never be hers. He looked like a groom and acted like a groom—but the cold glitter in his blue eyes told its own story.

He will never care for you, she told herself. So don't ever forget it.

During the drive to his apartment, she tugged the scarlet flowers from her head and shook little bits of confetti from her blonde hair. But she couldn't shake off her detachment as she and Ariston walked into the impressive foyer of his apartment building, where doormen and porters sprang to instant attention and a few men in suits shot her bemused glances. She hugged her pashmina around her shoulders in a vain attempt to hide as much of the scarlet dress as possible. Why on earth hadn't she changed into something more sensible first?

A private elevator zoomed them up to the penthouse suite, with its impressive views over many of London's iconic buildings and its seemingly endless suites of rooms. There was even a swimming pool and a gym in the basement—and the outside terraces were filled with a jungle of plants which temporarily made you forget that you were in the heart of the city. She had been there only once before—an awkward visit to oversee the installation of her new clothes in a large room which was now called her dressing room and where every item had been hung in neat and colour-coordinated lines by Ariston's housekeeper.

She hugged the pashmina as they stood in a hallway as big as her bedsit, where a marble statue of a man appeared to be glaring at her balefully.

'So now what do we do?' she said bluntly.

'Why don't you go and change out of that dress?' he suggested. 'You've been shivering since we left the reception. Come with me and I'll remind you where our bedroom is.'

Our? She looked up at him. Had he mentioned that to her before, or had she just not been concentrating? Probably not. His housekeeper had been hovering helpfully during her previous visit, so maybe it had only been alluded to. 'You mean we're going to be…sharing?'

'Don't be naïve, Keeley.' He glittered her a smile. 'Of course we are. I want to have sex with you. I thought I'd made that clear. That, surely, is the whole point of being man and wife.'

'But the vows we made weren't real.'

'No? Then we could make them real. Remember what I said about faking it to make it?' He gave an odd kind of laugh. 'And don't widen your eyes at me like that, *koukla mou*. You look like one of those women in an old film who has been tied to the railway line and only just noticed the train approaching. I don't intend behaving like a caveman, if that's what concerns you.'

'But you said—'

'I said I wanted to have sex with you. And I do. But it has to be consensual. You would need to give yourself to me wholeheartedly—and consciously,' he added with a cool smile. 'I'm not talking about one of those middle-of-the-night encounters, where two bodies collide…and before you know it we're having mind-blowing sex without a single word being exchanged.'

'You mean…' the tip of her tongue snaked over her top lip as she followed him along the corridor, to a room which contained a vast bed which reminded her of a sacrificial altar '…like the night our child was conceived?'

He gave a short laugh. 'That's exactly what I mean. But this time I want us both to be fully aware of what's happening.' There was a pause as he turned around to face her. 'Unless silent submission is what secretly turns you on?'

'I already told you—I have practically no experience of sex,' she said, because suddenly it became important that he stopped thinking of her as some kind of stereotype and started treating her like a real person. 'I…' She bit her lip and said it before she had time to think about the consequences. 'I'd never even had an orgasm before I slept with you.'

He looked at her and she could see a glint of something incomprehensible in his narrowed blue eyes.

'Maybe that's the reason why I'm not trying hard to seduce you,' he said unexpectedly. 'Maybe I want you to stop staring at me as if I was the big, bad wolf and to relax a little. Your dressing room is next door—so why don't you get out of your wedding dress and slip into something more comfortable?'

'Like…what?'

'Whatever makes you feel good. But don't worry,'

he said drily. 'I'm sure I'll be able to keep my hands off you, if that's what you want.'

'That's what I want,' she said, seeing his tight smile before he turned away and closed the door behind him. And wasn't human nature a funny thing? She'd been gearing herself up to fight off his advances, but the news that he wasn't actually going to make any left her with a distinct feeling of *disappointment*. She never knew where she stood with him. She felt as if she were walking along an emotional tightrope. Was that intentional—or just the way he always was around women? She undid the side zip of the red wedding dress, trying to get her head around the fact that this vast room with its amazing views over the darkening city was *hers*.

No. Not hers. His. He owned everything. The dress she stood in and the leather shoes she gratefully kicked off.

But not the child in her belly, she reminded herself fiercely as she walked into the gleaming en-suite bathroom. That child was hers, too.

Stripping off and piling her hair on top of her head, she ran a deep bath into which she poured a reckless amount of bath oil, before sinking gratefully into the steamy depths. It was the first time all day that she'd truly relaxed and she lay there for ages, studying the changing shape of her body as the scented water gradually cooled and she was startled by the sound of Ariston's voice from the other side of the bathroom door.

'Keeley?'

Instantly her nipples hardened and she swallowed. 'I'm in the bath.'

'I gathered that.' There was a pause. 'Are you coming out any time soon?'

She pulled out the plug and the water began to drain away. 'Well, I'm not planning on spending the night in here.'

She towelled herself dry and tied her damp hair in a ponytail. Then she pulled on a pair of palest grey sweatpants and a matching cloud-like cashmere sweater and found her way back through the maze of corridors to the sitting room, where the lights on the skyscrapers outside the enormous windows were beginning to twinkle like stars. Ariston had removed his tie and shoes and he lay on the sofa, leafing his way through a stack of closely printed papers. His partially unbuttoned white shirt gave a provocative glimpse of his chest and, with his long legs stretched out in front of him, his powerful body looked relaxed for once. He glanced up as she walked in, the expression on his shuttered face indefinable.

'Better?'

'Much better.'

'Stop hovering by the door like a visitor. This is your home now. Come and sit down. Can I get you anything? Some tea?'

'That would be great.' She thought how *formal* they sounded—like two total strangers who had suddenly found themselves locked up together. But wasn't that exactly what they were? What did she really *know* about Ariston Kavakos other than the superficial? She realised she'd been expecting him to ring a discreet bell and for his housekeeper to come scurrying from some unseen corner to do his bidding, just as she'd done on her previous visit. But to her surprise, he rose to his feet.

'I'll go and make some.'

'You?'

'I'm perfectly capable of boiling a kettle,' he said drily.

'But…isn't your housekeeper here?'

'Not tonight,' he said. 'I thought it might be preferable to spend the first night of our honeymoon alone and without interruption.'

Once he'd gone Keeley sank down on a squashy sofa, feeling relieved. At least she would be able to relax without the silent scrutiny of his domestic staff who might reasonably wonder why one of their number was now installed as their new mistress.

She glanced up as Ariston returned, carrying a tray, with peppermint tea for her and a glass of whisky for himself. He sat down opposite her and as he sipped his whisky she thought about all the contradictory aspects of his character which made him such an enigma. And suddenly she found herself wanting to know more. *Needing* to know more. She suspected that in normal circumstances he would bat off any questions she might have, with the impatience of a man who held no truck with questions. But these weren't normal circumstances and surely it wasn't possible to co-exist with a man she didn't really know? A man whose child she carried in her belly. She'd *humoured him* as he had requested earlier in the day, so wasn't it his turn to do the same for her?

'You remember asking whether I wanted my mother at the wedding?' she said.

His eyes narrowed. 'I do. And you told me she wasn't well enough to attend.'

'No. That's right. She wasn't.' She drew in a deep breath. 'But you didn't even mention your own mother and I suddenly realised I don't know anything about her.'

His fingers tightened around his whisky glass. 'Why should you?' he questioned coolly. 'My mother is dead. That's all you need to know.'

A few months ago, Keeley might have accepted this. She had known her place in society and had seen no reason to step off the humble path which life had led her down. She'd made the best of her circumstances and had attempted to improve them, with varying degrees of success. But things were different now. *She* was different. She carried Ariston's child beneath her heart.

'Forgive me if I find it intolerable to be fobbed off with an answer like that.'

'And forgive me if I tell you it's the only answer you're getting,' he clipped back.

'But we're married. It's funny.' She drew in a deep breath. 'You talk so openly—so unashamedly—about sex yet you shy away from intimacy.'

'Maybe that's because I don't *do* intimacy,' he snapped.

'Well, don't you think you ought to try? We can't keep talking about cups of tea and the weather.'

'Why are you so curious, Keeley? Do you want something to hold over me?' He slammed his whisky glass down on a nearby table so that the amber liquid sloshed around inside the crystal. 'Some juicy segments of information to provide you with a nice little nest egg should ever you wish to go to the papers?'

'You think I'd stoop to something as low as that?'

'You already did when you wanted to leave Lasia, remember? Or are you blaming a suddenly defective memory on your hormones?'

It took a moment or two for Keeley to recall her blustering bravado, spoken when she'd been swamped by humiliation and the realisation that he'd had sex with her for all the wrong reasons. 'That was then when you were intimating that you might not allow me to leave your island,' she retorted. 'This is now...and I'm having your baby.'

'And that changes things?' he demanded.

'Of course it does. It changes *everything*.'

'How?'

She licked her lips, feeling as if she were on trial, wishing her gaze wouldn't keep straying towards his hands and wishing they would touch her. 'What if our little boy...?' She saw his face change suddenly and dramatically. Saw the same look of fierce pride darkening his autocratic features, as it had done when the sonographer had skated a cold paddle over her jelly-covered bump and pointed out the unmistakable outline of their baby son. For a man who claimed not to do emotion it had been a startling about-turn.

'What if our little boy should start asking me questions about his family, as children do?' she continued. 'Isn't it going to be damaging if I can't answer a simple query about his grandma just because his daddy is uptight and doesn't *do* intimacy? Because he insists on keeping himself hidden away and won't even tell his wife?'

'I thought you said our vows weren't real?'

She met his eyes. 'Fake it to make it, remember?'

There was a pause. He picked up his glass and took a long mouthful of whisky before putting it down again. 'What do you want to know?' he growled.

There were a million things she could have asked him. She was curious to know what had made him so arrogant and controlling. Why he possessed a stony quality which made him seem so *distant*. But maybe the question she was about to ask might give her some kind of insight into his character. 'What happened to her, Ariston?' she questioned slowly and watched his face darken. 'What happened to your mother?'

CHAPTER NINE

Ariston's heart pumped violently as he looked into the grass-green of Keeley's eyes. And although deep down he knew she had every right to ask about his mother, every instinct he possessed urged him not to tell her. Because if he told her he would reveal his inner self to her, and that was something he liked to keep locked away.

He understood where his aversion to intimacy stemmed from but was content to maintain that state of affairs. He made the rules which governed his life and if other people didn't like them, that was too bad. His demanding lifestyle had suited him perfectly and, although his lovers had accused him of being cold and unfeeling, he'd seen no reason to change. He'd been self-sufficient for so long that it had become a habit.

Not even Pavlos knew about the dark memories which still haunted him when he was least expecting them. Especially not Pavlos—because hadn't protecting his brother been second nature to him and the highest thing on his list of priorities? But here was Keeley, his new and very pregnant wife, her face all bright and curious as she asked her question. And this wasn't some boardroom where he could quash any unwanted topic at a moment's notice, or a lover he could walk away from without a backward glance because she was being too intrusive. This was just him and her—a woman he was now legally tied to—and there was no way he could avoid answering.

He stared at her. 'My mother left us.'

She nodded and he could see the effort it took her to react as if he'd said nothing more controversial than a passing reference to the weather. 'I see. Well, that's... unusual, because usually it's the man who goes, but it's by no means—'

'No.' Impatiently he interrupted her. 'You want the truth, Keeley? The plain, unvarnished truth? Only I warn you, it's shocking.'

'I'm not easily shocked. You forget that my own mother pretty much broke every rule in the book.'

'Not like this.' There was a pause. 'She sold us.'

'She *sold* you?' Keeley's heart began to slam against her ribcage. 'Ariston, how is that even possible?'

'How do you think it's possible? Because my father offered her a big, fat cheque to get out of our lives and stay out, she did exactly that.'

'And she...never came back?'

'No, Keeley. She never came back.'

She blinked at him uncomprehendingly. 'But...*why*?'

Behind the hard set of his lips, Ariston ground his teeth, wishing she would stop now. He didn't want to probe any more because that would start the pain. The bitter, searing pain. Not for him, but for Pavlos—the little baby whose mama didn't want him enough to fight for him. He felt his heart clench as he started to speak and the bitter words just came bubbling out.

'I'm not saying my father was blameless,' he said. 'Far from it. He'd been brought up to believe he was some kind of god—the son of one of the wealthiest ship-owners in the world. He was what is known as a *player*, in every sense of the word. At a time when free love was common currency, there were always women—lots of women. From what I understand my mother decided she couldn't tolerate his infidelities any more and told him she'd had enough.'

'Right,' she said cautiously. 'So if that was the case, then why didn't she just divorce him?'

'Because he came up with something much more at-tractive than a messy divorce. He offered her a king's ransom if she would just walk away and leave us alone. A clean break, he called it. Better for him. Better for her. Better for everyone.' His mouth twisted. 'All she had to do was sign an agreement saying that she would never see her two sons again.'

'And she…signed it?'

'She did,' he affirmed grimly. 'She signed on the dotted line and went to live a new life in America, and that was the last we ever saw of her. Pavlos was…'

There was a pause and when he spoke it was in a voice devoid of all nuance. A voice, thought Keeley, which was enough to break your heart in two.

'Just a baby,' he finished.

'And you?'

'Ten.'

'So what happened? I mean, after she'd gone.'

He stood up, picking up his papers and stacking them on a nearby table, carefully aligning all the corners into a neat pile before answering her question. 'My father was busy celebrating the completion of what to him seemed like the perfect deal—being completely rid of an irritant of an ex-wife. In his absence he employed a series of nannies to look after us, but none of them could take the place of our mother. Even though I was a child I suspected that most of them had been chosen on account of their looks, rather than their ability to look after a confused and frightened little baby.'

He stared into space. 'I was the one who took care of Pavlos, right from the start. He was my responsibility. I wasn't going to risk anyone else getting close to him and leaving him again. So I bathed him and changed his nappies. I taught him how to swim and to fish. I taught him everything I knew—everything that was decent and good—because I wanted him to grow up to be a normal little boy. And when the time was right, I insisted he go to school in Switzerland because I wanted him as far away from my father's debauched lifestyle as possible. That's why I encouraged him to become a mariner afterwards, because when you're away at sea you don't get influenced or seduced by wealth. There's nothing around you but the wind and the ocean and the wildness of nature.'

And suddenly Keeley understood a lot more about Ariston Kavakos. What had seemed like an overprotective attitude towards his younger brother and his need to control now became clear, because as a child he had seen their lives dissolve into total chaos. That explained his reaction when he'd seen her with Pavlos because for him she had been her mother's child, and a harmful influence. He must have seen all his hard work threatened—his determination that Pavlos should have a decent, normal life about to go up in smoke.

And she understood why he had threatened to fight her for their child too, no matter how ruthless that might seem. Because Ariston didn't actually *like* women, and who could blame him? He was under no illusion that women were automatically the *better* parent who deserved to keep the child in the event of any split. He had seen a mockery made of the so-called maternal bond. He'd fought to protect his own flesh and blood in the shape of Pavlos, she realised—and he would do exactly the same for their own son.

Yet could his mother have been all bad? Wasn't he in danger of seeing only one side of the story? 'Maybe she couldn't have withstood your father's power if she'd attempted to fight for custody,' she ventured.

His voice was like stone. 'She could at least have *tried.* Or she could have visited. Wrote a letter. Made a phone call.'

'She wasn't depressed?' she said desperately, casting around for something—anything—to try to understand what could have motivated a woman to leave her baby behind like that. And her ten-year-old son, she reminded herself. Who had grown into the man who stood before her. The powerful man whose heart was made of stone. Had everyone been so busy looking out for the motherless little baby, that they'd forgotten his big brother must also be lost and hurting?

'No, Keeley, she wasn't depressed. Or if she was she hid it well behind her constant round of partying. I wrote to her once,' he said. 'Just before Pavlos's fifth birthday. I even sent a photo of him, playing with a sandcastle we'd built together on Assimenos beach. Maybe I thought that the cute little image might bring her back. Maybe I was still labouring under the illusion that deep down she might have loved him.'

'And?'

'And nothing. The letter was returned to me, unopened. And a couple of weeks later we found out that she'd taken a bigger dose of heroin than usual.' His voice faltered by a fraction and when he spoke again it was tinged with contempt. 'They found her on the bathroom floor with a syringe in her arm.'

Keeley rubbed her hands together, as if that would remove the sudden chill which had iced over her skin. She wasn't surprised when Ariston suddenly walked over to the window, his powerful body tense and alert, his broad shoulders looking as if he were carrying the weight of the world upon them. She wondered if he was really interested in gazing out at the tall skyscrapers, or whether he just didn't want to expose any more of the pain which had flashed across his shuttered features despite his obvious attempt to keep it at bay.

'Poor woman,' she said quietly.

He turned back to face her; his habitual composure was back and his eyes were as cold as a winter sea.

'You defend her? You defend the indefensible?' he iced out. 'Do you think that everybody has a redeeming feature, Keeley? Or just if it happens to be a member of your own sex?'

'I was just trying to see it from a different perspective, that's all.' She sucked in a deep breath. 'I'm sorry about what happened to you and to Pavlos.'

'Save your words.' He began to walk across the vast sitting room towards her. 'I didn't tell you because I wanted your sympathy.'

'No?' A shiver ran down the length of her spine as he approached. 'Then why *did* you tell me?'

He had reached her now and Keeley's breath caught in her throat because he was close. Close enough to touch—and she wanted him to touch her. So much. He was towering over her and she could detect the anger simmering darkly from his powerful frame.

'So that you recognise what is important to me,' he husked. 'And understand why I will never let my child go.'

She looked up at him, her heart beginning to pound. Yes, she could understand that perfectly, but where did that leave her? Old sins cast long shadows—was she to be punished for the sins of his mother? Would she be simply another woman for him to despise and mistrust—another woman to regard with suspicion? He'd told her unequivocally he wouldn't tolerate a sexless marriage and would take a mistress if he was forced to do so. But he had also promised her his fidelity if she took him as her lover, and she believed him. Why was that? Because she wanted to believe the best in people, or because she was empty and aching and wanted to reach out to him in the only way she suspected he would let her?

She shifted her gaze from the distraction of his handsome face to the hands which were clasped tightly in her lap. She studied the shiny golden ring which sat beneath the gleaming diamonds of her hastily bought engagement ring and thought about what those bands signified. Possession, mainly—but so far there had been no physical possession. He'd put his arm around her after the ceremony but that had been done purely for show. Yet despite everything she wanted him. Maybe even more than ever before—because didn't the things he'd told her just now make him seem more *human*? He'd revealed the darkness in his soul and she'd come to understand him a little better. Couldn't they draw closer to one another as a result? Couldn't they at least *try*?

She wanted to taste the subtle salt of his skin and to breathe in all his masculine virility. She wanted to feel him inside her again. And it was her call—he'd already told her that. She ran her fingertip over the cold diamonds. She could act all proud and distant and drive him into the arms of another woman if that was what she wanted, but something was making that idea seem repellent.

She snaked her tongue over bone-dry lips, because the alternative was not without its own pitfalls. Was he aware that she was crippled with shyness at the thought of trying to seduce a man as experienced as him? All they'd shared so far had been a mindless night of passion with the sound of the sea muffling their cries. It had happened so spontaneously that she hadn't had to think about it—while the thought of having sex now seemed so *calculated*. Was she expected to stand up and loop her arms around his neck—maybe shimmy her body against his, the way she'd seen people do in films? But if she tried to pretend to be something she wasn't—wouldn't he see right through that?

'Ariston?' she said, lifting her gaze to his at last in silent appeal.

Ariston read consent in the darkened pools of her green eyes and a powerful surge of desire shafted through him. He had revealed more to her than to another living soul and instinct told him it would be better to wait until he had fully composed himself before he touched her. Until the dark and bitter memories had faded. But his need was so strong that the thought of waiting was intolerable. How ironic that this woman carried his child and yet he scarcely knew her body! He'd barely explored the lushness of her breasts or stroked the bush of blonde hair which guarded her most precious of treasures. His heart was hammering as he pulled her to her feet and all he could feel was her soft flesh as she melted against him.

'A real marriage?' he demanded, tilting her chin with his fingers so that she could look nowhere but at him. 'Is that what you want, Keeley?'

'Yes,' she said simply. 'Or as real as we can make it.'

But as he pulled the ribbon from her ponytail, so that her hair fell in a pale waterfall of waves, Ariston knew he must be honest with her. She needed to realise that the confidences he'd shared today were not going to become a regular occurrence. He'd told her what she needed to know so she could understand where he was coming from. But she needed to accept his limitations, and one in particular.

'Don't expect me to be the man of your dreams, Keeley,' he husked. 'I will be the best father and husband that I can and I will drive you wild in bed—that much I promise you, but I can never love you. Do you understand? Because if you can accept that and are prepared to live with it, then we can make this work.'

She nodded, her lips opening as if to speak, but he crushed her words away with his kiss. Because he was done with talking. He wanted this. Now. But not here. He saw her startled look of pleasure as he picked her up and began to carry her towards the bedroom.

'I'm too heavy,' she protested, without much conviction.

'You think so?' He saw her eyes widen as he kicked open the bedroom door and too late he realised this was the kind of thing that women built their fantasies around. Well, that was too bad. He could only be the man he really was. Hadn't he warned her what he was and wasn't capable of? He laid her down fully clothed on the bed, but when her fingernails began to claw at his shoulders he gently removed them. 'Let me undress first,' he said unevenly.

His fingers were trembling like a drunk's as he unbuttoned his shirt and he noted that aberration with something like bemusement. What power did she have over him, this tiny blonde with her moon-pale hair and those green eyes which were forest-dark with desire? Was it because beneath that ridiculous fluffy sweater she carried their child—was it that which made him feel powerful and weak all at the same time?

He saw her eyes dilate as he dropped the shirt to the floor and stepped out of his trousers, yet the kind of flippant question he might *usually* have asked about whether she was enjoying the floorshow didn't seem appropriate. Because this felt…different. He felt the hard beat of rebellion. Surely those meaningless vows he'd made earlier hadn't got underneath his skin?

'Ariston,' Keeley whispered and suddenly she was feeling confused—wondering what had caused his face to darken like that. Was he having second thoughts? No. She swallowed. She could see for herself that was definitely not the case, and though she should have been daunted by all that hard, sexual hunger—the truth was that she was shivering with anticipation.

She raised her lips but his kiss was nothing but a perfunctory graze as he slid off the velour sweat-pants and pulled the voluminous sweater over her head, so she was left in nothing but her underwear. And she was glad she'd allowed the stylist to steer her towards the fancier end of maternity lingerie to buy a matching set of underwear which had cost the earth. The front-clipped lilac silk bra clung to her breasts and the matching bikini briefs made her legs look much longer than usual. As his dark gaze raked over her, the look of appraisal on his face made her feel intoxicatingly *feminine*, despite her shape.

His hand starfished darkly over one breast and as she felt the nipple tighten so presumably did he, because a brief smile curved his lips.

'I want you,' he said unsteadily.

'I want you, too,' she whispered.

He leaned over to skim down her little bikini briefs. 'I've never had sex with a pregnant woman before.'

Lifting her bottom to assist him, Keeley gave him a reproachful look. 'I should hope not.'

'So this is all very…' he undid the front fastening of her bra so that her breasts came spilling out and bent his head to capture one taut tipple between the controlled graze of his teeth '…new to me,' he rasped.

'New to me, too,' she moaned, her head falling back against the pillow.

He took his time. More time than she would have believed possible given his obvious state of arousal. His body was taut and tense as he stroked his fingertips over her skin—as if he was determined to reacquaint himself with this new, pregnant version of her body. And, oh, didn't she just love what he was doing to her? He palmed her breasts and traced tiny circles over her navel with the tip of his tongue. He tangled his fingertips in her pubic hair and then stroked her until she squirmed. Until every nerve ending was so aroused she didn't think she could bear it any more. Until she whispered his name on a breathless plea and at last he entered her. Keeley moaned as he filled her with that first thrust and he stilled immediately, his eyes shuttered as they searched her face.

'I'm hurting you?'

'No. Not at all. You're…' Some instinct made her thrust her hips forward so that he went deeper still— because surely that was safer than telling him he was the most gorgeous man she'd ever seen and she couldn't quite believe he was her husband. 'Oh, Ariston,' she gasped as he began to move inside her.

And Ariston smiled because this was a sound with which he was familiar. The sound of a woman gasping out his name like that. He forced himself to concentrate on her pleasure, to make this wedding-night sex something she would never forget. Because a satisfied woman was a compliant woman and that was what suited him best. His self-control was almost at breaking point by the time she shattered around him, her fleshy body spasming with release, and it was only then that he allowed himself the luxury of his own orgasm. But he was unprepared for the way it ripped through his body like a raging storm or for the raw, almost savage sound which was torn from his throat as he came.

CHAPTER TEN

A SOFT GLOW crept beneath Keeley's eyelids and in those few blurred seconds between sleeping and waking, she stirred lazily. Replete from pleasures of the night and with the musky scent of sex still lingering in the air, she reached out for Ariston—but the space beside her on the bed was empty, the sheet cold. Blinking, she reached for her wristwatch and glanced across the bedroom. Just after six on a Saturday morning and there, silhouetted by the light flooding in from the corridor, was the powerful figure of her husband, fastening his cufflinks. She levered herself up the bed a little. 'You're not going into work?'

He walked into the bedroom, one of the cufflinks catching the light and glinting gold. 'I have to, I'm afraid.'

'But it's Saturday.'

'And?'

Keeley pushed the duvet away, telling herself not to make waves. Hadn't they just had the most amazing night, with the most amazing sex—and hadn't those hours of darkness felt like perfect bliss? So what if he went to work when most of London was still fast asleep and getting ready for the weekend? She told herself that Ariston's dedication to work was the price you paid for being married to such a wealthy man. But it was hard not to feel disgruntled because it would have been nice to have spent the morning in bed for once. To have done stuff like normal newly-weds—moaning and giggling about crumbs in the bed or debating whose turn it was to make the coffee.

But she wasn't a normal newly-wed, was she? She was the wife of a powerful man who had married her solely for the sake of their baby.

She forced a smile to her lips. 'So what time will you be home?'

Reaching for his jacket, Ariston glanced across to where Keeley lay, looking delectably rumpled and oh-so-accessible. Her heavy breasts were spilling over the top of a silky nightgown, which somehow managed to make her look even more decadent than if she'd been naked. She must have slipped it on again during the night, he thought, swallowing down the sudden dryness which rose to his throat. A night when she had been even more sensual than usual, her uninhibited response to his first careless advances leaving him deliciously dazed afterwards.

He'd arrived home with an armful of flowers impulsively purchased from a street seller outside his office, a vibrant bouquet which bore no resemblance to the long-stemmed stately roses usually ordered by one of his secretaries to placate her when he had been held up by a meeting. And Keeley had fallen on them with delight, burying her nose in the colourful blooms and going to the kitchen to put them in water before his housekeeper had shooed her away and taken over the task.

His heart clenched as he remembered the soft flush of colour to her cheeks and the bright glitter of her eyes as she'd risen up on tiptoe to kiss him. He had pulled her onto his lap after dinner, playing idly with her hair until she'd turned to him in silent question and he'd carried her off to their bedroom with a primitive growl of possession. Had he once told her that he didn't play the caveman? Because it seemed that he'd been wrong. And he didn't like being wrong.

He watched as she tucked a lock of hair behind her ears, the movement making her breasts strain even more against the shiny satin of her nightgown, and he forced himself to look away. To align the pristine cuffs of his shirt beneath his suit jacket as if that were the single most important task of the day.

Was she aware of her growing power over him? A shimmer of unease iced over his skin. She must be. Even someone as relatively innocent as her couldn't be oblivious to the fact that sometimes he didn't know what day of the week it was when she turned those big green eyes on him. Perhaps she was trying to extend that subtle power. Perhaps *that* was the reason for the sudden look of determination which had crossed over her sleep-soft face.

'Ariston?' she prompted. '*Must* you go?'

'I'm afraid I must. Anatoly Bezrodny is flying over from Moscow on Monday and there are a few things I need to look at before he arrives.'

There was a pause as she snapped on the bedside light and pleated her lips into a pout which was just begging to be kissed. 'You spend more time at the office than you ever do at home.'

'Perhaps you'd like to dictate the terms of my diary for me?' he questioned silkily. 'Speak to my assistant and have her run my appointments past you first?'

'But you're the boss,' she protested, undeterred by his quiet reproof. 'And you don't have to put in those kind of hours. So why do it?'

'It's *because* I'm the boss that I do. I have to set an example, Keeley. That's why you have a beautiful home to live in and lots of pretty things to wear. So stop pouting and give your husband a kiss goodbye.' He walked over to the bed and leaned over her, breathing in the sexy, morning smell of her. 'You haven't forgotten we're having dinner out tonight?'

'Of course I haven't.' She lifted her lips to his. 'I'm looking forward to it.'

But he thought the kiss she gave him seemed dutiful rather than passionate, which naturally challenged him—because nothing other than complete capitulation ever satisfied him. Framing her face with his hands, he deepened the kiss until she began to moan and he was sorely tempted to give her what she wanted, until a swift glance at his watch reminded him that his car would be waiting downstairs.

'Later,' he promised, reluctantly drawing away from her.

After he'd gone, Keeley lay back against the pillows, blinking back the stupid tears which had sprung to her eyes. What *was* her problem—and why was she feeling so dissatisfied of late? It wasn't as if she hadn't known what she'd been getting herself into when she'd married Ariston. She'd known he was a workaholic and he'd never promised her his heart. He'd been honest from the start—some might say brutally so—by telling her he could never love her. And she had accepted that. *He was giving as much of himself as he was capable of giving*—that was what she told herself over and over. She closed her eyes and sighed. It wasn't his fault if her feelings for *him* were changing…if suddenly she found herself wanting more than he was prepared to give. And allowing those feelings to accelerate was fruitless; she told herself that too. She would be setting herself up for disappointment if she kept on yearning for what she could never have, instead of just making the most of what she *did* have.

So she ate the delicious breakfast prepared by Ariston's cook and told his driver that she didn't need him that day. She thought the chauffeur seemed almost *disappointed* to be dismissed and, not for the first time, she wondered if Ariston had asked him to keep an eye on her. No. She picked up her handbag and checked she had her mobile phone. She mustn't start thinking that way. That really *was* being paranoid.

She thought about going to look at the autumn leaves in Hyde Park, but something made her take the train to New Malden instead. Was it nostalgia which made her want to go back to where she used to live? To stare at the world she'd left behind and try to remember the person she had been before Ariston had blazed into her life and changed it beyond recognition? She found herself walking down familiar streets until at last she reached her old bedsit, and as she stood and looked up at the window she wondered if she was imagining the surreptitious glances of the passers-by. Did she look out of place with her quietly expensive clothes and extortionately priced handbag as she chased the ghosts of her past?

She ate lunch in a sandwich bar and spent the afternoon at the hairdresser's before going home to get ready for dinner, but she was unable to shake off her air of heaviness as the housekeeper let her in. She didn't know what she'd expected from marriage to Ariston, but it certainly hadn't been this increasing sense of isolation. She'd known he was tricky and distant and demanding, but she'd…well, she'd *hoped*.

Had she thought that living together and having amazing sex might bring them closer together? That what had started out as a marriage of convenience might become, if not the real thing, then something which bore echoes of it? Of course she had, because that was the way women were programmed to think. They wanted closeness and companionship—especially if they were going to have a baby. She knew she'd broken down some invisible barrier after he'd told her about the heartbreak of his childhood and she'd prayed that might signal a new openness. After the passion of their wedding night, she'd waited for that openness to happen. And then she'd waited some more.

And now?

Careful not to muss her hair, she pulled a silky black evening dress over her head. Now she was being forced to accept the harsh reality of being married to someone who barely seemed to notice her, unless she was naked. A man who left early each morning and returned in time for dinner. Who slotted in time with her as if she was just another appointment in his diary. Yes, he accompanied her to all her doctor's appointments and murmured all the right things when they saw their baby son high-kicking his way across the screen. And very occasionally they drove out to the countryside or watched a film together—small steps which made her hope that non-sexual intimacy might be on the cards. But every time her hopes were dashed as those steel shutters came crashing down and he pushed her away—Mr Enigmatic who was never going to make the mistake of confiding in her again.

Ariston arrived home in a rush and went straight to the shower, emerging from his dressing room looking a vision of alpha virility, in a dark dinner suit which matched the raven thickness of his hair. He walked over to the dressing table where she sat and began to massage her shoulders—bare except for the spaghetti straps of her black dress. Instantly she felt the predictable shimmerings of desire and her nipples hardened.

'Ariston,' she said huskily as his fingers dipped from her shoulder to caress her satin-covered ribcage.

'Ariston, what? I'm only making up for what I didn't have time for this morning. And how can I prevent myself from touching you when you look so damned beautiful?'

She clipped on an opal earring. 'I don't feel particularly beautiful.'

'Well, take it from me, you are. In fact, I'm tempted to carry you over to that bed right now to demonstrate how much you turn me on. Would you like that, Keeley?'

Did the leaves fall from the trees in autumn? Of *course* she would like it. But using sex as their only form of communication was starting to feel dangerous. The contrast between his physical passion and mental distance was disconcerting and…unsettling. Each time he made love to her it felt as if he were chipping away a little piece of her, and wasn't she worried that soon there would be nothing of the real Keeley left? That she would become nothing but an empty shell of a woman? She fixed the second earring in place. 'We don't have time.'

'Then let's make time.'

'No,' she said firmly, rising to her feet in shoes which probably weren't the most sensible choice for a pregnant woman, but this was the first time she'd met Ariston's colleagues and, naturally, she wanted to impress. 'I don't want to arrive with my cheeks all flushed and my hair all mussed, not when I've spent all afternoon at the hairdresser's.'

'Then perhaps you should skip the hairdresser's next time,' he commented drily as he glanced at the elaborate confection of curls piled high on her head. 'If it puts you in such a bad mood.'

It was one of those stupid little rows which spiralled up out of nowhere and Keeley knew she ought to dispel the atmosphere which was still with them when they got into their car. She wasn't going to improve matters by sulking, was she? Laying her carefully manicured hand on his knee, she felt the hard muscle flex beneath her fingers.

'I'm sorry I was grumpy.'

He turned towards her, the passing street lights flickering like gold over his rugged features. 'Don't worry about it,' he said smoothly. 'It's probably just your hormones.'

She wanted to scream that not everything involved her wretched *hormones*—but she was aware that such a reaction would make a mockery of her words. She stared down at her baby bump instead, before lifting her gaze to his. Why not tell him about what else had been bugging her lately—a practical issue they could address and which might improve the quality of their lives? 'Ariston.'

'Keeley?'

She hesitated. 'Do we have to have quite so many staff?'

His eyes narrowed. 'I'm not quite sure what you mean.'

She shrugged a little awkwardly and began to fiddle with her jewelled handbag. 'Well, we have a housekeeper, a cleaner, a cook, a driver and a secretary—as well as that man who comes once a week to water all the plants on the terrace.'

'And? It's a big apartment. They all have their necessary roles in my life.'

She didn't correct him by reminding him that it was her life, too. Choose your battles carefully, she reminded herself. 'I know that. I just thought that maybe I could, you know…help.'

'Help?' He furrowed his brows. 'Doing what?'

'Oh, I don't know. Chores. *Stuff.* Something to make me feel like a real person who's connected with the world, rather than some sort of mindless doll who gets everything done for her. A bit of cleaning, perhaps. Maybe even some cooking.' She bit her lip. 'But when I offered to peel some potatoes for Maria the other day, she acted like I'd threatened to detonate a bomb in the middle of the kitchen.'

He seemed to be picking each word carefully, like someone selecting diamonds from a barrel of stones. 'Probably because she didn't think it was appropriate.'

'And why wouldn't it be?'

'Because…' He sucked in a breath and made no attempt to hide his sudden irritation. 'You are not on my staff, Keeley, not any more. You are now the mistress of my household and I would prefer it if you acted that way.'

She sat up ramrod-straight. 'You sound like you're *ashamed* of me!'

'Don't be absurd,' he clipped out. 'But it isn't possible to flit between the two worlds—you must realise that. You can't be peeling potatoes one minute, and asking someone to serve you tea the next. You need to be clear about your new role and demonstrate it to everyone else, so nobody gets confused. Do you understand?'

She swallowed. 'I think I'm getting the general idea.'

He caught hold of her hand. 'And things will probably settle down once you've had the baby.'

'Yes, probably. At least that's something I *can* do,' she said lightly.

There was a pause as he circled his thumb over her palm. 'Though we will need a nurse, of course,' he added.

At first she thought she must have misheard him. 'I'm sorry?' she said, but her heart had started to race with some dark and nameless fear as she looked into his face.

'A nurse,' he reiterated. 'A nursery nurse, I believe they're called.'

'But...' She could feel tiny little beads of sweat pricking at her forehead. 'I thought since you'd been so hands-on with Pavlos, you wouldn't want us to have any outside help with the baby. Was I wrong about that too, Ariston?'

She saw his face darken. Was he angry at the mention of his brother's name—for her daring to bring up a subject he had very firmly closed on the night of their wedding?

'Obviously, you will do the lion's share but I shall be out at work for most of the day.'

'And?' she questioned in confusion as his voice tailed off.

His eyes briefly caught the gleam of lights as the car slid to a halt outside the restaurant. 'And we will need a nurse who speaks Greek, so that my son will grow up speaking my tongue. For that is vital, given the heritage which will one day be his.'

His words were still reeling around Keeley's head as they entered the upmarket Greek restaurant—one of very few in central London, or so Ariston informed her as they were led towards the best table in the room. But she didn't care about the stunning *trompe l'oeil* walls painted with bright blue skies and soaring marble pillars, which made you feel as if you were standing in the middle of an ancient Greek temple. She was so reeling at this latest bombshell that she could barely take in the names of Ariston's formidable-looking colleagues or their beautiful wives, who, to a woman, were sleek and dark and polished. She recited their names silently in her head, like a child learning tables. Theo and Anna. Nikios and Korinna.

And of course they all kept slipping into Greek from time to time. Why wouldn't they, when it was their first language? Even though they seamlessly switched to English to include her, Keeley still felt like a complete outsider. And this was what it would be like when she had the baby, she realised as she stared down at her glass of melon juice. She would be on the periphery of every conversation and event. The English mother who could not communicate with her half-Greek child. Who remained on the outskirts like some silent ghost. She swallowed. Unless she did something about it. Started being proactive instead of letting everyone else decide her destiny for her. Since when had she started behaving like such a *wuss*? If she didn't like something she ought to change it.

The men were deep in conversation as Keeley looked

across the table at Korinna, who was playing with her dish of apple sorbet instead of eating it.

'I'm thinking about learning Greek,' Keeley said suddenly.

'Good for you.' Korinna smiled before lifting her narrow shoulders in a shrug. 'Though it's not an easy language, of course.'

'No, I realise that,' said Keeley. 'But I'm going to give it my very best shot.'

She was just returning from the washroom when she crossed paths with the young waiter who had been looking after their table all evening, and he moved aside to let her pass.

'You are enjoying your meal, Kyria Kavakos?' he questioned solicitously.

'Oh, yes. It's delicious. My compliments to the chef.'

'You will forgive me for intruding?' he said, in his faultless English. 'But I couldn't help overhearing you saying you wanted to learn Greek.'

'I do. I'm just trying to work out the best way to go about it.'

He smiled. 'If you like, I could help. My sister is a teacher and she's very good. She teaches at the Greek school in Camden but she also gives private lessons and is very keen to expand. Would you like her card?'

Keeley hesitated as he offered her a small cream card. She told herself it would be rude to refuse such a kind offer and that perhaps this was an example of fate stepping in to help her. They said that working one-to-one was the best way to learn a new language and this could be an empowering gesture on her part. Wouldn't it be a brilliant surprise for Ariston if he realised she was making an effort to integrate into a culture which was so important to him?

She would show him what she was capable of, she thought. And he would be proud of her.

'Thank you,' she said with a smile, taking the card from the waiter and slipping it into her handbag.

CHAPTER ELEVEN

ARISTON LET HIMSELF quietly into the apartment to hear the unmistakable sounds of someone slowly reciting the Greek alphabet. He stood very still. They were coming from the music room, which was situated at the furthest end of the penthouse, and they were being spoken by a voice he didn't recognise. He frowned as he heard a second voice stumble over the letter *omicron*—traditionally a difficult letter for non-Greek speakers to pronounce—and suddenly realised that it was his wife who was now speaking. He began to walk along the corridor and the sight which greeted him took him completely by surprise. A beautiful young Greek girl wearing a sweater and a very short denim skirt was standing outlined against one of the giant windows and his wife was sitting near the piano, reading aloud from a textbook. They looked up as he walked in and he saw uncertainty cross over Keeley's features as her words died away.

The smile he gave was intended to be pleasant but his words didn't quite match. 'What's going on?' he questioned.

'Ariston! I wasn't expecting you.'

'Apparently not.' He raised his eyebrows. 'And this is?'

'Eva. She's my Greek teacher.'

There was a pause. 'I didn't know you had a Greek teacher.'

'That's because I didn't tell you. It was going to be a surprise.'

'Look, I can see you must be busy.' Eva was looking at each of them in turn and beginning to gather up a stack of papers before thrusting them hastily into a leather briefcase. 'I'd better go.'

'No,' said Keeley quickly. 'You don't have to do that, Eva. There's still half an hour of the lesson left to run.'

'I can always come back,' said Eva in a bright voice which suggested this was never going to be an option.

Ariston waited as Keeley showed the teacher out, listening to the sound of her rapid returning footsteps before she marched into the room and glared at him.

'What was *that* all about?' she demanded.

'I could ask you the same question. Who the hell is *Eva*?'

'I told you. She's my Greek teacher—isn't that obvious?'

'Your Greek teacher,' he repeated slowly. 'And you found her…where?'

She sighed. 'She's the sister of the waiter who served us the night we went to the Kastro restaurant. He overheard me saying to Korinna that I wanted to learn Greek and so he gave me Eva's card on my way back from the washroom.'

'Run that past me again,' he said. 'She's the *sister* of some random waiter you met in a restaurant?'

'What's wrong with that?'

'You're seriously asking a question like that?' he demanded. 'Think about it. You don't even *know* these people!'

'I do now.'

'Keeley,' he exploded. 'Don't you realise the potential consequences of inviting *strangers* into my home?'

'It's my home too,' she said in a shaky voice. 'Or at least, it's supposed to be.'

With an effort he altered the tone of his voice, trying to dampen down the anger which was rising up inside him like a dark tide. 'I'm not trying to be difficult, but my position is not like that of other men. I happen to be extremely wealthy. You know that.'

'Oh, yes—I know it. I'm never likely to forget it, am I?' she retorted hotly. 'What do you want me to do, Ariston—go around checking that Eva hasn't pocketed one of your precious Fabergé eggs?'

'Or maybe,' he continued, as if she hadn't spoken, 'maybe introducing you to the Greek teacher was simply a clever diversion and the pretty-boy waiter has designs on you himself?'

'You think he has designs on me?' She stood up and gave a disbelieving laugh as she angled her palms over the curve of her belly. 'Looking like *this*? How dare you? How *dare* you say such a thing to me?'

Ariston let her words wash over him but instead of being irritated by her defiance, all he could think about was how ravishing she looked in her anger. Her blonde hair was spilling wildly around her face and her green eyes were spitting emerald fire and automatically he reached out to pull her into his arms. That first contact made her pupils dilate and although she had started beating her hands furiously against his chest, she moaned when he started to kiss her and she moaned some more when he palmed her nipple and felt the tip pushing hungrily against his hand. She kissed him back and her kiss was hot and hard and angry, but the beating of her fists became less insistent. He levered her closer, and jutted his hips so that she could feel just how hard he was and she writhed against him in furious frustration.

Slipping his hand underneath her dress, he felt her bare thigh and as he began to stroke his fingers up towards her panties his desire went right off the scale. Just like hers. He could hear the unsteady rush of her breath as she scrabbled at his belt, and as she slipped the notch free he felt as if he might explode. He was rock-hard and the unmistakable scent of her arousal was in the air as his slowly moving fingers reached her panties to discover they were damp. So damp. He groaned again, and so did she as he pushed the taut panel aside and slicked his finger over her honeyed flesh, confident that sex would dissolve the tension between them as it always did. Couldn't he show her who was boss and wouldn't her hungry body accept that, the way it always did? Her arms wound themselves around his neck and he was about to pick her up and carry her over to the *chaise-longue* when suddenly he came to his senses.

'No,' he said suddenly, his heart pounding in protest

as he removed her hand from his trousers and pushed her away.

It took several moments before she spoke and when she did she looked at him in confusion. 'No?'

'I don't want you, Keeley. At least, not right now.'

'You don't?' she questioned, before giving a disbelieving laugh. 'Are you quite sure about that? Isn't that the way you like to settle any kind of disputes we have?'

He suppressed a ragged groan before forcing himself to step away from her. 'I'm not making love to you when we're in this kind of mood,' he said, his voice thick. 'I'm angry and so are you, and I fear I might be more...*physical* with you than I should be.'

'And?'

'And that's probably not the best idea given that you're pregnant.'

Keeley stared into his shuttered features as desire drained from her body, like water from the bathtub, and in its place came a horrible sinking realisation. Because no matter what she did or what she said—no matter how hard she tried or how long they stayed married—Ariston would always remain in command. She could learn Greek until the cows came home but it wouldn't make any difference. She could even try to find out more about ship-owning, but she would be wasting her time. Because what she wanted didn't count. It was what *Ariston* wanted which counted and it always would, because he ruled the roost and had been allowed to do so for years.

He liked her to know her place and to run everything past him first. He didn't like strangers in the house and now she knew that, she would be expected to respect his wishes. Her home had become her prison and her husband the rigid jailer. And the reason he didn't want to make love to her right now was nothing to do with his fears about her pregnancy. The expression on his face was as dark as the time he'd told her about his mother and suddenly she understood why. Because he didn't like the way she was making him react, she realised.

He didn't want to lose control or to be seen to lose control.

And she realised something else, too. That if she stayed, she would spend the rest of her life sublimating herself to *his* desires and *his* whims. The one thing she had asked for when she'd agreed to marry him hadn't materialised. They would never be equals—and what kind of an example would that be for her son?

Smoothing her hands over her hot cheeks, she stared at him. 'I'm done with this, Ariston,' she whispered hoarsely.

He narrowed his eyes. 'What are you talking about?'

'You. Me. Us. I'm sorry. I can't do this any more. I can't stay in this…this *mockery* of a marriage.'

His smile was cruel. She hadn't seen him look at her that way in a long time, but now she was reminded of the essential ruthlessness which lay at the very core of him.

'But you don't have any choice, Keeley,' he said silkily. 'You're pregnant with my child and there's no way I'm letting you go.'

She met the quiet fury in his eyes. 'You can't stop me.'

'Oh, I think you'll find I can,' he said. 'I have the

experience as well as the wherewithal. You have nothing while I have everything. I can get the full weight of any international court to rule in my favour in a custody battle—don't ever doubt that—though it's a path I'd rather not take. So don't make me, Keeley. Why don't we just calm down and recalibrate?' He fixed his steely blue gaze on her. 'Perhaps I *was* a little unreasonable—'

'Perhaps?' she demanded and she realised something else, too. That people didn't interrupt Ariston. His power had allowed him to build a wall around himself so high that nobody ever dared try. He'd made up all the rules and everyone else was supposed to just fall in and obey them. And everyone always had—until now. She was the only one who had dared to step out of line, but he couldn't wait to make her step right back in it again. 'You don't get it, do you?' she said shakily. 'This isn't a marriage, Ariston. It's a farce and a prison—and I'm not just talking about your lack of trust or the jailer-like behaviour you've demonstrated simply because I had the temerity to invite someone home!'

'Keeley—'

'No! You will hear me out. You will. Do you want to hear the reality of what it's like being married to you? Of how great it really is? You spend long hours in the office—and when you're back, at best you tolerate me. Guaranteed orgasms and the occasional trip to the theatre don't add up to intimacy, but I guess I shouldn't be surprised, because you don't *want* intimacy. You told me that yourself and at the time I thought I could live with it, or maybe even change it—but now I know I can't. Because you don't care about me, Ariston—

all you really care about is your baby. Sometimes you make me feel like a character in a science-fiction film, someone who is growing your child so that you can take him away from me just as soon as he's born! As if I'm nothing but a damned incubator!'

'Keeley—'

'Will you stop trying to interrupt me?' she yelled. 'When I mentioned that we were completely outnumbered by staff and spoke of my desire to help with a little housework, you looked at me as if I was some kind of freak. So what am I supposed to do all day? Haunt the shops like some well-dressed mannequin while I blitz your credit card?'

'Lots of women do.'

'Well, not me. If you must know, it bores the hell out of me. I had a brief love affair with excessive spending before we got married, but I'm over it now. It's an empty, meaningless existence. I'd rather give the money to charity than keep buying more overpriced handbags!'

'Keeley—'

'I haven't finished,' she continued icily. 'You speak Greek and I can't, which means I would always be the outsider—and when I do use my initiative to take lessons, I get accused of having the hots for my teacher's brother!'

'I hear what you're saying,' he said, sucking in an unsteady breath. 'And I realise I overreacted. Of course you must have lessons if you want them, but at least let me choose someone suitable to teach you. You can't just sign up with the sister of someone you've bumped into at a restaurant.'

'Why not?'

'Because they haven't been vetted,' he gritted out.

It was the final straw and it was at that point that Keeley knew there could be no going back. And no going forward either. Her heart was pounding fit to burst but somehow she kept her voice steady. 'So what am I supposed to do—be stuck in here while you vet anyone I might wish to see? Do you want to build barriers around me as high as the ones you've built around yourself?'

'*Now* who's overreacting?' he demanded.

'I'm not.' She shook her head. 'I thought things might change a little once we were married—but instead of the closeness I foolishly hoped might happen, all I get is anger and suspicion! I feel sorry for you, Ariston,' she added quietly. 'To view the world in such a cynical way means you'll never be happy and that will inevitably spill over into all our lives. And I'm not having any child of mine brought up in an atmosphere like that. I don't want our son to grow up knowing only distrust and cynicism—or to wonder why Mummy and Daddy never show each other any real affection. I want him to have a healthy view of the world, and that's why I'm leaving.'

'Just try,' he challenged softly.

She gave a nod of bitter understanding as she met his darkened eyes. 'Is that your way of saying you'll cut off my funds? Are you going to play the financial tyrant in addition to the emotional one? Would you really go that far, Ariston—after everything you've been through yourself? Well, go right ahead—be my guest! But if you do that I'll go straight to a lawyer and get them to slap a maintenance order on you. Or I'll sell *these*.' She pointed a shaking finger at the cold diamonds which flashed on her fingers, and then at the glittery tennis bracelet which was dangling from her wrist. 'Or *this*. Or if need be, I'll go to the papers. Yes. I'd do that, too. I'd sell my story and tell them what it was like being married to the Greek tycoon. I'd do anything to make sure you don't take my baby away, no matter how much you offer me to disappear from your life. Because I would never ever walk away from my baby and no amount of money could induce me to.' She sucked in a deep breath before her next words came out with a quiet intensity.

'I am not your mother, Ariston.'

She saw him flinch as if she'd hit him, but nothing was going to stop her now. 'Now, if you'll excuse me,' she said, her voice trembling, 'I'm going to pack my things and move out. And if you try to stop me, I'll… I'll call the police!'

His expression was unfathomable as their gazes clashed and she knew she'd pushed him as far as she possibly could. All the things she'd said had needed to be said and she'd meant every word of them, but that small glimmer of hope inside her refused to die. Could he read it in her eyes? Could he see the yearning she suspected still lingered there? The hope that maybe this showdown had cleared the air once and for all and he would let her get close enough to be the wife she really wanted to be. To show him all the love which was in her heart and maybe break down some of those formidable barriers he'd erected around his own. She swallowed. He might not ever be able to love her back, but couldn't he relax enough to *like* her and to *trust* her?

But the moment he opened his mouth she knew she had been wishing for the stars.

'I think, given your current state of hysteria, that you might be better to sleep on it. I will give you some space by moving into a hotel tonight—and hopefully, by morning, you might have calmed down a little.' His voice suddenly softened. 'Because getting yourself into this kind of state can't be good for the baby, Keeley.'

It was the final twist of the knife and Keeley wanted to howl with frustration. And sorrow. That too. She was glad he cared for his unborn son, but suddenly she needed him to care for her, too—and he was never going to do that. Quickly, she turned away from him, terrified he would see the heartbreak on her face or witness the tears which had begun to stream from her eyes as she stumbled her way towards the bedroom.

CHAPTER TWELVE

THE OCTOBER SKY was grey and brooding and Ariston was staring into space when the intercom on his desk buzzed and the disembodied voice of Dora, his assistant, spoke.

'I have Sheikh Azraq of Qaiyama on the line for you on one, Ariston.'

Restlessly, Ariston tapped his finger against the surface of the desk. He had been waiting for the call to confirm a deal he'd worked hard for. A deal which had the potential to increase the company's portfolio by many millions of dollars. He was about to accept the call when his mobile phone started ringing and he saw the name which was flashing up on the screen. Keeley. He felt the urgent crash of his heart and the sudden tightening of his throat.

'Tell the Sheikh I'll call him back later, Dora.'

'But, Ariston…'

It was rare for his assistant to even *attempt* to remonstrate with him but Ariston knew the reason for her unusual intervention. Sheikh Azraq Al-Haadi was one of the most powerful leaders of the desert lands and one who would not take kindly to his refusal to accept a phone call which had taken many days of planning to organise. But one thing he knew without a shadow of a doubt was that talking to Keeley was more important. His tapping ceased and Ariston's hand clenched into a tight fist as satisfaction hardened his lips into a smile. Was she regretting her decision to walk out on him? Finding that life wasn't quite so straightforward without the protection of her influential husband? Had she realised that he'd been right all along and that his concern about her associates had sprung solely from a need to protect her? He allowed himself a beat of anticipation. He would accept her back, yes, but she must understand that he would accept no similar tantrums or hysteria in the future—for all their sakes.

'Please tell the Sheikh I will move heaven and earth to arrange another call,' he said firmly. 'But for now I have someone else I need to speak to, so don't disturb me until I say so, Dora.'

He snatched up the mobile phone and clicked the connection, but took care to keep his voice bland and noncommittal. 'Hello?'

There was a breathless kind of pause. 'Ariston,' came the soft English voice which made his heart stab with a strange kind of pain. 'You took so long to answer that I thought you weren't going to pick up.'

Something inside him was urging him to make an attempt at conciliation but the anger he'd felt when she had carried through her threat and walked out on him had not left him.

'Well, I'm here now,' he said coolly. 'What is it you want, Keeley?'

The tone of her voice altered immediately and the stumbled apology he had been expecting was not forthcoming.

'As I'm having private healthcare, my obstetrician has fitted in an extra check-up for me and I'm due for a scan tomorrow,' she said, her voice now as cool as his. 'And I thought you might like to come. I realise it's very short notice and you might not be able to clear your diary in time—'

'Is that why you left it so late to invite me?'

He heard the unmistakable sound of a frustrated sigh. 'No, Ariston. But since you haven't bothered answering any of my emails—'

'You know I don't like communicating by email,' he said moodily.

'Yes, I realise that.' There was a pause. 'I just… I wasn't sure whether or not you'd want to see me. I thought about sending you a photo once I'd had the scan done, then thought that wouldn't be fair and so I—'

'What time,' he interrupted brutally, 'is it happening?'

'Midday. At the Princess Mary hospital. Where we went before—you remember?'

'I'll be there,' he said, before the voice of his conscience forced the next question from his lips. 'How are you?'

'I'm fine. All good.' He could hear her swallowing. 'The midwife is very pleased with my progress and I—'

'I'll see you tomorrow,' he said, and terminated the conversation.

He sat staring into space afterwards, angry with himself for being so short with her, but what the hell did she expect—that he would run around after her like some kind of puppy? He stared at the sky, whose dark clouds had now begun to empty slanting rods of rain onto the surrounding skyscrapers. After their blazing row he'd spent the night in a hotel to give her time to cool off, returning the following morning and expecting her to have changed her mind. In fact, he'd been expecting an apology. His mouth hardened. How wrong he had been. There had been no contrition or attempt to make things better. Her mood had been flat yet purposeful as she had repeated her determination to move out.

He'd tried being reasonable. He had not opposed her wishes, giving her free rein to move into her own place, telling himself that, if he gave her the freedom she thought she wanted and the space she thought she needed, it would bring her running right back. But it hadn't. On the contrary, she had made a cosy little nest out of her rented cottage on Wimbledon Common, as if she was planning to stay there for ever. During his one brief visit, he had stared in disbelief at the sunny yellow room, which she had made into a perfect nursery by adorning the walls with pictures of rabbits and such like. A shiny mobile of silvery fish had twirled above a brand-new crib and in the hallway had stood an old-fashioned pram. He had looked out of the window at the seemingly endless green grass of the Common and his heart had clenched with pain as he acknowledged his exclusion. And yet pride stopped him from showing it. He had given a cool shake of his head when she had offered him tea, citing a meeting in the city as the reason why.

She had told him she would be fair and that he could have paternal visiting rights as often as he liked and he believed her, but the idea of living without his son made his heart clench with pain. And yet the thought of an ugly legal battle for their baby had suddenly seemed all wrong.

Why?

Why?

He slept badly—something which was becoming a habit—and he was already waiting when Keeley arrived at the hospital, failing to hide the shock on her face when she saw him.

'Ariston!' Her cheeks went pink. 'You're early!'

'And?'

She looked as if she wanted to say something more but smiled instead, except that, as smiles went, it didn't look terribly convincing. Her mouth seemed strained but he thought he'd never seen her looking more beautiful, in a green velvet coat which matched her eyes and her fair hair hanging over one shoulder in a thick plait.

'Shall we go up to the scanning room?' she said.

'As you wish,' he growled.

The appointment couldn't have gone better. The radiographer smiled and pointed out things which didn't really need pointing out—even to Ariston's untutored eye. The rapidly beating little heart and the thumb which was jammed into a monochrome mouth. He could feel the salt taste of unwanted tears in the back of his throat and was glad that Keeley was busy wiping jelly from her stomach, giving him enough time to compose himself.

And when they emerged into the quiet London street it felt as if he had stepped into another world.

'Would you like lunch?' he questioned formally.

'I...no, thank you.'

'Coffee, then?'

She looked as if she wanted to say something important but although she had opened her lips, she quickly closed them again and shook her head. 'No, thanks. It's very kind of you but I'm off coffee at the moment and I'm...tired. I'd rather get home if it's all the same with you.'

'I'll have my driver drop you off.'

'No, honestly, Ariston. I'll get the bus or the Tube. It's no bother.'

'I'm not having you struggling across London on public transport in your condition. I will have my driver drop you off,' he repeated in a flat tone which didn't quite disguise his growing irritation. 'Don't worry, Keeley. I'll take a cab. I wouldn't dream of subjecting you to any more of my company since you clearly find the prospect so unappealing. Here. Get in.'

He pulled open the door of the limousine which Keeley hadn't even noticed and which had drawn to a smooth and noiseless halt beside them. He was watching her as she slid onto the back seat, the scent of leather and luxury seeming poignantly familiar as she stared into Ariston's blue eyes—those beautiful blue eyes which she had missed so much. Her mouth dried. Should she tell him to come round some time? Would that send out the wrong message—or maybe the real message—that it wasn't just his eyes she had missed?

'Ariston,' she began, but he had closed the car door and given an almost imperceptible nod to his driver as the powerful machine pulled away.

And Keeley turned round, slightly ungainly with her baby bump, wanting to catch a glimpse of his face as the car pulled away. Was she hoping for one of those movie endings, where she would surprise a look of longing on *his* face and she could yell at the driver to stop the car, and…

But he was walking away, striding purposefully towards a black cab which had just switched off its yellow light, and Keeley turned away, biting her lip as the limousine took her southwest, towards Wimbledon.

She was doing the right thing. She was. She kept telling herself that over and over. Why sit through a torturous lunch or even a cup of coffee when Ariston had a face like dark granite? He didn't love her and he never could. He was an unreasonably jealous and controlling man. He might have the power to turn her to jelly whenever he so much as looked at her but he was all the things she despised.

So how come she still wanted him with a longing which sometimes left her breathless with regret for what could never be?

And she was doing this for their baby, she reminded herself. Building respect between them and forging a relationship which would demonstrate what two adults could achieve if they only put their minds to it.

The journey to her cottage took for ever and in truth it would have been quicker getting the train, but the moment she walked up the path to her little house she could feel a slight lifting of her mood. Wimbledon Common had been one of those places she'd always drooled about when she'd lived in New Malden. She used to take the bus there on her day off. It had a villagey feel and a pond, plus lots of lovely little shops and restaurants. She'd seen other pregnant mothers giving her cautious smiles when she was out and about and she wanted to reach out and make friends, but something was holding her back. She shut the front door with a bang. She didn't want to let anyone close because then she would have to explain her circumstances and tell them that her brief marriage was over. Because if she admitted it to someone else, then she would have to accept it was true.

And she didn't want it to be true, she realised. She wanted…

She bit her lip as she batted the dark thoughts away. She didn't dare express what she wanted, not even to herself. All she knew was that she couldn't go back to that old way of living. Of feeling like a pampered doll in someone else's life. A decorative asset to be brought out whenever the situation merited it. She wanted to *connect* with the real world—not sit in her gilded penthouse and look down on it. And most of all she wanted a man who wouldn't make out that feelings were like poison—and you should avoid them whenever possible.

She lit a fire in the grate and had just made a pot

of tea when there was a ring on the bell. She peered through the peephole, shocked to see Ariston standing on her doorstep, his hands shoved deep in the pockets of his trousers, his face a dark glower. She pulled open the door and there he was, his black hair ruffled by the October wind and his jaw all shadowed.

Her heart missed a beat. 'Ariston,' she said, wondering if he could hear the slight quaver in her voice. 'What…what are you doing here?'

His shuttered features looked forbidding. 'Can I come in?'

She hesitated for only a moment before stepping aside to let him pass. 'Of course.'

She wasn't going to do that thing of offering him tea—of pretending this was some kind of social call. There wasn't going to be any of that fake stuff which just wasted time and meant nothing. She would hear him out and then he would go. But a shiver of apprehension whispered over her because an impromptu visit like this didn't bode well—not when his expression was so serious and so *brooding*. Had he decided he was being too soft with her and now that she was showing no signs of moving back, he was going to retaliate? Maybe instruct his lawyers to reduce the generous amount of income she was receiving—to shock her into seeing sense. Was he going to starve her out to make her come back to him? It was an unpalatable thought until she thought of one which was even worse.

That he didn't want her back.

Pain and panic rushed through her like a hot, fierce tide. What if he'd decided that life was easier without a wife who was constantly nagging him because he stayed late at the office? If he'd decided he'd had enough of domesticity and wanted to get back on the party scene. That she had been right all along and the marriage simply wasn't working.

'What do you want, Ariston?' she said, in a low voice. 'Why are you here?'

Ariston stared at her and the trilingual fluency of a lifetime suddenly deserted him. On the way here he'd worked out exactly what he was going to say to her but all the words seemed to have flown straight out of his head. But he knew what he wanted, didn't he? He was a man who was skilled in the art of negotiation. So wasn't it time to go all out and get it?

'I'm going to reduce my hours,' he said.

She looked taken aback, but she nodded. 'Okay.'

'Because I realise that you're right.' He rubbed his fingers over the faint stubble of his chin as if only just realising he'd forgotten to shave that morning. 'I've been working too hard.'

He looked at her expectantly, waiting for the praise which such a magnanimous gesture surely merited and for her to fling herself into his arms to thank him. But she didn't. She didn't move. She just stood there with her green eyes wary and her pale hair glowing in the thin autumn light which was streaming through the window.

'And your point is, what?' she questioned.

'That we'll spend more time together. Obviously.'

She gave an odd smile. 'So what has brought about this sudden revelation?'

He frowned, because her reaction was not what he had imagined it would be. 'I allowed myself to accept that the Kavakos company is in the black and is likely to stay that way for the foreseeable future,' he said slowly.

She screwed up her nose. 'And hasn't it always been?'

Raking his fingers back through his hair, he shook his head. 'No. I think I told you that when my father died, I discovered he'd blown most of the family fortune. For a while it was touch and go whether or not we'd make it. Suddenly I was looking into a big black hole where the future used to be and I had so many people relying on me. Not just Pavlos but all the staff we employed. People on Lasia whose livelihood depended on our success. People in cities all over the world.' He sucked in a deep breath. 'That's why I put the time in— long hours, every day, way past midnight. It took everything I possessed to turn things around and get the company back on an even keel.'

'But that was then, and this is now—and Kavakos is arguably the biggest shipping company in the world.'

He nodded. 'I know that. But hard work got to be such a habit that I let it take me over. And I'm not going to do that any more. I'm going to spend less time at the office and more time at home. With you.' He looked at her. 'That's all.'

The silence which followed seemed to go on and on and when she spoke her voice was trembling.

'But that's not all, Ariston,' she said. 'The reason you work so hard isn't because you've developed some kind of *habit* you can't break or because secretly you live in fear that all your profits are going to disappear

overnight. It's because at work you're the one in charge
and what you say goes. And you like to be in control,
don't you? Work has always provided you with an escape route. It's there for the taking when your wife
wants to get too close or tries to talk about stuff you
don't want to talk about.'

'Are you listening to a word I've just said?' he demanded. 'I've told you I'll reduce my hours, if that's
what it takes to get you back.'

'But don't you realise?' she whispered. 'That's not
enough.'

'Not *enough*?' he echoed, his blue eyes laced with
confusion. 'What else do you want from me, Keeley?'

And here it was, the question she'd wanted him to
ask ever since he had carried her to their bedroom on
their wedding night. A no-holds-barred question which
would make her vulnerable to so much potential pain
if she answered it honestly.

Did she dare?

Could she dare not to?

She'd once vowed never to put herself in a position
where she could be rejected again, but that was a vow
she'd made when she'd been hurt and humbled. All
these years later she was a grown woman who would
soon have a baby of her own. And it all boiled down to
whether she had the courage to put her pride and her
fears aside and to reach out for the one thing she wanted.

'I want your trust,' she said simply. 'I want you to
believe me when I tell you things and to stop imagining
the worst. I want you to stop trying to control me and let
me have the freedom to be myself. I want to stop feel-

ing as if I'm swimming against the tide whenever I try to get close to you. I want ours to be a marriage which *works*—but only if we're both prepared to work at it. I want us to be equals, Ariston. True equals.'

His eyes narrowed as he nodded his head. 'You sound like you've given this some thought.'

'Oh, I've given it plenty,' she said truthfully. 'Only I wasn't sure if I'd ever get the chance to say it.'

There was another silence and the haunted expression on his face tore at Keeley's heartstrings for she saw her own fears and insecurities reflected there. It made her want to go to him and hug him tightly—to offer him her strength and to feel his. But she said nothing. Nothing which would break the spell or the hope that he might just reveal what was hidden in his heart, instead of trying to blot it out and hide it away, the way he normally did. Because that was the only way they could go forward, she realised. If they both were honest enough to let the truth shine through.

'I didn't want to let you close because I sensed danger—the kind of danger I didn't know how to handle,' he said at last. 'I'd spent years perfecting an emotional control which enabled me to pick up the pieces and care for Pavlos when our mother left. A control which kept the world at a safe distance. A control which enabled me to keep all the balls spinning in the air. I was so busy protecting my brother and safeguarding his future, that I didn't have time for anything else. I didn't want anything else. And then I met you and suddenly everything changed. You started to get close. You drew me in, no matter how hard I tried to fight against it, and I recognised that you had the power to hurt me, Keeley.'

'But I don't want to hurt you, Ariston,' she said. 'I am not your mother and you can't judge all women by her standards. I want to be there for you—in every way. Won't you let me do that?'

'I don't think I have a choice,' he admitted huskily. 'Because my life has been hell without you. My apartment and my life are empty when you aren't in them, Keeley. Because you speak the truth to me in a way which is sometimes painful to hear—but out of that pain has grown the certainty that I love you. That perhaps I've always loved you—and I want to go on loving you for the rest of my life.'

And suddenly she could hold out no longer and crossed the room as quickly as her pregnant shape would allow. She went straight into his arms and at last he was holding her tightly and she closed her eyes against the sudden prick of tears.

'Keeley,' he whispered, his mouth pressed hard against her cheek. 'Oh, Keeley. I've been dishonest with myself—right from the start. I felt the thunderbolt the first time I set eyes on you and I'd never felt that way about a woman before. I told myself you were too young—way too young—but then I kissed you and you blew my world apart.' He pulled away and stroked an unsteady finger over her trembling lips. 'It was easier to convince myself that I despised you. To tell myself you were cut from the same cloth as your mother, and that I only wanted sex with you to extinguish the burning hunger inside of me. But you just kept igniting the flames. When you became pregnant—a part of me was exultant. I couldn't decide if it was destiny or fate I needed to thank for a reason to stay close to you. But then came the reality. And the way you made me feel was bigger than anything I've ever felt before. It felt...'

'Scary,' she finished, pulling back a little so that she could gaze deep into his eyes. 'I know. Scary for me, too. Because love is precious and rare and most of us don't know how to handle it, especially when we've grown up without it. But we're bright people, Ariston. We both know what we don't want—broken homes and lost children and bitter wounds which can never be completely healed. I just want to love you and our baby and to create a happy family life. Don't you want that too?'

Briefly, Ariston closed his eyes and when he opened them she was still there, just as she always would be. Because some things you just knew, if only you would let your defences down long enough for instinct to take over. And instinct told him that Keeley Kavakos would always love him, though maybe not quite as much as he loved her.

He pulled her closer, his breath warm against her skin. 'Can we please go to bed so we can plan our future?' he questioned urgently.

'Oh, Ariston.' She rose on tiptoe to wind her arms around his neck, and he could hear the relief which tinged her breathless sigh. 'I thought you'd never ask.'

EPILOGUE

'So, how are you feeling, my clever and very beautiful wife?'

Keeley lifted her gaze from the tiny black head which was cradled against her breast, to find the bright blue eyes of her husband trained on her.

How was she feeling? Tough question. How could words possibly convey the million sentiments which had rushed through her during a long labour, and which had ended just an hour ago with the birth of their son? Joy, contentment and disbelief were all there, that was for sure—along with a savage determination that she would love and protect their new baby with every fibre of her being. Baby Timon. Timon Pavlos Kavakos. She smiled as she traced a feather-light fingertip over his perfect, olive-skinned cheek.

'I feel like the luckiest woman in the world,' she said simply.

Ariston nodded. He didn't want to contradict her at such a time, but if luck was being handed out—then surely he was its biggest recipient? Watching Keeley go through labour had been something which had taught him the true meaning of powerlessness and silently he had cursed that he was unable to bear or share her pain with her. Yet hadn't it been yet another demonstration of his wife's formidable strength—to watch her cope so beautifully with each increasing contraction? A wife who was planning to join him in the family business, just as soon as the time was right. He remembered her reaction when he'd first put the idea to her and his tender smile in response to her disbelieving joy. But why wouldn't he want his capable and very able wife working beside him, with hours which would suit her and their son? Why wouldn't he want to enjoy her company as much as possible, especially since her command of Greek was getting better by the day?

But she'd told him that these days she studied his language with a passion born from wanting to fit in and not because she was terrified of being left out. Because she was determined to speak the same language as their child. And because family was more important than anything else. A fact which had been drummed home by the sudden death of her mother, a death which in truth had filled Keeley with a sad kind of gratitude, because Vivienne Turner was at peace at last. And it had focussed their minds on the things which mattered. They had decided to make their home on Lasia—on that exquisite paradise of a place, with its green mountains and sapphire sea and skies which were endlessly blue.

Ariston thought how beautiful she looked lying there, still a little pale and exhausted after her long labour, her blonde hair lying damply against her cheeks as she smiled up at him trustingly. 'Would you like to hold your son now?' she whispered.

A lump instantly constricted his throat. It was what he'd been waiting for. In fact, it felt as if he'd been waiting for this moment all his life. A little gingerly at first, Ariston took the sleeping bundle from her, and as he bent to kiss the baby's jet-black hair a fierce wave of love rushed over him. He was used to holding babies because he used to hold Pavlos most of the time—but this felt different. Very different. This child was *his* flesh. And Keeley's. Timon. The pounding of his heart was almost deafening and the lump in his throat was making speech difficult, but somehow he got the words out as he looked into the tear-filled eyes of his wife.

'Efkaristo,' he said softly.

'Thanks for what?' she questioned shakily as he put his free arm tightly around her shoulders and drew her close.

'For my son, for your love—and for giving me a life beyond my wildest dreams. How about that for starters, *koukla mou*?'

She was trying to blink them away but the tears of joy just kept rolling down her cheeks and Ariston smiled as he kissed each one away, while their son slept contentedly in his arms.

* * * * *

THE GREEK'S PREGNANT BRIDE

MICHELLE SMART

To the wonderful sisters in my life:
Jennie, Lulu & Joanne xxx

CHAPTER ONE

CHRISTIAN MARKOS TIPPED the last of his champagne down his throat and immediately refilled his glass.

He'd known today was going to be hard, but hadn't imagined quite how torturous it would be. Not even all the running around he'd done with Rocco that morning, in their seemingly desperate attempt to find the bride, had mitigated it.

Afterwards, he'd stood by the side of his closest friend on the happiest day of his life and all he'd been able to think was how deeply he'd betrayed him.

While Rocco had been exchanging his vows, Christian had been using all his willpower to stop his gaze flitting to Alessandra.

He was still fighting it.

Alessandra Mondelli: Rocco's baby sister. A pretty child who'd grown into a ravishingly beautiful woman. The one woman in the world who was totally off-limits.

Or should have been.

Attired in a long, sleeveless, silk mauve dress, with her glossy, dark-chestnut hair pulled back in a tight chignon, she'd arrived by boat with the radiant bride, the spring sun beaming down on her golden skin.

In his eyes the chief bridesmaid outshone everyone, including the famous supermodel bride.

The last time he'd seen Alessandra she'd been wearing a short, cream lace dress with black beading and a pair of black shoes so high he'd been amazed she could walk in them. But walk in them she had, beautifully, her delectable bottom swaying with every step. That was the last time he'd seen her clothed. The last time he'd seen her properly she'd been burrowed naked under the bed covers in her apartment.

The wedding party had moved from the beautiful gardens by Lake Como and into the Villa Mondelli ballroom. The wedding dinner was over, the evening celebration about to start. He'd made his best man's speech and managed to raise some laughs from the other guests, especially Stefan and Zayed, who'd substituted the speech he'd written with a bluer version. Instead of relaxing, knowing his job was done, Christian was on tenterhooks waiting for the music to strike up.

An American A-list starlet kept making eyes at him, a stunning woman with a body to die for. Just six weeks ago he would have been at her side like a shot. If not her, then one of the other gorgeous women littering this star-studded event already being labelled 'wedding of the century.' Supermodels, lingerie models, singers… It was like being a child in a sweetshop.

If that were the case, then he must have diabetes, because none of the sweets looked remotely tempting.

Except one. The forbidden one.

How could he have allowed things to get so out of hand? He might flit from bed to bed but he never lost control of himself.

To have lost his control with Alessandra…

He could blame it on all the champagne they'd drunk. He could blame it on a lot of things, but all the blame was on himself.

Alessandra had been vulnerable. Try as she'd done to hide it, she'd been a mess, grieving the loss of her grandfather, the man who'd raised her since she'd been a baby and who'd been buried barely two weeks before.

Christian had dropped in at the House of Mondelli, the

world-famous fashion house, on his way back from Hong Kong, expecting to take Rocco out for a night on the tiles, maybe spend the weekend together on his Italian friend's yacht. But Rocco had been in New York and he'd bumped into Alessandra, who'd insisted he take her out instead. Under normal circumstances he would have made his excuses and got back in his jet to fly on to Athens. If he hadn't caught the desperation in her beautiful honey-brown eyes, he would have done just that, not found himself recalling how she'd barely been able to stand during the funeral service.

When they'd set out for the evening, the last thing he'd expected was that they would end up in bed together.

Women came and went in his life on a regular basis. He could only assume that it was the fact Alessandra was someone who was *in* his life, so to speak, that meant he was having a hard job forgetting and moving on. That and the guilt of it all. She might have been the one to instigate the kiss that had led to them making love, but the blame for what followed lay firmly on *his* shoulders.

He should have been stronger.

In the six weeks since he'd seen her, he'd worked hard to push her from the forefront to the back of his mind, enough so that he'd arrived at Lake Como confident he could handle being in her presence without any problems.

He'd taken one look at her and all the guilt had churned itself back up. They'd exchanged a few brief words over the course of the day, the same basic pleasantries they'd exchanged with everyone else, but that was the extent of their interaction. So far, at least. There was still the dance to get through.

Whether he liked it or not, he would have to hold her in his arms one more time.

Stefan said something to him at the exact moment the band started their warm-up. As he spoke, Christian saw Olivia lean in close to press her ear to Rocco's mouth. It was a gesture that reminded him of his dinner with Alessandra, the way she'd leaned into him to hear him speak over the noise of the restaurant; the way her sultry scent had played under his nose…

From the corner of his eye he could see her chatting to the official photographer, the photographer probably getting tips from *her*. Alessandra Mondelli was one of the most famous fashion photographers in the world, a remarkable achievement, considering she was still only twenty-five. She'd made it all on her own. Just as he'd made his name on his own.

Stefan repeated himself; he'd been talking about the charitable foundation they and their friends had formed some years back.

Italian Rocco Mondelli, Sicilian Stefan Bianco, desert Prince Zayed Al Afzal and he had all taken a keen interest in running and raising money for their charity. They were the so-called Columbia Four, although he couldn't recall which of them had dubbed them so. Whoever had come up with it, it had stuck. They'd met during their first week at Columbia University and, as incredible as it was to look back on, the bond they'd formed had been instant. That bond had grown and a good few years later, when it had become obvious all four were heading towards the Forbes World's Billionaires List, they'd formed the charity. Christian was extremely proud of their charity, founded to ensure disadvantaged kids could get the education they deserved but were unable to afford. It felt good for them to be doing something together that didn't involve drinking and bedding as many beautiful women as they could.

They all believed the bond between them to be unbreakable.

But even the strongest steel could be destroyed.

He answered with what he hoped sounded like intelligence but, in truth, what came out of his mouth sounded so unintelligible he could be speaking Martian.

Luckily Stefan's attention was diverted by the band striking up their first song.

The bride and groom glided onto the dance floor to loud applause.

Christian's eyes drifted to his right, back to Alessandra. She was looking straight at him, a trapped expression in her eyes.

His chest tightened.

A powerful slap to his shoulder broke the spell.

'Time to get yourself on the dance floor,' Zayed said, sitting on the empty seat to Christian's left.

Theos. He had to dance with her. Olivia, the bride, had ordered it. The best man and chief bridesmaid…

Alessandra met him halfway, her obvious apprehension mirroring what raced inside him.

It would help if the band were playing one of the usual upbeat tunes that had made them one of the most famous groups in the world rather than the cover of a romantic ballad they were currently warbling.

Gritting his teeth, he walked by her side to the dance floor and took her into his arms.

His heart jolted at the first touch, a dozen memories playing in his mind. Her scent. Her taste…

The back of her dress was low, leaving him no option but to touch her silky skin. It was either that or hold on to her bottom. His hand lay rigid against her bare back, hardly touching her.

Yet, no matter the physical distance he tried to impose between himself and her slender form, his senses filled with Alessandra, her sultry scent playing tricks on him as they moved over the dance floor in a manner more akin to a pair of robots than a couple who'd had a wild night of sex just six weeks before. The stirring that had begun when he'd watched her walk up the aisle and had simmered since took on new life, an ache forming in his groin that he willed away with increasing frustration.

Think of Rocco, he ordered himself, staring at his loved-up friend who was locked in the arms of his equally loved-up wife. Rocco caught his eye and nodded briefly before leaning down to kiss his bride.

That one action felt like a knife in Christian's guts.

What would his friend say if he knew his best man had taken his sister's virginity?

The all-consuming desire he'd felt that night still dwelled in his blood. One night was all he usually needed, all he wanted. Once a woman had been enjoyed, there were no more mysteries to discover, no need for a repeat.

His skin felt as if it were dancing its own tune, his body out of kilter with what his head demanded.

He followed the words of the song they were dancing to, counting down the time to when the obligatory dance would be over. From the stiffness in Alessandra's stance, she was counting down the time too.

When the song finally came to an end and he made to pull away, she tilted her head to look at him, her doe-like eyes staring at him. *Theos,* she was so beautiful, those striking eyes set above a snub nose framed by slanting cheekbones. Her delicious plump lips parted. 'Christian, I…'

Whatever she was going to say was cut short when Zayed tapped her on the shoulder and threw Christian a conspiratorial wink. 'I do believe it's my turn to dance with the beautiful lady,' he said in a voice loud enough for Rocco to hear.

The groom turned his head towards the raised voice, his eyes narrowing before he broke into a wide grin.

It clearly didn't cross his mind that any of his friends would dream of doing anything with the sister he was so protective of.

Sickened with himself, Christian stepped back and forced a smile, mock-bowing. 'She's all yours.'

He waited for Alessandra to make a good-natured but cutting retort about not being anyone's property, but her eyes were stark on his face, a fleeting look of panic flashing over her which she quickly covered. But not quickly enough.

The ballroom of Villa Mondelli had enough waiting staff not to let any guest go thirsty for longer than thirty seconds but Christian wanted to get away from the hubbub of the mingling guests and headed to the bar.

After a shot of bourbon, he turned his head to see her now dancing with Stefan. She looked happy to be dancing with *him*, he thought, taken aback at the strength of his bitterness.

It was only natural she'd been stiff and awkward in Christian's arms. A one-night stand hadn't been on either of their minds when they'd set out that evening.

He'd been her first lover.

That, more than anything, was the thing that refused to dislodge from his mind.

The woman who'd been vilified by the press for an affair with a married man when she'd been a teenager had been a virgin. He'd always suspected there had been more to the story than had been written but the truth had come as a cataclysmic shock.

Whatever the truth, it was none of his business. Alessandra was none of his business. She couldn't be.

He took another shot to clear the bile crawling up his throat and watched Stefan place a hand to her waist. The bile almost choked him to see her laugh at something his friend said in her ear.

Zayed appeared at his side. 'Hiding yourself away, buddy?'

'Just taking a few moments.'

Stefan finished his dance and came over to join them. 'What are we all drinking?'

'Christian's already on the hard stuff,' Zayed said, indicating the empty shot glasses before them on the bar.

Christian hardly listened. Alessandra had left the dance floor. A quick scan of the ballroom found her sitting at a table with a group of people he didn't recognise. She was staring at him.

Their gazes held before he pulled away and fixed a smile on his face for his friends' benefit.

'Who's ready for a shot?' Before either could answer, he waved at the barman to pour them a bourbon each.

The three friends, sitting in a row at the bar, raised their glasses and chanted, *'Memento vivere!'* 'Remember to live,' the motto the four friends *did* live by, and downed their shots.

'I never thought I'd see us at a wedding for one of our own,' Zayed mused, wiping his mouth with the back of his hand. 'I still can't believe Rocco's got *married*. I mean… *married*?'

'Who would have thought he'd fall in *love*?' Stefan said with the same incredulous tone.

Christian grunted and caught the barman's attention for another round.

Call him cynical, but he couldn't help wonder how long it would be before the love they felt for each other turned into something ugly. Because that was what marriage did—turned two people full of hope and love into bitter caricatures of themselves.

Much safer for everyone's sake to avoid emotional entanglement. Christian conducted his own affairs by enjoying the moment and then moving on with the minimum of fuss. He had known before he was in double figures that marriage was not for him.

Zayed swivelled on his stool to cast his eyes over the ballroom. 'There are some hot women here.'

Stefan grinned. 'I noticed that lingerie model giving you the eye.'

'I thought she was an actress?'

'No, that was the other one.'

'I tell you who knocks spots off all these women,' Zayed said. 'Alessandra.'

Christian snapped his head round to stare at him. 'Don't even think about it.'

Zayed raised his hands. 'I'm just making an observation.'

'Well, don't.'

'Man, you know I wouldn't go there. I'd never do that to Rocco— Where are you going?' he added when Christian got up from his stool and made to leave.

'To get some air.'

'You not feeling well?' Stefan was looking at him closely.

'It's been a busy time. I'm probably jet-lagged. Get another round in—I'll be back in a few minutes.'

Instead of going outside, Christian went to the restroom and splashed cold water on his face.

He'd been a paper thickness away from punching Zayed. *Theos*, he needed to get a grip on himself.

This was *his* guilt and *his* problem. No one else's.

Back in the ballroom his eyes automatically sought Alessandra out. As he found her, she turned her head in his direction, as if some sixth sense told her he was there. Quickly she turned away.

He thought he was doing a good job of hiding his guilt-ridden inner turmoil. After that one close call of almost punching one of his oldest and closest friends for an innocuous remark, he joined in with the celebration they were there for, drinking, laughing and horsing about, being the same old Christian he always was when with them.

Except, every time he looked, he found Alessandra's gaze upon him. Their eyes would meet for a fraction of a second before jerking away. She certainly seemed to be enjoying herself, though, dancing with anyone who cared to ask, at one point stealing Olivia from Rocco and waltzing her around the floor to screams of delight.

Only when the bride and groom, their hands clenched tightly together, left to head off to their secret honeymoon destination did Christian determine his duty to have been done.

Exchanging bear hugs with Zayed and Stefan, who called him every laughably demeaning name under the sun for retiring to bed so early, he strode out of the ballroom, unable to resist one last glance at Alessandra. For once, she wasn't looking at him.

He was about to climb the stairs to the sleeping quarters when he heard his name called.

Stefan approached him and pulled him into another embrace. 'You are playing with fire, my friend,' he said into his ear.

'I don't know what you're talking about.'

'Sure you do.' He pulled back a little and brought his hands up to Christian's face, slapping both his cheeks lightly. 'You have to end it. *Now*.'

Christian's chest compressed. He couldn't lie to his friend. 'It was over before it started.'

'Good. Keep it that way. For all our sakes.'

Alessandra took a deep breath and knocked on the door. The party was still going strong, a DJ having replaced the band, music pounding through the walls. There were revellers all over the villa but thankfully this wing was quiet and devoid of people.

She waited a few moments before knocking again, louder.

Unless Christian had left without telling anyone, he was in there. The dim light seeping under the door testified to this. She'd casually asked Stefan and Zayed where their fellow musketeer had escaped to. She could only hope she'd imagined the suspicious but pitying look in Stefan's eyes when he'd told her Christian had gone to bed.

Please, God, let him be alone in there.

What were the chances?

She'd been nothing special, just another notch on a bedpost crammed with notches.

Christian Markos travelled with a trail of broken hearts

attached to him ranging from Hong Kong to London. Some sold their stories to the tabloids, tales of short-lived lust before being discarded. Some spoke with bitterness. Most spoke with longing. Most wanted him to break their hearts all over again.

It took an age before the handle turned and the door opened.

Christian stood clad in a pair of jeans. And nothing else.

He blinked narrowing eyes. 'What are you doing here?'

'I need to talk to you. Can I come in?'

His bronzed throat rose. 'That's not a good idea.'

'It's important.'

His firm lips, usually quirked in an easy smile, clamped together. He shifted past her, looking both directions down the wide corridor before ushering her in and swiftly closing the door.

His room was tidy, his tuxedo hanging neatly on the door of the wardrobe. The bed was rumpled; a tablet was on the bedside table next to a half-full bottle of bourbon and an empty glass.

'Are you drunk?' she challenged. This was a conversation she needed to have when he was sober.

'No.' He strode to the window and closed the heavy curtains. 'Believe me, I've been trying to reach that state.'

If only she were in a position to reach that state herself.

'Today went well,' she said, sitting gingerly on the corner chair. She could *really* do with a shot of that bourbon. It would make what was coming next easier to cope with, of that she was certain. 'Rocco and Liv looked really happy.'

Their obvious happiness had had the dual effect of making her heart lighten for her brother's sake and sink at the knowledge it was something she could never have for herself.

Christian propped himself against the wall by the window and crossed his arms over his broad chest. She hadn't really had the opportunity to study his torso in her apartment, and now she could look at it properly she felt the heat she'd experienced that night bloom anew.

Years of rowing and track had honed his physique, his form strong and athletic, his shoulders broad. Fine hair dusted across his bronzed chest and she felt an almost unbearable compulsion to hurtle herself into his arms and take solace in his strength.

Making love to him had been an experience she would never forget. The single best experience of her life.

Try as she had to expel the memories from her head, they'd stayed with her, tantalising her, taunting her with the knowledge it was an experience that could *never* be repeated.

The simple remembrance of his smooth skin flush against her nakedness made her feel as if her insides were being liquidised.

'What did you want to talk to me about?' he asked, cutting the preamble and pulling her back to the present. While he wasn't being unfriendly, there was none of the easy-going Christian she knew. She didn't have to be psychic to know he wanted her gone from his room.

His regret and self-loathing were obvious.

Her heart hammered beneath her ribs, her stomach roiling with nerves that threatened to overwhelm her.

This was all her fault...

'I'm pregnant.'

CHAPTER TWO

THE SILENCE THAT followed Alessandra's stark statement was total.

Christian seemed to deflate before her eyes, as if he'd suffered a body blow.

Which no doubt her news was, she thought miserably.

How she'd kept herself together throughout the day she would never know, her only thought having been that she *mustn't* ruin Rocco and Olivia's special day. *She mustn't.*

She'd spent pretty much her entire life trying to keep herself together in public, the hardest before tonight being two months ago when they'd buried her grandfather. The paparazzi had been out in force. She'd worn dark glasses until they'd entered the church, refusing to give them the money shot they so desired. Even when Sandro, her alcoholic father, had turned up drunk and made that dreadful scene, she'd kept her composure. Christian and Zayed had been the ones who'd calmly approached him and dragged him away.

Christian staggered over to the bed and sat heavily on it, clutching his head.

'Please. Say something,' she beseeched. The back of her retinas burned and she blinked furiously. No matter what happened in the next few minutes, she would not cry. She'd done enough of that.

He fixed his blue eyes on her. 'How long have you known?'

'A while, I guess, but I only took the test a couple of days ago.' She laughed, a hollow sound even to her own ears. 'I took three of them, hoping they were wrong.' At the third positive reading, she'd climbed onto her bed and sobbed.

'Have you seen a doctor?'

'Not yet.' She bit into her lip. It had taken her almost a fortnight to entertain the possibility that her late period might actually mean something, another fortnight before she'd unburied her head from the sand and crossed the threshold into the pharmacy.

She'd never believed she would be a mother. Motherhood went hand in hand with relationships and she certainly didn't believe in *them*.

'But you're certain?'

'Yes.' Once the reality of her condition had sunk into her shell-shocked brain, the tears had stopped.

Inside her, right in the heart of her womanhood, a tiny life grew.

Whatever the outcome of this conversation with Christian, nothing could change the fact that this life—her baby—was a part of her. Nothing could have prepared her for the host of emotions pregnancy would bring. It might be early days in pregnancy terms but already she loved it, this little alien developing within her; knew she would do anything to nurture and protect it. Anything.

Silence rang out, the only sound Christian's heavy breathing. She'd never seen his features—all angles and straight lines forming what had been dubbed one of the most handsome faces in Europe—look so empty.

'I'm so sorry.'

His brows drew together. 'Sorry for what?'

'I screwed up.' She forced herself to look him straight in the eye. 'I didn't take my pill properly.'

He shook his head and expelled a breath through his mouth, running a hand through his cropped dirty-blond hair. 'And you didn't think to tell me that?'

'I didn't know the dangers, not properly.'

'How could you not know? It's basic biology.' He swore under his breath.

'I was put on the pill because my periods were painful, not for the purpose of contraception.'

'You should have told me. *Theos*, if I'd known you didn't take it at regular intervals I would have made certain to use a condom.'

'I am sorry, truly sorry.'

The knuckles of his hands were white. She could see his temper hanging by a thread.

'You can't put this on yourself—*I* can't put it on you,' he eventually said. 'We were both there. I should have had the sense to use a condom like I normally do.'

She closed her eyes, pushing away thoughts of him with other women. 'Christian...I can't do this on my own. I need your support—not financially but in other ways.' Financially she could do it alone. She had her apartment, her career was thriving...

She opened her eyes and looked at his still-dazed face. 'I know I've had a head start getting my head around all this, and that's unfair on you, but I need your word—on your honour—that you'll be there for me and our baby.' Not that she could trust it. He was a man. Men always broke their promises.

All the same, she had to try and put a little faith in him. He was the father of her child. But then, her own father was the worst liar of all. He'd lied to her mother on her deathbed, promising to care for their children, never to leave them. That had been the biggest lie of all.

The only men she trusted were her brother and her grandfather. It had broken her grieving heart to learn recently that her grandfather had had his own dark secrets.

If it hadn't been for his death, she would never have slept with Christian. She'd bumped into him in the House of Mondelli headquarters after she'd had a meeting with the fashion director about a campaign she'd been hired to shoot. Christian had turned up to take her brother out but Rocco had been in New York.

She'd been in a bad place, she could see that now, trying to cope with her grief but not having a clue how to manage it. She'd never known pain like it. It still had the power to lance her.

Christian had presented the perfect opportunity for a night out where she could forget her pain for one evening, so she'd talked him into going out with her instead. Not for a minute had she imagined she would fall into bed with him.

But she had done just that and now she had to pay the consequences.

And so did Christian.

She might never be able to trust him but she'd had enough faith, whatever her state of mind, to lose her virginity to him. That had to account for something.

She wished he would say something. His frame was still but his eyes were alert. She couldn't read them. Couldn't read him.

'When news of the pregnancy comes out the press are going to swarm all over it. I've lived through one scandal and I can't go through that again on my own. I just can't.' Simply imagining going through it all again made her hands go clammy and her stomach churn. How clearly she remembered those awful days when the paparazzi had laid siege to Villa Mondelli, leaving her a prisoner in her own home. She'd never been so scared and alone in all her life. 'If I know I can rely on you for support when I need it, and later on when our baby needs it, I might be able to sleep again.'

Christian's throat rose before he twisted onto his side and grabbed his bourbon and glass. He poured a hefty measure and offered it to her.

She shook her head.

'Of course not,' he muttered, taking a large swallow of it. 'You're pregnant. Did you not drink today?'

'I had a small champagne during the toasts but that's all.'

He got to his feet and headed back to the window, peeking through the curtain.

'Will you support me?' she pressed. For her own peace of mind she needed to know. If he refused she didn't know what she would do other than fall into a crumpled ball. Or maybe join a convent.

No. She wouldn't do either. For the sake of the life inside her, she would endure.

'Will you support our baby and be its father?'

The ringing that had echoed in Christian's ears since Alessandra's pronouncement that she was pregnant subsided.

He gazed at her belly, still flat under the lilac of her dress, not a hint that within it lay the tiny seed of life.

The life they had created together.

His baby.

He was going to be a father.

As this knowledge seeped through him, he thought of his own father, a man who'd left before Christian had been old enough to memorise his features. He had no memories of him, no possessions to place a tangible hold on him. Nothing. Not even a photograph. His mother had burned them all.

If there was one thing he knew with bone-deep certainty, it was that he didn't want a child of his being raised without a father to look out for him or her.

From infancy it had been just him and his mother, a woman whose bitterness ran so deep it seemed to seep from her pores. His father had turned his back on them both and in turn had created the woman she'd become.

Christian would *not* be that man.

He raised his gaze from Alessandra's belly to meet her eyes, a sharpness driving in his chest to see all the fear and uncertainty contained in them. Despite the braveness she strove to convey, her hands trembled, her teeth driving in and out of her plump lips as she awaited his response.

He knew what his response must be.

'Yes,' he said, nodding slowly for emphasis. 'I will support you and our child. But in return I want you to marry me.'

The comb holding Alessandra's hair in place had been digging into her scalp all day, a minor irritation that suddenly felt magnified enough for her to yank it out. She got to her feet, swiping fallen hair off her face.

For a moment she couldn't speak, her brain struggling to find the English she'd spoken like a native since early childhood. 'I know this is a shock for you. I *know*, okay? But marriage?'

'Yes, marriage.'

She shook her head, trying her hardest not to let panic set in. 'Please, don't say anything you'll regret in the morning when you look at the situation with fresh eyes.'

'The morning won't change the situation. You'll still be pregnant.'

'And I still won't be marrying you.'

'Alessandra…' He bit back his rising voice. 'Alessandra, think about it. This is the obvious solution. Marriage will give legitimacy to our child.'

'This isn't the nineteenth century. There's no stigma to children born outside of wedlock.'

His eyes swirled with an emotion she didn't understand. 'Children need and deserve two parents. You know that as well as I do.'

One parent would have been nice in her case, she thought bitterly. Yes, her father was still alive, but he'd never been a real father to her. He'd abandoned her almost from her first breath. By the time of her first birthday, he'd gambled and drunk away their home and had foisted Rocco and her into the care of his elderly father.

She felt as if she'd been blindsided. Marriage was the last thing she'd expected Christian to suggest. The most she'd hoped for was public support for her and their child, and even that had felt like a pipe dream considering she was dealing with the commitment-phobic Christian Markos. He made Casanova look like a monk.

She hadn't allowed herself to hope for anything more substantial, had envisaged her and the baby's future with Christian flitting in and out when it suited him. She'd even prepared her 'please don't introduce our child to a succession of aunties' speech. In her head she'd prepared for just about every imaginable scenario. Apart from the scenario where he demanded marriage.

'Christian, please, be realistic. Marriage is…'

'Something neither of us wants,' he finished for her, meeting her gaze with steady eyes.

How clearly she remembered discussing marriage on their night out together, the night their baby had been conceived. *Fools* had been just one of the many words they'd used to describe people who willingly entered matrimony. They'd even toasted this rare meeting of minds.

'Exactly. Something neither of us wants.'

He finished his drink with a grimace. 'Seeing as neither of us has any intention of marrying in the conventional sense, marriage each other for the sake of our child isn't going to destroy either of our dreams. We won't be making a lifelong commitment to each other, just to our child.'

'But marriage…?'

'Marriage will legitimise the pregnancy and avert any scandal. The press will still swarm over the story, that's a given, but their angle will be softer towards you.'

'Accepting paternity will have the same effect. At this moment, that's all I need. Your acceptance. Everything else can be arranged between us later. There's plenty of time.'

'And what about what *I* need?' he challenged. 'You tell me I'm going to be a father and that you want my support but when I offer you the biggest support I can—marriage—you dismiss it out of hand.'

'What do *you* need?' she asked, now thoroughly confused. 'What will you get out of us marrying?'

'The chance to be a father,' he answered with a shrug. 'I've built up a multi-billion-dollar business and have no one to pass it to.'

She didn't bother to hide her scorn. *'Money.'* The only thing he enjoyed more than bedding women.

His blue eyes flashed sharply. 'No. A legacy. But even if I didn't have the wealth I would still want us to marry. I know what it's like growing up without a father and I will not have my child go through that. I want my child to have my name and know he—or she—is *mine.*'

How did he do it? No wonder he was reputed to be one of the greatest financial minds in the world. Money was what Christian dealt with every day, a world-renowned financial genius advising all the major corporations in all the different sectors.

She'd spent *days* agonising over all the possible details. He'd grasped the situation and dissected all the permutations in an instant. Having only known him as her brother's friend, she'd never appreciated this side of him before.

She appreciated it even less now.

'You can still be a father to our child without marriage.'

'And you can still be a single mother without any support other than financially,' he said, a warning note coming into his voice.

'I've already told you, I don't need or want your money.'

He inhaled a long breath. 'I'm trying to do what's right here. I don't want to force your hand but I have to think of our child. He or she deserves stability—marriage gives that. Or is your freedom more important?'

Christian watched Alessandra suck her cheeks in at his remark. He didn't blame her. Right then he was prepared to say whatever it took to get her to agree.

Theos, an hour ago the thought of marriage would have

made him run all the way to Hong Kong but now here he was, virtually coercing her into marrying him.

'That's not fair,' she said hoarsely.

'Life isn't fair.' He knew that all too well; it was the whole reason he was demanding this from her. 'Marriage needn't be a prison for either of us. You can carry on with your career.'

'How generous of you. You're welcome to carry on with your career too.'

He ignored her sarcasm, understanding the place of fear it came from. If he felt his world had just turned on its axis he could only imagine how it must be for her. She had to carry their baby into the world.

It was their baby he was thinking of. Christian had grown up knowing somewhere out there was the man who had fathered him but who wanted nothing to do with him, his own son. He had never understood why. He still didn't.

It had taken many years for him to accept his father's abandonment as a simple fact of life but as a child it had been a painful knowledge. He would *never* put his own child through that. *His* child would grow up feeling loved and secure with two parents who both wanted nothing more than to love and protect him or her.

Looking at Alessandra rest a protective hand against her still-flat stomach, he could see how deeply she already felt for their child.

Their child. His responsibility. Their responsibility, to be shouldered together.

'When we marry the world will see a united couple...' he started.

'Don't talk as if it's a done deal. Marriage changes *everything*. It's not just two people signing a piece of paper and exchanging a bit of jewellery. There are legal implications.'

'And it's those legal implications I want. I want our child to know their parents loved them enough to create a stable family for them.'

'This is too much.' She got to her feet. He experienced a sharp pang to see her tremble, to witness her keeping it all together, just as she'd done at her grandfather's funeral.

She carried herself so tall it was easy to overlook that she was a slip of a woman. Her glossy hair was sprawled over her shoulders, her golden skin pale.

The last thing he wanted was to hurt her but within him lay a deep-rooted certainty that this was the right path for them. It was the only path.

'I need to sleep on this,' she said, her honey eyes brimming with emotion, her usually accent-less English inflected with her Italian heritage. 'I can't agree to marriage just because you've clicked your fingers. You might change your mind. I've sprung this on you. Everything will look different in the morning.'

There were a dozen threats he could make to ensure her agreement. He bit them all back. He felt bad enough as it was without adding more ill deeds to the slate against him. There was one more thing he could add, though...

'I won't change my mind but you can go ahead and sleep on it,' he said. 'While you're lying in your bed thinking, consider the ramifications if you decide not to take me up on my proposal. If you marry me, scandal averted. If you don't, the press will crucify you and drag your brother and the entire House of Mondelli through the mud with you. Do you really want to go through all that again? Do you want *Rocco* to go through all that again?'

She stilled, stormy eyes locked on his.

'Do you want all the speculation over who the father is? The old scandal being raked up as the world wonders if you've been playing around with another married man?'

'But I never...'

He hated to see the hurt and bewilderment that flashed across her features but he had no choice. For their child's sake he would deploy every weapon in his arsenal to get her agreement. 'You know that and I know that. The rest of the world will believe what it wants to believe and, as it's doing so, the world's eyes will be on *you*.'

'You know how to play dirty,' she said hoarsely, her chest heaving.

'I could never have left Greece without learning how. If you refuse, you will have to deal with the press and the world's attention on your own. I will make no acknowledgement until our baby is born.'

Her throat moved as she swallowed, her eyes blazing their loathing at him. 'Do not think you can blackmail me, Markos.'

'I don't want to blackmail you,' he said, wondering why the sound of his surname being spat from her delicious, plump lips landed like a barb in his chest. 'But you leave me no choice.'

She backed to the door and gripped the handle. 'I'm going to my room now. I'll give you my answer in the morning.'

'There is only one answer.'

'You can still wait on it.'

CHAPTER THREE

HIS HEAD THUMPING, Christian entered the magnificent dining room where breakfast was being served. Alessandra was already there. So too were Stefan, Zayed and a handful of other guests who'd stayed the night rather than retire to their yachts or have their helicopters collect them.

It was little comfort that every person in the room looked exactly how he felt. *Skata*. Like crap.

He might not have been able to get himself as drunk as he'd wanted but his body was punishing him regardless for the quantity of alcohol he'd consumed.

Alessandra's gaze darted to him. Anyone looking at her could be forgiven for thinking she had a hangover too. Only he knew the dark rings under her bloodshot eyes were caused by a different reason.

He doubted she'd had any more sleep than the snatches he'd managed.

Even so, she still had that certain charisma that she carried like a second skin; her hair, left loose to tumble halfway down her back, as glossy as ever.

He took the seat next to Zayed, who was clutching a black coffee as if his life depended on it, and poured himself a cup of his own. He shook his head as a member of staff asked what he'd like to eat.

All he wanted at that moment was hot, sweet caffeine. And a dozen painkillers.

No sooner had he taken his first sip than Alessandra rose,

murmuring something to Stefan, who gave a pained laugh and immediately rubbed at his temples.

He waited long enough not to rouse any suspicion, making innocuous hangover talk with his buddies, before saying he was going for a lie down.

Alessandra's room was in a different wing from where he and his uni friends always slept when they stayed at the villa. He hadn't realised he knew exactly which room was hers until he knocked on the door. After a minute of no response, he nudged it open. It was empty.

Moving stealthily so as not to attract attention, he slipped out of the villa and into the gardens.

After much searching, he tracked her down. She was sitting on the stone steps that led into Lake Como. Only one yacht remained from the handful that had been moored overnight.

She didn't acknowledge his presence.

Today she was dressed in ankle-length tight white jeans and a pale-pink cashmere top, the V plunging down to display a hint of swollen cleavage, the only outward physical sign of the changes taking place within her.

What other changes were taking place within that gorgeous form…?

A stark image came into his mind of the perfection of her breasts, the way they seemed to have been made to fit his hands… If he closed his eyes he could still taste them, taste *her*…

'How are you feeling?' he asked abruptly, forcing thoughts of her naked body from his mind as he sat on the cold stone beside her.

'About as well as can be expected,' she replied after a long pause.

'I never asked last night how you're coping with the pregnancy—physically, I mean.'

Another pause. 'So far I've been lucky. No morning sickness or anything.'

'I've made a few calls and rearranged my schedule so I can stay in Milan for a few days. First thing tomorrow morning, we're going to see your doctor.'

'I've got a shoot to do.' She cast sharp eyes at him. 'And, before you accuse me of being selfish again, I'd like to point out that for me to cancel the shoot would mean a good dozen people's schedules being thrown. We can see the doctor in the afternoon.'

At least she was willing to see a doctor with him. That was a start.

'Does this mean you are in agreement to us marrying?'

She fell silent for a few moments, tucking a strand of hair behind an ear. 'If we marry, we both automatically become our child's legal guardian.'

'I am aware of that.' It was one of the things he wanted— his paternity to be recognised by law. Marriage might be destructive and capable of ruining people but it was the only way he could ensure his child had his protection. For that reason alone he was prepared to do it. For their child's sake, it was no sacrifice.

She stared at him. 'If anything happens to me, you have sole responsibility.'

He felt his blood chill at the sudden solemnity in her tone. 'Why are you talking like this?'

'Do you know how my mother died?' she asked in that same thoughtful tone.

'Rocco never liked to talk about her other than to say she'd died when he was seven.' Alessandra would have been a baby, he realised, doing the maths for the first time.

Her gaze didn't falter. 'She died having me.'

Theos...

'Rocco never said.' He shook his head, trying to digest her words.

'Rocco suffered the most out of all of us.' A faraway look formed in her eyes before she blinked it away and cleared her throat.

'What happened to her?' he asked, rubbing his chin, trying to imagine the Mondelli siblings as they'd been then: Rocco a child of seven, and Alessandra, so fresh and newborn she'd barely taken her first breath before her mother had been taken away from her forever.

He racked his pounding brain, trying to remember the age Rocco had been when he'd gone to live with Giovanni Mondelli, their grandfather. Eight, if he was recollecting correctly, which meant Alessandra had been a year at the most.

She'd never known the love of either a mother *or* a father.

At least his own mother had been there. For all her faults, she'd never abandoned him or reneged on her responsibility as a mother.

'She suffered from severe pre-eclampsia,' Alessandra said, her husky voice soft.

Red-hot anger flooded through him, pushing away the ache that had formed in his chest at learning of the tragic circumstances of her birth. '*Why the hell* haven't you seen a doctor yet?'

'It doesn't affect women until the later stages of pregnancy. For the time being, I'm fine. My mother didn't know what she was dealing with—she'd already given birth to a healthy child without any complications. Medicine has advanced a lot since then and we can prepare for it. The odds of anything happening to me are remote. But—and this is why I'm saying this now, before I agree to anything—if the worst happens then I need to know that you will rise to your legal and moral duty and raise our child.'

'I would *never* abandon our child,' he said harshly. 'I've lived without a father; I know what it's like to wonder where you're from. I will never let our child wonder who I am.'

'My father said that to my mother. He promised he would love and care for us but he broke it—he broke the promise he made to a dying woman. He abandoned me. He abandoned Rocco.'

'I am *not* your father. What he did was despicable. After the way my own father abandoned me, I would never give up my own flesh and blood.'

'I have to trust that you won't be like either of our fathers but I find trusting people, especially men, very hard. If I stay single, then I can nominate the guardian of my choosing.'

If fire could have shot from eyes then what burned from Christian's would have had her in flames.

'I will never allow that,' he ground out. 'I would fight for our child through every court in every land.'

The tension that had been cramping Alessandra's belly throughout the conversation loosened a touch.

She believed him.

Their child would have a father. A proper father.

She just had to hope her trust in this respect wasn't misplaced. For her child's sake, she had to try.

'I'm sorry for being melodramatic. I just need to be sure. We *both* need to be sure. If we marry then that's it—we're married. For better or worse. And, if I agree, I want you to promise that you will be discreet in your affairs.'

His head twisted at her abrupt change of direction. 'My affairs?'

'I'm not stupid,' she said with what she hoped sounded like nonchalance. If she was going to marry him, she would do it with her eyes open.

Christian was an attractive man—oh, to hell with such an insipid description, he was utterly gorgeous. He had the most beautiful eyes she'd ever seen in a man, a real crystal-blue that made her think of calm, sunlit oceans. When he fixed them on her, though, her internal reaction was turbulent; a crescendo of emotions she struggled to understand.

The way he'd made her feel that night…

He was used to women throwing themselves at him. She wasn't so naïve as to believe marriage would tame him. Theirs was not a love match. 'Our loyalty will be primarily to our child but I do not want the humiliation of your liaisons being paraded on the front pages of the tabloids. All I ask is that from now on you choose your lovers wisely.'

He inhaled sharply before expelling the air slowly. If his jaw became any more rigid she feared it would snap. 'Anything else?' he asked icily.

She refused to drop her gaze. 'Only that if we marry I won't be taking your name.'

Now she knew how it must have felt like to be glared at by Medusa. Forget mere fire; she could feel her blood turn to stone under his deadly stare.

'Why. Not?' he asked through gritted teeth.

'Because I like my name and I don't want to have to start all over again. I've spent the past seven years building my career but it's only been in the last few that my name has become famous for my work rather than my heritage and past exploits.' Alessandra wasn't prepared to fool herself. She might be famous at the moment for her photography but she didn't have the longevity that would still make her name roll off fashion editors' lips if she took months off. Her work as a photographer could quickly be forgotten, others taking her place.

More importantly, although this was something she chose not to share with Christian, figuring she'd pushed him far enough as it was, she didn't trust that their marriage would survive. If she was a betting girl, she would give them until their baby's first birthday. By then, Christian would be clamouring for his freedom.

'You can keep Mondelli as your business name but in our personal life you will be Markos.'

'Do not tell me what I can and can't do. Marriage will not make you my keeper.'

'I never said it would. However, one of the main factors in us marrying is to promote stability and unity. Sharing a surname is a part of that.'

'If you feel that strongly about it, you can change your name to Mondelli.'

'That is out of the question.'

'Why? Because you're a man? I never took you for a caveman.'

'It's the tradition of marriage.'

'We're not marrying for traditional reasons. As I pointed out last night, we're living in the twenty-first century. Plenty of couples marry without taking each other's surnames. I'm sorry if this disappoints you but I'm not changing my name. It's non-negotiable.'

'Our child will take *my* name.' He stared at her, the fire in his blue eyes, normally so warm and full of vitality, now turned icy cold. 'That is non-negotiable.'

'I can agree to that,' she said, matching his cool tone. It was one thing refusing to take his name for herself—refusing to let their child take his name too would feel as if she was being cruel for cruelty's sake.

'Good.' The coldness in his eyes thawed a fraction. 'Does this mean—finally—that you will agree to our marriage?'

'After all this you *still* want to marry me?' she asked, a tiny bubble of amusement breaking through the tension. If Christian wanted a wife he could walk all over, she was certain she'd just proved she wouldn't be that woman. She didn't want to be a harridan but she knew she needed to establish the ground rules first. She'd worked too hard to build a life that was all her own to give it up without a fight. For her baby it was easy, but for a man? *No.*

'All I want is what's best for our baby.'

'As do I.' If that meant marrying Christian, then so be it. Rocco had always described him as a man of his word—if she didn't agree, he would refuse to confirm paternity until after the birth. In the meantime, her name would be dragged through the mud again. She would have to cope with swarms of paparazzi hounding her; read the lies that would follow as speculation grew over who her baby's father was; listen to the taunts that would surely rain down on her. She would have to suffer it alone, just as she had the first time.

And it wasn't just she who would suffer. Rocco would too and God alone knew her brother had suffered enough at her hands.

But, above and beyond all that, her baby could be the one to suffer the most. Imagining—*knowing*—what people were thinking of her, were saying about her… It would contaminate her, just like it had the first time. She didn't want that bitterness and despair to infect her innocent baby.

No, whichever way she looked at it, marrying Christian was the obvious, *practical* thing to do. Her head knew it. Soon enough her twisted guts would believe it too.

'How will our marriage work on a practical level?' she asked, stalling the moment when she would have to say aloud the words agreeing to tie her life to this man beside her.

'We will lead our own lives.' His gaze bore into her. 'Our marriage will be private. We can keep separate rooms and lead independent lives so long as we show unity in public.'

'I can accept that,' she agreed.

'But on our wedding night and honeymoon we will need to share a bed.' Christian stared at her without blinking, making sure she understood. Alessandra's approach, blunt as it was, was for the best—neither of them wanted there to be any misunderstandings. They would both enter matrimony with their eyes open but their hearts closed.

Colour tinged her cheeks. 'Surely we don't need to go that far?'

'I want our marriage to be seen as legal in *every* respect. To protect our child from undue scandal and speculation, people must believe we're in love.' He tried to think about their marriage with his business head, consider it as just another merger between two companies. In essence, that was what it *would* be—a merger. The profit would come from the child they would raise together.

He'd craved isolation since he'd been a small child sharing cramped living space with his mother. His homes were his sanctuary, his space. Even his live-in staff had separate quarters.

Alessandra had been the first woman he'd woken next to and felt a tug of reluctance at having to leave.

He couldn't remember ever feeling so greedy for someone as he had that night, when he'd wanted her so badly it had been as if he were consuming her. If he hadn't been concerned that she might be feeling the physical soreness he assumed women must feel after losing their virginity, he would have made love to her all night long.

Her eyes didn't waver although more colour crept over her face. 'When you say you want it to be seen as legal in every respect, are you implying that we need to have sex?'

'No.' His voice dropped, heat unfurling within him as a memory of a dusky pink nipple floated into his mind. A small gust of wind fluttered across them, causing a strand of her hair to stray across her face. Unthinking, he reached out to brush it away. 'But we *will* be married—what couples choose to do in the privacy of their own home is entirely their own business.'

Her throat moved, a subtle movement, but one he recognised.

He leaned in closer. 'When we stay anywhere that is not under one of our own roofs, we will share a bed. What we choose to do in that bed is nobody's business but our own.'

Their marriage would be a merger, yes, but not a business merger. This was going to be a merger of two flesh-and-blood people.

Something pulsed in her eyes and he knew with certainty that she was remembering how good it had been between them.

They had been combustible.

All the supressed memories of that night came back in startling colour.

She'd been wild. Carnal. Eager to please and be pleased, to touch and be touched.

Her arousal had been a living thing…

She cleared her throat. 'And if I choose to sleep and *only* sleep…?'

Then his balls would probably turn blue.

'Then you will be left to sleep.' He let his voice drop further, inching his face closer to hers. 'But, if you choose not to sleep, you won't find me complaining.'

'Is that because you're not fussy about who you lie in bed with?' Her words had a breathless quality to them. He could feel the tension emanating from her.

'No.' He shook his head in emphasis and pressed his lips to her ear. 'It's because you're the sexiest woman I've ever known and I get hard every time I think of how you came undone in my arms.'

He moved back to see her lips part and her doe eyes widen.

'I understand your opinion of my sex life is less than flattering,' he said, thinking that she turned the most beautiful colour when she blushed. 'But, I assure you, I think with the head on my shoulders and not the one in my boxer shorts.'

She swallowed before saying, 'I think that's a matter of opinion.'

'Point proved,' he said. 'But, to prove *my* point, I will not make a move on you until we are legally married.'

Her eyes narrowed but he caught the spark that ignited in them.

'And, of course, you will still reserve your right to say no.' He dipped his head to whisper into her ear again, inhaling her scent for good measure.

All his senses heightened. He could feel the heat from her skin; knew the spark that had drawn them together in the first place was still well and truly alive. 'We're both going to have to make sacrifices for this to work—the bedroom is the one area where compromise and sacrifice are not needed, where our marriage can be about nothing but mutual pleasure.'

She raised a shoulder and exhaled a shuddering breath that sounded almost like a moan. It was a long moment before she next spoke, breaking the charged silence that had sprung up between them. 'I will not have sex with you just because it's expected.'

He pulled away, creating a little distance so he could look at her. 'My only expectation is that, when we're in public, we *both* put on a display of being in love.'

She held his gaze for a fraction longer before blowing out a puff of air and fixing her gaze back on the lake. *'Bene.'*

'So we are in agreement?'

'Yes. We are in agreement. I will marry you.'

It was Christian's turn to exhale. Who would have thought *he* would feel relief to hear a woman agree to marriage?

'It would be best to marry as soon as we can—before you start showing.'

'I don't want to arrange anything until I've spoken to Rocco.'

The mention of her brother's name hit him like a blow: the metaphorical elephant in the room spoken aloud.

'We will speak to him together.'

'It will be best if I speak to him alone. He's my brother.'

'And he's one of my closest friends. He's not going to be happy about this.'

'I would prefer it if he gave us his blessing but if he refuses…' She sighed, a troubled expression crossing her features.

'We will wait until he returns from his honeymoon,' Christian decided, although his guts made that familiar clenching motion they did whenever he thought of what his friend's reaction would be.

Rocco would never forgive him.

He didn't blame him.

Whatever was thrown his way, he would take. It would be no less than he deserved.

He remembered the first time he'd met Rocco, Stefan and Zayed during his first week at Columbia. He'd never left Athens before that, never mind Greece. New York had been a whole new world. He'd felt out of his depth on every level, especially when comparing himself to his new friends' wealth and good breeding. He'd had neither and hadn't been able to understand why they'd accepted him as one of their own.

Even now, a decade on when his own wealth rivalled the best in the world, he still struggled to understand what they'd seen in him.

He was Christian Markos, born a gutter rat without a penny to his name. She was Alessandra Mondelli, born into one of Italy's premiere families. She had class *and* breeding. She could be a princess.

In a perfect world she would marry someone from a similar background. Someone worthy of her.

All the same, they might be from disparate backgrounds but on marriage they had common ground: relationships were not for either of them. In that one respect they were perfect for each other. She would never *need* him or require more than he could give.

And he would never need her.

Messy, complicated emotions would never infect *their* marriage.

CHAPTER FOUR

ALESSANDRA PRESSED THE button allowing Christian into the building and took deep breaths to compose herself.

It would be the first time she'd seen him in ten days.

They'd spent a couple of days together in Milan, seeing her doctor then a private obstetrician. Both had confirmed that she and the baby were in excellent health. She'd known in her guts everything was well but hearing it vocalised had lifted a weight she hadn't been aware of carrying until it was gone.

A scan had been taken, a copy of which they had both taken before Christian had left. She'd spent hours gazing at that picture, making out the tiny head and limbs, so imperceptible she had to rely on memory from where the nurse had pointed. Sometimes, gazing hard, everything inside her would constrict, her throat closing so tight that she had to swallow to loosen it. Her beautiful baby. Her and *Christian*'s beautiful baby.

She hadn't see him since, all their communication coming via daily text messages and phone calls, during which he filled her in on all the wedding plans. He wanted a Greek wedding so it made sense for him to organise it. She didn't think she would have been able to handle getting involved anyway. She was having a hard enough time coping with the magnitude of what she'd agreed to.

She'd known Christian since she was twelve and Rocco had brought the Brat Pack—as she privately called her brother and his little gang of university friends—home for a week-long holiday at the family villa. But she didn't *know* him.

He drank bourbon rather than his national drink of ouzo. He was a snazzy dresser. His brain was lauded around the world. He was completely self-made. He liked rock music. He'd slept with a quarter of the world's most beautiful women, the others being shared out between her brother, Stefan and Zayed. He was used to getting his own way. And that was it. The rest was a mystery. She was marrying a stranger.

Dio l'aiuti—God help her—she would have to share a bed with him on occasion.

And, *dio l'aiuti*, the thought made her heat from the inside.

Ever since that particular aspect of their talk, it had felt as if a glow had been lit inside of her. His lips against her ear, his breath whispering on her skin…the heat it had ignited…

When he entered her apartment, impeccably dressed in a fashionable navy suit and striped pale-yellow tie, her heart made an involuntary skip. It skipped again when she caught his clean, freshly showered scent.

'My apologies for the delay,' he said, leaning in to give her the traditional kiss on each cheek.

Two little kisses; two tiny brushes of his lips against her skin, the hint of his warm breath on her…

The lit glow flickered and pulsated low within her, her body responding to his proximity like a bee to a field of pollen.

'It's fine,' she said, stepping away from him and opening her handbag on the pretext of checking her purse. If he looked at her now, he would see the colour she knew had bloomed on her face scorching up her neck.

Christian had been due at her apartment early that morning. He'd called late last night to say he'd been delayed but would make it to her before lunch. She hadn't been surprised. Men always made promises they had no intention of keeping. They told lies, whether deliberately or not. Even her grandfather, a man she'd thought full of morality, had lied. Only after his death had she learned he'd had an affair decades ago—with her new sister-in-law's mother, no less. If her grandfather could lie to the wife he loved so much, then what hope was there for anyone else?

The only man she trusted was her brother.

She didn't want to think what the cause of Christian's delay could have been.

'How did it go with the doctor?' he asked.

'Good.' She bit back the question of whether he would attend any further appointments with her. It would save him having to lie. It would save her having to pretend to believe it.

'Your blood pressure?'

'Normal. Everything is normal,' she said, anticipating further questions along the same vein. Feeling more on an even keel and in control of her reactions, she closed her handbag and looked at him.

He was watching her closely. 'It wasn't my intention to miss the appointment. There was a crisis at Bloomfield Bank and I had to attend an emergency board meeting.'

'You don't have to account for your whereabouts with me.' She forced a smile. 'After all, it's not as if we're married or anything.' She couldn't deny a tiny bit of the cramp in her belly lessened at knowing he hadn't been with another woman.

He'd given his word not to make a move on her until they married. He'd made no such promise about making a move on another woman.

So long as he was discreet, who he slept with was none of her business.

He laughed, a familiar sound that plunged her back to the meal they'd shared. Of the Brat Pack, he'd always been her favourite, the one she'd privately dubbed 'the Greek

Adonis.' A woman didn't need wine goggles to appreciate the strength of his jaw or the dimples that appeared when he gave one of his frequent smiles.

With wine goggles, though, even the most inhibited of females would be putty in his hands. She, the woman who'd thought herself immune to any man's charms, had been.

He hadn't even tried. A couple of glasses of champagne on an empty stomach and an aching heart and she'd felt her secret attraction towards him, locked away out of reach, escape and bloom. Like the gentleman he was—and he *was* a gentleman in the traditional, chivalrous term of the word—he'd walked her home and right up to her door. She'd been the one to kiss him, not the usual two-cheek kiss but one right on his mouth.

The feel of his lips upon hers, the scent of his skin and warm breath…the effect had been indescribable. It had unleashed something inside her, something craven, a side she'd spent years denying the existence of, telling herself she'd rather die a virgin than give herself to a man.

It hadn't felt like *giving* herself to Christian. *Giving* implied bestowing a favour, not the hot mix of desire and need that had made her desperate for his touch.

She could still feel and taste the heady heat of his breath…

But now she was stone-cold sober, her immunity back in its rightful place. Vivid memories might have the power to jolt her senses but they didn't have the power to knock her off balance. No man would ever have that power. Her body might have a Pavlovian response to him but intellectually and emotionally she was safe.

When they married he could see whoever he wanted. It made no difference to her. All she cared about was her baby. As long as her baby made it safely into this world, nothing else mattered.

Maybe when her baby was placed in her arms, her own place on this earth would make sense.

Maybe then she would lose the feeling she'd carried her entire life that she should never have been born.

Christian sensed a slight change in Alessandra's demeanour, an almost imperceptible straightening of the shoulders and stiffening of the spine.

She was looking good. She always looked good.

With her long hair loose around her shoulders, she wore faded tight-fitting jeans, a pale-blue cotton blouse unbuttoned to the top of her cleavage, a navy blazer and silver ankle boots with a slight heel. Heavy costume jewellery in shades of red hung round her neck and wrists, large, hooped gold earrings in her ears. Alessandra could wear a sack and carry it off, would still have that beautifully put-together air she carried so well.

Her apartment was the same: chic and beautifully put together, the walls and furniture muted but the furnishings bold and colourful. Giant prints of her work hung on the walls, enlarged, framed covers of *Vogue* and all the other glossy magazines she'd worked for.

He knew it would be a wrench for her to leave, but a third-floor apartment in the heart of Milan's fashion district was not a feasible place to bring up a child. He'd raised the subject of her selling it on the phone a few days ago. Her response had been non-committal to say the least.

He'd give her more time to get used to the idea before discussing it again.

'Are you ready to go?' he asked.

She nodded, her plump lips drawing together. 'Let's get this over with.'

Out in the courtyard at the back of the building, where his driver waited for them, her yellow Vespa gleamed from its parking space. 'I hope you're not riding on that thing any more,' he said, nodding at it.

'No,' she answered shortly, getting into the back of the car.

He followed her in, a pang hitting his stomach as he recalled the big beam on her face the one time he'd seen her ride on it—the day of their impromptu date. Another thing pregnancy would force her to give up.

When the car started to move, she turned to look at him, a set look on her face. 'Christian, let me make one thing quite clear. You are going to be my husband, not my keeper. Do not dictate to me.'

He sighed. 'Is this about the Vespa?'

'Yes.'

'I wasn't *dictating* to you. I was satisfying myself that you're not putting our child's life at risk by continuing to ride on it, especially here in Milan.'

'That is exactly what I mean. I don't need you to tell me the drivers here all approach the road as an assault course that must be beaten—I live here. I might not have a penis between my legs but my brain and rationality work perfectly well.'

'I never said it didn't,' he said, keeping his tone even. 'But you must appreciate that it is *my* child you are carrying and it is only right I take an interest in its welfare.'

'But it is *my* life. I will not be told what to do.'

'I am not telling you what to do.' How he held on to his patience, he did not know. 'All I'm saying is that having a child changes things…'

'You think I don't know that?' she said, her colour darkening. 'You think I'm not aware of the responsibility I have to bring our child safely into this world? Do you think I'm not *capable*?'

'Alessandra…' He took a breath and fisted his hands into balls. 'Will you stop putting words into my mouth? You're making assumptions.'

Her shoulders hunched before she flopped her head back and took a long breath. 'I'm sorry,' she muttered. 'I have an aversion to being told what to do.'

'I had already gathered that.'

She cast a sideways glance at him and tucked a strand of hair behind her ear. Her very pretty ear.

'As well as my aversion to being bossed around, I also have a tendency to get grumpy when I'm worried about something,' she admitted, her tone now rueful.

'You're worried about Rocco's reaction to our news?'

'Aren't you?'

He reached for her hand and squeezed it.

'Whatever happens with your brother, nothing will change. You and I will still marry. If he gives his blessing, then that will be beneficial, but if he doesn't then we will handle it together. Okay?' he added when she didn't answer, simply sank her teeth into her bottom lip and tugged her hand free from his clasp.

She nodded slowly, and absently rubbed at the top of her hand where his fingers had rested. 'Rocco is very protective of me. He always has been.'

'You're his sister; nothing will change that.' Christian was doing his best to project a positive frame of mind for Alessandra's benefit but was under no illusion about how hot-headed her brother could be. He knew that if the forthcoming meeting was badly handled, their friendship would be ruined.

Alessandra's lungs had closed up.

The intimacy of the cab, the forced proximity…

Worry about her brother's reaction faded as Christian's oaky cologne filled her senses, moisture filling her mouth and bubbling low in her most intimate area.

She pressed her thighs together and dragged out a short breath. It wasn't enough. She needed air.

There was nowhere to hide.

The traffic outside was atrocious. They were still a couple of streets away from the House of Mondelli, where her brother awaited her. If she were on her Vespa she would be there by now, able to weave in and out of the traffic while turning a deaf ear to the tooting horns.

'Let's walk the rest of the way,' she said. She needed air. She needed to breathe. 'It'll be quicker.'

Christian nodded and pressed the button to lower the partition, telling his driver to stop the car. As they were already stationary, this required no effort on the driver's part.

Alessandra immediately felt better out in the balmy spring air. She loved the sunshine; knew it was the reason her grandfather had left her the villa in St. Barts, so she had a bolt hole to escape to when the gloomy Milanese winter set in. She had no idea yet what she would do with the apartment in Paris he had also left her, but the villa would remain hers until she took her last breath. Which, if the Milanese drivers had anything to do with it, could be sooner rather than later.

They made it to the entrance of the luxurious building without being squashed by any moving vehicles and stepped inside. She smiled at the glamorous receptionists and, with Christian by her side, strode past the large rooms homing all the creative minds that made the House of Mondelli such a success, and through to her brother's office. His door was closed; Gabrielle, his PA, guarded it with her desk like a sentry. She stood to greet them.

Alessandra cast a quick glance at Christian, experiencing the strangest compulsion to grab hold of his hand. He inclined his head and threw a small, encouraging smile. She couldn't read his eyes.

Taking a deep breath, she rapped on the door and pushed it open.

Rocco was at his desk talking into his phone. A smile formed on his lips at seeing his sister, his eyes pulling into a question at seeing Christian follow her inside and shut the door behind him.

He ended the call and got to his feet, sidling round his desk to pull her into an embrace. 'You're looking well, *sorellina*.' Little sister.

'And you're looking tanned. Good honeymoon?'

'Perfetto.'

She didn't think she'd ever seen him so happy. 'How's Liv?'

Somehow his face lit up even more. 'She's wonderful.' Rocco moved on to Christian, giving him a bear hug, which he returned. 'What are you doing here?'

'I'm here to see you,' Christian said.

If Rocco heard the serious inflection in his friend's voice he made no sign of it. 'Alessandra and I have a lunch date—are you joining us?'

'Rocco,' said Alessandra, placing a hand on her brother's arm to get his attention. 'Christian is here with me. We have something to tell you.'

Immediately the light in her brother's eyes dimmed, became wary. 'Tell me what?'

Christian shifted slightly and placed an arm around her waist. The gesture felt almost protective. 'We're getting married,' he said, his tone serious.

Rocco shook his head as if clearing his ears of water. 'Married?'

'Yes. We wanted you to be the first to know.'

Alessandra pressed closer to Christian in a show of unity and forced a breezy laugh. If they could make this look and sound as natural as possible, then Rocco should be accepting of their plans. That was what she'd been telling herself for almost a fortnight. 'I want you to give me away.'

Rocco laughed with her, although not at his usual pitch. 'You two are getting married?'

'Si.'

'My little sister and my best friend?'

'Si! Isn't it wonderful?'

'That's one way to describe it. When did all this happen?'

'We bumped into each other when you were in New York.' She and Christian had agreed to stick with the truth as much as possible. Neither wanted to lie to Rocco. 'Christian had come to take *you* out but, as you were in New York,

I talked him into taking me out instead. Then, at your wedding we spent a bit more time together and realised our feelings for each other had changed.' That was the truth as well. How could someone be just a friend of your brother's if you were carrying his child?

'When do you hope to marry?'

'We've decided there's no point in hanging around so we've set the date for a fortnight. We're marrying in Athens.'

'That soon?'

Christian's hand brushed against her back as he pulled away from her and took a step closer to Rocco.

Neither man spoke.

Suddenly she became aware that the atmosphere in the office wasn't the warm bonhomie she'd intended. It was cold. Icy.

As she looked from her fiancé to her brother, taking in the two sets of lips clamped firmly together, her heart sank.

For all his outward amiability, Rocco hadn't bought a single word she'd said. And Christian knew it.

'Are you pregnant?' he asked, looking at her briefly, his tone casual.

She swallowed, stupidly unprepared for such a question. She placed her arm protectively across her waist.

This time he directed the same question to Christian. There was no denying the menace in his stance. 'Have you got my sister pregnant?'

Christian drew himself up to his full height. It was like watching two silverbacks square up to each other. Both men were equal in stature, both topping six foot by a good few inches, and both kept themselves in extremely good shape.

'Yes. Alessandra is pregnant with my baby and we have agreed to marry. We both want to do the right thing by our child.'

'The right thing by your child?' Rocco snarled, his face ablaze with fury. 'What about my sister? What the *hell* were you doing messing with her in the first place?'

'I'm not going to lie to you,' Christian said, his tone calm but with a hint of steel underlying his words. 'Neither of us meant for this to happen. But it *has* happened—Alessandra is pregnant with my child and I am going to support them both in every way I can.'

'So she was another of your one-night stands? Is that what you're telling me?'

Christian didn't answer, keeping his gaze fixed evenly on Rocco.

'You said neither of you meant it to happen, so I will ask you one more time: was she just a one-night stand to you?'

'Yes.'

If Christian intended to elaborate on his one-syllable answer, his words went unsaid when Rocco's arm shot out like a bullet.

'Rocco, *no!*' But her scream came too late to prevent her brother's fist connecting with Christian's nose, a resounding crack bouncing off the walls on impact.

Christian dropped to the floor with a thump.

Immediately Alessandra fell to her knees beside him. Vivid red blood seeped from his nose.

'What did you do that *for*?' she said, switching to Italian, half-shouting, half-screaming, not looking at Rocco, too busy checking Christian's vital signs. The pulse in his neck pumped strongly, the only blessing she could cling to. She looked up at her brother, who stood frozen. 'Don't just stand there—call for an ambulance.'

Rocco's broad chest heaved, his face a couple of shades paler than it had been when she'd walked into his office. 'He doesn't need an ambulance. He's already coming round.'

He was right. Christian's lips were moving.

'At least get some ice,' she snapped, somehow holding back the tears.

Not sure if she was doing the right thing or not, she carefully lifted Christian's head and placed it on her lap. Being as gentle as she could, she ran her fingers over his hair, not knowing or caring if she was comforting him or herself. Of all the scenarios that had played itself out in her head, this was not an outcome she had prepared for.

She should be getting used to that.

'Are you still here?' she snarled at her brother. 'He needs ice.'

'He needs castration.' He swore loudly. 'You're my sister and he's a playboy—'

'And you're a hypocrite!' she interrupted. 'The majority of the women you've slept with have been *someone's* sister. He's your best friend and you're just as big a playboy as he is.'

'Not any more, I'm not—and I'm not oblivious to those other women being someone's sister, but *you* are *my* sister.'

'No—I *was* your sister. After what you've just done, I will never call you my brother again. I'll walk myself up the aisle. Now, get an ice pack and then you can get the hell out of my life.'

Through the ringing in his ears Christian heard the sound of muffled talking. Arguing.

Was that *Alessandra* speaking so emotively?

Through the lancing pain in his face came the realisation that, yes, it was Alessandra—that it was her warm lap supporting his head, her gentle fingers lacing through his hair, her normally calm, husky voice pitched at a much higher octave than he had ever associated it with.

Footsteps left the room, the door slamming with a close.

He winced as the sound reverberated through his pounding head.

Well, that had gone better than he'd anticipated.

CHAPTER FIVE

BACK IN ALESSANDRA'S APARTMENT, Christian lay on the sofa, holding the ice pack in place to the bridge of his nose.

Eyes closed, he heard Alessandra pour fresh coffee out; listened as she padded over the thick rug and placed their drinks on the glass table in front of him.

Gabrielle had brought the ice pack to him, Rocco himself having disappeared from the building.

His old friend had seen straight through their deception, exactly as he'd known he would.

'You let him hit you, didn't you?'

He opened his eyes to find Alessandra glaring down at him. She'd changed into a short black skirt, the faded jeans she'd been wearing having been covered in his blood. Her golden legs were bare. Gorgeously bare.

He straightened and put the ice pack down beside his mug.

'Are you going to answer me?'

'Yes, I let him hit me.'

'Why?'

'Better to let him get it out of his system now than at the wedding.'

'He's not coming to the wedding. I've told him he's not welcome.'

Even though the movement hurt, he couldn't stop the smile forming. 'You don't mean that.'

'Don't I?'

'No, you don't.' He knew how close the Mondelli siblings were.

'I told you, I don't like being told what to do. I've had it up to here with my brother thinking he can run my life.' She slumped onto the single sofa and rubbed her eyes, smudging her make-up. 'Did you know I always refused to do any work for the House of Mondelli?'

'I was aware of that—Rocco always said he thought it was a shame, as your fashion shoots are some of the best in the business.'

'He said that?' A look of pleasure flashed over her, quickly replaced by another grimace. 'A few months ago he asked me to do all the photography for the new launch he was working on. For the first time, I said yes. I thought our relationship had reached the stage where he regarded me as his equal, as Alessandra Mondelli, not just as his little sister. I wanted to be employed for the quality of my work, not out of nepotism. I should have known better. He still thinks he knows best and can ride roughshod over my feelings.'

She made a noise that sounded like a choking growl and slumped on the sofa, bending her head forward, her long hair falling like a sheet before her until she tossed her head back and sighed. 'I love my brother but he has to accept I'm not a child any more. I'm an adult. I make my own decisions. He doesn't have to like them but he has to at least respect them and if he can't do that then he can keep away.'

'Our news was a shock to him. He'll come round.'

'I don't care if he does.' She blinked rapidly and swallowed. 'So much for averting a scandal; how long do you think it'll be before the press learns he hit you?'

'There's no need for the press to know anything.'

She arched a perfectly plucked dark brow. 'We were seen by at least a dozen people leaving the House of Mondelli, you with an ice pack stuck to your nose. Have you looked in the mirror?' She didn't give him the chance to reply.

'You've already got two black eyes forming. How are you going to explain that away?'

'I wear exceedingly dark sunglasses. No one will see my eyes.'

'That's not even funny.'

Seeing she was working herself into a state, he leaned forward and spoke forcefully. 'There will be no scandal. We will cut the press off at its head.'

'How?'

'By announcing our marriage. We will send out a press release today.'

She pulled a face. 'If we announce it now, the press will go into a frenzy.'

'They will,' he agreed. During their many phone conversations over the past ten days they'd discussed how to handle the press and had agreed to delay notifying them until a week before the wedding, at which point Alessandra would join him in Athens. All the guests they planned to invite could be relied on for their discretion. 'But it will be a controlled frenzy and give them something to write about that should, hopefully, supersede any rumour that may come about your brother hitting me. You will have to travel to Athens with me...'

'Absolutely not.'

'You've already agreed to join me there.'

'But not for another week.'

'It will be safer for you. Here, you're too exposed. The paparazzi can doorstep you.'

'I don't care.' Eyes blazing, she folded her arms across her chest. 'I can't go anywhere. I have work commitments. Lots of them. It's been hard enough trying to rearrange my schedule for the wedding and honeymoon but at least I've been able to give the editors and fashion houses I freelance for some notice. For me to come to Athens today means letting them all down at the last minute.'

'What's the alternative? For you to stay here in Milan to

face the press on your own? You wanted my support and I am trying to give it to you.'

'Why do I need to leave? Why can't you stay here?'

'I need to be in Athens. I have important business commitments coming up this week.'

'Are you saying your commitments are more important than mine?'

'No.' Swearing, he gripped hold of his mug. 'Yes.'

Looking at her, he could see she was fighting the urge to punch him in the face just as her brother had done.

Such passion.

On the surface, Alessandra Mondelli was the epitome of cool sophistication. Scratch beneath it and the passionate, sultry woman emerged like a vibrant butterfly emerging from a chrysalis.

Knowing he was the only man to have experienced that passion made his chest fill.

Her passion was *his*. All his.

One day, soon, he would sate himself in her arms again. He knew it and she knew it too; he could see it in the way the pupils of her eyes dilated when their gazes met, the way her breath hitched when they brushed against each other.

She still wanted him.

The thought of them sharing a bed again made his loins tighten and the dread of their forthcoming nuptials taste sweeter.

She would be his again.

For now, though, all thoughts of making love would have to wait. He'd given his word not to make a move on her until after their wedding and he intended to keep it.

'In the future we will arrange our schedules to accommodate both our obligations, but in this instance I'm afraid my commitments *are* more important than yours.'

One of Greece's major banks—one that had weathered the worst of the financial crisis—had been plunged into serious financial trouble and had called on Christian for help and advice. So many of his compatriots were struggling; it was like a constant pain in his chest. He'd been there once: impoverished. Desperate. He gave his assistance gladly.

'That's just…'

'There is another alternative,' he said, knowing perfectly well it was an alternative she would dismiss out of hand. 'You can stay at Villa Mondelli. The press won't be able to touch you there, not with all the security measures that have been put in place.'

'What, with my brother? I would rather stay in a convent.'

'Those are your options: stay here alone to deal with the press you hate so much, stay with the brother you've just disowned or come to Athens with me where the press can't touch you.'

'Then I stay.'

Theos, give him patience. The woman was even more stubborn than her brother. 'And deal with the press alone? When you hate them so much?'

'At least I know their comments will be kinder than they were before. I'd much rather they harass me by asking questions about our wedding than harass me by telling me who the latest person to call me a slut is.'

'They did that?' He'd seen much of the coverage, knew she'd had a rough time with the press, but had had no idea they had stooped so low as to tell a vulnerable teenager what despicable names people were calling her.

'That was then. I'm perfectly safe here in my apartment—the press can't get past the concierge.'

'Who are these people who called you a slut?' His brain refused to move on from that piece of information. When he learned who had said such insulting words towards her, he would hunt each and every one of them down. He would make them pay.

The sheer violence of his thoughts shocked him.

All his life he'd used his brains to better himself, only using his fists when it was a choice of fight or flight.

The kids in his neighbourhood had roamed the streets of Athens in packs while he had spent his precious free time with his head buried in books, determined to educate himself out of that life. They'd seen him as a freak.

Often they had lain in wait for him. Between the ages of ten and sixteen he'd been beaten up on average once a month. Always he'd fought back, sometimes more successfully than others. Then, aged sixteen, he'd experienced a monster of a growth spurt, growing six inches in six months. He'd also found himself an early-morning job at the fish market lugging heavy boxes of freshly caught mackerel and sardines. He'd filled out physically to match his new height.

He'd no longer been the skinny, bookish kid and the bullies had known it. After one particular fight, when he'd broken the nose of the ringleader and blackened the eyes of two others, they'd left him alone.

He hadn't wanted to hit anyone since then. Until now.

How could *anyone* call Alessandra a slut?

'Too many to name.' She answered his question with a shrug.

'How could they say such things? You were a child.'

'I was seventeen. Old enough to know better.'

'Do not tell me you blame yourself?'

'Only in the respect that I swallowed Javier's lies.' Her eyes pierced right through him. 'I should have known not to trust the word of a man.'

'Not all men are liars.'

'Aren't they?' She didn't elaborate. She continued staring at him with the same piercing expression.

'No!' he said forcefully.

'With the exception of my brother, all the men *I've* ever known have been liars. Trusting Javier cost me everything. My grandfather turned into my jailer, the few friends he'd permitted me to have turned their backs on me because their parents didn't want me corrupting them and Rocco had the humiliation of reading untrue, lewd comments about his baby sister. I'm sorry, but I will never trust you, Christian. All I can do is try and have faith that your indiscretions will be discreet.'

'I will never humiliate you or disrespect you.' He rose from his seat, ignoring the throbbing pain across the front of his face, and crouched on his haunches before her. Placing a hand on her neck, he rubbed his thumb over the soft skin.

Theos, one touch of her softness, one inhalation of her scent and his body responded, his groin tightening as memories of burying himself inside her assailed him.

'You are going to be my wife.' He spoke the words slowly. 'If you do not believe anything else, believe that that means something to me. I will take my vows seriously.'

'I'm sure Javier said the same thing to his wife.'

Christian swore and inhaled deeply.

Alessandra leant forward, matching the intensity of his stare, close enough for his oaky, masculine scent to swirl around her.

His hand was still pressed against her neck, heating her skin. For a moment she lost her train of thought, suddenly pulled back to that night two months ago, his naked body covering hers…

She blinked herself back to the present, grabbing onto his hand and lacing her fingers into his. She squeezed. 'When Javier's wife saw those photos of her husband kissing a girl half his age, she must have thought her heart was breaking.'

Those dreadful, incriminating pictures.

Her brother and grandfather had taken a business trip together to New York for a long weekend. The Mondelli housekeeper had taken the day off. Alessandra and the man who was supposed to be giving her private tuition in maths over the long summer holiday had had the villa to themselves for the very first time. They could have done anything.

It had been her suggestion that they go out for lunch at a

nearby hotel, famed for its discretion. Javier didn't live locally. No one would know him.

She'd *longed* to do something as a normal couple, not have to keep her feelings hidden away, and this had been the perfect opportunity. She'd believed him when he'd said they had to keep their love a secret until she turned eighteen and finished her schooling.

How grown up she'd felt, walking hand in hand with her would-be lover. How naïve she'd been.

They'd dined in the fine hotel restaurant using *her* allowance to pay the bill, oblivious to the fact that half a dozen paparazzi had swarmed the lobby, awaiting the rumoured arrival of one of Hollywood's most eligible bachelors.

While she'd been blithely oblivious, they'd recognised her in an instant. The photos they'd taken, published the next day across the whole of Italy, had been incriminating. Her and Javier holding hands, stealing kisses that looked a damn sight worse than the chaste kisses they'd actually been.

That was the last time she'd seen the coward. For a whole weekend, while her brother and grandfather had been in New York, she'd had to cope with a siege of paparazzi on her own. Those reporters had been there to witness Javier's wife arrive at the villa and bang on the door until a guilt-stricken Alessandra had answered it, her fulsome apology ready on her tongue. She'd never had the chance to say the words. As soon as she'd opened the door, Javier's wife had spat in her face, slapped her and called her a *puttana*— a whore. The press had caught every frame for posterity.

By the time her brother and grandfather had returned the damage had been done.

'Why didn't you ever put your side across?' Christian asked. If he felt any pain in his fingers he didn't show it, allowing her to continue squeezing tightly, as if he knew it to be an outward measure of the fury and pain recalling that awful time provoked.

'I wasn't allowed. Rocco and *Nonno* closed ranks.' She attempted a laugh. 'They were furious with me.'

'Why? Your tutor took advantage of you. If they were furious with anyone, it should have been him.'

'They *were* furious with him for taking advantage of me, but it didn't change the fact that I'd been sneaking around with a man almost twice my age. They forbade me from speaking to the press, saying I'd caused enough shame on the family name.' Even if she'd chosen to defy them, by the time she'd got over the shock that had rendered her virtually mute the press had moved on to its next victim. Alessandra Mondelli's affair with a married man had been old news. No one had cared for her side.

Christian disentangled his fingers from her grip and muttered another curse as he got to his feet.

The place where he'd rested his hand against her neck suddenly felt cold.

She shivered and rose to her feet to stand before him. 'If I leave with you today, my career will be ruined. No editor or fashion director will ever trust me again. It's the only thing I've got to hold onto, the only thing that gives my life any meaning.' How could she expect him to understand that? Her career was all her own. It had taken everything she had to get her name taken seriously and pull herself out from the cloud of scandal.

'And what about our child? Or does he or she not come into it?'

'Don't twist it like that. When our baby is born everything is going to change—I know that, and I'm preparing myself for the change it will bring, but right now I'm healthy and capable of working.'

'I'm not happy about this. You can't take risks with your health.'

'I don't expect you to be happy about it, but ultimately the decision is mine, so please don't patronise me about the health aspect—you were there when the doctor said I should live a normal life.'

He threw his hands in the air and shook his head, not bothering to hide his anger or frustration.

She continued speaking before he could open his mouth to argue any further. 'I will hire a bodyguard for when I leave the apartment—I promise I will protect our baby.'

'*I* will hire a bodyguard for you,' he insisted, looking only slightly mollified. 'And I want your word of honour that if at any time you feel in any kind of danger you will call me immediately.'

'I promise.'

He appraised her with narrowed eyes for a moment longer before inclining his head. 'Then I will have to trust you to keep to *your* word.'

She certainly deserved *that*.

Welcome to Athens.

No sooner had Alessandra stepped off Christian's private jet than two bodyguards appeared from nowhere. They took her luggage and escorted her to the waiting car with its bullet-proof, blacked-out windows.

A week ago she would have thought this overkill. She'd thought her brother was a pain when it came to being over-protective. Rocco had always been protective of her. After Javier, he'd become even more controlling. Her grandfather had been even worse. He'd withdrawn her allowance and curtailed her freedom, which had always been limited, to the point of non-existence. She'd returned to her private all-girls school when the holidays had finished to find he'd given strict instructions not to let Alessandra leave the grounds under any circumstances. This had been particularly humiliating, it being her final year, the school year when more adult freedoms were permitted. But not for her. All trust between her and her grandfather had broken down irrevocably.

She'd spent years breaking free and now, just as her life

and freedom were hers and hers alone, she found she was pledging herself to a man with the same controlling instinct she had spent so long kicking back from.

Christian had over-protectiveness down to an art.

He hadn't merely employed a bodyguard for her, he'd employed an elite squad of hardened ex-soldiers.

Unfortunately they didn't come with personalities, all having been highly trained never to crack a smile or share banter. In the safety of her apartment building she could forget all about them, but the second she stepped outside they would materialise.

As much as she found their presence stifling, she was grateful. She'd never imagined the paparazzi could be any worse than when she'd been seventeen. She'd been wrong. Eight years ago it had been mostly the Italian press with a handful of Brits thrown in. This time their number included Greeks—lots of them—Americans, French... She swore she'd even heard a Japanese voice throw questions at her. She'd known her engagement to Christian would generate a frenzy but had not been prepared for such madness.

The granddaughter of the great Giovanni Mondelli, a man of such stature he was regarded like royalty; the sister of Rocco Mondelli, the man credited with dragging the House of Mondelli kicking and screaming into the twenty-first century, a man who'd recently married one of the most famous supermodels in the world; Alessandra Mondelli, the former scandal-hit teenager who'd become one of the world's leading fashion photographers: for such a woman to be marrying the self-made Greek billionaire, the whizz of the financial world with the movie-star looks... For the press it was a dream combination.

For Alessandra it was a nightmare. She consoled herself that at least she wasn't being called a slut any more. She'd kept her dark sunglasses on and answered only one of the hundreds of questions that had been thrown her way over the past week.

'Are you looking forward to the wedding?' someone had asked.

'Of course,' she'd replied with what she hoped was an enigmatic smile.

She hadn't been the only target. Christian, his sunglasses permanently attached to his face too, had also been mobbed. As had Rocco, who ignored every single question. Rumours had started circulating in the past few days about the punch, a new frenzy ensuing.

Relieved to be away from the madness, she leaned back in the leather seat and gazed out at Athens, the city that would play a huge part of her life from this moment on.

She'd heard it referred to as 'the cradle of Western civilisation.' Even if she'd been unaware of its history, she would have recognised it. It had seeped into the walls, some pristine, some falling apart at the seams. With ugly apartment blocks and majestic buildings, it was a city that managed to be cosmopolitan yet obviously ancient and historic. A city of contradictions.

For the first time she felt something akin to excitement bubble in her veins.

She had six days in this city before she exchanged her vows. From worrying that she would be bored stuck in a place where she knew no one, she now saw a huge opportunity. If she could ever get anywhere. At this rate, she would be lucky to make it to the hotel before the sun set. She'd thought the traffic in Milan was bad...

Eventually, they came to a road with manned security gates that opened slowly and led to an enormous white building with pillars either side of the huge entrance. It was as though she was staring at a palace that had been home to the Greek gods themselves.

A fleet of staff was by her side within seconds of the car coming to a stop, her luggage whisked away while she was taken through to the marble foyer.

'Don't I need to sign in?' she asked when a woman, who

identified herself as the general manager, offered to take her straight to her room.

'No, *despinis*,' the woman replied. 'Everything is taken care of.'

Christian's work, Alessandra told herself, her belly tightening at the thought of seeing him again. She'd been so busy over the past week that she'd hardly had the time to think of him on anything other than a practical level. Her dreams, though, had been…disturbing. Enough that merely to think of him made her bones feel as if they'd been through a blender.

Pregnancy hormones. That was all it was, she told herself—pregnancy hormones playing with her emotions.

'Where are all the other guests?' she asked, following the manager to the lift.

'Today, you are our only guest. The others will be arriving from tomorrow.'

How strange. She'd never known a hotel to have only one guest before.

Her suite was one of two located on the top floor. She guessed the other had been reserved for Christian.

Stepping into it, she couldn't help the little thrill that ran through her at the opulent marvel of marble and the stunning views. The back window had a direct view of the Parthenon.

Over the years she'd stayed in many luxurious hotels but the lavishness of this suite had a magical quality to it.

'Will you require lunch in your room or would you prefer to eat in the restaurant?' the manager asked.

'I think I'll eat on my balcony.' She had a quick skim of the menu and selected a tomato salad with crusty bread. Nothing fancy, just something healthy to keep her going until Christian joined her that evening…

The same tightening in her belly happened as she thought of him again, her heart rate speeding up to a thrum.

CHAPTER SIX

AFTER A LAZY afternoon spent by the swimming pool, unwinding after a full-on week of work and the morning's travels, Alessandra was stepping out of the shower when the phone in her room rang out.

'*Ciao?*'

'Good evening, *agapi mou.*'

A tingle fluttered up her spine to hear his rich tones.

'Hello, Christian,' she said, keeping her voice formal. 'Does this call mean you're here?'

'It does. Can you be ready in a couple of hours?'

'Why?'

'I'm taking you out for dinner.'

Trying hard to dampen the excitement fluttering low in her stomach, she opened the large wardrobe where a maid had hung all her clothes. Amongst them was her wedding dress.

Her intention had been to buy the first dress that fitted and didn't make her look like a hag. Her intentions had gone to hell. Her brain had tried to hand over the cash in the first boutique but her heart had overruled it. It wasn't until the fourth boutique that she'd found The One, the dress that had made her heart want to burst with delight.

She didn't know what she'd been thinking when she had then parted with a large sum of cash for the lacy white lingerie she'd selected to wear with it.

No, that was a lie: she *did* know what she'd been thinking. She'd been thinking of Christian.

For now she selected a khaki shirt-dress that fell to mid-thigh. She stared with longing at her five-inch-high red Manolo Blahniks but ended up disregarding them for black strappy sandals with a more reasonable three-inch heel. She had a little life inside her to think of and to totter on sky-high heels was asking for trouble.

She wondered if her own mother had faced such trivial conundrums in her pregnancies. So many questions she would never hear the answer to.

She would give anything for one day—one hour, even—with her mother. One hour to be held in her arms, to inhale her scent and hear her voice.

She prayed her baby never grew up having the same longings: so many hopes and fears, a mountain of them. All that mattered was getting her baby safely into this world.

Accessorising with beaded orange jewellery and dangly ruby earrings, she'd just applied a second coat of matching ruby lipstick when she heard a rap on the main door of the suite.

She pressed a hand to her chest, a sop to trying to control her heart that had galloped at the first knock.

Opening the door, her stomach plunged to see Christian so tanned and gorgeous before her, dressed in a silver suit, tieless, the white shirt unbuttoned at the neck. She'd kissed that neck, remembered vividly its taste…

Their eyes met; there was nothing said for the breath of a moment before she stood aside to admit him.

'You're looking good,' he said.

'Thank you,' she said, striving for breeziness.

'Are you ready?'

'Let me get my bag and we can go.' The expansive room seemed to have shrunk in the space of seconds and she was glad to escape, if only for a moment.

In the sanctuary of the bedroom, she sat on the corner

of the bed and took some deep breaths. *Keep it together, Alessandra.*

Keep it together?

At Rocco and Olivia's wedding she'd been too worried about informing Christian of his impending fatherhood to read too much into the raging emotions sleeping with him had provoked. She'd assumed that, once she'd shared the news, her equilibrium would be restored. She hadn't thought for a minute it would become more unstable around him, an instability that seemed to increase with every moment spent with him.

She *would* keep it together. She would. She was a pro at it.

Getting to her feet, she grabbed the gold clutch bag off the dresser and strolled back into the living area. Christian was leaning against the dining table, doing something on his phone. As soon as he saw her, he pressed the button to turn the screen off and quickly put it in the inside pocket of his blazer.

'Everything okay?' he asked.

She mustn't question. It was none of her business. *None* of her business.

Javier had always been secretive over his phone: hiding to answer calls; speaking in hushed tones so she couldn't overhear him; telling her it was other private students who deserved his discretion. Naïve idiot that she was, she'd believed him, had never imagined for a moment that the reason his phone never left his person was because he was married to a woman who'd lived through one of his affairs before and checked on him constantly.

If Christian wanted to be secretive, then so be it. She had no emotional claim on him. He had no emotional claim on her.

She forced a smile. 'I couldn't remember where I'd left my bag.' What was a white lie in the scheme of things? She couldn't tell him his appearance had left her feeling so off-kilter she'd needed a moment to catch her breath and her thoughts.

'Where are we eating?' she asked, following him out of the door.

'At Titos, a French restaurant near the Panathinaikos Stadium.'

'French?'

'It is considered the best restaurant in Athens.'

She raised her brows. 'Can't we go somewhere…Greek?'

'This is the most exclusive restaurant in Greece. The waiting list is eighteen months long.'

She pulled a face. 'I like fine dining as much as the next person but, truly, you can't relax somewhere like that. Please, just for tonight, can't we go somewhere normal? You live here—you must know the place that serves the best Greek food.'

Something flickered in his eyes.

'You *do* know somewhere! Please, take me.'

'It's nothing special,' he said, his voice guarded.

'Good! Nothing special is exactly what I'm in the mood for. Plus, if we eat somewhere nondescript, the less chance we have of being spotted by the paparazzi.' They would be circling the city looking for them. They were nothing if not tenacious.

After what seemed an age, Christian gave an abrupt nod. 'I know a little taverna in Pangrati, a decent area of the city.'

She beamed. *'Perfetto.'*

They both nodded at the reception staff as they left the hotel and got into the waiting car.

'Can we walk some of the way?' she asked once they were enclosed in the back.

Christian stared at her, remembering how on their night in Milan she'd insisted they walk to the restaurant, happily tottering in the black stilettos that had displayed her slender yet shapely legs so well.

The dress she wore now showed them off too, golden thigh close to his…

He preferred to walk too. He'd especially enjoyed walking with Alessandra, the refreshing conversation, her obvious femininity without demureness. He'd enjoyed everything about that evening. He'd enjoyed everything about that night. Except for the guilt that had almost crippled him, especially the next morning.

It felt even worse now. Not only had he got her pregnant but he'd lost his friend. He could cope with that if he didn't feel so damn responsible for Alessandra and Rocco's estrangement. Even if he couldn't fix his own relationship with Rocco, he was determined to fix theirs.

'The driver can take us a little further in and then we'll walk the rest.'

'*Eccellente.* I want to see as much of your home city as I can.'

'There's plenty of time for that. In the meantime, how have you settled in? Do you have everything you need?'

'I'm finding it all a little strange,' she admitted. 'I assumed the hotel would be bursting with guests.'

'Usually it would be.'

'Did you have all the other guests kicked out?' She was only half-joking.

'Not exactly. Alternative accommodation was found for them. Hotel Parthenon is for the exclusive use of our wedding party for the next week.'

'However did you manage that?'

'It wasn't difficult. I own the place.'

Her brows knitted together in confusion. 'Seriously?'

'I assumed you knew.'

'I thought your business revolved around finance.'

'On the whole it does, but in Greece it's different. Greece is my home. I love my country but its economy is a mess. Anything I can do to invest and bring money into it, I will.' Hotel Parthenon had been an obvious place for him to start. He'd discovered it six years before, a shabby, run-down two-star hotel situated on a prime site. He'd paid over the odds for it then set about transforming it, employing local builders and architects to renovate it into the seven-star luxury hotel complete with heliport it was today. Its growing reputation meant it was fully booked all year round.

'I like that,' Alessandra said, nodding her approval. 'I always think people are too keen to disregard their roots.'

'That's easy for someone like you to say.'

'What do you mean?'

'You were born with every advantage. Your roots are something for you to be proud of.'

'You think?' Her eyes flashed. 'Please, tell me, what advantage did I have when my very existence is the reason for my mother's death?'

Shocked, he momentarily lost his voice. 'You can't believe that?'

Confusion flitted over her features as if she'd shocked herself with her own words. 'It's the truth,' she whispered.

'Ochi!' No.

'Si. My mother died so I could live. If I hadn't been conceived, she would still be here.'

A coldness lodged in his stomach. 'But *you* wouldn't be here. We wouldn't be sitting here now. Our child wouldn't be growing in your belly.'

Her eyes held his, a slight wobble in them, as if she were trying desperately not to let whatever driving emotion had caused her outburst to gain any further hold.

He could kick himself. 'I apologise. When I said you were born with every advantage, I meant it in the respect that you were born a Mondelli.'

Alessandra swallowed back bile. She didn't know where her outburst had come from. It was an outburst that had lived mutely on her tongue since she'd been a young girl made to feel as if she should be grateful for the privileges of her life. As if the fact she'd grown up with money could hide the circumstances of her birth and the knock-on effect that still echoed in Rocco's and her lives. Their father's life too, weak and spineless though he was. He'd effectively thrown his life away because he hadn't been able to cope without his beloved Letizia. Nor forgetting her grandfather, her *nonno*, who'd spent the last twenty-five years of his life raising his grandchildren while his own son and heir drowned in bottles of alcohol.

All those ruined lives. Ruined dreams. Rocco ripped away from the mother he'd worshipped. And for what? For *her*? Was one life really a fair exchange for so much misery?

'No, I'm the one who should apologise. You're right. Being a Mondelli is a privilege. I've been given every material advantage.'

'I didn't mean to imply that you were spoilt. I appreciate the Mondelli name has been a mixed blessing for you.'

'And the Markos name?' she said, glad to be able to turn the conversation onto him. 'Has that been a mixed blessing for you?'

He raised a shoulder. 'The Markos name is nothing special. It doesn't stand for anything.'

'Yes, it does. It stands for hard work, determination and guts.'

'Guts?'

'Rocco told me you got into Columbia on a scholarship. That alone tells me how hard you've had to work to get where you are.'

'We all have our crosses to bear, whatever background we're born into,' he said quietly. He tapped on the dividing window. Amidst a hail of tooting horns, the car came to a stop. 'We will walk from here.'

The taverna was exactly what Alessandra had been hoping for. Set off the beaten track, its marble tables with checked paper table-cloths were crammed inside and out, every one of them taken. Inside, a man played an accordion, the music only just audible above the raucous noise of the patrons, while pictures of celebrities lined the walls in haphazard fashion above empty bottles of wine with melted candles rammed into them.

Just as she was thinking they would never get a table, a balding man of about sixty wearing a white apron stretched around possibly the largest pot belly she'd ever seen ambled over to them, his arms outstretched. In a flurry of Greek, he pulled Christian into a tight embrace, slapping kisses on his cheeks, all of which Christian returned before stepping back and putting an arm around Alessandra's waist.

'Mikolaj—Alessandra,' he said, before adding, 'Mikolaj doesn't speak any English or Italian, *agapi mou*.'

Her offered hand was ignored as she was wrenched from Christian's hold and yanked into Mikolaj's embrace, which finished with an affectionate ruffle of her hair, much as if she were a child.

A small table materialised for them against the far wall. Mikolaj pulled the chair back for her, fussing over her until he was certain she was sitting comfortably—although how comfortable anyone could be when crammed like a sardine was debatable. He plonked a laminated menu in front of her then ruffled her hair again for good measure before disappearing into the throng.

Christian took the seat opposite. The table was so small his long legs brushed against hers. She waited for him to move them but realised there was literally nowhere else for them to go unless he twisted to the side and tripped up all the waiting staff.

She craned her neck around, trying to ignore the heat brushing up her legs. 'This place is wonderful.'

He raised his eyebrows. 'You like it?'

She nodded. 'This is exactly how I imagined a Greek restaurant to be. You can feel the energy—you don't get that in high-class restaurants.'

His eyes crinkled. Seeing it made her realise how tense he'd been up to that point. Although unfailingly polite, a barrier had been put up. Was it being here, in his home city, that had caused its construction? Or had she been so wrapped up in her own problems that she hadn't fully appreciated the effect their situation was having on him? Or a combination of both?

'The best thing about this place apart from the food?' he said. 'It's tourist-proof—all the people in here are locals.'

'Don't tell me you own it?'

'No. This is all Mikolaj's.'

'Is it always this busy?' It was a Monday evening, hardly the busiest night of the dining week.

'Always.'

Alessandra looked down at the menu. It was all in Greek.

'I can recommend the *stiffado*,' Christian said. 'Beef stewed in a wine and tomato sauce. The stuffed courgettes are good too.'

'Can I have both?'

He laughed. 'You can have whatever you like. It's all good.'

'Have you eaten everything on the menu?'

'A dozen times each.'

'No wonder Mikolaj treated you like his long-lost son.'

Before he could respond, a waiter appeared at their side, notebook at the ready.

'Shall I order us a selection of *meze* to start with?' Christian asked.

'You know all the best stuff,' she answered with a grin. Already the bustling, warm atmosphere of the place was easing the tension within her, making her relax in a way she hadn't since she'd taken the pregnancy test. 'Go ahead.'

She had no idea what he ordered, the waiter making squiggles on his note pad before bustling off, immediately to be replaced with Mikolaj, who carried a carafe of red wine and a jug of iced water.

'Do you want any wine?' Christian asked, knowing better than to tell her not to have any.

'I'll stick to water, thanks,' she said, her cheeks quirking as if she knew what he'd been thinking. As soon as they were alone again, she asked, 'How do you know Mikolaj? I'm guessing it's more than you being a good patron.'

'I have known him since I was small child.'

'Is he an old family friend?'

'Something like that.'

Her doe eyes were fixed on him with unashamed curiosity. 'Something like what?'

'My mother and I used to live in a room in the attic,' he supplied, adopting the tone he used to denote the end of a subject.

Alessandra ignored his tone and raised her eyes to gaze at the ceiling. 'You lived in the attic *here*?'

'Yes, here. My mother was a childhood friend of his. When we were kicked out of our old place, Mikolaj and his wife gave us the attic room.'

She looked back at him, her pretty brows drawing together. 'One room? For the both of you?'

'Yes.'

'That must have been hard.'

'You have no idea,' he said, more harshly than he'd intended. In those days, Mikolaj had been barely scraping a living for himself and his own family. If not for his incredibly generous heart, Christian and his mother would have lived on the streets. The attic room was given to them for free in exchange for his mother working in the kitchen. She'd been paid a share of the tips. It was all Mikolaj had been able to afford.

When Christian had made his first significant trade, a deal that had earned him a hundred thousand dollars, he'd sent Mikolaj a cheque for half the sum.

Looking back on those early years, it hadn't been the

poverty that had been the hardest to bear. The biggest cross had been living with his mother and her poisonous tongue.

Theos, but he didn't want to imagine Alessandra losing the spark that made her such a passionate, vivacious person and turning into one of the Furies, as his mother had. He wouldn't wish it on anyone but especially not her.

'Do you ever see your father?'

'No. He left when I was a baby.'

She leaned her elbows on the table and rested her hands on her chin. 'That must have been hard too.'

'It was hard for my mother, not me. I don't remember him.' He no longer wanted to remember him, although he had as a child, had been desperate to know any detail his mother could spare. As all her details had been disparaging at best, nothing concrete, he'd let his mind fly free to construct him. His father was a superhero who had gone to save a galaxy far, far away—unable to send his mother any money by dint of being in a galaxy far, far away. When that galaxy was saved, he would swoop back to Athens, and the little attic room his wife and son shared, and rescue them.

That fantasy sustained him for a few years until around the age of seven, when he'd overheard a conversation between Mikolaj and his eldest son. They'd been talking about Elena, Christian's mother.

'She can't help the way she is,' Mikolaj had said. 'When Stratos left her for that woman, it poisoned her. He packed his stuff and left her with no money when the boy was only six months old.'

Christian had tuned the rest of the conversation out. It had been enough to convince him all his mother's disparaging comments about his father were true. From that moment on, he'd no longer fantasised about his father. Stratos Markos was never going to swoop in to save them. That would be Christian's job.

CHAPTER SEVEN

'HAVE YOU EVER tried to find your father?' Alessandra asked a short while later, her eyes filled with curiosity.

'What for?' he dismissed. 'Why would I want to involve myself with a man who abandoned his wife and child?'

'I get that,' she said, pulling a face.

He closed his eyes. 'Your father is an alcoholic and a gambler. He was incapable of looking after you. He didn't abandon you. He's always been a fixture in your life. There's a difference.'

She laughed contemptuously. 'I thought you knew my background. My father dumped me on his father before I was a year old. Rocco took care of me from the moment I left hospital. My father wanted nothing to do with me—he still doesn't. He's never been there, not for any of the significant events in my life. My first Holy Communion, my Confirmation, the time I represented Milan in the under tens' gymnastics,' she said, ticking the events off on her fingers. 'He wasn't at any of them. The few times he's bothered to join us as a family, he won't speak to me. He's never *looked* at me. I was there, I was present and still he didn't want me. So don't try and make out I can't understand what it was like for you, growing up without a father, because my father abandoned me too, and, worst of all, he abandoned Rocco.'

He and Alessandra were like two peas but from pods grown in very different gardens, Christian realised. They'd both been abandoned by the people who should have been there for them. For good or ill, it had shaped them both. The distrust and avoidance of love and relationships.

They were more alike than he'd ever suspected.

Colour had heightened across Alessandra's high cheek-bones, her eyes ablaze with furious passion, the honey-brown a darkened swirl. He'd seen that swirl before, when she'd been pressed against the wall of her apartment.

Theos, she had felt unbelievably good in his arms, as if her contours had been shaped especially for him.

He regarded her carefully, pushing away thoughts of her naked: the way she had wrapped those lithe legs around him and clung to him, as if trying to burrow under his skin. Those same legs were pressed against his at that very moment…

The V of her dress had dipped, exposing the top of her golden cleavage, below which lay breasts that had become plumper since their time together.

What did they look like now? Did they still taste so sweet…?

This had to stop. Right now. Imagining them in bed to-gether was what had got him into all this trouble in the first place, sitting in that Milanese restaurant, fascinated by her plump lips, imagining them over his…

He would not touch her again until they were legally man and wife. He'd given her his word. He might have screwed things up but he was determined to do the right thing from here on in. On paper, his track record with women was less than complimentary. Given that and her own history, he could understand why Alessandra would be untrusting. It was down to him to prove himself to her.

Theoretically, it should be easy. Christian loved sex—what red-blooded man didn't?—but he'd never allowed his libido to run his life. With Alessandra… The longer she kept those gorgeous doe eyes fixed on him, the more his blood swirled with the need to consume her again. Every-thing about her spelled temptation, from the glossy chestnut hair that begged to have his fingers run through it to the toned golden arms his hands itched to trace. Every time she opened her mouth to speak, drink or eat, he would watch those beautiful lips and ache to press his own to them, to feel the heat of her breath merge with his.

Soon. Soon she would be his again.

'At least you had Rocco,' he said softly, thinking he would have given anything for a sibling when he'd been a child. It hadn't been until he'd met his fellow Columbia Four that he'd realised what had been missing in his life: true friendship.

'Emotionally, I had Rocco,' she conceded. 'But he's seven years older than me. By the time I was eleven he was at university, thousands of miles away. My grandfather loved me but he had no experience of raising girls and preferred to leave me in the hands of the household staff.'

'Our lives have been very different,' he said, choosing his words with care. 'It's pointless comparing them. You have lived yours and I have lived mine.'

'How has it been different?' she pressed, leaning forward.

'It just was.'

'But how?' A troubled look flitted over her face. 'Christian, we are marrying in five days. I don't want to marry a stranger.'

He reached for his wine and took a swallow. 'You, *agapi mou*, come from a world of glamour and money. You have no comprehension what it was like for us. We were so poor that for a whole year I went without shoelaces—trivial in the scheme of things but imagine it for a minute. I arrived at university with only one change of clothes. I was the child people like you pretended not to see.'

Alessandra was like one of those mythical creatures he had watched swish past this very taverna's front while he'd swept the floor. Unobtainable. Better than him. Better than he could ever be no matter how much money was held in his bank account.

Angry colour stained her cheeks, and she opened her mouth, surely to argue with him, before she visibly controlled herself. The outrage that had sparked in her eyes softened. 'Maybe you're right that I can't understand what your childhood was like. But I would like to try.'

He didn't *want* her to understand. Christian wanted her to remain untouched by the deprivation and misery that had sucked his mother down a black pit, turning her into a bitter woman who, even if presented with a glass three-quarters full would still regard it as being a quarter empty. All the riches and success in the world hadn't been enough to earn his mother's love.

He had no memory of the happy, vibrant woman Miko-laj assured him she had once been. Love that had turned sour had soured *her*, marking her with such blackness that nothing he'd done had been enough to turn it into a lighter shade of grey.

He didn't want that for Alessandra. Never for her.

Alessandra needed protection from it before it infected her too.

'We've had a good response from all the wedding invitations,' he said, deliberately and overtly changing the subject.

One hundred and fifty invites had been couriered across the world. It seemed even heads of state could drop commitments when it suited them and, with all the hype already surrounding their 'whirlwind courtship,' as the press was dubbing it, their wedding was shaping up to rival Rocco and Olivia's as Wedding of the Century. One of the British glossies had offered one million pounds for exclusive rights. They had, politely, ignored the offer. He liked that Alessandra hadn't been tempted to accept, one of the many ways she differed from all the other women he'd been with.

But wasn't that the reason he'd been with those women? Because he could see the pound signs ringing in their eyes and so knew there was absolutely no danger they could ever develop anything like a healthy—or unhealthy, depending on your point of view—attachment to him? He hadn't needed to protect those women from himself.

Her eyes sparked again before she sank back into her seat, gazing at him with a thoughtful expression.

'All but a handful have replied and all in the affirmative,' he added.

After too long a beat, she asked, 'What about Rocco? Has he replied?'

It had been at Christian's insistence that her brother had been invited. Left to Alessandra, he would have been ignored, something he knew she didn't mean, her pride and anger doing the talking for her. It would break her heart to walk up the aisle of the chapel in the grounds of the hotel without her brother on her arm.

'No,' he admitted reluctantly. 'He hasn't replied yet.' And neither had Rocco responded to the dozen emails and text messages he'd sent to him, entreating him not to abandon his sister. Rocco hadn't replied to a single one of them. He'd ignored all the messages and calls from Stefan and Zayed too.

The Columbia Four had been broken, just as he'd known they would be.

At least Stefan and Zayed were coming to the wedding. He would need his friends there. But not as much as Alessandra needed her brother.

If he had to get on his bended knee and beg, he would get Rocco to their wedding.

'I sent a bridesmaid dress to Olivia,' Alessandra blurted out, her cheeks staining with colour.

'Have you heard back from her?' he asked hopefully. If anyone could get through to Rocco, it would be his wife.

She shook her head. 'I didn't expect to. Her loyalty is with Rocco, not me.'

Conversation paused when a waiter arrived at their table laden with plates of steaming food.

Once they had helped themselves to a little of each *meze*, Alessandra said, 'Are many of your family coming?'

'I don't have any family.'

She looked confused. 'What about your mother?'

'I haven't invited her.'

'Why not?'

'We do not want my mother at our wedding.'

'Why not?' she repeated.

'Trust me.' He dipped some pitta bread into the hummus and popped it into his mouth, leaving her in no doubt that, as far as he was concerned, this thread of discussion was over.

Her eyes glittered with incredulity, as if to say, *trust you*?

Instead of arguing with him, she took a drink of water and allowed him to steer the conversation to innocuous small talk about music they liked and films they had both seen and enjoyed. Their tastes were surprisingly similar.

Theos, she was so easy to talk to; she had a way of fixing her honey eyes on him and making him feel he was the only man to exist in the world.

To know he was the only man to have tasted her delights and to imagine tasting them again made him feel as if he had heated syrup running through his veins. It wasn't just the contents of his trousers that stirred to be with her—everything felt heightened.

In that respect, the day of their wedding couldn't come fast enough.

The hotel was in silence when they returned. For the first time Christian regretted having the entire complex to themselves. There was no one—other than the handful of duty staff—to distract his attention away from Alessandra.

His fiancée.

She'd taken the hint and stopped digging for information on his past, although something in her eyes had warned him not to expect her silence to last for long. Instead, they had relaxed into easy conversation, just as they had on their one real date together. As on that night in Milan, he'd found his eyes drawn to her lips. They fascinated him. *She* fascinated him.

What was it with this woman? he wondered as they climbed the private lift to the top floor. His awareness of her was off the charts. His body reacted to everything, from the way her mouth moved to her husky laugh, to the way she smoothed her hair back to keep it from her face.

Alessandra's eyes had been as firmly fixed on him as his had been on her. She hadn't drunk any alcohol but he recognised the signs of inhibitions loosening. Just as they had that night in Milan.

He would not act on it. Not tonight. Not until they were legally man and wife.

Man and wife.

Three words he would never have put together with himself and, he knew, Alessandra would never have put with herself.

If he were being honest, he would have to admit that, if someone had put a gun against his head and said he had to choose one woman of all the women he'd been with to marry and have a baby with, Alessandra would have topped the list. All the other women had been fun and flirty but without an ounce of substance. Exactly the way he'd liked them. No commitment, no emotions. No chance of them falling in love and that love turning into bitterness.

Alessandra had a fun and flirty streak in her but she also had substance by the barrel. Her emotions were right there on the surface, no pretence, no subterfuge and, *Theos*, she was sexier than any mortal had a right to be.

He'd spent half the evening fantasising about those luscious lips.

They reached the door to her suite.

'Thank you for a lovely evening,' she said, leaning against the wall by the door. Her eyes were wide; even under the soft lighting he could see the dilation of her pupils.

'It's been my pleasure.'

And it had been.

He didn't want the evening to end.

What was there to stop him leaning in for a kiss?

Nothing.

Except he'd given his word that nothing physical would happen between them again until they were legally married and he would keep that promise even if his testicles exploded with frustration.

'Are you working tomorrow?' She rubbed a hand up her arm, the movement pushing her breasts together. The image of dusky pink nipples immediately floated into his mind and with it came the thickening of his blood he was fast associating to feeling when with her.

He had to assume it was a simple case of forbidden fruit tasting sweeter. Like the child in the sweet shop who had no money and salivated over every piece of delicious confectionery on offer.

'Yes. Some of our guests are arriving in the evening. I should be back to greet them with you.'

'I guess this will be the first public display of our love and unity,' she said, an ironic smile whispering across her face.

He palmed her cheek and rubbed his thumb over the soft skin. He could do that much without breaking his vow. 'Can you handle it?'

'Can you?'

'For the sake of our child, yes, I can.'

Her eyes held his. She raised a hand and pressed it to his fingers still resting against her cheek. 'Then I can too.'

Alessandra was certain he was going to kiss her. She recognised the look in his eyes, the desire in them that darkened the blue. She'd seen that look before, right before she'd pressed her lips to his in her apartment…

He stepped away before either of them had the chance to act on it, dragging his thumb down her cheek one last time.

'Sleep well, *agapi mou*,' he said, bowing his head, then turning on his heel and striding down the corridor to his own suite.

She didn't know if the breath she expelled was one of relief or disappointment.

After yet another unsettled night, Alessandra got out of bed early, not long after the sun had begun to rise.

Showering quickly, she shrugged on a short, lime-green sundress and slid her feet into a pair of wedged espadrilles, then grabbed her camera and headed out of her suite. As she made her way up the corridor, she passed Christian's room.

Was he still sleeping?

He'd been as good as his word yesterday, arriving back from his busy day twenty minutes before their first guests had arrived. They'd spent the evening glued to each other's side, laughing and joking. At one point he had leaned in to whisper into her ear.

'I think we're convincing them,' he'd said. At least, that was what she thought he'd said, the feel of his hot breath against her skin turning her brain to mush in less than a second.

Dio, what was he doing to her?

Was it any wonder she couldn't sleep?

She'd spent years believing marriage and babies would never be in her future. Sexual relationships had been consigned to the same void: not for her. No messy emotions to contend with, no lies for her ears to disbelieve, no truths for her eyes to avoid. Once the dust had settled with the fall-out over Javier's lies, she'd come to the conclusion that living a life of solitude was the best for her.

Other than her brother, she'd effectively been alone since birth. Her grandfather had controlled every aspect of her life, from the food she ate to the clothes she wore to the friends she was allowed—but always remotely, Alessandra another tick on his daily to-do list, his directives adhered to by the many members of the Villa Mondelli staff. She'd *longed* for someone to want to be with her for her, not because they were paid to be or because she'd passed some kind of wealth and social standing test, but for *her*. She'd truly believed Javier had seen beyond the surface but it had been a lie that had shattered her.

All the protections she'd placed around herself since those awful, lonely days were crumbling at the edges.

In three days she would be pledging her life, her future, to Christian Markos. How could she keep her emotions in a box if she had to share the bed with him occasionally?

One night: that was all it had taken. She'd watched him sleep, her chest clenched so tightly she'd fought for air.

She needed air now.

She wandered to the end of the corridor and climbed the stairs that led up to the roof terrace.

Their wedding was three days away but already a huge transformation was taking place for the party they would be having there once the nuptials were done. White tables and chairs were laid out to the specifications of their wedding planner. She stared at what was to be the top table, a sharp pang lancing her as she thought of sitting there without either her grandfather or her brother by her side.

A part of her wanted to call Rocco, was desperate to hear his voice. But she would not. Christian still bore the remnants of the punch Rocco had given him, the black eye now a pale yellow, but still evident if you looked closely enough. Unless he was prepared to apologise and accept her marriage, he could stay away.

Forcing her thoughts away from her brother, she headed to the back of the terrace, the part that overlooked the huge gardens. Far in the distance sat the whitewashed chapel they were to marry in. It gleamed under the morning sun, as if it were winking at her. She readied her camera and fired off a couple of shots.

She much preferred taking photos of people but one day

she wanted to be able to show her child everything about their parents' big day. She'd been nine when she'd stumbled across her own parents' wedding photos. Until that time she'd never believed her father had *ever* smiled, not once in his whole life. But, of course, it had been the pictures of her mother that had meant the most to her.

Whenever she was asked the question of who her biggest influences were as a photographer, she always said Annie Leibovitz and Mario Testino, but in truth it was her parents' wedding photographer. He had brought them to life in a manner that had touched her deeply and made her see them as people in love.

She wondered if Christian had photos of *his* parents' wedding day and if he ever looked at them.

Christian. It disturbed her how badly she wanted to know everything about him, to understand everything that made him tick, everything that had shaped him. The pieces were coming together but it was like a semi-filled photo album with pictures missing.

Resolve filled her. She looked at her watch. If she hurried, she should be able to catch him before he left the hotel for his first appointment of the day.

CHAPTER EIGHT

Minutes later she knocked on his door, her camera still slung round her neck.

She sensed movement behind the door before it opened, sensed him peering through the spyhole.

And there he stood, skin damp, hair wet…and with nothing but a towel wrapped around his hips.

'Sorry; I've caught you at a bad time,' she said, having to fight to get her vocal cords to work properly and not stammer.

'Not at all. Come in.' He stood aside to admit her into his suite.

She stepped past him, moistening suddenly dry lips.

Dio, was he naked beneath that towel?

Her arid mouth suddenly filled with moisture.

'Is there a reason you've come to my suite so early, *agapi mou*?' he asked, a smile playing on his lips, as if he knew exactly what was going on beneath her skin.

'No.' She blinked sharply. 'Yes. Do you want to get dressed before we talk?'

'I'm good.'

'Please?'

'Does the sight of me undressed disturb you?'

'It makes it hard for me to think straight,' she admitted, wishing she could think of a decent lie.

'That is good.'

'It is?'

'The thought of you naked makes it hard for me to think straight too. So, we are even.'

'You think of me naked?' Did she *have* to sound like a breathless imbecile?

The smile dropped. He closed the distance between them and inhaled deeply.

His voice dropped to a husky whisper. 'All the time. I've just thought of you while I showered, imagining you sharing it with me.'

She swallowed. Was he suggesting what she thought he was…?

His lips brushed against her earlobe. 'Until we are legally married I will have to satisfy myself with memories of our night together in Milan.'

Her skin fizzed beneath the warmth of his breath while heat such as she had never experienced surged through her, settling in the V of her thighs. He stepped closer still and placed a hand on her thigh, close enough that she could feel his erection jut through the cotton of his towel and press against her belly.

She tilted her head back and gazed into his eyes. It was there, that desire: stark, open, unashamed.

What would he do if she were to loop her arms around his neck and kiss him? If she were to clasp his towel and yank it off him…?

He must have read her mind for his lips brushed against her ear again. 'Anticipation makes fulfilment taste so much sweeter.'

She pulled away. 'Do you know that from experience?'

A strange look came into his eyes, a half-smile tugging on his lips. 'Only in a professional sense. I look forward to finding out if it's as sweet when it comes to us making love again.'

'I thought you said it would depend on whether I wanted anything to happen,' she said, her voice hoarse.

'And it will.' Now his eyes glittered, no mistaking the

feeling behind them. 'But we both know the anticipation is driving you crazy too.'

While Alessandra stood there, unable to deny what he'd said, too full of the heavy, pulsating thickness swirling through the very fabric of her to think clearly, Christian strode into the bedroom of his suite.

'So, what did you want to see me for?' he asked, disappearing from view.

Forcing her brain to unfog itself, she followed him to the door but stopped at her side of the threshold.

She took a moment to compose herself, but that very composure almost fell to ruins when he emerged back in view, now wearing a pair of black boxer shorts that only enhanced his strong physique.

He opened his dressing-room door and disappeared again, re-emerging moments later with a pair of grey trousers on. Looking at her, he slipped his arms into a pale blue shirt. 'Alessandra?'

'Sorry.' She put her hand to her mouth and cleared her throat. 'I just wanted to discuss the guest list.'

'Everyone has accepted.'

'Apart from Rocco?'

He nodded, his mouth tightening.

She watched as he deftly did the buttons of his shirt up.

'I think you should reconsider inviting your mother,' she said.

He didn't react, other than a slight narrowing of his eyes.

'It doesn't feel right, us marrying without you having any family there.'

'You haven't invited your father,' he said pointedly.

'That's because my father is an alcoholic who likes to pretend I don't exist. She's your mum—wouldn't she *want* to see her only child get married?'

'Just drop it. She's not coming and that's final.' He tucked his shirt in and pulled the zip of his trousers up.

'No. I won't drop it. If you won't invite her then can you at least tell me why?'

His mouth set in a forbidding line, he reached for the silver tie on his bed and walked over to the mirror on the wall, his back to her. He met her eye in the reflection.

'No. I can't.'

'Why not? Christian, we're getting married in three days. You know everything about me and my past—what is so bad that you don't want me to meet your mother? Are you ashamed of her or something?'

'*Or something* about sums it up,' he said grimly. 'But, no, I'm not ashamed of her.'

'Really? Because it looks like you're ashamed of her from where I'm standing.'

His nostrils flaring, his jaw clenched tight, he knotted his tie. 'Can you not take my word for it?'

'I'm sorry, but no.' This was too important a topic to back down from.

He must have seen something in her reflection that made him read the stubbornness of her thoughts. He shook his head angrily. 'If it means that much to you, I will show you.'

'Show me what?'

He straightened his shirt, then turned back to face her. 'I'll take you to meet her. You can see for yourself why I don't want my mother anywhere near our wedding.'

The car came to a stop outside an immaculate two-storey house in a quiet Athenian suburb.

No sooner had the engine been turned off than Christian got out, not bothering to wait for the driver to open the door for him.

The entire drive had been conducted in silence, Christian sitting ramrod-straight, only the whiteness of his knuckles betraying what lay beneath his skin.

It was a demeanour Alessandra had never seen from him before. It unnerved her.

That he'd cancelled his first appointment of the day had unnerved her even more; that, and the grim way he'd said, 'Let's get it over with.'

It was with a deep sense of dread that she followed him out of the car and up the small driveway.

A tall, thin woman with short white hair appeared at the door, lines all over her weathered face, her thin lips clamped together in an obvious display of disapproval.

Wordlessly, she turned on her heel and walked back inside, leaving the door open for them to follow.

The house itself was pristine, a strong smell of bleach pervading the air.

There was nothing homely about it. What could have been a beautiful home was nothing but a carcass, sanitised functionality at its best.

If Elena Markos could speak English, she made a good show of hiding it. She made no show of hiding her disdain for Alessandra, refusing her hand when Christian introduced them, and looking through her when Alessandra said, *'Hárika ya tin gnorimía,'*— 'pleased to meet you'—a phrase she'd practised with the girl who'd brought breakfast to her suite that morning after Christian had grudgingly agreed to bring her here.

They gathered together in the immaculate kitchen, where the stench of bleach was even stronger. No refreshments were offered.

Alessandra might as well have been invisible. All of Elena's attention was on her son. She was speaking harshly to him in quick-fire Greek, whatever she said enough to make the pulse in his jawline throb. When he replied, his answers were short but measured. At one point he seemed to be the one doing the talking rather than the listening, his words making Elena dart her blue eyes to the stranger in the midst, a sneer forming on her face.

In all her twenty-five years, Alessandra had never sat in such a poisonous atmosphere as this, or felt as unwelcome.

There was something almost unhinged in Elena Markos's demeanour. Her eyes were the same blue as Christian's but were like a frozen winter morning without an ounce of her son's warmth.

Simply imagining being raised by this woman made her skin feel as icy as Elena's eyes. But Christian couldn't leave it to imaginings. He'd lived it, every cold, emotionless second.

Was it any wonder Christian eschewed any form of emotional entanglement when *this* was what he'd grown up with?

Her mind flitted back to their many conversations at Mikolaj's taverna. She'd said the name Markos stood for guts and determination but had not appreciated then exactly how great his determination must have been, not just to drag himself and his mother out of poverty but to keep his humanity.

Mikolaj. She recalled the obvious affection between the two men. Surely it was from this man Christian had learned to form real human bonds? It soothed her to know he hadn't been completely alone in his childhood.

So much for the couple of hours Alessandra had anticipated spending there. After twenty minutes, Christian took her hand and said, 'We're leaving.'

'Already?'

'Now.'

Elena glared at them, her eyes like lasers.

When they reached the door to leave she gave what Alessandra assumed was supposed to be a laugh.

'Fool girl,' she said, her accent thick. 'Marry fools. He kill you heart.'

Alarmed and not a little scared, Alessandra nodded weakly, squeezing Christian's hand so tightly her blood screamed for circulation.

Nothing was said until they were back in the car and moving, both pressed against their respective doors.

'What did you think of my mother?' Christian asked, amusement and bitterness both vying for control in his voice.

Alessandra was unable to do anything but raise her shoulders and blow air out of her mouth.

That had to be the most surreal experience of her life, like stepping into some parallel universe where poison ivy grew instead of roses.

'Do you understand now why I don't want her at our wedding?'

'I think so.' She shook her head some more. She could still taste the acrid atmosphere, overwhelming even the cloying bleach. 'What did she say to you?'

'The usual. That I'm a useless son for leaving it so long between visits; that her house isn't good enough for her; that the house is too big for her, that it's too small, that her car is getting old. The usual.'

'You bought the house for her?'

'It's the third house I've bought for her—the other two didn't *match her needs*. I buy her a new car every year. I give her a large allowance. It's never enough. I could give her my entire fortune and it wouldn't be enough. If she came to the wedding, she'd spend the day complaining. Nothing would be good enough for her, and when she isn't complaining she'll be telling all our guests about my no-good bastard of a father who broke her heart and deserves castration without anaesthetic.'

His father's desertion and betrayal had shattered her. Whatever love had once resided in his mother's bones had been destroyed, leaving nothing but the toxic shell of the woman she must have once been. Christian understood it, could see how she had become like that. Stratos Markos hadn't just walked away from her, he had walked away from the child they had created together—that was how little she had meant to him. He had wanted no part of her, so worthless that their baby meant nothing to him either.

'Has she always been like this?' she asked, her husky voice stark.

'All my life. She thinks all men are like my father—that's what she was saying to you when we left, that you're a fool to be marrying me and that I'm going to break your heart.'

Alessandra's shock was palpable. 'She said that about her own son?'

'She also said it would be kinder for me to rip your heart out now—you forget, *agapi mou*, that I am my father's son, something she never lets me forget. In my mother's world, all men are liars and cheats, especially those with the name of Markos.'

Her doe eyes widened, full of sympathy. 'You're not to blame for your father's actions.'

'I know that.' But right then he didn't want to hear any platitudes. A coldness had settled in his chest, bearing down on him.

It was always the same after he visited his mother. Regardless of the heat outside, inside all he felt was compressing ice.

'And it's not fair for her to label all men as bastards because of the misdeeds of one.'

'But do you not believe that yourself?' he said roughly. 'That all men are scum?'

She swallowed, her eyes dimming as if in confusion. 'I don't hate men, I just don't trust them.'

What would it take to get her to trust *him*? If she'd taken him at his word he would never have had to bring her here.

He wished he could demand it of her, as if trust were like a tap that could be turned on and off at a whim.

After a long pause, he said, 'We're lucky we both know how destructive love can be. We won't fall into the trap our parents fell into. Our child will never have to deal with parents whose love has turned to bitterness and recrimination.'

Their child wouldn't have to deal with his or her parents

loving each other at all. All the love would be reserved for their child and only their child.

He exhaled slowly, waiting for the chill in his chest to lessen but it continued to cling to him like a thick, cold fog.

He hadn't expected anything different from his mother; he was more or less immune to it. It had been witnessing Alessandra's visible shock at it all that had really set the cold in, had brought the old feelings and memories hurtling back.

The empathy shining from her eyes had been too much.

He'd never introduced his mother to any of his friends or lovers before. His mother had her own special compartment in his life. He'd long ago accepted that she wouldn't change, that no matter how he succeeded in life it would never be enough for her. Even the news of being a grandmother had failed to elicit a smile. She would never love him.

Far from repelling Alessandra, his mother's behaviour had elicited her sympathy, her empathy: towards him.

He didn't want her pity.

She was getting too close; he could feel it.

Any closer and she'd be able to see the gutter rat who lived in the blackness of his heart.

Christian's driver dropped Alessandra back at the hotel before taking Christian to his offices.

A dozen more guests had arrived while they'd been at his mother's house. It amazed her that so many super-wealthy and famous people were able to drop their commitments for what was essentially a free holiday, but surprisingly their presence worked in her favour, distracting her thoughts from their visit to Christian's mother.

Every time she closed her eyes she saw the laser glare of Elena Markos's eyes and she wondered how Christian had endured living with such coldness.

That he had dragged himself out, turned it around and made something of himself only added to what had been a slowly growing admiration towards him. That admiration had now accelerated.

Although she was suffering a large dose of guilt for forcing the issue, she was glad they'd gone. Her understanding of the man she was going to marry was growing by the day.

She spent the rest of the day mingling with their guests, some of whom she actually knew, lazing by the pool, playing cards, drinking non-alcoholic cocktails. It was fun, but she wished Christian could be there to enjoy it too. He worked so hard, just like her brother.

Maybe he would kick back and relax when they went on their short honeymoon. She hoped so. He deserved it.

She headed back to her suite late afternoon and had a long soak in the sunken bath, already looking forward to the evening meal which Christian had said he'd be back for.

As she slipped into a red tunic dress, she realised that there hadn't been a single minute when she hadn't thought of him. The thought was like a jolt, enough to make her hands tremble, making it hard for her to apply her make-up.

She'd just regained her equilibrium when there was a knock on her door.

And there he stood, wearing the same suit she'd seen him change into that morning in his suite but with the tie removed and the top three buttons of his shirt undone, exposing the top of his bronzed chest.

Finding him there sent a huge surge through her, making her heart pump and her pulses race. *Dio*, the man was divine. In *all* ways.

'I thought I should let you know I'm going to New York,' he said as he stepped into her suite.

'Okay. When's that?'

'I'll be leaving for the airport in a few minutes.'

His words had the effect of making her heart sink to her knees. 'Are you kidding with me? You're leaving *now*?'

Dio l'aiuti, was he getting cold feet?

'It's only for a couple of nights—I'll be back Friday evening.'

She forced her voice to remain calm. 'We're getting married on Saturday.'

'I'll be back in plenty of time.'

A little distance was all Christian needed. Distance away from Alessandra, time to clear the coldness on his chest that still hadn't shifted. Time to track her brother down and force him to listen.

'I thought we were supposed to be putting on a united front?'

'We have been. Our guests will understand.'

'But these are *our* guests. I've completely rearranged my schedule to be here this week so we can entertain them together and convince them that we're the real deal.' The brightness of her welcome had cooled considerably.

'This is my life, Alessandra. I warn you now, there will be plenty of occasions when I have to fly off at a moment's notice.'

She eyed him, lines appearing in her brow. 'And what if *I* have to *fly off at a moment's notice*? Will you show me the same latitude?' The challenge was there, from the jut of her chin to the tone of her voice. 'I have a career of my own too, remember?'

'Our marriage is going to take time to shake down,' he conceded, wishing he could be in his jet *right now*. He didn't want to deal with her anger or acknowledge the suspicion emanating from her eyes. That was not what they were about. They were two individuals able to lead their lives to their own needs, not justify their whims and absences to each other. He shouldn't feel any guilt. 'We will find a path that suits us both.'

She nodded slowly but when she spoke her voice was fractionally warmer. 'So long as you don't expect all the compromise and sacrifice to come from my end.'

'I don't expect that.'

'Good.' After a moment of silence, she jerked her head in another nod. 'Have a safe trip.'

He mimicked her movement. 'I'll see you at the chapel.'

CHAPTER NINE

ALESSANDRA STARED AT her reflection. She'd been primped and preened by an army of beauticians and now she was ready.

Ready?

She would never be ready. Not for this.

But it had to be done.

She had to marry Christian and she would do it alone.

Sebastian and Zayed, who had arrived together the night before, had both offered to give her away. She'd been touched by the offers but had declined. They were there for Christian, not her.

There were only two people she would have wanted to walk her down the aisle and one of those was dead. The other hadn't even had the courtesy to respond to his invitation.

She straightened her spine. It wasn't as if this would be a real marriage. This wedding was going ahead for one reason and one reason only: their baby. That was what she needed to focus on. It was *all* she should focus on—not Christian or the way he'd flown off to New York at a moment's notice. Or her suspicions that there was more to his impromptu trip than business. Or those horrible hours waiting for him to return while the cynical part of her brain had thrown taunts that he wouldn't be coming back, that he'd abandoned her. Just like her father had.

Do. Not. Trust.

She *had* to trust him with regard to their child. She had to.

Christian was not her father. And he hadn't abandoned her. Right at that very moment he stood in the chapel waiting for her. Exactly as he'd said he would be.

The relief she'd felt late last night when he'd called to say he was back in Athens had been so powerful it scared her to remember the physicality of her reaction.

It was simply relief that he hadn't humiliated her by standing her up, she insisted to herself. Nothing more than that. Nothing.

She checked her watch. It was time. In approximately one hour she would be married. Christian would be her husband.

She watched her reflected cheeks flush, her blood heating at the remembrances of their one night together, the night that had led to this very moment. Vivid memories of it played in her dreams every night, teasing her, haunting her.

People always said you couldn't miss what you'd never had and in the sexual aspect of her life that had held true. Now that she *had* tried it…

But it wasn't sex on its own that she wanted, that her body responded to. It was sex with Christian. Whether it was the alcohol loosening her inhibitions or something else undefined, he'd awoken her. He did things to her.

Before she'd put her wedding dress on, she'd stepped into her lacy white knickers, imagining him sliding them off; had put her lacy white bra on, imagining him unclasping it; had rolled the silk white stockings up her legs, imagining his strong fingers trailing over her skin as he slid them off.

Dio, how many times had she picked up her phone to call him before slamming it back down? Too many to count.

He'd called her a couple of times, though, conversations that had left her feeling all knotted yet incredibly warm inside. There was something about his voice that set tiny little bolts darting through her skin…

She hadn't been able to shake the feeling that he was hiding something from her, though.

Per favore, not another woman.

Do. Not. Trust.

How she could she trust him? She didn't know how.

She did know that she wanted to. She wanted to believe he would treat her with respect, that maybe one day…

A rap on her door jolted her out of the trance she'd worked herself into.

It was probably a member of staff, come to escort her to the chapel. The sweet girl who brought her breakfast every morning had been shocked when Alessandra had told her she would be walking to the chapel alone.

Always alone.

How she wished she'd swallowed her pride and called her brother and begged him to come. Deep inside, a part of her had believed he *would* come, that he wouldn't leave her to do this alone. That he'd forgive her.

This was his flesh and blood growing in her belly, the very reason she and Christian were prepared to take this ultimate step.

Alone or not, she should have left already.

Her stomach clenched.

She gazed at the French doors.

She didn't have to do this. She could step out onto her balcony, unfold the emergency stairs and escape. Everyone was at the chapel. The staff was busy organising all the celebrations. It could be ages before anyone realised she wasn't being traditionally late.

She pictured Christian's face when he realised she'd stood him up.

She couldn't do that to him. Alessandra knew all about humiliation and would never intentionally inflict it on someone else, least of all him.

And what would their innocent baby say when, at some

point in the future, he or she learned what their mother had done to their father?

Another rap on the door reminded her that someone stood on the other side waiting for her.

Hurrying over, she opened it, pulling a smile onto her face that dropped as soon as she saw who it was.

Dressed in a morning suit, stood her brother.

For a moment she didn't say anything.

Then she burst into tears.

Christian stood with Zayed and Stefan at his side, his two best men—or, as they were called here in their shared role, his *koumbaros*—eyes fixed on the chapel door.

Where was she?

It was traditional for the bride to be late but half an hour? If Stefan hadn't taken his phone from him after Christian had texted her to say he was at the chapel, he would have called and demanded to know where she was.

A face in the congregation caused him momentarily to lose track of his thoughts.

There in the third row sat Mikolaj, an enormous beam on his face. Beside him sat his wife, Tanya, and three of their seven children.

Alessandra must have invited them.

His stomach curled.

She'd done that for him.

Christian nodded a greeting to them but was unable to return the smiles.

Where was she?

The priest continued to smile reassurance but Christian could see the doubt now plaguing his jovial demeanour.

At least the chapel belonged to the hotel and thus was owned by him. They would wait.

Another ten minutes passed. Just as his guts were really starting to churn, the door swung open and there she appeared, the sunshine illuminating her in a golden glow that made the white of her dress sparkle.

It was like gazing at an angel, a moment so beautiful that the relief that should have overwhelmed him faded into nothing, leaving only wonder.

The sound of Pachelbel's *Canon in D* began, played by the string quartet hired for the occasion.

Alessandra walked towards him, an ethereal smile on her face, her steps slow.

His eyes fixed solely on her, it took a good few beats before he registered the arm she held on to.

Rocco had come. He hadn't abandoned his sister. Christian's trip to New York had paid off.

Behind them walked Olivia, stunning in emerald green.

As the bridal party stepped closer to him, a lump formed in his throat that grew larger with every one of Alessandra's steps until she was there before him.

Unlike most brides, who pinned their hair up into an elaborate creation, she'd left hers loose, tumbling around her shoulders in dark chestnut waves. She looked amazing. Her dress a work of art: thin lace-embellished straps with tiny diamonds curved down and across her cleavage like a heart, the sheer material wrapping around her waist to showcase the flare of her hips, then floating to the floor and resting in a white circle.

He looked for a sign of apprehension but none was there. Her beautiful honey-brown eyes, artfully made-up, were clear. Remarkably clear.

He reached out a hand, and as she took it he caught Rocco's eye. The look he gave said: *she's all yours now. Hurt her and you will spend the rest of your life paying for it.*

He'd never understood the full weight of what 'giving the bride away' meant until that moment.

From here on in, the role of her protector passed to him, an antiquated sentiment, but one he felt keenly.

Alessandra would never be his possession but for good or for ill they would be bound together.

The service was anticipated to last around an hour. For the congregation, it no doubt dragged. For Christian, time accelerated, the moment to exchanging their vows speeding up until it was time for them to make their promises to each other—not a requirement of the church but something they had agreed upon between themselves for the benefit of their guests.

He said his first, then Alessandra recited hers, her husky voice true and strong, her Greek practised and flawless. The look in her eyes, fixed on his, was full of meaning. It was a sight that made his chest feel as if a weight had been placed inside him, squeezing down.

There was no time to consider it as now was the time for what was, to many Greeks, the most important part of the ceremony: the crowning. The priest blessed the two floral-wreath crowns, then Zayed took the lead, passing the crowns back and forth over them three times before carefully placing them on their heads.

Finally they were done.

It was time to kiss the bride.

He searched again for her apprehension. It was still missing, a smile playing in the corner of her delicious lips. Lips he hadn't felt upon his since the night they had conceived the child that grew in her belly. Lips he'd spent the past couple of months dreaming of.

Swallowing away the lump in his throat, he placed a hand to her still-slender hip and leaned down. Her small hand reached up to rest on his lapel.

He closed his eyes and pressed his lips to hers, just the breath of a kiss, but enough for the softest mouth he'd ever known to reawaken more memories of their night together and make his pulses race.

When the kiss ended, the congregation, no doubt led by Mikolaj, burst into applause. Alessandra grinned, her whole face smiling, her happiness transparent. She placed a hand on his shoulder and straightened to whisper into his ear, 'Thank you.'

He knew without her having to explain that she was talking about Rocco.

'Thank *you*,' he whispered back.

She'd brought Mikolaj to their wedding. Christian hadn't thought he wanted him there, thought he hadn't wanted any associations with his past. He hadn't appreciated how much it would mean. He'd thought having Stefan and Zayed there would be enough but, no matter how close they all were, Mikolaj had been there his entire life. He was family. Knowing he and Tanya were there to witness it all warmed him right down to his toes.

A sharp pang of regret rent him that his mother wasn't there to witness this day too. But, unlike Mikolaj, his mother would have taken no joy from it. The opposite, in fact.

One look at Mikolaj's beaming, proud face showed how much being there meant to him.

Alessandra had done that for him. Before he could consider what that actually meant, she kissed him, a kiss containing more than a hint of promise. That promise was reflected in her sparkling eyes.

The coldness that had remained within him since their visit to his mother suddenly lifted, pushed out by the desire this beautiful woman—his bride—elicited in him.

For a moment he was tempted to say, to hell with the reception, and whisk her straight off to his suite.

A knowing look played on her beautiful features, a look that said *just a few more hours and I will be yours*.

And she would be—his. Every inch of her.

A short time later they left the chapel, officially husband and wife.

Most of the non-Greek guests had brought confetti to throw over them, but Mikolaj and Tanya had come prepared, handing out paper cups full of rice to throw, as was the proper tradition in Greece.

Amidst howls of laughter, thousands of hard grains were chucked over them from every possible angle. Zayed and Stefan got hold of him and tipped a cupful down the back of his morning suit, rubbing them into his back for extra effect.

The official photos were taken in the grounds before the chapel, and then the entire wedding party headed back to the hotel for the proper celebrations to begin.

The terraced roof of the hotel had been transformed. An abundance of balloons and beautiful flowers covered the entire perimeter, the Parthenon clear in the distance, but close enough that from certain aspects it felt as if you could reach out and touch it.

The day had turned into something magical.

All Alessandra could think was how much work and effort Christian had put into making this a special day for them. Sure, he'd outsourced it all, but he'd been the one to do the outsourcing.

All she'd done was buy her dress. And lingerie…

Crying in her brother's arms had had the effect of clearing her head.

Rocco had urged her to abandon the whole thing. He and Olivia would take care of her.

Alessandra didn't need taking care of—her baby did. Christian was her baby's father. They belonged in each other's lives.

She'd washed her face and reapplied her make-up and then, when she'd looked back in the mirror, the truth had been reflected back at her in startling clarity.

She was committing her life to Christian and their baby. It was time to embrace it for all their sakes.

Done with taking pictures of her husband and their

guests—it truly was a photographer's dream here—she put her camera back into its case and sat back down at the top table.

Staring at him now—holding court with Zayed, Stefan and Stefan's date, Clio, on the edge of the dance floor—her heart clenched, packing into a tight little ball.

Christian must have felt her gaze upon him for he met her eyes, raising his glass of champagne to her.

She raised her lemonade back, her skin dancing as if his gaze had physically touched her.

He said something to his friends which made them all laugh. It pained her that Rocco refused to join them, keeping his distance in the far corner of the room with Olivia and an earnest A-list Hollywood superstar. Her brother had spelled out in no uncertain terms that he was there to do his duty and nothing else.

Her suspicions about Christian's trip to New York had been correct—he *had* gone there with an ulterior motive. But her fears had been wildly off the mark. He hadn't gone to meet up with a secret woman. He'd gone in an attempt to make her brother see sense and attend their wedding.

He'd turned up at their New York home and told her brother in no uncertain terms that Alessandra needed him. When he'd left, Olivia had taken up the cause, essentially bullying Rocco into attending.

Knowing Christian had done that for her...*è stato incredibile*.

She only wished Rocco would see what an amazing thing it was too. To her knowledge, he hadn't exchanged a word with Christian all day.

Whatever his reasons, and however great his reluctance, she was glad he'd come. More than glad. She hoped with all her heart that one day he would come to accept them and accept that their marriage was the right thing for all of them. He might infuriate her but he was her brother and she loved him.

Christian weaved his way through the dancing guests and took his seat at the top table beside her. 'How are you feeling?' he asked, leaning back into his chair.

'Perfetto.' She smiled. 'This has all been amazing, *grazie mille.'*

He slung an arm around the back of her chair. 'It is my pleasure.'

The sound of rotor blades in full motion caught their attention.

'Paparazzi,' he spat, getting back to his feet and kicking his chair back. Immediately he pulled his phone from his pocket and dialled a number, speaking into it with a low voice packed full of menace.

'I had arranged that no helicopter fly within a mile of the hotel today,' he explained tightly when he finished his call, his face taut. 'I will not have our wedding day turned into a circus.'

She shrugged. 'They're tenacious. It was to be expected.'

'They're like locusts.' He laid his palms on the table, his face stark with anger.

Not wanting all the good feeling ruined, she raised a hand to his face and palmed his cheek. 'Thank you.'

The blue in his eyes darkened, his frame stilling. 'For what?'

'For trying to keep them away from me.'

His nostrils flared a touch. He didn't answer, simply stared at her as if trying to peer into her mind.

She gazed back, drinking him in, the heat inside her—so constant when with him—bubbling beneath her...

And then he dipped his head and covered her mouth with his, holding it there, not moving, just breathing into her, warm champagne-scented air filling her senses until he gently slid his mouth across her cheek and brushed his lips against her ear. 'Soon, *agapi mou*, I will do more than just kiss you.'

Her insides melted. Her heart racing at a gallop, she was about to grab his hand and beg him to whisk her away to somewhere private when Zayed joined them, announcing his presence by slapping Christian hard on the back.

'Come on, newlyweds, it is time for the Kalamatianos,' he said, referring to the traditional wedding dance adored by all Greeks. Over his shoulder, Mikolaj and Tanya grinned and waved, already tapping their feet in anticipation.

She was so glad she'd gone behind his back and invited them. It hadn't sat well with her, knowing he would have no one from his childhood there. Knowing Christian was happy she had done so lightened her further.

It made her feel all warm and fuzzy inside, thinking they had gone behind each other's back to bring someone important to their big day.

Soon she was on her feet with Christian in the centre of the dance floor, each holding an end of a scarf that had been thrust at them. With traditional Greek music playing, Zayed and Stefan chivvied everyone up to form a circle around them, the guests linking hands and, following Mikolaj and the other Greek guests' example, swirling around them like a circling snake, shouts of, *'Opa!'* ringing out.

Alessandra had the time of her life. When the Kalamatianos was over, everyone, including the bride and groom, stayed on the dance floor. They danced together, slow songs, fast songs, their hands entwined, their eyes only for each other.

She wanted the wedding and all the good feelings it evoked in her to last forever, to hold on to this moment for as long as she could. Contrarily, she wanted it to end now, wanted the sensuous promise ringing from Christian's eyes to become reality.

Soon…

Soon it would be time to retire to his suite and begin their newly married life in a manner that sent heat surging through her just to think about it.

Christian opened the door of the suite and, keeping hold of Alessandra's hand, closed it behind them.

'Someone's been busy,' he observed, burrowing his face into the nape of her neck. At long last, he was free to touch her and taste her and do all the things he'd wanted to do for so long the ache in his groin had become a permanent part of him.

His suite—*their* suite, now all of Alessandra's possessions had been moved in while their celebrations had been going on—had been decorated. Flowers were artfully arranged in vases, rose petals had been scattered over the bed and a bottle of champagne sat in an ice bucket next to two champagne flutes.

'Clichéd but very romantic,' she said, twisting round to face him.

All the dancing had left her cheeks flushed and her eyes alive with pleasure.

He wanted those eyes glowing with pleasure for a different reason.

Gripping her hip, he pulled her to him and snaked his arm around her waist.

He gazed down into those striking eyes and those more-ish lips. His to taste.

She was his to taste.

As he bent his head to claim her mouth, she darted gracefully out of his clasp, laughing softly. 'Not yet.'

'You're making me wait?' he said, his words coming out with an animalistic growl.

'I'm going to freshen up. Remember, *anticipation makes fulfilment taste all the sweeter.*' She sashayed to one of the bathrooms, flashed him a smile full of promise and locked the door behind her.

* * *

Alessandra applied a touch more lipstick then tightened the sash of her silk white robe.

Who needed alcohol?

Desire pulsed through her, making her pulses race uncontrollably.

She hadn't expected that a ring on her finger and a signed piece of paper could make her feel so different but it did.

Christian was the only man she'd ever truly wanted.

She remembered the first time she'd met him, when she'd been twelve and Rocco had brought the Brat Pack to Lake Como for a break. How young and naïve she'd been, still believing in love and romance. She'd taken one look at Adonis and her heart had skipped into her mouth.

He'd hardly noticed her existence.

Looking back with the benefit of hindsight on her illfated tryst with Javier, she could see it was the flattery she'd responded to, not *him*. She'd swallowed all his lies because she'd been flattered a man, not an immature boy, was showing an interest in her.

With Christian, it was the man himself she responded to.

She dabbed some perfume behind her ear and onto her wrists and left the privacy of the bathroom. It was time to see her husband as his wife.

CHAPTER TEN

WHEN ALESSANDRA EMERGED from the bathroom and closed the door softly behind her, the only sound Christian could hear was his own heartbeat. Drumming. Thundering in his ears.

He'd stripped naked, shedding his clothes in front of the mirror, staring closely at his reflection.

He didn't know what it could be but he felt different.

He looked the same. The desire he felt for his beautiful bride still burned deep inside him.

But something had changed.

Now he sat in the huge bed, leant back against the headboard, the bed sheets draped across his lap, a dim light glowing. And she was here with him, her dress removed, only a white robe covering her beautiful figure.

Slowly she stepped to him until she reached his side.

'Take your robe off.' He could hear the thickness in the timbre of his voice.

Her hands trembled, but a knowing smile pulled at her lips. She tugged at the sash of her robe and parted it, letting it drop to the floor.

Christian couldn't have torn his gaze away if he'd wanted to.

He didn't want to.

He wanted to capture this moment so he could replay it forever.

Theos but she was more beautiful than he remembered,

the white of her lacy lingerie contrasting against the golden hue of her skin.

Her breasts were swollen, the bra pushing them up to display her cleavage, only just hiding the dusky nipples he remembered so well.

Sitting upright, he extended a hand to grip onto her curved hip, sliding a finger under the strap of her suspender belt.

He ran his other hand up the soft swell of her belly, only slightly thickened since he'd last seen her unclothed.

She dropped a hand onto his shoulder, a cloud of her sultry scent releasing and filling his senses. He'd never known a scent like it, so perfectly matching its owner, a sweet yet musky fragrance, with depth.

He traced his hand back down her belly and clasped hold of her other hip, tugging her to him.

Inhaling her scent deeply into his lungs, he pressed a kiss into the curve of her neck, felt her quiver.

The ache in his groin, that constant state of affairs whenever he was with her, magnified by a thousand, his entire body coming alive to her sweet touch and even sweeter taste.

Using gentle manipulation, he pulled her onto the bed facing him, so she straddled his still-covered lap.

Her eyes darkened and swirled, arousal and desire burning strongly.

The first time they'd made love he'd plunged into her without a thought. His shock at discovering she was a virgin had been masked by concern that he'd hurt her. Her breath had hitched, a tiny mew escaping her throat. He'd held her tightly, stroking her hair, her body, raining kisses over her face until he'd felt her relax, seen her pupils dilate...

She'd been so responsive to everything he'd done to her, so eager to give in return.

She'd been a revelation.

And now he got to experience and taste her all over again.

But this time there would be no pain. Only pleasure.

Wrapping an arm around her and cradling the back of her head with his other hand, he pulled her flush against him and slanted his mouth over the soft, plump lips he'd spent the past two months dreaming about.

She sighed into him and rested her hands on his shoulders, her nails digging into him as her lips parted to allow his tongue to sweep into her warmth.

He stroked her back, up and down, exploring the silky skin anew, then down her sides to the top of her stockings.

She broke the kiss, nuzzling her mouth against his jaw and down into his neck, her hair tickling him.

'You taste divine,' she murmured, the first words she'd uttered since she'd left the bathroom.

Her compliment made his chest heave.

He speared her hair and tugged it back gently so he could look into her eyes. '*You* are divine.'

A small, almost shy, smile spread across her face, and she leaned forward to kiss him, deeply, passionately, her hands crawling up to his scalp and holding on to it.

He found the clasp of her bra and undid it. She released her hold on him, enabling him to pull the straps down her arms and discard the bra on the floor beside him.

When they'd made love the first time, he'd been enraptured with her breasts, their size, their taste, the way his hands could cup them perfectly, everything about them. Pregnancy had swollen them. He didn't know if it was a trick of the light but her dusky nipples seemed darker than he remembered, contrasting against the paleness of her breasts.

He was the only person in the world who knew Alessandra's breasts were the palest part of her body.

It was because his child was growing inside her that these small, subtle changes were taking place.

Using his hands to lift her a touch, he dipped his head and captured one of those beautiful, dusky nipples in his mouth.

Alessandra moaned and ran her fingers through his hair, arching her back to thrust her chest forward and into him.

He flattened a palm against the small of her back to steady her, his free hand roaming until he found the clasp of her suspenders. Before he released it he stroked the exposed flesh above the stockings. Her skin felt better than any material ever could.

When he played with the clasp he was shocked to find himself all thumbs, the deftness he'd acquired over the years gone. It was as if he'd never tried to undo a suspender belt before.

Spearing her hair again, he kissed her, filling his senses with her sultry, sweet taste, driving all thoughts from his mind.

Frustrated at the suspender belt, he tugged at a stocking and felt the material rip in his fingers. He grabbed the material of the other and did the same, then clasped her bottom and leaned forward, using his strength to lay her flat on her back. The movement caused the bed sheet to fall from his lap, freeing his erection which brushed against her thigh, sending deep pulsations firing through his blood, his loins, everywhere.

He sat back to gaze at her, noting everything, from her short, shallow breaths to the jutting of her erect nipples.

Unable to resist, he kissed her again, hard. Alessandra's arms looped around his neck, her legs lifting to hook around him, clasping him to her.

'Not yet,' he murmured, kneeling upright.

She pouted and raised herself onto her elbows. Her breaths came in shallow pants.

'Soon,' he promised, leaning forward to kiss her neck and push her flat again.

A sound like a purr came from her as he kissed his way down her chest and belly and slipped a hand round her back to undo the clasp at the back of her suspender belt. Discarding it, he flattened a hand over her thigh and caught the top of the ripped stocking. Slowly, he pulled it down, past her knee, over her calf and down to the delicate ankle.

'I've dreamed of you doing that,' she said, her husky voice almost breathless.

She'd dreamt of him...?

In response, he leaned down to press a kiss to her now bare foot, then followed the trail he'd just made with his hands with his tongue, darting licks and kisses all the way up to her inner thigh and up to the very heart of her. Pressing his mouth onto her knickers, he inhaled deeply, the scent of her heat almost making him dizzy with desire.

Checking himself, he gritted his teeth before gripping hold of her remaining stocking and slowly sliding it off.

Now she was naked save for her lacy knickers. He took a moment to stare at her, taking every inch of her in.

She was perfect.

She was *his*.

The look on her face was something to be savoured, a knowing yet shy quirk of the lips.

She levered herself up until she knelt before him, face to face.

'My turn,' she whispered, her eyes sparkling.

For such a slight woman she had a hidden strength, able, with a push of her hand, to shove him onto his back.

She laughed softly, taking hold of his wrists and pulling them up and over his head.

This had to count as the single most erotic moment of his life: Alessa straddling him, pinning him down, her swollen breasts brushing against his face. Every time he made to capture one in his mouth, she would move just out of reach.

Her teasing was deliberate, as was the way she straddled him, positioning herself on his erection. Every time she moved out of the reach of his mouth her crotch rubbed the length of his erection, the material of her knickers preventing any penetration.

She leaned down to kiss him on the mouth, still holding his wrists.

With a simple flick he could be free from her clasp.

Instead, he kissed her back, succumbing to the delights she wanted to bestow on him.

Her soft mouth pressed along his jaw then she released her hold on his wrists and slowly made her descent. No part of his chest was left unkissed or unstroked, his skin alive under the trail she made.

When she reached his groin she completely ignored his erection, her mouth working around it, her hands cupping his balls while her tongue darted out to taste them.

Her movements were clumsy, a sign of her inexperience, but this only added to the eroticism of the moment.

This was all for him.

Her tongue flickered onto the base of his shaft.

A powerful bolt shot through him, a groan escaping his lips.

He gripped the bed sheets in his fists and clenched his teeth even tighter, finding a spot on the ceiling to focus on.

For a moment he'd been certain he was going to come.

'Is something wrong?' she asked, stopping what she was doing to look at him, her eyes clouding with doubt.

Speech wouldn't form. He shook his head and sat up, leaning forward to clasp her cheeks and pull her into another kiss. In a tangle of arms and legs they collapsed together, Alessandra beneath him, devouring each other with their mouths.

He tugged at her knickers, pushing them down her hips, using his thighs and legs to pull them down. When they reached her ankles she kicked them off then wrapped her legs around him, raising her bottom so her heat rubbed against his erection.

And then he was inside her, burrowed in her tight heat, the relief giddying.

The first time they'd made love he'd been blown away

with how deeply he'd felt everything, every touch, every movement magnified.

This was something else completely.

Slowing their kisses, he began to move, keeping his groin ground to hers.

Her soft moans fired him, her kisses fuelled him, her roaming hands and fingers burning through his skin.

He opened his eyes to find her gazing at him in a dazed wonder.

Reaching for her hand, he brought it up to rest by the side of her head and clasped it tightly, kissing her with renewed passion as his thrusts deepened. It was as if he'd fused into one with her.

He felt rather than heard her come. Her grip around his erection thickened and tightened, her lips freezing on his, her only sound a tiny, almost breathless mew.

He was hardly aware of his own release. His senses were too full of Alessandra, watching every last moment of her climax.

Finally spent, he burrowed his face into her neck, careful not to put too much weight on her belly, and savoured the most delicious warmth he'd ever known spread through him.

The heavy weight of sleep soon came to claim him, and he shifted his weight off her. She followed his movements and settled into the crook of his arm with a contented sigh.

He awoke a few hours later. The suite was in darkness, a sliver of moonlight shining through.

Alessandra was draped over him, breathing deeply, her hair tickling his neck and chin. He smoothed it down, marvelling at its silkiness.

He tried to doze but sleep refused to return.

How could he sleep with so much racing through his mind? When there were so many emotions racing through his chest, it was a struggle to catch his breath.

The first time he'd slept with her, in her apartment in Milan... He'd struggled for thoughts and breath then too.

This was much worse.

He'd felt her getting too close in Mikolaj's restaurant, that feeling she could see through the veneer of his skin and through to the heart of him. That feeling had been compounded after the visit to his mother's house. He'd retreated to New York partly to talk sense into Rocco but mostly for space to compose himself in preparation for his new life.

Marriage wouldn't change anything, he'd convinced himself. He would compartmentalise Alessandra's presence in his life just as he did with his mother. They would live together but they wouldn't *be* together.

Making love to her again... Something had come alive inside him. He'd felt it uncoiling when they'd exchanged their vows but with everything going on that day had put it to one side. Now it, whatever *it* was, had uncoiled and bitten him, hard enough that it felt like a physical pain.

Before he could hope to decipher it, she roused in his arms, pulling herself up enough to kiss him, deeply, passionately, awakening in an instant.

He responded as if he'd been lying there waiting for her to wake, groaning when she slid onto his already hard length.

Doing nothing but hold on to her waist to support her, he let her take the lead. The moonlight bathed her, letting him watch as she took her pleasure, watch the lips that parted, the eyes that glazed. Her soft moans deepened until she ground herself onto him. He felt her release as deeply as he felt his own, revelled in the pulsations that seemed to draw his own orgasm into unquantifiable realms.

Afterwards, when he thought she was falling back into slumber, she pressed a kiss to his chest.

'I could get used to this,' she said, her voice sleepy but tinged with a smile.

And tinged with something that sounded like hope.

His eyes opened with a jerk.

He remembered the look in her eyes when they'd exchanged their vows. Now he knew what it had been: hope.

Alessandra had hopes for their future as a married couple.

She was changing towards him—she *had* changed towards him.

And with that change came the realisation that he could forget sharing a bed with her when they both wanted it.

Unless he kept a proper distance from her, he would soon have the power to hurt her.

Carefully he disentangled himself from her arms and got out of bed.

'Where are you going?' she mumbled.

'To get a drink. Go to sleep. I'll be back in a minute.' But he knew his words were a lie even as he spoke them.

He needed to protect her.

He needed to protect her from himself.

Alessandra slipped into her robe and headed to the bathroom where she could hear the shower running.

Her skin flushed to think of joining Christian in there, lathering his gorgeous body...

She stretched for the third time, shaking the lingering sleepiness off, and turned the door handle. It was locked.

She tried the handle again and still the door didn't budge.

She didn't know why—what experience did she have of men in a sensual sense?—but it surprised her that he might want his privacy whilst he showered. After the things they'd done to each other...

The flush on her skin deepened, penetrating through her flesh and down low, erotic memories of what they had done together, making her glow from the inside out.

It had been even better than she remembered. The alcohol during their first time might have been enough to loosen her inhibitions but it must have dulled her senses a fraction too.

Or maybe it was because this time there was something real between them that surpassed mere lust.

All Alessandra knew was that she wanted nothing more than to spend the day in bed with him. The only thing to spoil her memories was awakening to find his side of the bed empty.

Instead of waiting for him, she dived into the adjoining bathroom and deliberately kept the door ajar, an open invitation for *him* to join *her*.

After a good few minutes of soaping herself under the powerful walk-in shower and washing her hair, boredom kicked in.

She dried herself quickly, rubbed the towel over her hair and moisturised her face.

She made to leave the bathroom, pausing at the last moment to put her robe back on, not yet confident enough to walk around stark naked in broad daylight.

The door of the bathroom he'd been using was open. Masculine scents mingled with the steam of the shower, filling the empty bedroom.

Maybe he was ordering breakfast for them.

She wandered through to the main living area of the suite and found him at the dining table—fully dressed and working on his laptop.

He looked up and flashed a quick smile. 'Good morning.'

She nodded slowly, caught off-guard to find him working. For surely he must be working? He hadn't even donned casual clothes but wore a white shirt and blue pinstriped trousers.

'Are you planning on wearing that to Marrakech?' she asked. They were due to fly there later that afternoon for a four-day honeymoon.

An uncomfortable look spread over his face, quickly gone, but there long enough for her chest to sink down to her feet.

'I'm afraid we will have to take our honeymoon another time,' he said calmly, looking back at his laptop. 'An emergency has come up.'

'Another one?'

He threw her a smile that was clearly intended to bestow patience when all it did was make her want to throw something at him.

'You know my job is all about finance. When financial problems hit companies, prompt action is needed.'

'I appreciate that. What I don't get is why it has to be you—why can't someone else step in and act as saviour?'

'There is no one else.'

Her eyes narrowed in suspicion. 'What about our honeymoon and the way it's supposed to convince the world we're in love?' Why did her heart clench to say that?

'I joined the board of an Athens shipping company last month in an advisory capacity. One of my staff has been going through the accounts and has discovered a large hole in the company's finances. Unless we plug that hole in the next two days, fifty thousand people will not receive their pay cheques. That's fifty thousand people who will struggle to pay their bills, their mortgages, feed their children. We will go to Marrakech at a later date.'

How could she argue with that? She couldn't, not unless she wanted to sound like the most selfish person in the world.

She eyed him coolly, trying to decide if the whiff of duplicity she detected was real or the workings of a tired, disappointed mind. Four days in Marrakech with nothing to do but laze under the sun and make love had sounded like heaven.

She didn't dispute the crisis he'd described was real. What she did dispute was his assertion that he was the only person in the world able to resolve it.

Throwing a tight smile, determined not to show her disappointment, she said, 'Seeing as you're going to be busy,

I'll return to Milan. There's a lot of stuff there I need to be getting on with.'

'No, you will stay here in Athens with me.'

'Are you giving me an order?'

He sighed. 'If you return to Milan on your own, the day after our wedding, suspicions will be aroused. People will understand the postponement of a honeymoon because of a financial crisis. This is Greece; the whole country's in crisis. They will not understand a new wife who is not at her husband's side during it. We need to live together full-time as man and wife for a few months to keep the doubters at bay. We already agreed this.'

Alessandra's teeth were clenched so tightly against the metaphorical kicking they'd just received that she had to fight to prise them apart.

Suspicions would be aroused?

That was one way to bring her back down to earth.

While she fought the despondency crashing through her like a wave, she fought even harder to keep her composure.

This was a timely reminder that theirs was not a real marriage. The romance of their wedding day— what Christian had done to get her brother there, the wondrousness of their love-making—all must have combined to set off some new hormones within her that made her look at Christian in a fuzzy light.

Dio, she must have been cast under a spell.

She blinked rapidly to clear the fuzzy light, wishing she could clear the churning in her belly with the same ease.

'Okay, I'll stay in Athens with you, but remember I've a shoot scheduled for next Thursday so we need to be back in Milan for that.'

He bowed his head. 'I'm sure that won't be a problem.'

'Good.' She didn't add that should a 'problem' occur she would fly to Milan and do her work regardless. 'I'm going to order some breakfast. Do you want anything?'

'Just a pot of coffee, thank you.'

Christian watched her pick up the suite phone and place their order then turned his attention back to the screen in front of him.

His eyes wouldn't focus.

After the incredible night they'd shared he'd been expecting much greater resistance from Alessandra about the postponed honeymoon, had braced himself for the worst.

If he hadn't seen the flare of despondency in her eyes he would believe her understanding and calmness at the situation was genuine.

As much as it hurt him to hurt her, he knew it was for the best.

He *had* to put their marriage on the footing they had originally agreed.

There were women who could separate love and sex. He no longer believed Alessandra to be one of them.

The hope he'd seen in her eyes as they'd exchanged their vows and then the hope he'd heard in her voice after they'd made love…

What did he, the gutter rat from Athens, know about love?

All he knew about it was that it broke hearts and destroyed people. It had destroyed his mother and Alessandra's father.

He wouldn't know how to love or show love if he tried. All he knew was how to make money. A woman like Alessandra deserved so much more.

Physical distance wasn't enough. He needed to put emotional distance between them too. Now. Before he hurt her.

If he allowed their sexual relationship to develop, her feelings would likely develop too while his…

He'd never had a proper relationship before. Never. He had no idea how long it would take for boredom to set in, when the thrill of making love to the one woman would abate and he'd be looking for a new challenge.

If her feelings grew stronger whilst his decreased, the pain it would cause her would be immense.

He had to nip it in the bud now. For both their sakes.

CHAPTER ELEVEN

CHRISTIAN'S HOME WAS a pebblestone villa in a private enclave of Athens, set away from the hustle and bustle of the city. Surrounded by acres of green land, the villa itself was found by means of a private driveway; indeed, the one word that sprang to Alessandra's mind as she got out of the car was *private*. They could be anywhere. They could be nowhere.

The villa was beautiful, there was no denying that—picture perfect—but the silence was deafening. Villa Mondelli had been much the same, the majority of her childhood spent in its splendid isolation. She'd adored the infrequent trips to Milan Rocco would take her on when he was home from university—loved the noise, the smells and the bustle of the big city, that feeling of being a small cog in a big wheel where all the tiny component parts jostled together nicely to make the big picture.

They'd left the hotel after breakfast, waved off by their remaining guests. She'd forced a bright smile, forced jollity.

On the drive to his home he'd explained in more detail what he was working on. She'd tried hard to be sympathetic and understanding about the importance that the situation be speedily resolved. That did nothing to prevent the underlying resentment.

She was used to workaholics. She'd been raised by the various nannies her workaholic grandfather had employed for her. Her brother was of an identical mould.

But she was one hundred per cent certain that, if such a situation had occurred hours before Rocco's honeymoon, he would have put Olivia first. At the very least he would have discussed the matter with her and taken her input before making a decision.

The big difference was that Rocco loved Olivia. She was his world.

All Alessandra was to Christian was the vessel carrying his child, married to secure his heir and avert a scandal. Love did not and never would feature in it, no matter what foolish feelings had been stoked on her wedding day.

Against her better judgement she'd allowed hope to rear its head.

Sex was a dangerous game to play. It evoked feelings that had no business being conjured.

In future she would make love with her body and detach her mind. Somehow. She was certain it could be done. Lots of other women were able to do it so why should she be any different?

The vows she'd made had been given honestly but for the sake of the little life growing in her belly, not for herself.

It would be wise for her to remember that and stop letting her hormones off the leash.

Christian followed her out of the car and walked her to the large front door, the driver tasked with bringing her luggage in.

A woman who Alessandra judged to be in her mid-forties opened the door to greet them. Christian introduced her as Evanthia, his head of housekeeping.

Evanthia took Alessandra's extended hand, uttered a friendly greeting in Greek then stood back so they could enter.

The interior was every bit what the average person would expect a bachelor billionaire's home to look like: lavish. Ostentatious. Cold. All vaulted ceilings, white walls and lots of marble.

The reception area where they stood led through to an enormous open-plan living space. While she stood at the threshold, craning her neck to take it all in, Christian and Evanthia had a quick conversation.

'I need to go,' he said to Alessandra a few moments later. 'Evanthia will show you around and show you where your room is.'

'Where *my* room is?' she interrupted, snapped out of her musings about his interior decoration.

He nodded. 'If you're not happy with it then let Evanthia know and she can move you to a different one.'

'Oh.'

He looked at her with calm eyes. 'Is there a problem?'

She forced her own eyes to be bright and wide. 'Not at all.'

'Then make yourself comfortable—this is your home now. It is doubtful I will be back before the evening but you have my number if you need me for anything.'

With that he left, leaving Alessandra feeling as if a rug had been pulled out from under her.

They were to have separate rooms.

That meant they would be sleeping in separate beds.

Her reality check that morning when he'd cancelled their short honeymoon hadn't been a reality check enough.

The talking-to about having sex with her body and not her heart now sounded presumptuous and silly, even if she'd only been talking to herself.

Silly, silly Alessandra. When would she learn?

She placed a hand to her stomach, refusing to let the swell of hopelessness pull her down.

Evanthia said something in Greek, beckoning for Alessandra to follow her.

Time to pull herself together.

All her love would be reserved for her baby.

With many gestures, Evanthia gave her the tour: the huge living area with its 'hidden' library, a bar nestled in a cut-out section of wall and a dining area with a table that could fit two dozen comfortably. She was also shown the enormous kitchen, the indoor swimming pool and the gymnasium that would put any private member's club to shame. Through a back door she was shown two outdoor swimming pools and a lawn tennis court, then it was time to head upstairs. They climbed one of three sets of winding stairs and walked along a landing that overlooked the living area, a four-foot-high length of impossibly clear Perspex barrier there to stop anyone plunging headfirst to the first floor.

Her room was at the far end of the landing. Her luggage had been placed inside.

'Clothes,' Evanthia said, pointing at an internal door. Alessandra opened the door to find a dressing room.

'I do?' Evanthia asked, picking one of the suitcases up.

'I can do it,' Alessandra answered with a smile. 'Thank you for the offer.'

Evanthia started talking, gesturing wildly.

Not having the faintest idea what the housekeeper was saying or what her gestures meant, Alessandra smiled and nodded politely. Eventually Evanthia bustled off after making gestures Alessandra thought might have indicated food.

As soon as she was alone in her room she set about unpacking, hanging her clothes in the empty dressing room.

A dressing room that would only ever contain feminine clothes.

Silly little Alessandra, she thought, folding into drawers the new underwear she'd brought expecting her husband to remove them.

She could wear bloomers and he would neither know nor care.

At some point in the preceding weeks she'd allowed herself to believe their marriage could be like a small nursery garden that, with some care and attention, might—just might—bloom into something substantial. Something real.

She'd even allowed herself to believe that Christian could

be someone in whom she could trust, not only with her baby but with *her*.

Christian had taken all those little seedlings and ripped them up, a reminder that he'd never wanted the garden in the first place. He'd put her subtly but firmly in her place.

So why had he made love to her on their wedding night? Out of duty? To consummate it and make it legal?

No. He must have made love to her because she was there and he could. She could have been any woman in that bed.

It was her own lack of sexual experience that had failed to recognise it for what it was.

Did he expect them to sleep together again or was that it?

Her cheeks burned just imagining asking that question. The humiliation of his answer would be too much.

But it hurt so much to know that an experience she'd found so special and fulfilling had been all one-sided. Christian had been going through the motions, his tenderness part of those motions.

He probably had sex with all his lovers in the same way. Why did she think she was so special that Casanova Markos would want to share a bed with her more than once? She'd shared two nights with him; she should feel special. She'd had a one hundred per cent higher success rate than his other women.

She rubbed her itchy eyes and chided herself. Christian wasn't doing anything they hadn't previously agreed. She had to accept things as they were, not as she now wished they could be.

Their marriage would be like the green land surrounding the villa. Flat and one-dimensional and not a single different colour in sight.

Alessandra hovered the photo over the place on screen until she was happy with the position then clicked to release it. She stared for an age, trying to think of a witty caption to go with it. Inspiration struck. She typed it in, clicking the save button at the exact moment Christian stepped into the hidden library.

She'd heard movements, had assumed it was members of the household staff.

She hadn't for a minute thought it was her husband actually returning home at what would be regarded by a normal person as a decent time.

How she wished her pulses didn't race at the mere sight of him.

'What are you doing?' he asked, leaning against the oak desk she'd appropriated for her purpose.

'A wedding montage.' She made sure to keep her tone neutral. 'I'm making what is basically an electronic magazine with pictures of all the people who were there to share our happy day.' How she stopped her tongue curdling over 'happy day' she didn't know. 'When it's done I'll email it to all of them as a keepsake.' She would also print and frame a copy and hang it beside her bed where it could be a daily reminder that her life with Christian was a sham, a marriage for appearances.

It felt good to have something to occupy her. Since their wedding three weeks ago, they'd travelled to Milan together for a few days so she could do her prearranged shoot and meet her obstetrician, flown on to Hong Kong where they'd stayed in his penthouse apartment—in separate rooms—for a week then travelled to London for a day's shoot. They'd been back in Athens ever since.

Having no work to occupy her here, she'd spent a day sightseeing, undetected by any paparazzi. Far from being able to enthuse about all the ancient relics at the Acropolis, she'd felt lonely surrounded by couples and groups of people all chattering happily together.

Christian's home was so remote and her grasp of the Greek language so weak that the chances of making any friendships almost impossible. At least his apartment in Hong Kong was central, allowing her plenty of freedom to explore and occupy herself.

Being in Athens reminded her too strongly of being back at Villa Mondelli, when her grandfather had always been too busy working to take any notice of her. Rocco had been of the same mould. She'd learned as a child that moping about didn't change anything. Keeping busy was the solution to curbing isolation. As a child she would bury her head in books, draw pictures and practise her gymnastics. She'd needed something, a project here in Athens, to keep the isolation at bay and it had been while going through the photos she'd taken on their wedding day, trying hard to look at them objectively and not through maudlin eyes, that inspiration had struck.

'May I look?'

'It isn't finished yet—I'm about two-thirds done, but help yourself.' She pushed her chair back to give him access to her laptop. She didn't push back far enough, catching that gorgeous oaky scent that made her mouth water.

She closed her eyes in a futile attempt to curb the longing sweeping through her at his proximity.

In three weeks he hadn't once attempted to seduce her, not even with his eyes, as he had done so many times before they'd made their vows.

One night had been enough for him to bore of her sexually. Okay; two nights. But they'd been months apart.

If only she could get her body to believe it was bored of him too.

Time would curb it, she told herself. Eventually his lack of interest would creep through her like a pollutant and she would be able to stop tossing and turning throughout the night, wishing he would come to her.

After three weeks of no physical attention she accepted that wasn't going to happen.

It had done nothing to cure her longing.

'This is incredible,' Christian said, clicking his way

through the pages she'd created. 'The glossy magazines would pay you a fortune to get hold of your memory stick.'

'I'm sure they would,' she agreed drily.

Silently she congratulated herself on another coherent conversation with him.

It would have been easy to slip into self-pity after his rejection.

She would not do that. She would not infect her baby with negativity.

In fairness, he hadn't lied to her. On the contrary, their marriage was shaping up to be exactly how they'd devised when they'd first agreed to it.

She only wished she'd known how heartsick it would make her.

Pushing her chair farther back, she got to her feet. 'Are we still going out tonight?' She refused to make assumptions. He might have only popped home for a fleeting visit between appointments.

Christian worked ridiculous hours. Even in Milan, where they'd stayed so she could work, he'd holed himself up in the spare room of her apartment, which he'd turned into a bedroom-cum-office, working until the early hours and joining her for an evening meal before disappearing again.

'Yes. We don't need to leave until eight. There's plenty of time.'

They were going to a party at the British Embassy, their first official function as man and wife.

She looked at her watch. 'I suppose two hours is adequate time to get ready for a night out.'

'You suppose?' he echoed with a droll tone.

Christian put his cufflinks on then slipped into his tuxedo jacket and straightened his black bowtie. He would do.

He headed downstairs and poured himself a small shot of bourbon.

It had been a hard few weeks and now he was looking

forward to an evening out. Yes, it would be a networking evening, but with Alessandra by his side it would be bearable.

It was strange to think of himself merely enjoying a woman's company for company's sake but with Alessandra he did. Until their impromptu date, all his dealings with women had been for two reasons: business, at which he refused to blur the lines between personal and professional; and pleasure, the women he dated with the sole intention of bedding them. He'd enjoyed the time spent with them but it had been a means to an end, the end being in bed naked.

Alessandra was the first woman he'd gone on a date with whom he'd had no intention of bedding. He'd found her wildly attractive but she'd been so off-limits he'd curbed that side of his thought process with her. After a few glasses of champagne had loosened them both up, he'd found himself wildly fascinated by *her*, the mind beneath the beautiful face, not just the body beneath the dress she'd worn.

For the first time, he looked back on his behaviour before he'd met Alessandra with a sense of shame.

How many women had he bedded in his thirty-two years?

He couldn't even hazard a guess.

He'd hopped from bed to bed without a second thought.

For the first time, he considered he'd been running, not hopping. Running as fast as he could.

Alessandra was the only woman whose bed he'd run from without immediately hopping into another.

From their first night together until she'd approached him at Rocco and Olivia's wedding, there had been no one else. There still hadn't been.

He hadn't promised fidelity to her. So long as he was discreet, he could bed whomever he chose.

The problem, as he was learning, was that just because he could act like a kid in a sweetshop, his taste at that moment was for only one particular sweet. That sweet went by the name of Alessandra.

He didn't believe he'd ever worked as hard as he had these past three weeks. He'd always been a hard, diligent worker but since his university days he'd always ensured there was time for fun.

The only fun he wanted now came in a slender package with a mane of glossy chestnut hair. There were times, especially late at night, when he heard movement from her room, when he would fight to remind himself why he couldn't allow their relationship to be anything but platonic.

In his eyes, she was a princess.

He was a gutter rat.

He wasn't good enough for her.

He would only bring her misery.

Better to keep things platonic for both their sakes *and* for the sake of their unborn baby.

It was harder than he'd ever imagined.

He straightened as Alessandra descended the stairs, the jewellery she wore around her wrist clanging against the railing she lightly gripped.

She never failed to take his breath away.

Tonight she wore a floor-length turquoise silk gown with only one long sleeve, gold and diamond beading around the neck line that slashed under her bare arm. The material layered like descending waves down to her feet, displaying her slender curves but hiding the slight burgeoning of her waistline. Tonight her neck was bare, the only complementary jewellery a chunky Egyptian bracelet and a pair of gold teardrop earrings. Her hair had been swept up into an elegant knot, her eyes dramatically darkened, her lips conversely painted a nude colour.

The Egyptian bracelet only accentuated the idea of an Egyptian queen having sprung to life.

An ache formed in his chest, a much different ache to the one coursing through his loins.

That bare, golden arm and shoulder were her only real

bits of bodily flesh on display but the effect on him was as dramatic as if she'd walked down the stairs naked.

His mind filled with visions of peeling the dress from her...

He swallowed the imagery away and stepped forward to her, being greeted with a cloud of her sultry perfume in return.

'You're beautiful,' he said.

She smiled. '*Grazie*. You look good yourself.'

Alessandra had always found men wearing dinner jackets attractive—there was something so sophisticated and suave about the look—but Christian made other men's attempts look like little boys playing dress-up. There was something about the way he filled it that made her pulses skip and her skin tingle.

If they had a proper marriage she would at least have the anticipation of ripping it off him when they got home...

Stop it, she scolded herself. Thoughts like that did nothing for her private mission of gaining immunity against him.

And nor did the darkening of his eyes, that look as if he wanted nothing more than to rip her clothes off too.

A rush of warm heat pooled in the apex of her thighs, so deep and sudden her legs weakened.

It was a look she hadn't seen in three weeks.

Any immunity she might have managed to attain was ripped away in one fell swoop.

CHAPTER TWELVE

CHRISTIAN'S DRIVER PULLED up outside the embassy. No sooner had the engine been turned off than the door was opened for them and they were ushered out of the car amidst a hail of flashbulbs from the waiting paparazzi, who'd been tipped off that they were attending.

As they crossed the threshold of the historic building, Alessandra almost jumped out of her skin to feel Christian place his hand on the small of her back.

It was the first time he'd touched her since their wedding night.

It's for the paparazzi's benefit, she told herself.

When he clasped her hand into his much larger one, threading his fingers through hers, the nerves on her skin tingled with warmth, her fingers yearning to squeeze their possession.

Keeping a firm grip of her hand, he steered her around the room, introducing her to various bankers, investors and their partners and spouses.

She found it hard keeping track of names. Every time Christian's body brushed against hers, her heart would skip and her mind would lose its train of thought.

When a waiter passed carrying a tray of canapés, she pounced, glad of a decent excuse to drop her husband's hand.

It wasn't just money and finance people wanted to talk to them about, though; many were keen to discuss the wedding, eager for the intimate details the press had only been able to guess at. They'd released a couple of photos to the media in the hope that having something publishable would help them lose interest.

'They should give everyone name tags,' she said after a few hours of small talk and endless canapés. Christian had noticed her springing lightly on her aching legs and, insisting she rest for a few minutes, had borne her off to some empty seats in an alcove.

A smile tugged at his lips. 'It would make life easier.'

'How many of these people do you actually know?'

'Far too many of them.'

'You don't sound very enthusiastic.'

'Finance doesn't always attract the most charismatic of people.'

'It attracted you.'

'You think I'm charismatic?'

'You know you are,' she said with deliberate dismissal.

'Is that a compliment?' he asked, raising a brow in bemusement while his beautiful eyes glittered.

'Take it however you want.' She smiled at a passing woman they'd spoken to earlier, the wife of a diplomat. She couldn't help but notice the woman's gaze linger a touch too long on Christian.

Did she think he was charismatic?

Christian had more charisma than anyone she'd known. People were drawn to him. *Women* especially were drawn to him and it wasn't the sole result of his good looks. She doubted the size of his bank account had much affect either—the magnetism he carried came from him.

'Then I will take it as a compliment.'

'Why finance?' she asked, her interest piqued. 'Of all the jobs and careers out there, why go that route?'

The bemusement dropped, the warmth in his eyes cooling. For a moment she thought he was going to ignore her innocent question.

Instead, he held her gaze. 'When I was a small child, every night before she slept my mother would get the few drachmas she had to her name, place them in front of her and count them.' He spoke slowly and concisely, as if he were thinking carefully about his answer. 'I think she hoped that if she counted them enough times they would magically double. The only time I was ever able to make her happy was if I found a stray coin and brought it home to her.'

He shook his head, distaste pouring off him. 'She worked so hard but we were so poor she couldn't afford to pay for my school books. We had food in our belly from Mikolaj— whatever was left over from the day before—but there was no money for anything—not birthdays, not Christmas, not anything.'

Alessandra swallowed, the familiar ache forming in her belly that always came when she thought of his childhood. She hated imagining what he'd lived through.

His gaze bore into her. 'I was obsessed with people like you.'

'Me?' she queried faintly.

'I would see men and women like you, people who were clean and wore beautiful clothes, and wonder why we were so different, why the clothes my mother and I wore were falling into rags. Then I realised what the difference was: money. They had it and we didn't. So that became my obsession. Money. I was determined to learn everything about it: how to earn it, how to make it grow and how to keep it so that my mother and I too could be clean and wear beautiful clothes.'

'You certainly realised your dreams,' she said quietly. 'Did you have to study hard for it or did it come naturally to you?'

She thought back to her own single-sex education and how she had resented the strictness, rebelling by refusing to pay attention or do homework until it had become likely she would fail all her exams. If she'd applied herself a bit more, her grandfather would never have felt the need to employ a private tutor to help her catch up. Javier would never have entered her life. Who knew how different her life would have been if she'd never met him?

Would she have stayed a virgin until the age of twenty-five?

She hadn't been ready for sex with Javier but with hindsight it was because she'd known, even without being aware of his wife and children, that a sexual affair between them was wrong. The balance of power had been too one-sided, in his favour.

But Javier was her reality. She didn't know if she would have stayed a virgin until the age of twenty-five if she hadn't met him because that would have been a different Alessandra, not the Alessandra she was today.

'I studied every hour I could,' Christian said, adopting the same quiet tone as she. 'I must have been ten when I realised education was the only way either I or my mother could escape.'

'I'm so sorry,' she said softly after a long silence had formed between them.

'For what?'

'I don't know.' She raised her shoulders, wishing she could articulate the shame churning within her. She recalled the little rant she'd had in Mikolaj's taverna when she'd put Christian in his place about him not having a monopoly on childhood pain and abandonment.

At least she'd always had clean clothes and fresh food. Materially she'd had everything she could have wished for; the things she'd been denied were to stop her being spoiled and not due to a lack of finances.

After the mess that had been her relationship with Javier, her grandfather had used money—her allowance—as another means to control her. No allowance meant no money; no money meant she stayed prisoner in the villa without the means to bring any more shame to the good Mondelli name.

A prisoner?

What a self-absorbed brat she had been.

Christian's whole life came into sharp focus. No more potted snapshots of her Adonis, the hard working but poor scholarship student, the small child sharing a mattress in a cramped attic room with his harridan of a mother...

Now the snapshots formed a whole picture. Formed the man before her; everything it must have taken for him to drag himself out of the slum. Two decades of suffering before he'd had the opportunity to shower daily.

What must he think of her, the spoiled little rich kid? *She* knew she'd never been spoiled but in comparison to Christian she might as well have been Imelda Marcos. So her grandfather had been a workaholic and happy to pass the actual raising of his granddaughter to the female staff of his household? At least she'd never doubted his love. So he'd cut off her allowance? Oh, boo hoo. Her grandfather had been teaching her a lesson. Without it she would never have felt compelled to get herself a job, would never have answered the advertisement to be a photographer's assistant and taken the first steps on the career she loved.

She'd been self-sufficient ever since.

She might not have had a mother or a father but she'd had her grandfather, strict as he was, and her brother, as protective as he was. Things might be tense at the moment but Rocco would always be there for her.

Christian hadn't had any of that. Mikolaj had been there as best he could but with a business to run and seven kids of his own to raise it hadn't been enough. Christian had basically been alone until he'd established the strong friendship group with her brother, Stefan and Zayed. A friendship that had been destroyed because of her.

'Your mother...'

'What about her?' he asked tersely.

'However crazy she makes you feel, you must love her very much.'

He breathed deeply. 'I respect what she did for me as a child. She could have abandoned me but she didn't. I do my duty towards her and will never abandon her. But love? She poisoned any notion I ever had of love.'

As Alessandra digested this, a silver fox of a man came over to join them in the alcove, a German she recalled Christian telling her was head of one of Europe's major private banks.

'Have I introduced you to my daughter?' he asked, indicating a woman of around the same age as Alessandra who was hovering behind him.

'I don't believe so,' Christian answered.

Silver Fox pulled his daughter to him. 'Kerstin, this is Christian Markos and his wife, Alessandra.'

Kerstin's eyes gleamed as she leaned in to kiss Christian's cheeks, lingering to whisper something in his ear. A tall, blonde, impossibly glamorous and beautiful woman, she reminded Alessandra of old Hollywood. Her kisses to Alessandra were quick and perfunctory, the first thing that caused the word *bitch* to float in Alessandra's mind.

'Kerstin graduated a few years ago from your Alma Mater,' Silver Fox said when the introductions were complete.

'You studied at Columbia?' Christian asked with interest.

'I did,' she said with a knowing smile.

So she had brains as well as beauty?

'I seem to recall your father saying something about it, but that was quite a few years ago,' he mused. 'Are you planning on following in his footsteps?'

'*Ja*—when Papa retires the plan is for me to take over his role.'

'That's something I wanted to talk to you about,' Silver Fox said, addressing Christian. 'Kerstin and I feel she needs to expand her horizons. We would like you to taking her under your wing for a year or two so she can learn directly from you different aspects of our business.'

Over my dead body.

'That's an interesting idea,' Christian said, turning his attention directly to Kerstin. 'What are you hoping to learn from me?'

'Everything!' Thus said, Kerstin proceeded to discuss in great detail what she hoped to achieve under his tutelage, most of which went straight over Alessandra's head. This wasn't through a lack of understanding on her part, more to do with the raging burn in her brain that glowed so brightly, nothing else could penetrate.

If she had claws she would scratch Kerstin's eyes out without a second thought.

With a snap, she knew who Kerstin reminded her of and why she'd taken such an instant dislike to her.

She reminded her of all the women she'd ever seen photographed on Christian's arm.

His interest in her—the way he leaned in closely to hear what she had to say, the obvious interest in his expression— was all so clear a highly polished window couldn't have been more transparent.

Feeling everything inside her clench, she forced her ears to tune in to the conversation.

Now it really did fly over her head.

When it came to financial matters, the most Alessandra ever needed to know was the amount in her personal and business bank accounts and what income and outgoings she had. When she heard the word *securities* banded about in all earnestness, the only thing her brain conjured up were her bodyguards.

She wasn't stupid; she knew that. But finance was its own separate language, one she didn't know how to translate.

Kerstin did. Kerstin spoke fluent finance.

Alessandra placed a hand on her belly as if by covering it she could protect the tiny life within from the thoughts raging through its mother's head.

By marrying her, Christian had deprived himself of a marriage that would be far better suited to him.

Kerstin would be perfect. She had the physical attributes he so desired—Alessandra doubted any man would get bored of making love to *her*—but, more importantly from her husband's point of view, there would be no juggling of time, no compromise. Kerstin would flit into his life as if she'd been born there and then, when her father retired, she and Christian would take over the running of his bank together.

Dio, now her brain was running away from her. She couldn't make it stop.

They'd been in the woman's company for twenty minutes and already Alessandra had mapped her entire future out for her.

Christian had never wanted to marry. He'd given up his freedom for their baby. He was trying to accommodate the mother of his baby into his life as well as he could.

He might never have wanted to marry but he *did* want children.

If he'd met Kerstin tonight as a single man, would he too have grasped what an ideal wife she would have made for him?

They'd have been perfect together, could have made beautiful babies over a set of spreadsheets then whispered sweet nothings about the world of finance into each other's ears until the early hours of every morning.

'Are you okay?' Christian asked quietly, breaking into her runaway thoughts.

She swallowed and jerked a nod. 'I think I have indigestion,' she said, uttering the first thing that came into her mind.

His blue eyes studied her, a question mark in them.

'I must have eaten too many *spanakopita*,' she expanded, referring to the mini filo-pastry pies stuffed with spinach and feta she'd taken a liking to. At her last count she'd eaten eight of them.

Her appetite had deserted her now. Her stomach felt so tight she doubted anything would go down.

'Would you like to go home?' Did he have to look so concerned when she was playing an imaginary game of marrying him off to someone else? A more suitable someone else.

'No, I'll be fine.' She forced a smile. 'Carry on with your conversation—I need to visit the bathroom.'

A few minutes later, after a sharp talking to herself in the privacy of a cubicle, she was washing her hands when Kerstin walked in.

The hot, burning feeling in Alessandra's brain immediately started up again.

'Is something the matter?' Kerstin asked.

Dio, now Christian's future imaginary wife was looking at her with concern.

'Not at all.' She forced another brittle smile.

A knowing expression came into Kerstin's eyes. 'My sister have a baby soon. You are the same, *ja*?'

'How can you tell?' Not only was she beautiful and intelligent but also psychic.

'My sister has had many babies,' Kerstin said with a laugh.

'Please don't tell anyone,' Alessandra beseeched. 'We're not ready for the world to know.'

'All those men chasing you with their cameras...is not nice.'

Beautiful, intelligent, psychic *and* empathetic?

Had a more perfect woman ever been born?

Kerstin looked openly at Alessandra's belly. 'I think you hide it for not much longer. Soon you will show.'

She stated the latter with such certainty that for a moment Alessandra was tempted to ask exactly how much later, right down to the hour.

Instead she fought back the sudden spring of hot tears welling in her eyes.

Kerstin saw them too and placed a comforting arm around her shoulder. 'Your hormone will feel better soon.'

Alessandra gave a shaky laugh, accepting the tissue Kerstin magically produced.

At least she had one advantage over the beautiful German woman. Her own English was much better.

'You're very quiet,' Christian said. They'd been in the car for ten minutes since leaving the embassy and Alessandra had spent the entire time gazing out of the window.

She'd become increasingly quiet since their wedding. It was only tonight, when she'd been her old, sociable self, that he'd realised quite how withdrawn she'd become.

Was he the cause? Had his mother's prediction already started coming true?

He wanted to reach out to her and find out what troubled her but didn't know how.

She raised a shoulder—the bare shoulder he'd spent the evening trying not to stare at. It had been an effort of epic proportions that had failed. That one naked limb had acted like a beacon to his eyes. The rest of her had acted as a beacon to his senses.

Holding her hand, feeling her warm, slender body brushing against him…

All the good work he'd done in recent weeks building a distance from her had crumbled.

Theos, he *ached* for her. Ached to possess her all over again with a burn so deep it was like fighting through treacle fog to remember why he had to keep his distance.

'Are you going to take Kerstin on?' she surprised him by asking.

'I haven't decided.' On paper Kerstin was an ideal candidate for his ever-growing empire, having the perfect qualifications and aptitude. Her father was a long-standing, respected member of the finance community. Yes, on paper she was ideal.

But he hadn't imagined the tension emanating from Alessandra when he'd been talking to her. He didn't want to do anything that would make his wife uncomfortable.

'I think you should.'

'What? Take her on?'

Alessandra turned her head to look at him. Her features were still, sombre, even. 'She's perfect.'

It was too dark to read her eyes.

'If I were to take her on in the capacity she and her father have requested, she will do a lot of travelling with us,' he stated carefully.

'She will do a lot of travelling with *you*,' Alessandra clarified. 'In another month or so, we can stop zigzagging the world together. Our schedules will thank us for it,' she added drily.

'Let us consider that in another month,' he said, his mouth filling with an acrid taste at the thought of travelling without Alessandra by his side. The acridness turned sweet as he thought of how travelling made her sleep. How many hours had he spent these past few weeks on his jet, taking advantage of her oblivion to study her sleeping form, reminding himself over and over why he could only look at her? *Theos*, he wanted to touch her so badly.

She raised her shoulders in a sign of nonchalance, a smile playing on her lips. It was too dark to tell if her eyes smiled too. 'I do think you should consider taking Kerstin on. Every billionaire should have a decent protégée.'

'I thought our child would be a good candidate as my protégé.'

'It will be a long time before our child is old enough for that. Consider Kerstin as practice.'

'That's not a bad idea,' he mused. Taking Kerstin under his wing would certainly strengthen the ties between himself and her father, Gregor, a very powerful man in the

European banking world. To take Kerstin under his wing would put Gregor in his debt. Debts of a personal nature were their own form of currency.

Under normal circumstances, he wouldn't hesitate. As Alessandra had pointed out, Kerstin was perfect. She was highly intelligent, multilingual and already had an excellent grasp of his business. His job would involve fine-tuning that grasp.

Moonlight seeped in the windows, the light bouncing off Alessandra's bare arm, giving it a silver glow.

That naked arm. How could any man concentrate on anything for longer than a few seconds with that in his eyeline?

All it made him think of was the rest of her naked too.

Do not think of her naked.

It was hard enough sitting in an enclosed cabin in the back of a car with her without bringing memories of her beautiful naked form to his mind's eye.

Self-enforced celibacy clearly did not agree with him.

How could any man cope with celibacy whilst living with such temptation?

He gave a silent prayer of thanks as his driver turned the car into the long driveway.

They were home.

In silence they entered the villa. The live-in staff had long since retired to their own quarters for the night.

Tiny nightlights glowed from the reception through to the living area and up the stairs, bathing Alessandra in a dim light that magnified her sultry beauty.

The ache in his groin, far from diminishing as he'd valiantly willed it to do in the car, increased, his arousal spreading from his loins…

That damn bare arm…

She paused at the bottom of the staircase to look at him. 'Thank you for a nice evening—'

'You have enjoyed yourself?' he cut in, delaying the time she would climb the stairs and head to her room.

'I wouldn't go that far,' she answered with a wry smile. 'It was hardly a night of music and dancing but it was a lot less stuffy than I expected.'

'That's good. I don't want you feeling uncomfortable when we go to these functions.'

She nodded, looking away. 'Well, good night.'

He inclined his head in return, fighting to keep his feet from crossing the marble floor to her. 'Good night.'

Holding on to the rail, she climbed the stairs and crossed the landing to her bedroom. Only when she reached her door did she turn her head to look back round and gaze down at him.

Then she disappeared inside her room, closing the door firmly behind her.

CHAPTER THIRTEEN

ALESSANDRA'S PHONE VIBRATED in her pocket. Grimacing, she fired off a couple more shots then carefully let go of her camera, which she kept around her neck. 'You can change into the next set now,' she said to the model standing in front of the white board, wearing nothing but a pair of skimpy knickers and bra.

She'd spent the past three days working on a shoot for a well-known lingerie brand. With a waist that seemed to be thickening by the day, spending days with semi-clad underwear models was not doing a great deal for her ego. Her pregnancy would soon be obvious to everyone.

She pulled her phone out, her heart skipping to see Christian's name flash up. She read his message:

Just landed. How long are you going to be?

She fired off a quick reply.

A couple of hours. Meet you at my apartment.

When they weren't physically together, most communication between them was done via messaging. She'd steered it that way. The first time he'd called after the embassy do a month ago, her hands had gone clammy just to see his name flash up in the screen. She'd stared at it until it had gone to voicemail, wiped her hands and written a quick message back, apologising that she'd missed his call. He'd messaged straight back. The next few times she'd done the same—avoided the call and then messaged him. Since then, he'd taken to messaging her without bothering to call. It made it easier for her. Having his rich tones play directly into her ear made more than her hands clammy.

Shoving her phone back in her pocket, she forced her concentration back to the skinny model, who'd changed into another lacy number with the help of an assistant, uncaring of who in the studio saw her fully naked.

'Left arm in an arc above your head please,' she said, lifting her camera back up to her face.

When the final frame was taken she packed her camera away, had a quick chat with her assistant, who was happy to pack everything else up, and left the building.

Soon she was nodding at the concierge and climbing the stairs to her apartment, grabbing the extra seconds gained by not using the lift to compose her thoughts and get her emotions in check.

Only three days apart, the longest since they'd been married.

She'd hoped the distance would be good for her.

Christian sat at the dining table, cradling a coffee and eating a bowl of pasta.

'I saved you some,' he said by way of greeting. 'I thought you might be getting hungry.'

Alessandra had taken her health seriously from the moment she'd realised she was pregnant but since she'd entered the second trimester, she'd become fanatical about her diet.

Food and calorie intake she could control and she did so rigidly, making sure everything she ingested was as nutritionally perfect for her baby as it could be.

It was the only thing she could control. Everything else seemed to be slipping through her fingers.

'How was Hong Kong?' she asked, walking over to her little office space in the corner which was a little too close to the dining table than she liked. Being in Milan made it harder for her to tune Christian out. The apartment she'd always thought of as wonderfully spacious seemed to shrink whenever he was there with her.

God knew she was trying to keep her distance from him, trying to be as unobtrusive as possible.

Thankfully her work load had increased. The days she wasn't on shoots were spent developing the results, spent in meetings with directors whether in person or via conference calls; being busy.

Conversely, Christian's workload had seemed to abate. He now made it home at a decent time most evenings.

Now it was Alessandra holing herself away, burying herself in work. Avoiding him as much as she could.

It was the only way she could keep herself sane.

She'd never imagined marriage would be so hard emotionally, a feeling exacerbated at Stefan's wedding to the beautiful Clio a couple of weeks ago. It had been a wonderful occasion but watching them exchange their vows had brought everything back about her own wedding day and the hope she'd been foolish enough to allow through.

She'd never imagined she would feel so emotional towards him.

'No problems,' he said. 'The contract was signed.'

'How did Kerstin get on?' Good. Her voice was normal as she spoke the German's name.

'Very well. She's staying in Hong Kong for a few days.'

Kerstin had started working for him a couple of weeks before. Right at the exact time as Alessandra's nutrition control had taken on a life of its own.

Typically of Christian, as soon as he'd decided on a course of action he implemented it immediately. He'd decided they should marry—a month later it was done. He'd decided to employ Kerstin—a fortnight later she was his new protégée.

'That's good.' Taking a seat at her desk, she fired up her laptop.

'Are you working?'

'We don't have to leave for half an hour.'

'I wanted to talk.'

'About?'

'We need to start looking for a proper house here in Milan. One we can raise a child in.'

She shrugged. 'Go ahead.'

'I've spoken to a property agent.'

'Naturally.'

'I've shortlisted a couple of homes we can look at after we've seen the obstetrician.'

She could feel his eyes upon her as she placed her memory stick into the side of the laptop. Her hands trembled.

'We need to get moving on this,' he continued. 'I've asked the agent to provide a valuation for this place too.'

She snapped her head round to stare at him. 'I don't want to sell it.'

His eyes narrowed. 'We agreed…'

'No, *you* agreed. I'll let you know when I'm ready.'

Christian counted to ten in his head, fighting to keep his features neutral.

He pushed his bowl across the table and got to his feet. 'We should leave now.'

'We've plenty of time.'

'It's always good to be ahead of the traffic.'

He didn't want to argue with her, especially not prior to their appointment with the obstetrician, but if he stayed another minute in this damned apartment he would go crazy.

He'd given her carte blanche to redecorate all his homes to her own taste so she would come to think of them as her homes too, and what did he get in return? Nothing.

This was Alessandra's apartment, not his. She had no intention of ever making it *theirs*.

It probably wouldn't bother him so much if not for the

fact that the distance between them now came from *her*, a state of affairs that had grown since the embassy function. Even at Stefan's wedding she'd been distant, when normally she thrived at social events.

If he'd thought she was happy with the status quo it wouldn't disturb him so much but, whenever he looked in her eyes, all he saw was unhappiness. When she was with him, she withdrew into herself. He was doing everything in his power to bring her spark back but she resisted at every turn. There were times when he thought he saw glimmers of it, generally if a magazine was released with her photography in it or if they passed a billboard she'd created—her face would light up like an enchanted child's.

It pained him to see her so withdrawn. It unnerved him. It reminded him too much of how things had been with his mother, when nothing he did made any difference to her mood.

Today, he was determined to get to the bottom of it—he would learn whatever it was troubling her and fix it, whether she wanted to talk about it or not.

She must have seen the no-nonsense light in his eyes for she pursed her lips together, slapped the lid of her laptop down and grabbed her handbag.

'Let's go, then.'

All was good with the obstetrician. Alessandra was healthy. Her blood pressure was normal. Their baby's heartbeat was strong. Yes. All was good. Christian always left those appointments feeling lighter.

The good feelings dissipated quicker than normal this time. They'd visited a number of homes in excellent parts of Milan, all large enough to raise a football team, if they so wished, with rooms to spare. Alessandra's interest had been minimal. Grudging.

It only added to his intuition that something was seriously wrong with her.

'Let's get something to eat,' he said after the third viewing. Maybe she was tired.

She didn't argue. 'Where do you want to go?'

He was about to suggest somewhere quiet where they could talk but had a flashback of their date and the trendy restaurant she had led them to. The lively atmosphere there had certainly played its part, along with the alcohol, in loosening them up. Maybe it would have the same effect on her again. 'Let's go to Nandini's.'

He shook the agent by the hand, promised to be in touch soon and waited for Alessandra to get into the back of the waiting car.

Instead she met his eye. 'Can we walk? It's not far.'

He gazed down at her feet. Only small heels on the black boots she wore. Almost practical. Ever the fashionista, though, she wore a black-and-white drop-waisted mini-dress. The gap between the hem of the dress and the top of her boots was tantalising him to the point of distraction.

If anyone looked closely or from a profile view, they would see the hint of a burgeoning bump beneath it.

They walked in silence down the bustling streets, past tourists and locals alike, gazing through windows at the glamorous wares of the now closed shops, and into a narrow street packed with cafés and bars. People sat on tables outside, smoking, eating, drinking and enjoying the weather.

When they'd dined in Nandini's that last time, it had been a Friday evening and the place had been full of people ready to let their hair down after a hard week of work.

Tonight, a Wednesday, it was much quieter. Even the music was on a lower setting, no longer loud enough to burst your eardrums.

A waiter took her jacket then showed them to their booth. She slid onto the long leather seat with obvious relief.

'Are your feet hurting?' he asked.

'A little.' She opened the menu. 'I've been on them all day.'

'Then why did you want to walk?' It made no sense to him. That was why he had a driver at his disposal at all times.

Alessandra shrugged. 'I like walking.' She didn't add that she couldn't face sitting in the back of the car with him any more.

She'd felt his irritation at her attitude to the beautiful homes they'd been shown round. And they *were* beautiful, palatial in size and structure, the kind of homes any little girl dreaming of being a princess would love to live in. But those little girls also dreamt of living in their palatial homes with their princes, not with the man who'd married them so he could have legal rights to their child.

It wasn't that she worried he would bawl her out for her ungrateful attitude—God alone knew, she wished she'd been blessed with acting genes so she could fake pleasure for him—because he didn't bawl her out over *anything*. She knew when she displeased him, though. He might not verbalise it, keeping his anger contained within him, but it was there in his eyes and the tone of his voice when he wasn't quick enough to curb it.

She wished he *would* bawl her out. At least it would show he felt something for her, that she was worth expending some hot air arguing with.

The main reason she hadn't wanted to sit in the back of the car with him was because spending time alone with him had the effect of turbo-charging her emotions. It would be easier to contain if it were just sexual feelings but it ran so much deeper than that. Whenever they listened to their baby's heartbeat, she longed to reach out to him and clasp his hand, to unite for those few magical seconds.

Sitting alone in the back of the car with him, his hard, warm body so close…

She wanted to reach out and grab more than his hand. She wanted to climb onto his lap and nuzzle into that strong neck that smelled so good, taste the smooth skin…

Far from the distance she'd imposed lessening these longings, it had only increased them. She needed proper physical distance, and not just emotional distance, because keeping only an emotional distance wasn't working. The three days apart they'd just had were nothing. Three months might do the trick.

At least tomorrow she had an overnight trip to London without him.

They ordered their meals and drinks, both opting to go straight into the main course. While they waited, they chewed on breadsticks and made idle small talk.

She remembered that first date, here in this restaurant. They'd had to sit close to each other to make themselves heard. They'd talked about anything and everything, their conversation easy.

Tonight it felt as if she were dragging barbed wire from her throat.

As was normal, Christian's phone vibrated at regular intervals.

'You should answer it,' she said upon the fourth vibration.

He shrugged. 'Whoever it is can wait.'

'It might be important.'

His eyes fixed on hers. '*This* is important.'

'*Si*, food is very important,' she answered, as if making light of it could evaporate the growing tension.

A bowl of butternut squash and spinach ravioli with strips of crispy pancetta and flakes of parmesan was placed before her. She didn't know which dish she liked the look of more, hers or Christian's *cotoletta alla Milanese* which looked equally divine.

'Would you like to try some?' He held up his fork, a good helping of breaded cutlet on it.

'No, no, you eat it.' Quickly she forked a delicate raviolo into her mouth, dropping her eyes away from his thoughtful expression.

'Are you still travelling to Tokyo next week?' he asked,

referring to a fashion shoot she'd been booked for for one of Japan's up-and-coming fashion houses. She was looking forward to the trip. Five whole days away from him.

'I was thinking I'd meet up with you there,' he added. 'I've some clients in Tokyo I need to touch base with.'

'Don't rearrange your schedule on my behalf.' Never mind the distance she wanted to take advantage of, he'd made enough sacrifices for her. If all his sacrifices had been purely for the baby's sake, she could have lived with it. But they weren't. He'd made sacrifices for her too. The more she thought of them all, the more nauseous it made her feel.

'I want to,' he said, his voice dropping.

'I think the press are convinced about our marriage now,' she said, keeping her attention firmly on the bowl of food before her. 'I haven't been stalked for days.'

'I'm surprised they haven't picked up on the pregnancy yet.'

'So am I.' It was only a matter of time.

'I will still travel with you. I don't like the thought of you being away for a week without me.'

'It's only five days, not a week,' she corrected. 'I've been travelling with my job since I was eighteen. I'm perfectly capable of looking after myself.'

'You weren't my wife then. Is there something wrong with me wanting to spend time with you?'

Yes, she wanted to scream. There was everything wrong with it. Every minute they spent together made her heart hurt even more that their marriage could never be real, that the love she felt for him could never be reciprocated...

Love?

Where had that thought sprung from?

Amore?

Frantically she fought with herself to deny it, to refute the obvious.

Dear God, had she really fallen in love with her husband?

No. She couldn't be that foolish. She wouldn't be.

In a flash, she remembered the first time she'd seen him, sitting with the rest of the Brat Pack in her brother's den, drinking beer and watching football.

Little Alessandra had taken one look at the blond Adonis and immediately pictured him on a white horse coming to rescue her from the tower where the evil witch held her.

A young girl's crush, that was all it had been. She'd had plenty of them: pop stars, film stars—her bedroom walls had been littered with posters of her favourites. Christian had seemed as remote to her young self as they had been.

Whenever she'd studied the tabloids with stories and pictures of him, and whoever was the latest woman hanging off his arm, she'd felt a funny tugging deep in the pit of her belly. She'd never understood the feeling or what it meant. But now she did understand it.

Her heart had belonged to Christian from that first look.

She'd never imagined any of the pop stars or film stars rescuing her on a white steed. Only Christian.

He hadn't rescued her. He hadn't saved her. All he'd done was unlock her heart.

She'd always wondered how his women could swallow his lies, had assumed he *must* have lied to them to get so many of them into his bed.

He didn't lie. He didn't need to. Women wanted him regardless. *She* wanted him regardless.

She always had.

'Alessandra?'

She darted her eyes to him.

'Is something the matter? You've gone very pale.'

She shook her head with vigour, part in denial and part to clear the burn scratching the back of her retinas. 'Will Kerstin come to Tokyo with us?'

'I don't know. I haven't thought about it.'

'Have you slept with her yet?' The question escaped before she could contain it.

'*Ochi!* What kind of question is that?'

'An obvious one.'

'No, I have not slept with Kerstin, and I am insulted you would think I have.'

'Don't be insulted. It's only a matter of time.'

A dangerous silence followed.

When she looked at him, Christian's eyes had darkened and fixed on her, a pulse throbbing at the junction where his earlobe met his jaw.

Not taking his eyes from her face, he put his knife and fork together on his half-eaten meal and dabbed at his mouth with his napkin, which he then screwed into a ball and released onto his plate.

'Get your things together,' he said, rising to his feet and throwing some euros onto the table. 'We're leaving. I'll wait outside for you.'

She watched him retreat, her heart hammering so hard she could feel the beats in her mouth.

Even her legs were shaking, her whole body one mass vibration of cold fear and misery.

Their waiter appeared with her jacket. 'Is something wrong with your meal?' he asked anxiously.

'No, it's delicious. My husband's remembered an appointment, that's all.'

As promised, Christian stood outside on the pavement with his arms folded.

His car pulled up in front of them. Christian didn't wait for the driver to get out, opening the back door himself and indicating for Alessandra to get in.

She waited until the car was in motion before attempting to apologise. 'I'm sorry if I…'

'I am not prepared to have this discussion in the back of a car,' he said grimly.

'But…'

'Ochi!' he said with such finality she clamped her lips together lest she say anything else.

CHAPTER FOURTEEN

ONCE INSIDE THE APARTMENT, Alessandra hurried to hang up her jacket and remove her boots. 'I'm going to make myself a camomile tea. Do you want anything?'

'No.' Christian's answer was curt. She could feel his anger rippling beneath the surface, just as it had on the drive back from the restaurant when he'd sat beside her with arms folded so tightly she could see the muscles bunched beneath his shirt.

Now his hands were rammed firmly into his pockets.

She headed straight for the kitchen area and with shaking hands filled the kettle. Camomile tea, while not the most palatable of hot drinks, was famed for its calming abilities. Maybe it would help soothe the tumult of emotions shredding her.

Dio l'aiuti, she loved him.

'I'm struggling to understand some things,' Christian said in a tone calm and reasonable. She could hear the undercurrent of wrath beneath it, though. 'I took Kerstin on at your behest.'

Keeping her back to him, she took a teabag from the container. 'You wanted her anyway.' How could he not? Kerstin was *perfect*. She was everything that she, Alessandra, was not. For a start, Kerstin would never be so careless about contraception. If Christian was to have a family with the German woman it would be because they both chose it and not out of a sense of duty.

'Not in the way you're implying.'

'You should.'

'What should I want? To *sleep* with her?'

Did he really expect her to believe his incredulity? This from the man who hadn't touched her, his wife, since the night they'd exchanged their vows. He hadn't laid a single finger on her.

'Why not? She's a beautiful, intelligent woman.'

'Yes,' he agreed. 'That doesn't mean I want to have sex with her.'

'Of course you do. She's exactly your type, all long legs and blonde hair.' Deliberately, she tossed her hair back and flashed a smile. *Hold it together, Alessandra, please; just a few more minutes, keep it together, then this conversation will be over and you can breathe again.* Her fingers dug into the palm of her hands so tightly she could feel her nails pierce the skin. 'Honestly, Christian, I think you're mad for *not* wanting to sleep with her. She's perfect for you.'

'I'm married to *you*. I chose *you*.'

His words cut through her, slicing through her heart and deep into her marrow.

Lies. Lies. Lies.

'You chose me?' she asked slowly, her ears ringing, her heart thundering so hard it reverberated through her skin.

'You know I did. I made my vows to *you*.'

Alessandra twisted round so quickly Christian could have sworn she'd performed a pirouette.

The smile she'd been wearing since their return to the apartment had been nothing but a mask that now ripped away to reveal the savagery beneath the surface.

'You *chose* me?'

'Alessandra…'

'You chose me?' Her husky voice rose with every syllable. Before he knew what was happening, she'd grabbed her cup and thrown it at the far wall. White china exploded upon impact, large chunks flying onto the wooden floor, smaller shards landing like darts around the larger pieces.

'What the…?'

'You didn't *choose* me. You didn't choose to be my husband; you chose to be a father.' Her face was dark with colour, her eyes wild, feral.

He strove for composure. '*Parakalo*. Please, *agapi mou*, I need you to calm down.'

'Do *not* call me that. Whatever it means, *you* don't mean it.'

'It means—'

'I don't care what it means!' Her voice had risen to a scream. 'You want me to calm down? Don't you like me throwing cups? Well, how about plates? Is that what Greek housewives do when their husbands don't want them? Do they throw plates?'

The bowl of pasta Christian had been eating out of earlier, which had been left in the sink, went flying the same way as the cup. Without pausing for breath, she swung open the door of the cupboard that contained all the crockery.

'Alessandra, that's enough,' he commanded.

'Don't tell me what's enough.'

He lunged for her before she could throw the plate she'd taken hold of, grabbing her wrist with one hand and relieving her of the plate with the other. 'I said that's enough.'

Heart pounding, blood surging with adrenaline, he kicked the cupboard door shut, flung the plate on the work surface then pressed her against it, using his strength and height to trap her.

She pushed against him furiously, bucking. '*Bastardo!* Let me go.'

'I will let you go when you've calmed down.'

'I am calm!' she shouted.

'Listen to me,' he said, trapping her face in his hands, forcing her to look at him. 'I do not want to sleep with Kerstin. The only woman I want to sleep with is you.'

Her eyes raged with so many emotions he didn't know where to begin counting them. '*Bugiardo*. Liar.'

'When have I ever lied to you? Name one instance.'

'I...' Her voice trailed off, became smaller. 'You don't want me. You've rejected me since we married.'

'Not want you? Can you not feel how turned on I am?' He laughed cynically. As if she could fail to feel his erection pressed against her abdomen.

That was what happened when you were starved for the woman you wanted more than you'd thought humanly possible. One touch and the body turned to lava, no matter how inappropriate the situation or how vainly you tried to control it.

'I thought I was doing the right thing.'

Her plump lips parted, closed then parted again. 'Why?'

The solitary word came out as a breathless rush, but air did escape, warm, sweet air that filled his nostrils and penetrated down, burrowing through his skin, his veins, down into his arteries and pumping through him in a great rush of need.

Why? All he saw were those lips, luscious invitations to sin.

Why?

He no longer knew. All he knew for certain in that moment was that if he didn't feel those plump lips on his again he would never know the answer to anything.

He crushed his mouth to hers.

There was no resistance.

A tiny, guttural noise came from her throat and she melted into him, weaving her arms around his neck, her nails scraping the nape of his neck, her mouth moving beneath his as she kissed him back, kissing him with a violence that made the heat deep within him enflame and his heart beat like a thousand drums had been let loose within him.

Still devouring her with his mouth, he raised her onto the work surface, her legs parting to wrap around his waist.

Her hands were everywhere, yanking at his shirt to loosen it from his trousers and burrowing up, her small fingers sweeping up his chest, marking him with her heat.

Theos, but she felt amazing.

He found the zip of her dress, was about to tug it down, when Alessandra suddenly wrenched her mouth away from his, pressed a hand to his chest and pushed.

'No,' she said, her tone biting. 'Do not try and distract me by trying to have sex with me. I am not a toy to be played with and then discarded.' She slid down onto the floor and glared at him. Her chest heaved. 'You were going to tell me why you've rejected me since our wedding night.'

Christian raked a hand through his hair, trying valiantly to stem the pumping of his blood. Her taste was there on his tongue, under his nose.

Theos, he wanted to be inside her.

Taking deep breaths, he turned away to rummage through a cupboard. Weeks ago she'd brought a bottle of bourbon to keep in her apartment for him, a gesture that had touched him. A gesture he was now thankful for as a method of numbing his heightened body a fraction.

He'd been on the brink of losing his control with her. Again.

He poured himself a measure and downed it before facing her.

She leant back against the work surface, arms folded across her chest.

This was what he'd wanted just ten minutes ago. For them to talk. For her to tell him what was troubling her. Was it really the lack of sex within their marriage that had caused it? Or something deeper?

What he hadn't expected or wanted was for her to demand the conversation start with him.

'We married for one reason and one reason only,' he reminded her.

'Our baby,' she supplied flatly.

'Yes. For our baby. It's the only reason we married. We did not marry for ourselves. I became concerned that your feelings for me had developed beyond mere convenience.'

Her eyebrows shot upwards. 'You were concerned about my *feelings*?'

'Alessandra…you are an incredibly sexy woman. I would have shared your bed every night since our wedding but I didn't want you mistaking good sex for real emotions.'

'Why would you have thought that? Because I'm a woman and incapable of separating my emotions?'

'No.' It was the light and hope in her eyes when she'd looked at him at their wedding. It was the desolation he'd caught glimpses of these past few weeks.

Alessandra rolled her eyes but there was a definite tremor in her voice. 'And you wonder why I don't want to sell my apartment? Where else am I supposed to go when our marriage falls apart?'

'That is not going to happen. There is no reason for us to fall apart provided we stick to our original agreement.'

'And what if our original agreement doesn't suit me any more?'

A cold chill swept up his spine.

'This is my *home*,' she continued. 'You talk about wanting to leave a legacy for our child? Well, this place is *my* legacy. It's the only thing that's all mine, that I can leave. I'm not prepared to give it up for a man who can't commit to a real marriage.'

'We have a real marriage. Real to us. We both meant our vows.'

'No, we do *not*. Our marriage is no more real than a winged unicorn.'

'Where is all this coming from?' he demanded. The thumping in his ribs no longer had any connection to desire or lust. Fear knotted in his guts but he knew not what the fear was of. 'You knew the score from the start—it's what we agreed on. It's what we both wanted.'

'But now I want something else. I want something more.' Alessandra had seen the way Rocco and Olivia were together. If her brother could find love and be happy...

She had found love too. The problem was she had found it with her husband.

'More? What kind of *more*?' He spoke as if it were a dirty word.

'I want *everything*. I want a husband to sleep with every night, not just for sex but to curl up to. I want to wake up every morning and know that the man I love loves me in return and doesn't regard me as a means to an end. I want it all.'

Christian looked as if he'd been sucker-punched. 'Have you met someone else—is that what all this is about?'

'No.' She stared at him, willing him to understand.

She couldn't hide any more. This was the point of no return. Time for her to lay her cards on the table and see where it took them, for good or ill. 'There is only you.'

She watched as his powerful body froze, the only movement coming from his blue eyes which darkened and pulsed, the look in them as if he were seeing her for the very first time.

'Please, say something,' she beseeched.

'For the love of God—Alessandra, that is not what our marriage is about.'

Her heart lurching so violently she feared she would be sick, she brushed past him, reached for the bottle of bourbon, poured a measure then thrust the glass into his hand.

After he'd downed it and slammed the glass on the work surface, she stood before him and gazed right into his eyes. 'Can you ever love me?'

His face went so white it would have been comical had the situation not been so serious.

'Neither of us believe in love. It's what makes us so compatible.'

How she wished she could have a proper drink too. Just as well she couldn't—the aroma of bourbon playing under her nose made her belly recoil. Or was that terror of where this conversation was going?

Retreat wasn't an option. Not any more. Their time had come.

'This is all your fault,' she said starkly, holding his eyes, refusing to let their hold drop. 'When we married, all I felt towards you was a severe degree of lust. If we'd kept it at sex, I probably would have been fine—lust is intransigent. It would have fizzled out eventually.' But as she spoke the words, she realised them to be a lie. She'd already been in love with him.

'Instead, you withdrew physically,' she continued. 'But you've been…good to me. You look out for me but don't try and inhibit or stifle me. You're supportive and enthusiastic. You made me trust you.'

Something flickered in his eyes at her utterance of the word *trust*. She hardly believed it herself but it was the truth. Somewhere along the line she had begun to trust him. She'd fought it and fought it but it had crept up on her all the same. Just as her love for him had.

'If I'm such a good guy then what is the problem here?'

'This pregnancy has changed me. *You've* changed me. I deserve love and all that it can give. And so do you.'

'Do you hear what you're saying?' he asked roughly, his eyes wild as he took a step back. 'All this crap about love when we both know all it does is destroy people.'

'*No, it does not!* Love only destroys if the person allows it. My father allowed it and so did your mother. We don't have to be like them.'

'You're right—we don't. And we won't. People who take the risk are weak and foolish and I am neither of those things. I thought you were better than that too.'

'Then I must be weak and stupid.'

'I can't be the man you think you want,' he warned. 'I have no capacity to love and, even if I did, I've grown up seeing how dangerous it can be and the knock-on effects it has on everyone else.

'Where are you going?' he demanded when she suddenly turned away and headed for her bedroom.

'To pack.'

'For where?'

'London.'

'Your flight doesn't leave until the morning.'

'I'll see if I can get a sooner one.' She flung her wardrobe doors open, pulled out her small carry-on case and placed it on the bed.

He didn't love her.

He would never love her. He wouldn't even try.

'Can you call me a cab, please?'

'You're not going anywhere. Not until we've talked this through.'

'We're talking it through right now.' She selected some clothes and placed them neatly in the case, then dug her phone from her pocket and pressed the app that would send a taxi straight to the apartment building. 'We can stay married until the baby is born, so you can have the legal rights you want, and then we can divorce. I'm sure we can find an amicable solution to custody—'

She started to zip her case but Christian wrenched it from her, whipping it away and hurtling it to the floor with a slam. She didn't think she had ever seen him so angry. Not that *anger* was the correct word for the wildness surrounding him.

She could hardly blame him. She was destroying the future they had planned. But that had been a future before she'd fallen in love with him.

He gripped her shoulders. 'We made a promise to each

other and our child to be a family. You're breaking that promise. I will not agree to any divorce.'

'Why are you being so unreasonable?' she demanded, her own temper rising back up. 'You're still going to get what you want. You're still going to be a father.'

His hands slid off her shoulders and balled into fists. 'Why are you doing this?'

Because I love you. And I know you will never fall in love with me. And to continue living with you knowing I will never have your love will eventually destroy me just as it destroyed your mother and my father. But not to their extent. Never to their extent. Our child will never suffer for it, I swear.

But the words went unsaid. If she thought for a second there was a chance that in the future his feelings could develop as hers had, she would say them.

What kind of idiot fell in love with a man incapable of returning it?

Had she been fool enough to hope his feelings would change as hers had? *No*, she hadn't been stupid enough to think that. But still she'd fallen for him.

'What do you think the press are going to say when they learn our marriage barely lasted two months?' he asked, his voice cold and terse.

'Let them think and write what they like. I have finally grown an immunity to them.' Three months ago, the thought of them crucifying her for the whole of Italy's delectation had made her want to vomit. Now…let them write what they liked. The fear she had felt of the press since she'd been seventeen had gone. She didn't know when it had happened, only that it had.

She was an adult. *She* controlled her life, not the press.

'And what about when our child grows up and reads about it?' he snarled.

'Then we will tell our child the truth. There's been enough lies.'

Every feature on his face was taut but his eyes were hard. 'If you're so determined to go, then go. Take the time to think. When you get back we can discuss this like rational adults and find a way to thrash out a marriage that suits us both.'

'There's no way thrashing anything out will change my mind. We're over.'

He got back to his feet and strolled past her and into the spare room. *His* room. He'd never wanted to share hers. He shut the door behind him with a slam.

Blinking back tears which served no useful purpose other than to blind her, Alessandra scraped her hair into a tight ponytail, carried her suitcase into the living area and quickly gathered her work stuff together.

Dio, Dio, Dio, get me out of here before he comes back out. Please, before my strength deserts me and I throw myself at his feet and beg for his love.

She left the building and walked straight into a media scrum.

Dozens of paparazzi swarmed her, closing in, leaving her trapped between them and the door she had already closed.

'Alessandra, when is the baby due?'

'Alessandra, how do you feel about becoming a mother?'

'Alessandra, was the baby planned?'

She never got the chance even to think of a response or a way to escape. The door behind her flew open with such force she lost her footing. Were it not for the strong arms there to catch her, she would surely have fallen. As it was, Christian gathered her to him, protecting her with his strength, and marched her and her luggage deftly through the mob and into the back of the waiting cab.

Her last glimpse of him was when he tapped the top of the car to indicate the driver should leave, turned on his heel and marched back through the swarm, parting it as if he were Moses and they were the Red Sea.

* * *

Christian poured himself another bourbon.

He should check himself into a hotel and out of Alessandra's apartment. She'd spelt out in no uncertain terms that this was her home. Not theirs. His homes weren't enough for her.

He wasn't enough.

Did it really matter if they divorced? He'd still have his legal rights with regard to their baby. He would still be a father. Alessandra would never deny him access; that he knew with as deep a certainty as he knew anything. She would do the right thing by all of them.

So why did it feel as if his world had toppled upside down?

And why did he feel so full and nauseous?

He finished his drink and poured another. The bottle was now empty.

Yes. Time to leave.

The freedom and space he'd always cherished so much but had gladly sacrificed for his unborn baby was his again to do with as he pleased.

Under normal circumstances he would hunt down Rocco, Stefan or Zayed and talk them into a night out. But these weren't normal circumstances. Not for any of them. Rocco would sooner spit on him than see him. Stefan had recently shocked them all by marrying Clio—he hadn't seen that coming—while Zayed was spending increasing time in Gazbiyaa, preparing to take over the throne.

All their lives were changing.

He went to grab his briefcase, which he'd left by Alessandra's corner office. Instead of picking it up and leaving, he found himself sitting at her desk, flipping through the portfolios of her work.

As much as he admired all her work, it was their wedding album he spent the most time looking through. These were the unofficial ones taken by Alessandra, a timeline from the start of their wedding week, when their first guests had arrived, right up to the moment they'd got on the dance floor for the Kalamatianos. His lips quirked to see a picture of a particularly beautiful but notoriously moody actress smiling for the camera with something black in her teeth.

His heart jolted when he turned the page over to find a montage of photos of the same face. All different angles, all different moods: some smiling, others distant, a couple frowning... One in particular held his attention. The face was staring directly into the camera, a wide, relaxed grin on the face, a soft yet suggestive look in the eyes, as if the person wanted nothing more than to take the photographer to a private room and make love to them.

Not have sex.

Make love.

The subject of the photographs was him.

Christian pulled up outside Villa Mondelli. Turning off the engine, he stared at it in the same way he had stared at it as a poor eighteen-year-old boy on the cusp of becoming a man. He'd seen lavish splendour before, had walked past the mansions in the most affluent parts of Athens vowing that, one day, he too would live in a home like these. Villa Mondelli was the first of that particular type he'd actually been invited into. Not only invited to cross the threshold but to stay there for a week—and many more weeks later on throughout his life, but of course at the time he wasn't to know that. The Mondellis had welcomed him, Stefan and Zayed into their home and treated him *as if he were their equal*, as if he were more than a dirt-poor gutter rat raised by a single woman with callused hands.

Now, fourteen years later, with homes every bit as opulent as the villa and wealth beyond his dreams, he still felt that same tug in his heart. But this tug was for Alessandra.

When he'd first visited he'd been full of envy for the

people who lived there, brought up with such easy wealth. Or so it had seemed to his eyes.

Alessandra had lived in this house almost her whole life, brought here when her father had lost his own house and abdicated responsibility for his children onto his own father. Alessandra had been a baby. She'd grown up feeling responsible for her mother's death, shunned by her father and raised by an often austere man who'd thought his child-rearing days long finished with. Her only source of love had been her older brother whom, despite all her grumbles at his interfering, she worshipped. For much of Alessandra's life in this home, that same brother had been absent, away in the US studying, graduating to become a workaholic.

More often than not, her only company in this vast house were the staff, people sharing a roof with her because they were paid to.

All the envy he'd felt fourteen years ago had gone, replaced with the sad knowledge that even the richest of people could lead the poorest of lives.

Look at him. He, Christian Markos, was now regarded as one of the richest men in the world. He had all the wealth and all the trappings such wealth brought, but in his heart he was still poor.

It was only now, at the age of thirty-two, that he'd discovered the path to true richness.

He hadn't even placed a foot on the bottom step when Rocco answered the door.

Christian looked up at him. 'I'm here to see Alessandra.' He hadn't seen her in a fortnight. They'd exchanged a couple of text messages. She'd agreed to meet him in Milan for her next obstetrician appointment, but until then she wanted some space.

He'd needed space too, to get his head together. To get his heart together.

Rocco looked him up and down. 'And what if she doesn't want to see you?'

'Has she said that?' A puff of relief escaped from him. His hunch had been right. For all Alessandra's proclamations that she'd rather live in a convent than stay with her brother, this was the first place Christian had looked when she'd failed to return to her apartment after her Tokyo trip.

He'd been there waiting for her.

A long pause. 'No. She doesn't need to.' Rocco made no effort to move.

'Either let me in or I let myself in.'

Now Rocco's face did show some animation, a snarl flitting over it. 'You enter my home when *I* say you do.'

Christian had had enough. He was there to see his wife, not debase himself by getting into a fight with his brother-in-law. Raising himself to his full height, he climbed the steps and stood eye to eye with him. 'I know Alessandra is your sister but she is *my* wife and the baby she is carrying in her womb is mine—*mine*—and I will fight with every breath in my body to protect them. I am going to see her whether you like it or not, so, are you going to let me the easy way or the hard way?'

He couldn't believe it had come to this, two old friends squaring up to each other. If he wasn't so heartsick about his wife there would be some room in his heart to mourn the death of a friendship he'd valued so highly and had hoped, until this precise moment, could one day be mended.

To his surprise, Rocco's stance relaxed a fraction. He looked him over, nodding slowly, his eyes thawing. 'She's in the summer room.'

Christian waited for the catch. When no catch seemed forthcoming, he headed off in the direction he remembered.

'*Memento vivere*,' Rocco called out.

The words made him pause in his tracks. He turned his head and supplied, 'Remember to live.'

Finally a smile attached itself to Rocco's face. 'The best life to live is with the woman you love, *si*?'

He agreed with a nod. 'Living without the woman you love is no life.'

Rocco laughed. 'My sister is going to run rings around you.'

'She already is.' As quickly as Christian's cheeks raised up into a quick grin, he felt a fragmented piece of him re-attach itself.

Now to find his wife and see if all the other broken pieces could be fixed too.

He found her curled up on the daybed, a cross between a *chaise longue* and a sofa, reading a glossy magazine. Beneath the simple black dress she wore, he could see the definite rounding of her belly, safely protecting their baby in its confines.

He would give his life to keep Alessandra and their baby safe from harm.

She glanced up, her eyes widening to see him there. 'Christian.' Her voice sounded hoarse. 'What are you doing here?'

'I've come to bring you home.'

She raised a brow. 'Home?'

'Home. With me. Where you belong.'

Sighing, she put the magazine down and swung her legs round, dipping her head. 'I told you I wanted some space.' Her words were muffled behind the sheath of her hair that had fallen in front of her face.

'You've had enough space from me to last you forever.'

'Nothing's changed…'

'Everything's changed.' Crouching down on his haunches before her, he gently swiped her hair away and placed a finger under her chin.

Her gaze met his for a brief moment, honeyed eyes wide with pain.

'Answer me one question. Do you love me?'

'Are you trying to humiliate me? Is that why you've come here?'

'I found the pictures you took of me.'

Her mouth curled in bitterness. 'Then you already know the answer.'

'I want to hear it from your lips.'

'Why? Let me have *some* dignity, please.'

'Because I've never heard the words before.'

A glimmer of shock passed over her. She sat up straight and looked at him—really looked at him. 'Never?'

'Never.' Not from his mother. Not from any of the scores of women he'd had throughout the years, which wasn't surprising, considering he would leave before the beds had cooled. 'Please, *agapi mou*, if the words are true then say them.'

She'd lost so much colour he feared she would faint. But that was not Alessandra's style. This was not a woman who wilted under pressure. Her lips clamped together, her eyes brimming with tears, he watched her fight to stop from falling.

'Shall I make it easy for you?' he said quietly. 'How about if I were to tell you that I love you? Would that make it easier for you to say the words?'

Her chest hitched as she gave a sharp nod, still not speaking.

'I love you.'

One solitary tear did break free, trickling down her cheek. He wiped it with his thumb.

'I've spent many hours these past couple of weeks looking at those photos you took of me. You see something in me no one else can. The thing I never wanted you or anyone to see.'

'What thing?' she whispered.

'The man inside. The gutter rat who grew up feeling dirty and unworthy and unlovable.'

'You're *not*…'

He placed a finger to her lips, though the sound of her outrage warmed the coldness inside him. 'I've been fighting to stop you getting too close since before our wedding night because I knew you were so near to seeing what's inside me. I thought it would repel you as it does my mother. I knew when you spoke of love in our apartment what you were trying to tell me, but I refused to listen. I didn't think I deserved your love. I was scared that to fall in love with you would be to destroy you—and you, Alessandra Mondelli, whom I so wish would be Alessandra Markos, are the most precious person in the world to me. Without you, I am nothing. I accept that I'm not good enough for you…'

'Will you *stop* saying that?' She dug her nails into his skin. 'You are not a gutter rat. You are…*everything*. Everything you've achieved with your life, everything you've done… If anyone's undeserving, it's me.'

'To me, you are a princess. You deserve all the richness this world can bring, *agapi mou*, and I will do everything in my power to give it to you—if you'll let me. I love you and I don't want to live another day without you.'

Alessandra felt a whoosh of air leave her body. He loved her?

He loved her?

He loved her!

He placed her hands to his chest. She could feel his heartbeat thrumming wildly beneath his shirt. 'I thought I could compartmentalise our marriage in the same way I compartmentalise my relationship with my mother. She lives in a corner of my life, safely hidden away from everyone so she cannot hurt me or anyone else. I told myself I would marry you to become a father and not a husband but I was wrong—I wanted you as much as the baby and was desperate to make you mine. I tried to compartmentalise you, not because I was scared of hurting you, but because deep down I knew *you* had the power to hurt *me*.'

'I have the power to hurt you?' she whispered, gazing at the man she loved so much.

'More than you could ever know. Throughout my childhood I wanted nothing more than to make my mother proud and for her to love me. The power she had over me, the power to hurt me... I swore no one else would ever have that power. But then you came into my life and nestled straight into my heart and there was nothing I could do to stop it. I used to fear that falling in love with someone would curse them, make them turn into her. But you could never be like her. She took her heartbreak and bitterness out on me. You would never do that to our child. There hasn't been anyone else since that first night we had and I know there never will be. Only you.'

He brushed a thumb over her lips. 'I was desperate for you to sell your apartment, not because I thought it made sense in any way but because I felt excluded from it.' He allowed himself a crooked smile. 'I was jealous of an apartment.'

She leaned forward and rubbed the tip of her nose to his, unable to believe this was really happening.

From feeling as if she would never feel the sun on her face again she could feel its beams spread through her.

He loved her!

'I was also afraid that if you had a bolt hole to escape to you would be more tempted to use it,' he continued. 'I should have guessed you would use this place as your bolt hole.'

'I couldn't face being in the apartment without you,' she confessed. 'So I turned up at Rocco's door claiming asylum.'

He laughed. 'He must have been delighted to know we'd fallen apart.'

'No,' she said thoughtfully. 'When he realised I was actually in love with you, the chip he'd been carrying went. He became my brother again.'

His lips were so close to hers. She craned her neck forward, suddenly desperate to feel them upon her, to be cradled in his embrace but he gripped her neck at the side, gently but with enough firmness to stop her moving.

'So, you do love me?' For the first time she saw his vulnerability.

'Yes. I love you. With everything I have.'

She'd hardly finished speaking before his mouth crushed hers, his essence filling her with such sweetness the tears really did fall.

'Oh, my love,' he said, wiping her tears away. 'I never want to see you cry.'

'They're happy tears,' she said with a sniff. 'You're not the only one who's always felt unworthy—I've spent my whole life feeling like a poisoned chalice, put on Earth to destroy anyone who gets close to me.' She stroked his cheek. 'I wanted you to employ Kerstin because I thought she was the perfect woman for you.'

Incredulity spread over his face. 'You were trying to *engineer* me being with her?'

'I thought she could make you happy. You wouldn't have to compromise your time or sacrifice...'

Her words were cut off by a hard, possessive kiss.

'You're perfect for me,' he said when he pulled away, cradling her cheeks to gaze into her eyes. 'Just you. We've both made sacrifices. I would make them again a thousand times over.' He bowed his head and brushed his lips against hers. 'I love you. You're my world.'

'And you're my everything,' she answered softly.

For the first time Alessandra felt a tinge of sympathy for her father, who had gone so off the rails when he'd lost the love of his life. After a fortnight without Christian, she had a little insight into what he must have gone through. She would never be able to forgive him, not for the way his actions had so hurt Rocco—and they had hurt her brother more than her because Rocco remembered a time when their father was a loving man who had adored his small family—but a whole chunk of the bitterness she felt towards him fell away.

'I love you, Christian.'

'Always.'

'Always.'

And they did.

EPILOGUE

'IT'S A GIRL!'

Alessandra didn't know who was the most excited at the giving of the news—the obstetrician or her husband, who announced it in unison while the midwife held the baby—her daughter—up for a few brief seconds before the cord was cut and they whisked her away to clean her up

Christian was back at the top of the table, bed or whatever it was she was laid upon, raining kisses all over her face, muttering prayers and thanks in Greek, English, Japanese, Cantonese and any other language he could conjure.

'You are wonderful,' he said into her ear in a reverential fashion.

'You're pretty wonderful yourself.' She laughed, stroking his hair.

It felt good to laugh.

It felt even better when they placed her daughter on her, allowing a little skin-on-skin time before whisking her back off for swaddling.

'Look in my bag,' she whispered.

'Why?'

'Just look. There's an envelope in the side pocket.'

Doing as he was bid, Christian tore the envelope open and studied the document inside.

After long moments he faced her, his eyes brimming with so much emotion it was like looking into an overflowing bucket.

'Thank you, *Kiria* Markos.'

'You're welcome *Kyrios* Markos.'

It was a document making official Alessandra's name change from Mondelli to Markos.

This was her gift to him, her statement to them both as much as to the world that they were a unit. Their love was for keeps. Cut one and both would bleed. Their baby made them a family. She wanted their little family all to have the same name.

'There is one little problem.'

'Oh?'

He reached into his back pocket and pulled out an envelope.

Inside was a document making official Christian's name from Markos to Mondelli.

Thus, when their swaddled baby was handed to them properly to begin their journey as a family, the first thing their daughter heard was the sound of her parents' laughter.

As beginnings went, it couldn't be bettered.

'Three, two, one, drink!'

In unison, Christian and Rocco raised their glasses to their mouths and downed their shots.

'To Letizia Markos,' said Rocco, picking up his next shot.

'To my beautiful baby,' Christian agreed. 'And to my beautiful wife.'

'Three, two, one, drink!'

Christian had already celebrated the birth of his baby with Rocco, Zayed and Stefan four months before.

Tonight it was Alessandra's turn. She was having her own version of wetting the baby's head in the bar next door with her sister-in-law and some other friends. He suspected theirs would be a much more civilised affair than his had been. But not by much.

Thinking about it, he realised Alessandra hadn't drunk

any alcohol for well over a year, what with the pregnancy and then the four months of breast-feeding she'd done.

Her tolerance would be minimal.

Theos, and she'd insisted on wearing her five-inch heels.

He was all set to bolt out of the bar and hover over her like her own personal guard when Rocco called the barman over for another round.

'Now we need to drink to baby Mondelli,' Rocco said with a knowing look.

'Baby Mondelli?' It took a moment for the penny to drop. 'Olivia, she is…?'

Rocco couldn't hide the beam on his face. 'Yes. I'm going to be a father.'

'That is wonderful news!' Embracing in a manly fashion, the two men then downed their final shots, got to their feet, walked out of the bar and into the next one, both eager to be with the women they loved above all else.

* * * * *

BOUGHT FOR
HER INNOCENCE

TARA PAMMI

CHAPTER ONE

"I HAVE A proposition for you, Jasmine, that would allow you to pay off your brother's debt within a year."

Fear was a cold fist clamped over her spine, but Jasmine Douglas forced herself to stare steadily into the chilly green eyes of Noah King.

That word *proposition* from any other man of her acquaintance, while wholly unwelcome but an awful reality of her life, was something she was used to.

The clientele of the club where she worked, owned by Noah, was constantly under the impression that her scantily clad, gyrating-around-a-pole body was up for sale. That *she* was for sale.

She wasn't and never would be.

Only soul-wrenching fear of the consequences of owing a debt to this man who owned three underground gambling clubs in London, and who was even now contemplating her future without blinking, had forced her into it.

She had barely buried her brother Andrew when she had learned of the debt he had piled up with *Noah King*, of all people. Desperation to resolve this debt and a need for survival forced her every night to take the stage.

So coming from Noah, that dangerous word turned the very blood in her veins into ice. "I've not missed a single payment, Noah," she finally said through a dry mouth.

"Yes, but you're barely making a dent. You have no assets that you could sell off, either."

Her skin turned cold in the comfortably warm warehouse that was the headquarters of Noah's empire. A couple of completely harmless-looking men had showed up at her flat this morning and very politely accompanied her to see Noah here.

Sweat pooling over her neck, Jasmine realized how foolish she was to assume that anything related to Noah King was harmless.

"Am I a prisoner, then?" she said, before she could hold back the reckless question.

Noah didn't even blink as he casually peeled an orange and offered her some. "Until we find a satisfactory resolution, yes."

Her gut dropped and she fought the instinct to turn around and run. No phrase had ever scared the daylights out of her like *satisfactory resolution*.

Why, oh, why hadn't Andrew thought of where his debt would lead him one day? How could he have left her to deal with this dangerous man?

How, after all the promises he had made to her, could he have left her even worse than they had already been?

She had slaved for five years and was still stuck in this man's power, like a fly stuck in a spider's web. The more she tried to get out, the more she was ensnared.

On the heels of that thought came instant guilt. Andrew's face flashed in front of her, his eagerness shining in his eyes, his expression so kind, lodging a lump in her throat.

We'll get out of this dump one day, Jas. You just wait and watch. I'll get us out of here.

Her brother had only wanted what was best for her, had only wanted to improve their lot in life. Had watched out for her for years.

Equipped with no skills, saddled with their mother's

drinking and responsibility for Jas, he had seen no other way out of the hellhole they had been born into except by trying his luck in Noah's gambling den.

Not his fault that he had died so suddenly at only twenty-nine in an accident. Not his fault that everyone they had counted on had disappointed them.

And just like that, as though he was a thorn forever lodged under her skin, like a memory that had been burned into her brain, Dmitri came to mind.

Dmitri Karegas—godson of Giannis Katrakis, textile tycoon and internationally renowned playboy, collector of expensive toys like yachts and Bugattis and...*beautiful women.*

Dmitri, who had grown up along with them on the streets of London after his English father's business went into bankruptcy, whom Andrew had shielded from his alcoholic father numerous times, Dmitri, whom Andrew had treated like a brother, Dmitri, to whom Andrew had gone in need and who had refused to help an old friend while he led a filthy rich life, who had looked at her so coldly at Andrew's funeral and offered her cash.

Dmitri, whose exploits she followed with something bordering on obsession.

Thinking of Andrew would only weaken her; thinking of the man who might have helped was definitely a certain waste of her energies now.

It was as if there was glass in her throat as she looked back at Noah. "How much do I owe?"

"Thirty thousand pounds. It would take you another decade to pay it off if you continue as you do. But if you added a little something more personal to your menu at the club, then I see this going somewhere. You're a huge hit, Jasmine, and I've been getting offer after offer..."

Noah's words came as if from a distance, as if it was

happening to some other person, as if it was the only way
her mind could deal with it… Sweat gathered over her
forehead and the back of her neck, the pungent odor of
alcohol and sweaty bodies that clung to the walls of the
warehouse cutting off her breath.

The only thing that did burn into her mind was that
she would be one step closer to selling herself, if not all
the way. That was what Noah had decided for her. If she
didn't get out now, she never would.

But how? Her lungs burned with the effort to draw
breath; her knees locked in utter fear.

"…unless someone offers to buy out your debt, you
have no choice." Noah's words floated into her mind again.

That was it. That was all she needed—someone to pay
off her debt, to buy her from Noah.

And that someone had to be Dmitri.

No, that ashamed part of her screamed. If she went to
him for help, he would know how low she had fallen. He
would…

Better to sell herself to a known devil than an unknown
one, the rational part of her asserted.

But even Dmitri couldn't just extract her from Noah
King with all the power he had amassed. Not after he had
turned his back on this life and everything in it.

Not if he had become a soft man who spent his days
lounging about on his yacht and nights with women who
did his every bidding.

Jasmine would have to provide Dmitri an opening and
pray that he would take the bait. And if he didn't, the consequences didn't bear thinking about.

The article she had seen in the tech magazine that had
been wrapped around the loaf of warm bread she had
bought at the bakery only last week came to her. She had
nothing to lose at this point and still, everything to gain.

"Put my virginity up for an auction," she said loudly,

the words burning her lips. "Give me a chance to pay it off at once."

A deafening silence filled the hall. Jasmine could feel ten sets of eyes on her, her skin crawling at the obviously male interest in her. Steadily, she held Noah's gaze, immensely grateful that at least his gaze was free of the openly nauseating lust she usually found herself the target of.

But then, Noah was, first and always, a businessman.

His silent appraisal of her gave Jasmine hope. Her breath ballooned up in her chest, crushing her lungs as she waited for his reply.

"You think someone will buy you," he finally said, a greedy glint in his eye. She had caught his interest, she realized, a shaky relief filling her inside out.

"Yes," she said, putting all her confidence in that single word. "Give me a week, Noah, please," she added, desperation coating her throat.

"Three days," Noah finally said.

A shake of his head had one of his thugs accompanying Jasmine to the room she had been brought to earlier.

For a second, Jasmine shook violently from head to toe, utter fear drenching her.

No, she couldn't lose her nerve now.

Switching her prepaid cell phone on, Jasmine clicked the number she had memorized years ago on the clunky keys, every breath coming like a chore. It had been years; he wouldn't probably have the same number anymore.

Even if he did have it, he might not care.

Pressing the cold phone to her forehead, Jasmine held back the hot sting of tears.

This had to work.

She backspaced a few times as her fingers shook on the phone screen. Her stomach tight, her hands clammy, she hit Send and crumpled against the floor.

* * *

In the process of putting his discarded shirt on, Dmitri Karegas flicked a glance toward the blonde provocatively stretched over his bed.

"Come back to bed," she whispered without any fabricated coyness.

What was her name? Mandy? Maddie?

For the life of him, Dmitri couldn't remember such a simple thing. And couldn't manage any shame over it, either.

Work, party, sex—these were the parameters of his life. He didn't hate women, didn't remember deciding to make his life so. But there it was.

He had worked around the clock for the past two months, trying to undo the damage his business partner and oldest friend, Stavros, had wreaked on Katrakis Textiles' stock with his uncharacteristic behavior, and finalizing a coup that had finally landed a nightclub he had been dying to acquire on his portfolio.

So he had found the blonde at the nightclub on his first night looking over his new toy.

She was everything he liked in a woman—willing, wanton, with a wicked tongue to boot. Even better, she didn't fill the silence with inane chatter and hadn't even dropped those usual hints about a budding relationship.

One creamy thigh bared as she slid upward in the bed. Yet as her rose-colored nipples puckered into tight buds under his continued stare, all he felt was an echo of arousal, the way a dog would lift its muzzle at the scent of meat.

Nothing else. Just like the numerous times over the past decade.

He worked, he collected his toys, he slept with willing women, yet somehow Dmitri never felt anything but a surface reaction, as if he was skimming through the very edge of life, incapable of sinking beneath the surface, forever on the outsides of it.

As if what he had turned off all those years ago to live through another day could never be turned on again. Even when he had helped Anya, who had become a sort of a friend, it had been a shallow echo of a different reality, another life where he had saved his mother that night.

Laughter, gravelly and as shocking as if a mountain rose in the midst of the sea, reached his ears, cutting off his unnerving reverie.

It was the afternoon that Leah had invited Stavros and herself to lunch aboard his yacht.

Looking around, he found his jeans and pulled them on.

He had always liked his godfather's granddaughter. But ever since Leah and Stavros had found their way to each other, which he had been damn glad about because all the drama around their marriage had caused the Katrakis Textiles' stock to sink, he had begun finding it distinctly uneasy to be in their company.

He knew what the source of that unease was but he was damned if he gave it voice. Neither did he feel up to the disapproving glance that would come from Stavros.

Even though he was only older by three years, Stavros treated him as if Dmitri was still the sixteen-year-old thug that their godfather Giannis had brought to his estate.

"Leave as soon as you can," he told the woman without meeting her gaze.

As soon as he stepped on the upper deck, Leah pulled away from Stavros and gave him a loose hug. "It's good to see you, Dmitri."

The familiar warmth of her slender body chased a sudden shiver through him, as shocking as if a cavern of emotion had opened up amongst the emptiness. Something must have flickered in his face because Stavros studied him closely.

Ever since Stavros had accepted that he was in love with Leah, after years of scorning Dmitri for what he called his reckless, hedonistic lifestyle, Stavros knew how empty Dmitri felt inside.

"I liked you better before," he said roughly, warning Stavros away.

Leah looked between them, frowning. "What?"

"Nothing," Stavros delivered in a flat tone. The knot of his gut relented a little and Dmitri breathed easy, slipping into the mode of that reckless playboy that was bone-deep now.

He pulled a chair for Leah and signaled to his staff to serve lunch. Pulling on a practiced smile, he looked at Leah. "So what has prompted you two to emerge from your love nest a week before the wedding?"

Leah sighed. "I would like for you to give me away at the wedding. Giannis is not here and you mean a lot to me, Dmitri."

"How many more times do I have to give you away?" he teased while intensely glad that she had asked him.

Her gaze twinkling, Leah grabbed Stavros's hand and laced her fingers through his. "Just this one more time."

After years of shouldering duty and knowing nothing but rules, Stavros had finally found a measure of happiness with Leah.

Holding Stavros's gaze, because he would die rather than betray anything else that he might be feeling to his friend, Dmitri said, "It will be my pleasure, Leah."

The sharp chime of his cell phone drew his attention. Frowning at the strange number, he clicked it.

I need help, Dmitri. Call Noah and find out. Do this for Andrew.

A cold nail raking over his spine, Dmitri stared at the message.

Images and sensations—his father's drunken rages, his mother's tired face, his own powerlessness, stinking alleys filled with Dumpsters, fistfights and broken noses, sobbing when Andrew held him hard, and a girl with huge, dark eyes in her oval face...

Jasmine...

Christos, the message is from Jasmine.

His gut clenched so hard that he pushed at the table and stood with a growl, a violence of emotion he hadn't known in years holding him in its feral grip.

Noah... Noah King... The man who ruled over the lowlifes of London like a king ran his empire... Lending and extortion, bars and nightclubs, pimps and prostitution, there was no pie that Noah didn't have a finger in.

And Jasmine was caught in it.

A soft hand on his arm brought him back from the pounding fury... He turned to see Leah staring at him with such shock that his breath burst into him in a wild rush.

On his other side stood Stavros, his gaze filled with concern. "Dmitri, who was that text from?"

"Jasmine." Even saying her name sent a pulse of something through Dmitri. As if he was opening a door he had closed on the worst night of his life. As if he was suddenly a spiraling vortex of emotion instead of empty inside.

"Jasmine, as in Andrew's sister?" Stavros's understanding was instant.

"Yes, she is in trouble," he replied, running his hand through his hair.

His muscles pumped with the need for action; he wanted to smash something, he...

"Dmitri, let's discuss what needs to be done," Stavros interjected calmly, as if aware of how raw he felt. Of course, his friend knew.

He opened the message and read it again. He had thought Jasmine better off without his interest and instead, she had been right there in that veritable hell all these years.

How? How was Jasmine in trouble with Noah King? What had Andrew done?

Instructing Stavros to wait, he made a series of calls, pulling every contact he had made during his life on the streets of London.

In twenty minutes, he had the gist of the situation, and it sent his sanity reeling.

Noah King had set Jasmine's virginity up for an auction and she was texting for help.

If he hadn't spent the first fifteen years of his life in that pit, he wouldn't have believed it. The thing that burned him, though, was that she didn't ask for help. Not even now.

Instead, she'd reminded him that he owed Andrew for the countless times he had saved Dmitri from his alcoholic father's rages and then from any number of fistfights that could have killed him.

Did she think he wouldn't come unless it was to pay off a debt?

Shoving away the infernal questions, he turned to Stavros. "I…need as much cash as we can drum up instantly, upward of a hundred thousand pounds at least."

Stavros didn't even hesitate before he called their accountant. "Anything else?" he asked after he had finished.

"You're the only one I trust. If this goes sideways, I want you to…take care of Jasmine."

Stavros didn't even try to stop him, only nodded. He had taught Dmitri what it meant to do his duty.

Maybe this was his chance to start afresh. Maybe he

would have his own freedom from the guilt and emptiness that had plagued him for more than a decade once he'd set Jasmine free.

Jasmine was startled awake from a fitful sleep by the soft creaking of the door. Adrenaline deluged her and she choked down on the scream building in her chest. Slowly, she reached for the knife and sat up toward the edge of the bed. She wasn't going to leave her safety to chance.

Thankfully, the bed was in the darkest part of the room.

Noah, for all the ruthless chill in his eyes, wouldn't lay a finger on her. But John, his younger brother… She had seen that lust in his eyes every time she had run into him at the club.

She would have only one chance at striking out and she intended to take it without fail. She didn't wonder if there was a chance to escape or if Noah would rip into her for attacking his brother.

All she cared in that moment was that no one pinned her on that bed, that no one touched her.

Footsteps that were as light as her own treaded the cheap linoleum floor and she waited, crouching.

The moment the faint shadow moved, she attacked soundlessly. Her knife sliced through the air and scratched at something before she was plucked off the bed as if she was a feather.

She lashed out with her fists and legs, her screams choked by a rough hand that found her mouth effortlessly.

Her struggle lasted all of two seconds. She was grabbed and hauled against a hard body, knocking the breath out of her while a viselike arm clamped around her middle.

"Stop struggling or I will walk out and not look back."

Mindless with fear, Jasmine dug her teeth into the hard

palm, squeezing and pushing against the steel cage that clamped her.

The hold against her waist tightened, long fingers pressing into her belly and almost grazing the underside of her breasts.

But John's body wasn't honed to steel like the one holding her was, the thought pulsed through the fear. John was fleshy, round. John was... The body that held her tight was all hard muscles and sharp angles, the scent that filled her nostrils not of sweat and other body fluids but clean with a touch of water to it.

Like the ocean breeze. And only one man she knew had that intoxicating scent that had muddled her senses the last time, too.

She had been drowning in grief at Andrew's funeral, and the sight of him, all stunning and sophisticated and so different, that crisp scent of him as he had neared her had sent her on a tailspin.

"Dmitri?" she whispered, every hope, every breath hinged in that name, her pulse fluttering so fast that it whooshed in her ears.

The tightness of his hold relented, a sudden shift in the hardness that encased her. His breath landed on the rim of her ear, tickling her. "At your service, Jasmine."

Relief came at her in shuddering waves, her lungs expanding, her throat thick with pent-up fear.

Long fingers moved up and down her arms, stroking her. "Breathe, *pethi mou*."

A streak of longing rent through her at the endearment, tearing at the hardened chunk of self-imposed loneliness that was her core. God, she hadn't been held like that in forever.

"You came," she whispered, feeling light-headed and shivery.

"Your faith in me will bloat my ego." Silky smooth and

dripping with sarcasm, his words were a whiplash against her fading willpower.

Anchoring her fingers on his forearms, she forced her spine to straighten. "From everything I hear about you," she said, her relief fading with a welcome burn of anger and grief she had nursed for the past few years, "your ego, *among other things*, is apparently already big enough."

Waves of his laughter enveloped her. His mouth opened in a smile against her jaw, sending a burst of such shocking heat through her nerves. She didn't dare turn and glance at him, for fear of combusting alive on the spot.

Why was she reacting like this to him? Was it shock?

"John's lying outside—"

She tried to jerk away from him. "God, you killed him?"

Another lethal smile flashed at her. "I promised my godfather I wouldn't waste the life he gave me."

"Nice to know you keep some of your promises."

"And then there is Stavros," he continued smoothly, ignoring her ungrateful little remark, "whose wedding is in a week, and he would not appreciate being dragged into my mess." He sighed. "So tempted as I was, I didn't kill him. I don't even use my fists anymore except to hit Stavros," he added. "And believe me, if that isn't exercising self-control, I don't know what is."

Jasmine had no idea if he was serious or joking. The fact that he had answered her request for help, even though it was what she had fervently prayed for, hit her hard now.

Was it because she hadn't expected the infamous playboy to come himself? Because she had relentlessly, *and a little obsessively*, hoped that the soft lifestyle had softened him?

Had somehow made him less?

Instead, the body that encased her felt as if it was made of steel. Realizing that she was leaning into him, she threw her elbow out.

His breath hissed out of him. "Now that we have finished our introductions, are you ready to leave this dump?"

"Dmitri…why did you attack John? Why're you here in the middle of the night?"

Darkness shadowed his face, the fluorescent light caressing his face here and there. The light gray of his eyes was the only thing she could see. And in one glimpse, they burned with such ferocity that Jasmine dropped her gaze. "I hit him because I remembered how much of a bully John was and because he was sniffing around outside your door. And I'm here at midnight because I don't trust Noah not to up the ante by morning—"

One question burned on her lips. "Did you…pay off the debt, Dmitri?"

"I didn't just pay off the debt, Jasmine. I won the—" he slipped into Greek and Jasmine had no interest in learning what the pithy word was "—*auction*. Now stop acting the damsel in distress and move, *thee mou*."

The endearment, echoing with mockery, lanced at her. "I'm not a damsel, neither am I naive enough to assume that you're a white knight."

The second her words left her, she wanted to snatch them back.

His teeth gleamed in the dark. "It heartens me to know that you know the score. I'm no white knight, neither will I risk loss of limb to save your hide."

"No?"

"No. But you already know that. What did you call me at Andrew's funeral—a self-serving bastard who doesn't know the meaning of honor or loyalty? Throwing some money at Noah to *buy* you is one thing. But my generosity doesn't stretch far enough to risk myself. So how about we postpone our chat?"

The dark of dawn cloaked them as they exited into the

street. A gasp left her as she saw the sleek Bugatti motorcycle tucked neatly out of sight.

So what the dirty rags reported about his lifestyle was true. Bugatti bikes, and a yacht and countless women—Dmitri Karegas finally had everything he had ever wanted.

And he hadn't lifted even a finger to help Andrew.

I have asked Dmitri for help and he cut me off, Jas. He's not the boy we knew once. Andrew's words resonated in her head, building a fire of hatred in her gut. But he had helped her today, the sensible part of her piped up.

"You're staring at it as if it were a viper that would strike you."

Feeling the intensity of his perusal, she shook her head.

It didn't matter what Dmitri had become. It *couldn't* matter to her.

He was an old friend who happened to have enough money to bail her out of a sticky situation. She would pay him back, even if it meant she would have to go hungry half the time, and they would be through with each other and that would be that.

"Jasmine?" Dmitri probed softly.

Cold October wind pressed against the exposed skin at her neck, sinking and seeping into her flesh. The worn-out sweatshirt she had pulled on last night offered meager protection. Her muscles shivered at the biting cold.

He chucked off his leather jacket. And held it out to her.

Her hands wrapped around herself to ward off the cold, she stared back at him.

"I don't need it…" Her teeth chattered right in the middle of her sentence. Bloody traitorous body! "I'm fine," she finished lamely.

He said nothing, his hand still stretched out toward her.

The silence between them stretched, sharply contrasted by the growing traffic around them. He pushed the helmet down onto his head. Though his face was hidden by the visor, Jasmine could feel the thread of his fury beneath it.

His very stillness in the wake of it was disconcerting and she marveled at his control.

Why? Why was he so angry with her? Why couldn't he take the damn helmet off so that she could properly look at him, so that she could at least guess his thoughts?

She must still be under shock after the past few days because somehow the latter mattered more to her than his anger.

She wanted to see those solemn gray eyes; she wanted to see that broken blade of his nose, the tender smile that had always curved his mouth just for her. The strength of how fiercely she wanted to feel those arms around her once again… It was insanity.

More than anything, she wanted to see how much he'd changed from the sixteen-year-old who had left with his wealthy godfather.

From as far back as she could remember, Dmitri had been rough, almost violent, got into every fight he could manage. Only Andrew had been able to calm him, reach him at a level that no one could.

His mother's death did that to him was all her brother would say when she probed. She remembered how fiercely Dmitri had fought against leaving with his godfather. It had taken Andrew countless hours to convince him.

But once he'd left, Dmitri hadn't looked back. Not once.

He had easily forsaken Andrew and all the promises he'd made, had become the überwealthy playboy who cared nothing for those he had left behind.

And then he'd started appearing in the gossip columns, his wild parties, expensive toys and the countless women he dated—*dated* being a euphemism—making him infamous. One time, he had even come close to marrying a Russian supermodel.

In short, his life now was spheres away from hers.

"Before you read something into this—" she sensed his sardonic smile rather than seeing it "—it's like putting a tarp on my Ferrari or a fresh coat of paint on my yacht, Jasmine. It's about protecting my possessions."

A gasp escaped her at how effortlessly cruel he was. "I still don't want it."

"Fine, freeze to your death, then."

He pushed the helmet over her head. With precise movements, he tugged the ends of the strap together tight around her chin. Jasmine jerked at the touch of his long fingers against her jaw and cheeks, a searing heat stroking her skin. The click of the strap reverberated in tune with the thud of her heart.

"I don't need—"

"I'm very possessive of all my toys."

She slapped his hand away from her chin, her rising temper drowning out the confusion. With movements as measured as she could make them, she got on the bike.

"I'm not a bloody toy that you acquired. You're just as bad as the lot of them."

Her words got cut off as the bike started with a sleek purr, pulled off like a cannon and the momentum almost threw her off the backseat.

The very real risk of flying off the bike claiming her, Jasmine held on to his shoulders, taking care to not touch him more than necessary.

A distinct sense of unease settled between her shoulder blades. What had she risked by trusting a man who had no loyalty, who thought his roots were nothing but a dirty stain that had to be removed?

CHAPTER TWO

THROUGH LITTERED STREETS and narrow alleys, Dmitri drove on and on, feeling as if the very devil was on his heels.

Usually, he felt as if he was the king of the world as the sleek machine responded to his every request, purred into a beauty of motion. Usually, he found escape from the emptiness in his gut when he drove his bike or when he took his yacht out onto the ocean.

With the wind whipping at him and the world going motionless around him, the pure throttling power of it had always calmed him.

He knew nothing of that calm now. A cascade of emotions and feelings deluged him, and it was as if he was still trying to breathe, trying to stay afloat.

It was going back to that neighborhood, he decided with a choked-back growl.

His life had been a veritable hell all those years ago and not for the reason that Stavros and Giannis assumed. Being there, he thought, would surely send him spiraling into that angry, violent teenager Giannis had suddenly found on his hands.

And it had.

That same anger and fear and shame had instantly corralled him the moment he had seen the familiarly grungy warehouse, smelled the nearby leather factory. The suffocating stench of his failure clung to his pores.

Like an invisible rope had loosened the tether he kept

on the memories he locked away, like his skin could flinch and smart again from scars that had healed on the surface long ago.

He hadn't felt this out of control since…since the night his mother had died. The road curved dangerously ahead and he throttled the gear, curving into it.

A tentative hand pressed into his shoulder, his name a soft whisper on the periphery of his roiling emotions. Jasmine's slender body slammed into him from behind, her arms vining around his midriff like clinging ropes. Her mouth was near his ear and her terrified voice broke through the black shroud of past.

"Dmitri, *please*…slow down."

Her soft entreaty finally punctured through him and he slowed.

Her hands wound around his waist snugly. She was plastered to his back from cheek to chest, and a sigh left her mouth. He clutched her hand at his waist and she pressed back silently. He didn't know who sought comfort from whom, but there was something about her embrace that calmed the turmoil inside him.

That life was over, he reminded himself. Andrew was far beyond his help. His mother was far beyond his help.

He had nothing to recommend about himself to a woman, but he had oodles of money. And with it, he would ensure Jasmine never went back to that world, would set her up for the rest of her life and walk away.

They stopped finally after an hour, dawn streaking the sky a faint pink. Her muscles cramping at sitting so still and erect on the bike, Jasmine got off the bike shakily, her legs barely holding her up.

From a dingy, neon-lit back alley to the sophisticated elegance of The Chatsfield, London, it was as if she had fallen through a tear in the fabric of the city.

Chauffeured luxury vehicles rounded the courtyard even at this time, designer-clad men and women making their way to the entrance.

Her neck craned back, she took in the majestic building and then looked down at herself. Dressed in washed-out jeans and a thin, baggy sweater, she felt like a mangy dog that the liveried bellboy would shoo away any second.

With a masculine elegance, Dmitri got off the bike and handed the keys to an eagerly waiting, uniformed valet. He came to stand next to her and instantly, a storm of butterflies unleashed in her belly.

Heat crept up her chest as she remembered the restrained power in his leanly coiled body.

After years of dreaming about getting out of that life, the reality of it happening had hit her hard. Driven by a growing sense of freedom and fear at how fast he had been going, she had wrapped herself around him. She had only sought comfort in a distressing moment, and yet now it felt shameless and weak, smacking of a familiarity that she didn't want him to think she presumed.

He hadn't pushed her off the bike, so that had to count for something.

The frigid air that met her nostrils was coated with the scent of him, and somehow became the familiar anchor in a sea of strangeness.

"You should have told me where we were going," she said, aware of the belligerence in her tone and not able to stop it.

She hated feeling as if she didn't belong. And the sad truth of her life was that she belonged in that dingy alley rather than here. She belonged more in that club that catered to the most basic sins than in this posh elegance, with men like Noah and John rather than the man Dmitri had become.

He took her elbow and pulled her forward. "You don't sound happy to be out of there."

Keeping her gaze ahead, which was sure going to break her neck, she quipped, "More like not happy to be out here. I don't want to go in there, Dmitri. I just need a few more minutes of your—"

"We're going to need a lot more than a few minutes to sort things out, Jasmine. And if I can belong here," he threw at her arrogantly, "then you can."

"Sort out...what? Why?"

His long fingers dug into her flesh as if to jostle her. She pulled at his grip with her fingers but he didn't relent. "You will not look at me. Why?"

She angled her head and caught a quick glimpse just to defy him.

Piercing gray eyes held hers in an open challenge and she turned away.

The doorman held out the door for them, a familiar smile on his face. Dmitri greeted him by name and Jasmine followed slowly. He had been so close all these years. And she had never known.

"You stay here regularly?"

"Yes."

"I didn't realize you visited London anymore."

"And you would know because you have kept in touch?" An impression of contained energy and a barely civil smile hit her. "Stavros prefers to look after the Athens side of the business."

Entering the brilliantly lit lobby from the dark, hushed luxury of the outside was like stepping into a different world. Jasmine blinked and stared around, losing her bearings for a few minutes.

Black-and-white art deco flooring complemented soft beige walls while a stunning, magnificent chandelier took center stage in the vast space. Bold lines and sweeping curves made the hotel look timelessly elegant.

And Dmitri stood in the center of it all.

Black jeans and black leather jacket made him look effortlessly breathtaking, the long, lean lines of his body drawing looks from more than one woman even in the predawn hours.

He might have started where she did, but there was an aura of casual power and panache that made Dmitri not just blend, but stand out amidst the extravagant grandeur of the hotel.

At five-ten, she matched his six-three stride easily. She only wished she could say the same of her clothes and more important, her insides. The vast foyer felt as if it would take forever to cross and all she wanted to do was to fade away from the brilliant lights.

It was not that she thought herself plain. On the contrary, she had heard all her life, and felt nauseous, that she was exotic, lush, possessed of perfect voluptuousness for her vocation. She was stared at six nights of the week and earned her living making love to a pole, but it was how she felt next to the casual elegance of the man next to her that bothered her.

The shame that always clung to her, as if it was etched into her very skin, was amplified when she stood next to him. Just as it stung her that he had seen her at such a weak moment.

As if suddenly he was a measure of her looks, her world, her very life.

She flinched when he pulled her away from the reception area toward the bank of elevators. He held her loosely and yet a thread of his emotions, not so contained, brimmed within him.

Beneath that polite smile, she had a feeling he was ragingly furious. And she was afraid of finding out why.

"The hotel is fit for a king," she said, trying to keep the utter awe she felt out of her words.

"I have a feeling that you're the opposite of impressed."

The doors of the lift closed with a soft *ping*, trapping them inside. Her heart beat like the thundering hooves of a horse when he hit the stop button.

"You have to look at me now, Jasmine" came his soft command.

"You're making a big deal out of..."

"Are you afraid of me, *thee mou*?"

Shaking her head, she looked up.

The four walls of the lift were glittering mirrors that showed her a stunningly gorgeous face.

Her femininity, beaten down and stuffed into a bag, roared a primal scream of joy at the sight of the magnificent man in front of her. Every inch of her—from her skin to her breasts, from her cells to her core—stood to attention.

His legs crossed at the ankles, his hands gripping the wall behind him, he filled the space with his masculinity. Something else burst into life in that enclosed space, swelling and arching, until Jasmine felt as though there was a hum inside her every nerve.

Even at sixteen, he had had arresting features, but now...the power he exuded and his command of the world filled the planes and angles of his face, making him a lethal combination of stunning looks and effortless masculinity.

Long, curly lashes kissed cheekbones that were honed so sharp that it was like looking at the work of a master sculptor. Deep-set gray eyes studied her just as hungrily as she studied him. As if he knew her volatile reaction to his nearness.

Of course he knew, Jasmine scolded herself. There couldn't be a man alive who looked like Dmitri and didn't know it, didn't wield it to his advantage. And the fact that she, too, with all the rules she had set in place to be able to face herself in the mirror, was staring at him with googly eyes, measuring herself against him… That woke up Jasmine like nothing else could.

Now she understood the sense of danger that had skittered through her very blood when he had held her from behind so intimately.

The danger to her didn't come from him. The danger to her came from her reaction to him.

CHAPTER THREE

DECIDING THAT HE would protect her at any cost was one thing, Dmitri thought as Jasmine devoured him with those wide eyes.

The actual logistics of what he would do with this wild creature were quite another. With lush breasts and narrow hips that swayed with every step she took, from the way she tucked that tumbling jet-black hair behind her ear to the pouty mouth that came from no injection, Jasmine was not simply beautiful, but stunningly sexy.

Was that the reason for that ridiculous auction? Had some man coveted her because of those Arab genes that she had inherited from an absentee father, and Noah had turned it to his advantage? What horrific scheme had she caught herself in?

Round jet-black eyes, dark arched eyebrows that suited perfectly those big eyes, a sharp, bladelike nose and a pointed chin.

There was not an ounce of extra flesh on her face, giving her a lean, sharp look. As if every bone in that face had been sculpted by years of hunger and sleepless nights. Her hair, jet-black and thickly curling, was pulled back tightly, exaggerating the feral sharpness of her features. One curl dangled alongside a sharply defined jawline.

There was an alert look in her eyes even now, just as there had been in that warehouse. The straight, tense line of her shoulders, her sharp breaths... He realized how alien this was to her.

How alien he was to her...

When he had seen her five years ago, she had barely turned eighteen, and had looked nothing like this...except for that wary distrust.

It had been there then, too. But where she had barely glanced at him then, her bold gaze drank him in today.

He had never experienced such a thorough, artless appraisal. Women came on to him all the time and he enjoyed it, but Jasmine's searing gaze was more than basic female curiosity.

It was as though she was looking for something, or someone. And instead of that shallow echo he was so used to, he felt something inside him vibrate in response to her look.

As if a part of him that had lain dormant and unfeeling for so long suddenly uncoiled itself at the sight of her. Dangerously tempting and thoroughly unwise... He wondered how to distance himself from it.

Because as hungry as he'd been to feel something like that, he had nothing to give her.

"No one would know you were from the streets," she said with a brittleness that he wouldn't have associated with her.

"And why do you sound as if that's the worst thing in the world, Jasmine?" He would not call her Jas even though it fluttered on his tongue. Which was strange, because how could a woman's name have so much power over him? "It's a pit of desperation and addiction and violence. Why should I ever want to look as if I belonged there once? Why should anyone who had a chance to get out of there still cling to it?" Steel resonated in his voice at the end there but he couldn't help it.

Her eyelashes fluttered, and he had a feeling she was

trying to calm herself down. She failed. When she looked at him, she fairly bristled with aggressiveness. "Of course not. And God forbid anything stand in the way of you leaving the past behind, Dmitri, anything even remotely dirty and poor taint your extravagant lifestyle now."

He pushed off the wall, furious energy burning through his veins. Instantly, she flattened herself against the wall. And the startled look in her eyes more than anything calmed him down.

Let her think what she wants, he told himself.

He had never cared what the world thought of him. Why would he care about what Jasmine said? But he couldn't allow her to taunt him like that; he couldn't allow her to think even for a second that she knew him.

He turned all the energy in him into cutting scorn, delivering it in a silky-smooth tone. "Before you castigate me for wanting out of that life, let's not forget how this night started, *thee mou*. Let's not forget whose money and power saved whose ass in this story, *ne*?

"Maybe you believe your life is not valuable enough to get out of there, but I will not feel guilty for thinking mine is. Nor will I feel guilty about enjoying the fruits of my hard labor. Giannis might have—"

"Pulled you out of the hellhole that was our life, but I know that it was you and your friend…"

"Stavros Sporades," he added.

"That it was you two that put his textile company on the global map, especially when everything else is folding in this economy," she added, as if she was offering him recompense for angering him. "I have followed your—" he had a feeling she wouldn't say the actual word that she wanted to "—success the past few years."

And suddenly, it was as though a hard fist jammed into his throat. She had known he was rich, then. She had known that he could have helped. Even as she refused to admit it, she had known, all along, that he would come if she asked.

And yet, she had waited so long… Which night would have made it too long?

Fury, reminding him of broken bones and painful fists, flew hot through him. "Have you? Gratifying to know that I held your interest for so many years, *pethi mou*. And a little shocking that you have somehow lost the good sense I thought you possessed."

The lift opened just then and he walked out without checking to see if she followed.

By the time she walked past the dramatic reception hall into the sitting lounge of the suite, Jasmine felt numb to the extravagance of her surroundings.

It was a toss-up between the electricity that burned between Dmitri and her and the reach of his wealth and sphere.

A finely carved wood and marble fireplace dominated the lounge, which was decorated with black leather furniture.

Her running shoes sank into the thick carpet with a soft hiss.

Jasmine had barely caught her breath when a woman walked into the lounge. Her hair was mussed around her fragile, sleep-ruffled face, her long legs bared in shorts.

"Dmitri?" she whispered, her shocked glance taking in the both of them. "You took so long…"

"Leah? What are you doing here?" The concern in Dmitri's voice was as unmistakable as the lacerating sarcasm when he addressed Jasmine.

Suddenly, being a spectator to a romantic reunion between Dmitri and his latest girlfriend was the last thing Jasmine wanted to be.

The woman crossed the last few steps, genuine worry

etched on her brow. Dmitri enfolded her so gently that it sent a pang through Jasmine. "When you were taking so long, he dropped me off here. He's been calling every fifteen minutes..." Her gasp pierced through Jasmine.

"Dmitri, you're bleeding." With that, Leah clicked her cell phone on and left the room.

The sharp hiss of his exhale, the way he had held himself so rigidly on the bike... Her gut heaving, Jasmine turned him around roughly and lifted his leather jacket.

A patch of red stained the tear on his pristine white shirt around his abdomen, a stark contrast against the rest of it.

Jasmine stared at the dried blood and the way the shirt clung to his skin. Bile filled her throat as the metallic scent washed over her. Shivers set forth from the base of her spine. As if her attacking Dmitri when he had come to save her was the last straw...

Pressing her hand to her forehead, she tried to breathe past the rawness in her throat. "I could have killed you... I thought John would sneak in in the middle of the night and I was just being cautious... I never..."

"I did not ask why you attacked me," he said in that monotone voice again. He sounded angrier at her being upset than that she had wounded him. "*Theos*, I don't care that you tried to protect yourself. I care that you have led a life that requires that you sleep with a knife under your pillow."

She flinched at the disgust in his words.

For as long as she had known, men had only looked at her cheaply, with lust glimmering in their eyes. And once she had started working her current job four years ago, it had only gotten worse, shame and self-disgust her only companions.

So why the hell did she care what Dmitri thought of her?

His hand under her chin, he lifted it up. She clutched her eyes closed to lock away the tears. The depth of her reaction to him, his words scared her.

"Look at me, Jasmine." Something rumbled in that soft command. She would have called it desperation if she thought she could hold together one sane thought at the moment.

His hands moved up and down her arms as if he was calming down a spooked animal. "You're shaking again. *Theos*, stop being afraid of me."

"I'm not afraid of you," she whispered, opening her eyes. Dark stubble surrounded that carved mouth. "I'm so sorry, Dmitri..."

He shook his head. "You grazed me really good with the serrated edge but it's only a flesh wound."

She ran a shaking finger over the mended bridge of his shattered nose, a tendril of desperate emotion engulfing her.

"I don't remember ever being so terrified as that night when John punched you," she said, remembering the horrific night when John had broken Dmitri's nose. "I thought you would kill him."

A haunting memory flashed through those deceptively calm eyes. "If not for Andrew, I would have." A smile cut his mouth then, transforming his face again. It was like seeing someone intensely familiar slip on a mask and become a stranger. "For a woman who defends that filthy world, you're acting strange at the sight of a little blood."

Her finger moved down his nose, hovered over his mouth, her heart thundering in her chest.

"Jas..." Her name was a raw warning on his lips.

An immense stillness seemed to come over him, the faintest of shudders moving his narrow seamed mouth. His fingers clasped her wrist tight, as if he was truly afraid of her touching his mouth. "You're still in shock."

Was he convincing her or himself? she wondered. She had seen her mum waste herself away in a bottle of rum, had seen Andrew breathe his last... Grief and fear for her life had all been consuming her since Noah's men had arrived at her doorstep three days ago, and yet it was this moment that threatened to shove her heart out of her chest...

This craven yearning to touch him, to discover if there was anything left of the boy who had treated her as if she was the most precious thing he had ever held... It was madness.

Because he had left that boy behind a long time ago when he had walked out with his godfather. Leaving Andrew and her behind.

Far, far behind.

"Dmitri?" a man's deep voice called.

It jolted her out of her feverlike delirium and Jasmine tried to collect her breath.

"It might be a flesh wound, but you should still have it sterilized and cleaned up," the man continued. "It doesn't look as though Jasmine uses that knife for chopping vegetables."

She looked up to find Dmitri looking at her with a sardonic gleam in his eyes, his brows raised in question.

He held her wrist aloft and returned it to her side. Then he gently nudged her back. To his friend, he added, "Hand me the first-aid kit, Stavros."

Enough, Jas!

Was she so desperate for a connection from their awful past, so lonely that even Dmitri's begrudging help would do?

She was damned, however, if she let his posh friends walk all over her, or insult her dirty roots.

Stavros, whose face was a study in austerity and cold arrogance, gazed at her, his expression inscrutable.

"I assure you, Mr. Sporades, my knife is not as filthy as you imagine."

A smile touched the man's mouth but his expression didn't lose the severity. "You mistake me, Jasmine," he said, assuming a familiarity that shocked her. "I'm in awe of how cunningly you found a way out of your predicament. Although I—"

"He wishes, *rightly*—" Dmitri cut in, frost turning his eyes into a thundering gray "—that you had not put yourself in such a dangerous situation in the first place."

"Put myself in that situation? You talk as if this was a game to me. You think I...I wanted to *sell* myself like that?"

Such a savage growl erupted from Dmitri that it was like seeing a cat transform into a tiger, vicious claws unsheathed. "You don't want to know how I dare ask that question, *yineka mou*, not in front of company. That is a discussion you and I will have later, when I'm not in danger of strangling you for the company you keep."

The silence that followed the softly spoken threat was deafening, the shock on his friends' faces sending a ripple down Jasmine's spine.

Jasmine felt as if she had been slapped, as if her shame was written all over her face. There was none of that easy humor, that uncaring attitude that he had worn in the past couple of hours. "I've had enough of you and your insulting—"

She had barely turned around when his broad frame, bursting with contained violence, blocked her. "Do not test my patience, Jasmine."

Something in the glint of his eye warned Jasmine to shut up.

"How bad is that cut?" Stavros intervened as if the room wasn't crackling with furious energy.

"I can attend to it myself." Dmitri turned and grinned,

a wicked glint in his eyes. The transformation from brooding violence to charming rogue was so swift that Jasmine did a double take. "Or Leah can attend to me."

Jasmine had never seen him smile like that.

Innocence had never been a luxury they had been afforded, and for as long back as she could remember of her childhood, Dmitri had been in it. And not this smiling, outrageous playboy who looked as though nothing touched him...

The expression in his eyes was dazzling, wicked and not...completely real. He knew what his outrageous remark would do and he had used it to deflect attention from him and his wound.

That smile was a practiced facade, she thought with a frown.

Leah shook her head. "Dmitri, stop taunting him. And, Stavros, really, enough with the caveman—"

"Tell your husband that I'm not sixteen anymore and he doesn't need to patch me up." This was Dmitri again, winking wickedly at Leah. "I had hoped you would have cured him of all this duty nonsense in your bed, *pethi mou.*"

A curse flew from the deceptively calm Stavros.

"You're his wife?" Jasmine said to the blushing Leah, realizing she had spoken out loud when Dmitri looked at her.

"Who did you think she was?"

Challenge. Dare. Belligerence. All of it wrapped in a smooth tone.

With three sets of eyes resting on her, Jasmine flushed but refused to let him embarrass her. She poured defiance into her tone. "Your current squeeze.

"I'm sorry." She said this to Leah, who was shaking her head at both men.

"Don't be." Leah smiled. "Dmitri is being his usual

beastly self. I'm Leah Sporades. Giannis, their godfather, was my grandfather."

Jasmine stood awkwardly as Stavros and Leah argued with Dmitri with an obvious familiarity while he threw outrageous remarks at them.

I knew him before you did.

The errant thought dropped into her head and she sent a startled glance toward Dmitri.

His gaze stayed on her, intense and brooding, as if he would like nothing but to skin her alive with his words. Seconds piled on as that same awareness locked them in their own little world. What would happen when his friends left?

Running a hand over her forehead, she looked away. The faster she got out of here the better.

She grabbed the kit from the unsuspecting Stavros and turned to Dmitri. "Stop with the macho posturing and sit down. The cut is on the far left side and you're left-handed."

His grin vanishing, Dmitri looked at her as if she had suddenly sprouted two heads.

She sighed. That mutinous, wary expression in his eyes... *That* she remembered.

"Strip, Dmitri."

"Usually I'm filled with uncontainable anticipation at that command from a woman," he said with an exaggerated leer, "but give back the kit to Stavros, Jasmine."

Unbuttoning his shirt, Dmitri pulled it off his wound. Only a jerk of his mouth betrayed his pain. Ridges of leanly sculpted muscles defined his broad chest, only a smattering of dark hair dotting the olive-toned skin.

Her cheeks instantly tightened, her mouth dry as Jasmine tried to not stare. She took a step toward him, determined to act normal. "I'll make it fast."

Dmitri glared at her. "I'd rather you not touch me at all."

"Why not? I've sewed up so many of Andrew's wounds growing up that I—"

"Like Stavros pointed out so well, we don't know where *you and your hands* have been. And yes, you are super-tough to have made it all on your own for so many years... But we both know that you are a little fragile right now, *ne*? You were crawling all over me on the bike and—"

"Because you were driving like a maniac," she yelled, her face heating up.

"—and a minute ago, you got upset at the sight of the small gash. I'd rather you not look at me with those sad, puppy eyes while you tend to me as if this was some grand reunion that we both have been breathlessly waiting for for years. My generosity toward you is fast disappearing and the cut burns like hell."

The kit fell from her fingers, thudding like a drum in the silence.

There were so many offensive things in there that for a second, she couldn't even sift through them all. Only stood weightless while the cruelty in his words carved through her.

Then the slow, merciful burn of humiliation spread across her throat and cheeks, merciful because anything was better than that hollow ache, her ribs squeezing her lungs tighter and tighter.

His words should not have touched her. He was nothing to her. She had hated him for years on principle. And yet his words knocked the breath out of her.

Was it because she had never been so *literally* saved from a situation before? Because, for most of her life, she had only depended on herself, and seeing a man like Dmitri come to her aid was warping her sense of reality?

Or was she just like her mum after all? One kind word from a man and she was ready to fall over herself and into his arms?

She struggled to hold his gaze but she did, pouring all the hatred, *for him and for herself,* into that look.

"You're right. I'm not myself…" She drew in a shuddering breath. "And you… You're not…"

His face was a tight mask over his angular features, his eyes suddenly hauntingly vulnerable. "Do not assume to know me, Jasmine."

She shook her head, feeling immensely weary. "No, I don't, do I? Have your cut looked at or let it fester and rot you, for all I care. I need a little more of your precious time and then I want out of here."

Holding her shoulders rigidly, she turned.

The sympathy in Leah's eyes was much too real, and Jasmine steeled herself against it. Stumbling through the lounge, she ducked into the first room and closed the door behind her and then walked into the en-suite bathroom.

A sea of white marble greeted her. With a tub long and wide enough for her to swim in, with gleaming gold taps, cold porcelain tiles and thick, fluffy towels, it was her version of paradise.

Tempted as she was to soak in the bath, she stripped and headed for the shower, needing to wash off the fear and grime of the past two days. If only she could so easily wash off the stink of her life…

The moment the water hit her, something in her unraveled. With a deep breath, Jasmine let the tears that had been threatening all night, out.

Only once, Jas, she warned herself.

She would cry just this once, without caring what it meant. She would let herself be weak just this one time. And then she would walk out and not look back.

She had been right in rejecting his offer of money when Andrew had died.

With the hatred of a thousand suns, she promised herself she would never set eyes on Dmitri Karegas again after tonight.

CHAPTER FOUR

DMITRI HISSED OUT a sharp breath as Stavros dabbed his wound with an alcohol wipe. Yet the burn of it over the open flesh was nothing compared to the burn in his gut.

The image of Jas's face, her mouth trembling, her wide eyes stricken with hurt, would haunt him for the rest of his life. Along with a hundred other images of her.

Jas, looking at him with a toothless smile, Jas, at nine, sitting by him in companionable silence while he nursed a broken nose, Jas, her tears overflowing onto her cheeks as he said goodbye to her and Andrew…

Jas, as she glared at him with bristling hatred and fury at Andrew's funeral five years ago…

And now this Jas, who saw through his veneer to the real him, who had melted into his arms with such vulnerability in her eyes…

Who had looked at him as if he was everything…

A furious cascade of such hunger churned in his gut that he had to grasp the handrest to anchor himself. Just the torrent of emotions that had deluged him ever since she had come at him with that knife was proof enough.

No! That look had been nothing but a result of shock.

He didn't want her to look at him like that, as if he was her hero and knight wrapped in one.

He was no one's hero, and definitely not hers. He shattered women's silly romantic notions of him on a regular basis.

Yet the hurt in her eyes disturbed him far more than it should have.

Theos, where was the woman who had so thoroughly despised him that day?

Setting Jasmine's expectations regarding him shouldn't require this much thought and second-guessing.

"You know," Leah's voice cut in, "I always thought you were the kinder one between Stavros and you." She sighed. "I'll wait in the limo, Stavros. I don't want to embarrass Jasmine anymore but if possible, please convince her to come with us."

"She won't accept anyone's charity," Dmitri said, before he could curb the words. Because he had tried once and she had bristled as if he had made an indecent proposition.

Leah's displeasure swelled in the silence even after she left.

Unrolling gauze, Stavros leveled him a flat look. Dmitri refused to take the bait.

Stavros cut up a strip of medicinal gauze and covered up the wound and then neatly put on a plaster. Then he shut the plastic case and tucked it away. Uncoiling to his height, he finally met Dmitri's gaze. "She seems...very innocent, Dmitri."

He understood the awe in Stavros's voice. Dmitri had been prepared for the shock of seeing Jasmine after all these years, but she was nothing like he had imagined.

From the moment he had entered that house, a tight fist had formed in his gut and it showed no signs of loosening. To find her like he did today, to imagine what would have happened if he had been late... Everything inside him ignited into a mindless fury, every lesson he had learned in controlling his temper consumed by that fear.

"Something I didn't have when Giannis plucked me from there, you mean?" he challenged Stavros.

"Yes."

Stavros's unsaid question reverberated in that single word, but Dmitri was in no mood to talk about the lack of his innocence. Stavros had come to mean more to him than even his godfather but he wouldn't go into his past even for him.

He refused to let it leave a mark on him.

"You don't know to handle her," Stavros said in that arrogant tone of his that drove Leah crazy.

"You're afraid I'm going to corrupt that innocence," Dmitri stated flatly.

Jasmine was like the key to the Pandora's box he had left behind a long time ago. And all he wanted with the key was to throw it away and not look back.

"No," Stavros replied, surprising him. "But it is also obvious that she—"

"She's a debt, Stavros, and I pay them."

A lethal smile touched his friend's mouth. "Tell me your plans for her."

He remained silent, drawing a complete blank.

What was he supposed to do with her now? She had no place in his life, even a minuscule one.

"We both know that you can't just let her walk out of here. Not without ensuring she's not going to be a danger to herself."

"Danger she's courted recklessly." The words rattled out of Dmitri on a wave of anger.

Why the hell hadn't she come to him before this? *Theos*, he understood addictions and the damage they caused, but for Andrew to leave her with so much debt, a debt that Dmitri had no doubt was the result of his gambling…?

Fury and powerlessness flew in his veins because Andrew wasn't even here anymore for Dmitri to take it out on.

"So she deserves to be left to her fate?" Stavros asked

with rising incredulity. "Is this how you would've helped if Calista had been in trouble?"

"*Christos*, she's not going to…" The horror of the night when Stavros's sister had died cut him off.

But then, none of them had known Calista had been on such a self-destructive path until it had been years too late. Pain pounded through his veins at the thought of Jasmine going down that path. Look at the situation she had found herself in. "She's not going to calmly accept whatever I propose."

"I know you hate responsibility of any kind, Dmitri, but this is—"

"*Theos*, Stavros, she does not belong with me. Not for a moment, much less for days."

Stavros looked at him again, something emerging in his gaze. As if he could sense the panic in Dmitri's words. As if he could see the noose tightening around Dmitri's throat. "Then, you should have never answered her call for help.

"What about her is bothering you so much, Dmitri? I have never seen you in such a…*state* when it comes to a woman. You change them on a weekly basis. Why is she different?"

Dmitri pushed a hand through his hair, feeling as though his life was slipping out of his hands. How he wished he could fob her off on Stavros…

"You don't want to be responsible for her and yet your conscience won't let her walk away. How about you do not anger her, then?"

"Where was this infinite wisdom when it was Leah we were dealing with?" he couldn't help pointing out.

"Learn from my lesson, then, won't you?" Stavros growled, steel edging into his tone. As it always did when even the mention of how close he had come to losing Leah came up. "If you hurt her again, the damage she does to you might not be so minimal. Or even worse, she could just turn around and go back to that same world."

"Her feelings are not my concern." That was it. Jasmine could rant and rage at him all she wanted. All he cared about was that the woman was alive. If he had to shred her to pieces to do it, he would, again and again. But he wouldn't let her return to that life.

He had failed so many people in his life, but he couldn't fail Jasmine.

Jasmine stepped into the elegantly decorated bedroom and flopped onto the bed. The robe she had put on slid silkily against her skin but she just couldn't get herself to wear the same jeans and sweater again. Not until she got them washed, at least.

Only silence came from the front lounge. Her heart thudding loudly, she looked up.

Dmitri prowled into the room and leaned against the wall, the movement pulling one lapel of his unbuttoned shirt higher, exposing a rope of leanly sculpted muscle. A gauze pad near his abdomen stood out white against his olive skin.

One of his brows lifted, a sardonic smile twisting his mouth.

Sinuous heat bloomed low in her belly, the sight of his naked torso a temptation like she had never imagined.

The luxurious black satin scrunched in her fingers painted a picture of her writhing beneath that leanly coiled frame, all of that simmering intensity unleashed on her, while he worshipped her with the mouth that had pierced her so much...

"Jasmine?"

His frown prompted her out of her fantasies, her skin heating up.

She was used to attention of the most extreme kind,

knew lust in all its forms. And yet, when Dmitri looked at her, even innocently as he was doing now, as if he could see into her head and soul, she was extremely aware of it.

Of all the men in the world, something inside her reacted with a violent energy to Dmitri. Maybe it was because she had known him as a kid. Maybe because, for the first time in years, she was with a man and she didn't have to worry about whether he was motivated by lust or some other inferior motive.

That was it.

Dmitri, for all his crushing words, was safe.

For years, she had wondered if the life she had adapted to to survive had somehow corrupted her ability to feel this kind of need, if her body would ever feel like it was anything but an instrument she had honed to make a living…if she would feel free enough…wondered if there was anything pure left in her thoughts except for the technicality of it…

Yet that it was Dmitri that incited her like this… It left her shaking to her very bones.

Didn't her body know that she was supposed to hate him even if he looked like a Greek god? That he was a man who turned his back on friends because they didn't fit into his new life?

She was like a deer planning her escape route, Dmitri decided, leaning against the door. Not that he didn't think it was for the best.

The moment he saw her on the bed, *his bed*, in his robe, even if it fell to her ankles, his blood had vanished south.

She had looked so lovely for a second there, claws withdrawn. Like a lioness who wanted to be petted for a little while. Before she most likely ate you.

"You look as if you have a fever."

She nodded. "I don't feel… I'm just achy all over."

Her words emerged as a rough croak. The soft admission from her was as strange as the feverish look in those dark black eyes. Scrubbed of sleep and any lingering softness that he had ruthlessly pushed away, they glowed with determination. And regret punched him in the gut even as he knew that it was better this way.

He didn't want her all soft and melting. He wanted her to fight him and hate him.

Had she been hurt in their tussle? he thought then, the very idea horrifying him. Frowning, he took a step forward and clasped her cheek.

She flinched away from him. A silent roar burst into life inside of him, and he forced himself to take multiple breaths.

Theos, he hated when she flinched at his nearness like that...

Which was a thousand kinds of insanity because he had practically yelled at her to not come near him.

Stavros had taught him well. It took all of his willpower to control that wild thing inside him that wanted her hands on him. All of her on him. Reminded himself that all he offered a woman was sex. And Jasmine deserved a lot more.

Clenching his jaw, he fought for composure. "Did I hurt you when I tackled you?"

"No. I just... I pulled a muscle the other day and it's still bothering me."

"Let me see it."

"No." Jasmine drew in a deep breath and forced the words to come out evenly. "Thanks for coming so promptly today, Dmitri. For literally coming to my rescue."

"You almost choked on that, *ne*?"

She shrugged, refusing to take the bait.

He entered the bedroom and went to the wardrobe.

Panic blooming in her gut, she looked around the bedroom she had run into.

It was his bedroom, of course.

She tried to slide off the silky sheets. And lost the little dignity she had in the process when he turned around, his brows raised.

Sleeping in Dmitri's bed was the last thing she needed. It was far too intimate for the little peace that she needed for her overactive mind.

She dangled her legs on the side of the bed. "I didn't realize this was your bedroom. I will just…"

"Stay," he ordered her softly.

With his back still against the wardrobe, he extracted a perfectly pressed white cotton shirt with sure precision, shrugged off the bloodied shirt. Too mesmerized by the sight of his corded biceps and chest to even pretend otherwise, Jasmine watched as he pulled on the fresh shirt.

"I will sleep in the longue or order housekeeping to clean up Stavros's room." He buttoned it down, his gaze taking in her flushed face with a casual indifference. "Are you hungry?"

Getting up and padding away from the bed, she walked to the chaise longue. "No. And you don't have to babysit me. I just want to crash for a few hours."

"I have no interest in spending the night babysitting you. Tell me…how did Noah agree to this outrageous idea of an auction?"

"You know how."

Another step closer. But caught between the bed and him, there was no way to escape. Retribution that he had threatened shone in every line of his body. "Dmitri…"

"Enlighten me again how it happened."

"Even after all these years, we still owed him money. Noah would have liked for me to sign away my entire life and I didn't want to continue—" a shudder went through her spine "—there anymore. I thought of you and suggested he put me up for auction."

He stared down at her as if he could see through her skin and into the very heart of her. "Where was he going to find buyers if not for me?"

Something in his question struck a chord of fear in Jasmine. "There weren't any others."

"Noah is not famous for his kindness. I don't understand how he agreed to your condition."

"Because all the world knows that you're a gazillionaire and Noah just happens to know that at one time you used to have a conscience. I gave him an opening to exploit that. If you're through being disgusted with me—"

"Disgusted? *Theos*, what the hell was Andrew thinking to leave you with so much debt? Why didn't he—"

Just hearing her brother judged for what little he could have done inflamed her. "Don't speak his name."

"He should have taken better care of you. I don't understand—"

Shivering from head to toe, she struggled to keep the grief at bay. Even after five years, it shredded her strength and composure with its claws. "How do you know what he did or didn't do? You left us."

Was that it? Had she hated him all these years because he had left her alone with an alcoholic mother and a brother addicted to gambling away the very little they had ever had? Was her bitter envy over his better life at the root of it all?

"I didn't have a choice, Jasmine."

"You didn't have a choice except to forget us? He always watched your back, stopped you from getting yourself killed. If not for him, you would have died a violent death a long time ago."

Every inch of his face became immobile under her attack. He stood absolutely still, calmly absorbing her insults.

Only the haunting depths of his eyes betrayed his shock. "You think I need a reminder, *Theos mou*, that without Andrew, there would have been nothing left of me for Giannis to save…"

God, what the hell had she said?

The cynical curve of his mouth… The emptiness in his eyes… She never wanted to be witness to that ever again.

She didn't want to see that flash of pain in his eyes ever again, much less cause it.

"That…that came out wrong. I just… I don't know what's wrong with me. I've never…" She took a bracing breath. "Seeing you just reminds me that he's forever gone, Dmitri. That he never had a single chance to break away from it all."

He stepped away from her as if to avoid the poison of her words. "Until I can ensure that there's no danger to you, you have no choice but to face me, Jasmine." Still, he didn't sound angry or upset. Still, he only spoke about her safety.

As if it was an onerous duty he had to take on even if she was ungrateful.

Jasmine wanted to kick herself for her impulsive mouth. Or curl into a ball and cry. In one swoop, she had spewed out all the bitterness she had struggled to keep at bay for years. She couldn't bear to look at herself, much less at Dmitri. She couldn't bear to be in his presence for a second longer without wanting to slap herself.

It was being near him, she realized. From the moment he had stepped in there, it was as if she had lost all sense of herself. It was as if she had forgotten all the hard lessons she had learned so early in life.

"I have seven thousand and change saved that I can pay you instantly. The rest of it will take me time, but I will pay you back even if I have to…"

A slow grin spread across his devilish mouth. He

shifted his feet, bit his lower lip, as if to contain the laughter spilling out, leaned his hip against the wall as if he were posing for a photo shoot and smiled again. The veins in his forearms stood out as he folded his arms, oozing sex appeal.

Jasmine's breath caught at the sheer, stark beauty of it.

There was nothing false or practiced about the curve of his mouth now.

It lit up his light gray eyes, carved a dimple in his cheek. Her knees turned to mush as he dipped his head low and batted at her with his shoulder. "So you're determined to pay me back, then, *yes*?"

Of course, the man didn't need his fists anymore. He could charm the birds from the sky with that smile. Was it any wonder that women threw themselves at his feet? What woman wouldn't want him to look at her with need in those gorgeous eyes? What woman wouldn't want those rough hands on her, that luscious mouth driving her wild?

She was getting hot just thinking about it. "Every last penny," she croaked out.

"How?"

"I'll come up with something."

"You know, Jas…" He pressed the heels of his palms to his eyes in an exaggerated show of patience. "Spanking's never been my thing but, *Theos*, I'm *so tempted* to give it a try right now. You and your ideas and your plans…"

She gasped, heat streaking her cheeks. "I was running out of options."

He prowled toward her like a predator. Heat from his body enveloped her, coating her very breath.

"And what if someone else ended up buying…*you*?"

"You're trying to scare me."

"There was someone else, Jas, someone who was willing to pay a lot of money to own you."

Jas remained silent, fear and confusion stealing rational thought from her.

"Didn't you think of contacting me even once? Did you have to wait until it got this desperate?"

She had. She had thought of him countless times, her body and mind weary after another long night, after facing another of her mother's drunken episodes. After feeling as if she would never make a dent in her debt, after facing another man look at her as if he could own her body and soul for a few bucks. After seeing her life pass day after day in that pit.

In a moment of weakness, she had called Katrakis Textiles in Athens once. The receptionist had even politely asked her for her name. In the end, she had chickened out.

In the end, it had been easier to hate him from a distance than take his pity.

"I don't like depending on anyone for anything," she said instead.

"Fate has a way of punching us with exactly what we don't want. There was someone else who bid for you. Which meant Noah had two dogs out for the same bone, and he let us go at it."

Another bidder? Her knees gave out and she sank to the longue.

Sweat beaded her brow, nausea climbing up her throat. Noah had tricked her. If Dmitri hadn't come along, he would have sold her virginity to someone else.

The horror of what could have happened filled her with dread.

"Noah said you called it a virginity auction. And that's what it truly was. What I can't figure out is who else wanted to pay off that debt and why."

Her head spun in a thousand different directions and Jasmine struggled to hold on to her sanity. Clutching her head, she walked away from him.

Just leave. Don't care what he paid, Jas. He can afford it.

Walk away, the survivor in her begged.

"How much did you pay Noah?"

"You're not my priciest toy, if that's what worries you."

Her gut heaved with anticipated dread, her right eye twitching uncontrollably from keeping her gaze so straight. Something was very wrong; she knew it in her bones.

"Stop taunting me, Dmitri. How much do I owe you?"

"A hundred and thirty thousand pounds, but since I'm feeling generous I'll round it down to an even hundred."

A hundred thousand pounds? Her gut flopped to her feet. "That can't be true. That much money… It's ridiculous, God…"

Clutching the wall behind her, she gasped for breath. "This is my worst nightmare come true… *Oh, God…*" It would take her ten lifetimes to make so much money. She would never be able to pay him back, never walk away from this.

"Being saved from a life of trading your body is your worst nightmare?"

Uncontrollable shivers overtook her. Hunger and lack of sleep from the past two days hit her like a battering ram, the sheer willpower with which she had kept herself going, shattering finally. "No. Bound to you eternally by this debt is."

She swayed and sank to the thickly carpeted floor.

A soft curse ripped through the air before she was pulled up like a rag doll. "*Theos,* Jas." His voice wasn't loud, yet it carried something. His gaze searched her, his fingers splayed against her jaw, a strange glitter darkening his eyes. "Now is not the time to lose that reckless pride."

Pushing his hands away, she sank back onto the chaise

longue. Her body felt boneless, as if she would never stop falling.

All she wanted was to curl up and sleep for the next decade. All she wanted was to let someone else bear the burden, just once. "How am I going to pay you back? Lord, what am I going to do?" she muttered to herself.

The bedroom door opened and an army of uniformed staff set down an array of dishes that had her gut twisting with hunger. She looked at the clock, which said five in the morning.

The staff vanished just as they had appeared, with minimal fuss, making her wonder if she had imagined them.

"Until you figure out a way, you will eat, sleep and generally keep your presence in my life to a minimum."

Swallowing at the mouthwatering aroma from the dishes, she nodded. Eyed the distance from the chaise to the table and groaned.

With a curse that sounded filthy to even her untrained ears, he stopped by the table and lifted a silver dome off a plate. "When did you eat last?"

"A cheeseburger about twenty hours ago," she whispered pathetically.

Pushing her legs out of his way none too gently, and careful enough to not even accidentally touch her hip that was propped up, he sat down at the foot of the chaise. Forking pasta with his left hand, which was such a familiarly intimate gesture from her childhood that a lump formed in her throat, he brought it to her mouth.

Jasmine closed her mouth over the farfalle eagerly.

"Don't make a habit of this, Jas."

He sounded uncomfortable, wary. Was he afraid that she would climb all over him again and embarrass them both?

Closing her eyes, Jas chewed, relishing the thick white sauce. "Won't even remember this, Dmitri."

She ate in silence while the influx of carbs lulled her

to sleep. She finished off a bottle of water and stretched back down on the chaise.

"I'll see you later."

She lifted her thumbs as he stilled by the door, pensive. She felt like that mangy dog again. Only instead of letting the doorman kick her, Dmitri had decided to keep her.

Something strange was going on with him. The fleeting thought came to her even as her head felt as if it was filled with cotton candy.

One minute, he was shredding her into pieces with such ruthlessness, and the next…such tenderness showed in his eyes that she thought she would shatter in the face of it.

"Where are you going? When will you return?"

He stared at her for a long, disturbing, soul-crushing moment before he covered the distance between them. Still reclining on the chaise, she waited with bated breath, her heart hammering behind her rib cage.

He would surely cut her to pieces for asking that question, for assuming such…

Kneeling down to her level, he took her hand in his. Her hand was delicately slender in his huge one, and suddenly, she felt a sense of security she hadn't known in a long time. It was as if a fuzzy feeling unspooled in her gut.

"I have a very irate portfolio manager that I have to mollify after my latest bout of shopping frenzy," he whispered, and she laughed through the weariness.

"Tonight I can sleep, can't I? For as long as I want?"

He squeezed her hand, and she thought how rough his palm was. "Yes, you can, Jas. No one will come in. You're…safe here."

Her eyelids felt as if they would glue together forever. Jas squeezed his hand back and whispered, "Thank you," before giving in to the sleep claiming her.

Maybe she didn't have to hate Dmitri so thoroughly, the

thought came to her. She would still pay him back, yes, but they could at least be friends, couldn't they?

As much friends as she could be with a man who had bought her and who set her pulse racing like nothing in life ever had.

A man who was making it harder for her to hate him.

CHAPTER FIVE

DMITRI RETURNED WELL past eleven, his entire morning spent in a fruitless search. He still had no answers whatsoever as to what Noah had intended. He had been shut down at every avenue he had pursued and he knew why. Noah didn't want word getting out about Jasmine getting out of her debt. Even though the greedy old bastard had milked the occasion for all its worth.

Bad for his business.

And he knew he could expect no answers from the infuriatingly deceptive woman herself.

There were too many unknowns about what she had done these past few years. And then there was her assumption that he had never looked back for Andrew or her.

Even though he had.

Andrew had been viciously angry with Dmitri that last time they had met, just months before he had died, because Dmitri had refused to give him any more money. Because Dmitri had wrongly hoped that cutting Andrew off after so many years would curb his gambling habit.

He had never thought Andrew would poison Jasmine against him, however, that he would lie about all the times Dmitri had lent him money.

But then he shouldn't have been shocked. Didn't he know firsthand the consequences of addiction and self-loathing it built up? How it only looked for a scapegoat?

For years, Dmitri had faced his father's fists just because his father hadn't been man enough to accept that his alcoholism had been responsible for the miserable state of their lives. No, his cowardly father had blamed his mother instead.

After everything he and Andrew had been to each other, Dmitri had become that scapegoat for Andrew.

No wonder Jasmine despised him. And he had no intention of telling her the truth, either. He needed the distance her hatred for him put between them.

But the sense of honor Giannis and Stavros had instilled in him wouldn't let him wash his hands of her.

It meant he couldn't just pad her bank balance and remove her from his life. Not until he figured out this whole auction mystery about her. Not until he was completely sure that Jasmine could walk away from that life.

Unbuttoning his shirt, he entered the bedroom and stilled.

The blinds were open and the sunlight made every inch of the room glitter with a soft, golden glow.

And in the middle of it, on the chaise longue, lay Jasmine. Her hands were folded under her cheek, her long legs half dangling on the other side revealed delicate feet with red-tipped toes.

She was only a few inches shorter than him, which meant she had to be uncomfortable as hell on the chaise. While a perfectly good king-size bed lay in touching distance.

Stubborn woman!

If not for sheer exhaustion, she would have crawled out to the corridor rather than take his help, he knew.

Without intending to, he found himself moving closer to her.

Her dark hair was finally out of the knot and spread against the beige upholstery like nightfall, lustrous and wavy. Spiky eyelashes curved against her cheeks, her plump, wide mouth, for once not pursed in disapproval.

She looked like a wild, beautiful horse he had once seen on Stavros's farm, a horse that had refused to be mounted by anyone. An incongruous, irresistible combination of untouched innocence and untamed wildness.

One minute, she was consigning him to hell for his sins and more, the next, melting into him.

He sank to the floor and leaned his head against the bed, memories he had locked away rushing at him.

He didn't remember a moment of his childhood without her in it.

She had been such a tall, gangly little girl when he had left, her black eyes filled with fat tears when she had said goodbye.

For years, after he had moved in with Giannis, he remembered that face and her wet kiss on his cheek.

Even now, at first glance, she looked scrawny, the robe sticking on her angular shoulders, drowning her lithe form. But that was where the girl he remembered with such fondness ended.

Honey-gold and smooth, her skin shone with a brilliance no amount of makeup could achieve, transforming her face. There was a lean, tensile strength to her body, a fluid grace and energy that had slammed into him when he had tackled her.

Curves that had pressed against his forearm that he couldn't see now…

Theos, was he so shallow that he was this desperate for a peek at what she so desperately wanted to hide? Had he truly become that playboy who had the hots for every woman that came into his life?

Was there nothing he wouldn't take to sate that perpetual emptiness within him?

Because, for once, Stavros was wrong, his faith in Dmitri misplaced. There was something between Jasmine and him, and every inch of him wanted to explore what it was, and she…she was no match for him.

Theos, this was Andrew's little sister, the last woman he needed to tangle with, however much she made him feel things he had never felt before.

He pushed himself off the floor, called Reception and requested a different suite.

He had plans for tomorrow, for next week, for the next month. And he intended to keep those plans.

And that meant the bachelor party he was throwing Stavros at a strip club in Monaco. Something he had been looking forward to ever since Stavros had pronounced that he was marrying Leah again, properly this time.

By the end of the next three days, Jasmine was ready to throttle Dmitri with her very hands. And more than annoyed with herself for being a naive idiot.

She had woken up long past midday, feeling as if a speeding bus had run her down. Her body was a mass of bruises from being tackled by the giant brute, her neck ached from sleeping at an awkward angle for so long on the chaise longue, which she kicked out of a perverse anger when she was up, and of course, her foot hurt because of that.

The worst was the feeling of being caged in the sophisticated but deafeningly silent hotel suite. What had seemed so secure in the dark of the dawn now felt like a jail that cut her off from the rest of the world.

Looking out of the French windows, she had seen the bustle of Bond Street and yet, she felt worlds away.

She hadn't minded it so much the first day, having spent two hours soaking in the decadent marble tub. Not even when the hotel physician and a nurse had arrived, *on the orders of Mr. Karegas of course*, to ensure Ms. Douglas suffered no ill effects after the stress of her previous day.

Not when she had been served a five-course meal with as much aplomb as if she were the queen.

In fact, she had been impressed and softened and whatnot by the time she'd finished her chocolate-dipped strawberries and mint tea. Even convinced herself that she had been extremely stupid in not coming to Dmitri for help sooner.

By the evening of the second day, she was ready to hitch herself up on the prestigious artwork and climb the walls.

So dressed again in her freshly laundered old jeans and one of Dmitri's Savile Row dress shirts—she couldn't bear to even look at her old sweater—she had stepped out of the suite and found a hulking giant following her down the corridor and into the lift.

He had appeared by her side as she waited for the doorman, his hand on her wrist sending a current of fury through her.

"You're not to leave the premises of the hotel, miss," he had replied when she had glared at him. "Mr. Karegas ordered that you stay put until he's sure you're safe," he had said with a repressive shudder.

Flushing as if she had been caught out being particularly naughty, she had mumbled off something and dutifully headed back into the room. Only later had she realized that Dmitri had practically made her a prisoner.

Even then, she had warmed up, so devoid of basic security her life had been.

So she had waited, over the next day and another day. Patiently and with even a growing sense of gratitude and warmth, her gullible, ever-ready-to-succumb-to-temptation mind painting pictures of their blossoming friendship.

Until she had surfed the channels and seen the latest tabloid channel report.

Dmitri Karegas was living it up at the illustrious bachelor party he was throwing his best friend and business partner of years, Stavros Sporades.

Hadn't Leah said she was Stavros's wife?

The feature went on to talk about the world-famous strip club, the hundred different champagnes that had been served, a burlesque show that apparently was the raciest thing ever and the sexiest, the most raucous bachelors from the world attending, including a Hollywood movie star, a sheikh from the middle east and a Japanese media mogul…and Dmitri Karegas.

Stavros, the supposed groom, Jasmine realized, was conspicuously absent.

Somehow, she had a hard time imagining that austere, almost forbidding man giving in to the kind of excesses that would go on at the party that feature boasted about.

Because her job had given her ample exposure to it, especially when she had waitressed at a private party once, too terrified of taking on her usual duties.

Drinks, dancing, women…and Dmitri, with his reputation for a voracious sexual appetite in the middle of it all…

Her gut heaved so violently at the very thought that she pressed her hand to it…

What the hell was wrong with her? She was acting as if they were…

No, she wouldn't even think it.

Two photos of the party had been leaked through the usual social media sites.

One showed two buxom blondes—really there was no other way to describe the décolletage of the two women—corralling him on either side, holding their empty champagne flutes aloft while Dmitri popped the cork open with a thousand-kilowatt smile for the flashing camera bulbs.

The second one was a close-up of him, a grainy shot clicked with a cell phone camera. Those hauntingly beautiful eyes of his held a smirk...a challenge? A chasm of emptiness that she wished she understood...

Did no one else get glimpses of the man she did? It felt as if only she could see beneath the mask he wore to the real man.

Something swelled in her chest, so intense was her longing to understand him again like she had once.

Her cell phone's chirp, a text from her mother pleading with Jas for any cash she could spare, pulled her from the trance. A technologically delivered slap to pull her back to her reality, so to speak.

Of course, Dmitri wasn't worried about her. It was nothing but a ruse to scare her into staying put just so he could feel better about his unwanted duty toward her.

Hadn't she started this whole thing because she didn't want to be anyone's prisoner?

There was an ongoing...*negotiation* between Dmitri and her, that was all.

A string of softly spoken words, a kind glance and some pasta Alfredo and she was ready to turn into his next groupie.

He owed her nothing, having paid a thousand times over. He had clearly told her that she was but an inconvenience, ordered her to stay on the periphery of his life.

Where was this sense of betrayal coming from then? *Dear Lord*, how desperate was she for some kind of connection that she projected it onto the first man who had looked at her with nothing but a begrudging kindness? One who had been disgusted by her lifestyle?

The next two hours she spent in the suite waiting for the giant security guard to change shifts was the longest of her life. The minute the clock struck four, she grabbed her handbag, stepped into the lift and ran out of the building.

If she hurried, she could make it to her bank on time and withdraw cash for her mum.

Ten minutes into walking into the neighborhood she grew up in, unease gripped Jasmine.

Something sinuous settled in her belly at the thought of going back to her dinky flat. *No*, it wasn't the flat as much as it was the life she didn't want to lead anymore.

She needed to start a new chapter in her life. Needed to use this time to make a clean break of it, once and for all.

Tomorrow, she would start looking for a new job. As soon as she thought it, her heart sank. The only connections or contacts she had were the ones revolving around the nightclub, her brother's friends and Noah's men.

Except for Dmitri.

Dmitri, who it seemed could turn her inside out just by existing.

She spent the next few hours running errands—withdrawing cash, buying groceries and mulling over new career possibilities that would help her earn a hundred thousand pounds fast enough. And catching quite a bit of gossip at her old haunts.

Apparently, the fact that Dmitri had bought her was something of news in their little flea-infested, junkie-ridden neighborhood and she was the star of the feature. The almost envious lewdness that dripped from the comments that in the end she would go in the same career route as her mother, of course with a bit of an upgrade to it, what with Dmitri being a billionaire and all, had been extremely hard to swallow.

Had she thought she was better off here for even a minute? She had no education, no job training, and she knew nothing except keeping herself in good shape and keeping her head down. Hours of rigid exercise and practice had made her a good pole dancer, but what other job could use that?

Her skin clammy with sweat, she packed a quick bag, stuffing in underwear, another pair of jeans, a few blouses and the few cosmetics that she owned.

And the diamond pendant, her one precious belonging, that Andrew had given her for her eighteenth birthday.

This was it.

She was saying goodbye to this life. Her pride and her curious weakness when it came to Dmitri... She would have to find a way to deal with it.

It was past eight when she finally reached her mum's flat. The same frustration built up inside her as she borrowed the keys from old Mrs. Davies, but this responsibility, Jasmine realized, she couldn't walk away from. Not until one of them was dead.

She cleaned up the one-bedroom flat, emptied the grocery bags and then loaded up the cardboard boxes with empty bottles. She put the check she had made out at the bank in an envelope and left it on the counter.

The bulky box in hand, she had barely made it down the steps when the hairs on her neck stood up, like the antenna on her mother's old TV.

The long lines of a dark limo slowly materialized under the sadly flickering streetlight, the sleek vehicle a stark contrast against the dirty pavement.

And leaning against it, his long coat fluttering against the wind, his denim-clad legs crossed at his ankles, stood Dmitri. Moonlight illuminated his face in shadows and strips but still enough for her to see the arctic blaze in his eyes.

Soundlessly, he moved toward her and Jasmine let out a yelp, trying to escape him.

The cardboard box slipped from her fingers and thudded to the ground, the bottles causing a loud tinkling sound. Anything she had been about to say fell away from her in a horrified squeak as he lifted her off the ground, threw her over his shoulder, waited for his chauffeur to open the door.

And then threw her onto the long leather seat as if he was dumping out yesterday's garbage.

Undignified protests sputtering from her mouth, she had barely even straightened on the seat when the limo took off.

"What the hell do you…"

The dark scowl etched on his brow shut her up instantly, his silver-plated watch glinting in the dark as he barked out commands in Greek.

Jasmine pressed her fingers to her temple and forced herself to breathe in and out. She sat up straight and looked out the window, struggling to rein in her temper. Of course, the tinted glass offered up a reflection of the man's aquiline nose, sculpted cheeks and a mouth made for sin.

He didn't get off the phone all through their drive through the city. They had left her dirty neighborhood, drove for a long while and finally had crossed the motorway when the limo came to a stop. Even then, he didn't look at her. Only waited patiently when the door was opened.

Jasmine scrambled out with as much dignity as she could muster, given that he was dragging her with him as if she were a recalcitrant child.

"Oh, wow…" she said, as she finally noticed the sleek lines of the jet that was already idling. Glancing around only now, she saw the acres of empty land stretched out on all sides, a string of lights marking a couple of runways. They were at a private airstrip, miles away from the city.

She pulled at her arm. His fingers dug into her flesh.

"Ow, ow… Dmitri, you're hurting me."

He let her go so suddenly and with such force that she half stumbled. She couldn't believe it was the same man who had fed her pasta with such tenderness. "What is wrong with you?" she yelled.

Fury gripped his features. "You were not supposed to leave the hotel suite. There was a report of a young woman's body found near the…"

Turning around, he kicked at the ground, causing asphalt to fly around them.

She put her hand on his arm and he tensed. "I was never in any danger."

"*Theos*, Jas, do you want to go back to that life? Is that it? You're just as addicted to the danger and desperation of it as him? Like the whole infernal lot of people I've been cursed to know?

"If you are, tell me now. Because I won't have your death on my conscience, too."

Andrew. He was talking about Andrew, Jas realized slowly—about Andrew's lifelong gambling addiction.

How long had he known? Had he found out after he had talked to Noah?

But Jasmine couldn't bring his name up. Not when the very subject of Andrew seemed to push them both into a dangerous territory. Not when she didn't trust herself to say something nasty just because Dmitri was here and her brother wasn't.

Dmitri had had a benevolent godfather who had come for him just at the right time, true. But the whole world knew how hard he and Stavros had worked to turn their godfather's small factory into a global empire.

While Andrew had only continued to make worse and worse choices.

"I'm not Stavros. I won't save someone against their own wishes to self-annihilate, Jas. If I walk away now, I will never come back."

"No, I don't want to go back," she answered, all her fury fizzling out at the anguish in his words. "Not for a day. I was angry that you…" Her claim sounded so childish to her own ears. It wasn't his fault that she was feeling so fragile.

She met his gaze squarely. "I only went back to collect a few things, Dmitri. I was going to beg you to…" She paused, realizing she hadn't actually come up with a plan except to throw herself at his mercy.

Again.

"Beg me for what?"

"A job. Or something."

His fury shifted as he assessed her with disbelieving eyes. He ran a hand through his hair. "That's the first sensible thing you've said to me. And you wasted my entire evening."

She did seem to have a death wish, because the words poured out of her without the basic check her brain was supposed to engage. "An evening of more festivities in Monaco?"

Instantly his expression shuttered, changed. An infinitesimal moment in which she caught a glimpse of something, a hunger, beneath the surface. Just as she had seen in the photo in the newspaper.

When he looked at her again, the careless indifference was back in place. "My activities or my personal life is none of your business, so stay out of it."

When she dug in her feet, he turned around with a sigh. "And before you waste another few minutes, yes, your life, at least for now, is my business."

"How, except that I owe you money that I could never repay?"

"Five years ago, when Andrew died, I should have dragged you out of that hellhole. I didn't, and that decision has cost me a hundred thousand pounds and an ever-increasing amount of havoc on my life. Until I ensure you won't end up on the streets again, you'll stay with me."

Oh, how she wanted to smack the arrogance off his

face, but he was right. She had nowhere to go. So she followed him up the stairs and into the…most luxuriously chic aircraft she had ever seen.

Hanging on to her foolish pride because really, no one could expect her to get used to this kind of wealth when she had lived hand to mouth all her life, she tried very hard to act as if she traveled in first-class luxury with a textile tycoon every other day.

If the outside of the Learjet was all sleek lines and thrumming power, the inside was world-class spacious luxury she had only ever seen in glossy magazines. Power seats in cream leather so soft that she was scared of scratching it sat in two different clusters with legroom enough to accommodate a giraffe. *Or her.*

Two flat-screen monitors whirred out of the ceiling as she watched while the flight attendant rattled off a wine selection, half of which she had never even heard of. Sparkling water was all she had ever allowed herself, before, during or after work, resolved to never blunt her senses in any way.

"Just water for me, thanks," she finally said, just to stop the woman from figuring out she wasn't Dmitri's usual caliber guest.

The moment the thought crossed her mind, she felt ashamed of herself. That she wasn't sophisticated or educated had never bothered her before.

"Where are we going?" she asked when they settled down.

"We're not returning. Not unless my business dictates it. You'll travel with me until I…until you get back on your feet. But not in London, not when you'll only be tempted to go back to that life."

Her mum hadn't cared about Andrew or her for as long as she could remember. Only about her broken dreams and drowning them in alcohol…

Even Andrew's legacy for her had been crushing debt, debt that had turned her life in a direction she had never wanted it to take.

"There's something to be said for a clean break, Jas. Believe me."

Jasmine exhaled roughly, realizing he was right. "Can you please have someone check in on my mum once in a while?"

"Already taken care of."

Her nerves jangled with excitement and fear and so many more feelings she couldn't name. But at least there was no regret for the life she was leaving behind.

CHAPTER SIX

DMITRI HAD NEVER considered the private jet owned by Katrakis Textiles small by any standard before tonight. It was not his favorite, as anything—bike, car or flight—that boasted size over speed wasn't.

But the spacious front cabin with a king-size bed in the rear had served him well on his cross-Atlantic trips, especially when he was traveling on business with a team in tow.

The constantly fidgeting woman sitting across from him, however, made him reconsider this view.

She was making him reconsider too many decidedly sure things he had designed for his life, things that gave him shallow and transient pleasure at the least, things he had become used to…

Theos, he had looked forward to that bachelor party for months.

But the weekend in Monaco had turned out to be torturously boring for him, his mind pushing the picture of Jasmine sleeping so peacefully in his bedroom, to the fore.

There was something utterly satisfying about keeping her safe. And after his failure to save his mother, he didn't misunderstand where the feeling came from, either. But even then…

The sight of a woman had never transfixed him like that.

Like a treasure that called to seamen, luring them, her

stunning face had come to him in the strangest of moments, stealing away whatever satisfaction the moment would have presented.

So here he was, his usually uncaring mood roused to a temper, his libido unsatisfied, while the confounding woman's presence in his life spread as if it was a stubborn virus.

The picture she presented, everything covered up from top to bottom, shouldn't have snagged his attention at all.

Her jeans, while obviously worn out and of cheap quality, were snug and tight, encasing her long, long legs like a glove.

He had received an eyeful of her mouthwateringly pert bottom while she had knelt in the seat and tugged viciously at the poor, unsuspecting seat belt, not realizing that all she had to do was to click on the latch for it to pull.

And then there was the real culprit that sent a simmering awareness through his blood for the sheer intimacy of it.

His pristine white, custom-made Armani dress shirt that she wore.

He was bulkier and broader and she was thin, waiflike… The shirt should have looked like a bag on her scrawny build.

The shoulder seam fell to her upper arms, while she had rolled up the sleeves. Tucked into those tight jeans, it billowed over her torso. But with the outline of her black bra visible through the thin cotton, the wide collar flashing peeks at golden honeyed skin every time she moved, it was the most erotically feminine thing he had ever seen.

Never had a woman so thoroughly covered up fired his curiosity to such depths.

She made his shirt her own in such a sexy way that he wanted to rip it off her, press his mouth to that silk-like skin, so that he could discover, for himself and for her, what lay beneath.

Theos, he was turning rock hard and he hadn't even touched her…

No other woman in the world had ever baffled Dmitri like her; no other woman shook his compass in such a shattering way.

Despite everything, there was an inner strength to Jasmine that scorched him every time he looked into her eyes. Add to that, that instant charge whenever she looked at him out of those big black eyes.

"Is your mother well?" he said, choosing a topic that would surely defuse that charge.

A line of tension immediately bunched her shoulders tight before she slowly turned toward him. Her mouth closed on the bottle as she took a long sip. His blood rushed south as a picture of that saucy mouth wrapped around him came forth…

He pressed his fingers to his temple, searching for a shred of decency.

"As fine as she can be." She screwed the cap back slowly. "Even Andrew's death changed nothing for her."

The bitterness in her tone took him aback first. Then it cycled to guilt and frustration.

He should have gone back for her after Andrew's death, shouldn't have walked away just because of his past failures. He knew, firsthand, the price a child paid for a parent's destructive addiction. Even if her mother's alcoholism had resulted in neglect of her children and not something much worse. A cold chill climbed up his spine. "Does she still—"

"Drink like a fish and then spiral into pitiful sobs remembering Andrew's dad and then mine in that order? Yep… The worst are the stories about me turning into some Arab princess overnight when my father comes back for her after all these years. Thinks it's going to be *Princess Diaries*—Jasmine-style."

Her smile too wide, the glitter in her eyes too bright, she looked as if she would break with a gentle tap. Tenderness like he had never known engulfed Dmitri. He didn't know what to do with it, didn't know how to stop feeling it.

He had no words of comfort to offer. "Do you want me to look for him?"

Shock widened her eyes. "My father?"

He nodded. "It might not be that hard now that—"

"He spun stories, used her for a year and skipped town the moment she told him she was pregnant. She was nothing but a convenient mistress for a visiting diplomat. He had twenty-four years to change his mind. I don't need another parent who looks at me as if I was the reason their life took a miserable turn."

"Then, why did you go to see her again?" Frustration mounted inside him. "Why were you running around all evening loading up groceries, cleaning up?"

She frowned. "I haven't checked on her in a week."

"How much did you end up giving her this time?"

Her neck moved this way and that, that ugly knot at the back of her head making his fingers itch with the urge to unravel it. She was stalling, he knew.

That run-down flat was in a dilapidated part of the city; the empty bottles she carried out, the way she had almost cringed into herself in the darkness… Image after image flashed in front of his eyes… *Theos*, how did you protect someone from their own naïveté?

Suddenly, he had newfound respect for what Stavros went through with Leah.

Studying her neatly trimmed nails, she cleared her throat. "You're making too much of…"

"How much, Jas?"

It felt as if a vein would burst in his temple, as if his very life was shifting in front of his eyes.

He hadn't meant to shout. He hadn't meant to get so

angry. He hadn't meant to spend every waking minute thinking of the infuriating woman or wanting to wring her neck. Or kiss her senseless.

"Just a little…" She swallowed when he continued to glare at her. "Okay, fine, most of what I saved. Her rent was overdue by two months and she had—"

His filthy curse rang around the cabin, but did nothing to alleviate his frustration.

Jasmine looked at him with wide eyes, more alert than shocked at his outburst.

"So all of the seven thousand pounds you were boasting about? No wonder you weren't making any dent in—"

"Yes, okay. I have done this before."

He shot up from his seat, like a wild animal that had forced itself to be peaceful until now. That was what always made her curious.

That carefree, reckless, unemotional demeanor he put on—that wasn't the natural state for Dmitri.

His jeans outlined those powerful thighs and tight butt, his gray shirt molding to the hard planes of his lean stomach. It was impossible to be in the same room as him and not be aware of his every breath, every movement.

Before she could blink, he was bending over her seat, his breath whispering against her cheek.

Every inch of her uncoiled at the latent power of his body caging her against the seat. Heat from his lean frame stroked her, and she gripped the leather seat tight. "You do know that she will just drink all your hard-earned cash, don't you?"

She nodded, mesmerized by the molten depths of his eyes.

"Then, it hasn't sunk into that stubborn skull of yours that she's only manipulating you? That she will suck the blood out of you but not stop? That you're nothing but a crutch that she'll use for the rest of your life?"

"She's still my bloody mother." She was shouting now, her eyes filling with furious tears. "Would you rather I walk away like you did, wash my hands off, turn away from that dirty world? Pretend as though I never came from there in the first place, as if I never had a weakness or a flaw to begin with? Spend the rest of my life pursuing mindless pleasure in every corner of the world as if it was my due?"

A flicker of something molten flashed in his eyes, a flinch to his mouth.

She had surely angered him now. But instead of fear, she felt only exhilaration. As if the blood pounded harder in her veins.

He dipped his head even lower, bringing his mouth so close to hers. *God*, all she had to do was tilt her chin up and her lips would graze his. She would finally know how he tasted; she would know what she had already imagined a thousand times over.

Just one taste, that was all she wanted of this man who set her senses aflame without even trying.

"So whatever little you had to pay me back is gone now, *ne*?" he finally said in a silkily dangerous voice.

It made her feel oddly hollow, weightless.

"What happened to your pride, Jas? What happened to paying me back even if it killed you? What happened to not depending on me for anything ever again?" His thumb traced her lower lip, as if he was testing the shape and softness of it.

It was not affectionate or tender...and yet, the ache between her legs was long, low and instantaneous.

Instead of slamming his hand away, she froze.

"You don't have a job. You donated your meager savings because you're weak enough to still want to matter to her." He traced the seam of her collar with a long finger, and her skin tingled as if he had drawn a line of fire down her throat. "Even the shirt you're wearing is mine." Her heart threatened to rip out of her chest as he scrunched the fabric with one hand and pulled her forward.

He whispered the words against the corner of her mouth. "How exactly do you think you're going to pay me back now that you're penniless?"

Incendiary heat sparked from that small patch of skin, and she shivered violently. His fingers pressing into her jaw, his body locking her against the seat, there was nowhere for her to go, even if she would have wanted to.

"Or is it that," he continued, a certain relish to the way he enunciated every word, "your pride and outrage at being in my debt was just an elaborate farce? Did you envision living a cozy and comfortable life off my goodwill and wealth? A rich benefactor was what you were looking for all along? Does Noah get a cut?"

She felt her chest tighten at the very picture he painted in such a honeyed tone, as if he very thoroughly relished twisting the knife as deep as he could.

A soundless scream ricocheted inside her, leaving marks, while she still grappled with the poison in his words, with that savagely satisfied glint in his gaze.

He's doing this on purpose, some naive, weak part of her moaned.

But she squashed that stupid, wanting, weak Jas.

It didn't matter how much he believed his own outrageous claim; it didn't matter if he truly thought her a scheming witch out to snare a better lifestyle.

What mattered was that he had chosen to say those words out loud, that with every word he spoke, with every look he cast at her, Dmitri pushed her away, hated her very presence in his life.

Dmitri, she realized with a painful breath, was so dangerous to her. All she wanted at that moment was to pay his debt, walk out of his life and never see him again. Never subject herself to this hollow weakness, to this constant shame and inadequacy clinging to her every pore.

And there was only one way she could do both: take something she seemed to want with a longing like she never had, and pay off his debt.

The only way, as crazily desperate as it was…

Clasping his cheek, she covered the last bit of distance between them. Pressed her mouth against his, her teeth grinding against his lips. A tremendous stillness came over him while an inferno of heat and shame and fury raged inside her.

She could feel her heart hammer against her chest, like a bullet would ricochet in a closed room, punching holes through it…

And then it slowed down as his gaze clung to hers, a palette of emotions burning through it.

His mouth…oh, that sinful mouth was so hot and soft, seemed to fit so perfectly against her…and everything inside her sobbed and reveled at how intoxicatingly good he tasted. Everything inside her wanted to sink and burrow into him… All this in the space of one jagged breath.

Time itself seemed to come to a screeching halt, and Jas slanted her mouth afresh against his again, arching into his body, and tasted him, again and again…this way and that, moving and lapping while his bristly chin scratched her, while his breath infused hers…

The scent and taste and heat of him exploded inside her and she wanted more of this madness; she wanted him to kiss her back if it was the last thing she knew, so she dug her teeth into that sculpted lower lip…

And he turned into a burst of violent energy around her. His fingers crawled into her hair, molded her scalp roughly and slammed her against him. Her breath shoved out of her lungs.

Sweet victory was hers, she thought, drowning in the storm in his gray eyes...

He growled against her mouth, hot and hungry. And her aching sex pulsed in tune with that feral sound. The sweep of his tongue, the biting grasp of his mouth... It was like a furnace had been stoked into life inside her.

His mouth clung to hers with an erotic heat. Pleasure suffused her every nerve until she thought she would burst from the inside out. That mouth—*oh, God, that mouth*—it devoured her softness, pressing and plunging, licking and nipping, biting and bruising, one hand splayed against her scalp, one hand holding her shoulder in a bruising grip so that she didn't lean into him.

A moan, drugged and delirious and, oh, so wicked, rang around the cabin, and she realized that it was she who made that sound. That she was panting and moaning, that a rush of wet heat filled her core, that an ache zoomed from her mouth to every inch of her, that Dmitri's kiss was more real, more him than anything else he did or said.

It was as if she had found the Dmitri that she had been waiting for all these years, here of all places.

In his kiss.

Her soft, tentative mouth was like pouring kerosene onto a thin flicker of fire, working him into such a state of arousal that Dmitri felt it burn his throat.

Then her tongue licked his lower lip and his erection became thick against his jeans, as if it could imagine those licks against itself...

It was unlike anything he had ever known in the past decade or with another woman. But it was the vulnerability that she strove so hard to hide in her eyes that captured him.

Her eyes held that perpetual longing for something, that same hungry look that he saw when he looked at himself in the mirror. Something inside her had always calmed him, and now it was as though the effect had grown up along with them, morphed into pure sexual hunger.

It stirred into fire that unquenchable hunger inside him, filled the void that resonated inside him whatever he did, however far he went to fill it...

She would be different, he knew. She would be an experience he would never forget in his life. She would be the drop that would finally quench his thirst.

Because Jasmine knew him, the real him. Not this charming, pleasure-seeking playboy that he had become to hide the reality.

And she would give him everything she had. He could see it in her eyes, in the way her eyes turned molten, in the way her mouth trembled when he came near.

What will happen after that, Dmitri? a voice very much like Stavros needled. *Christos*, that bastard had really become his conscience over the years, hadn't he?

And the voice that was full of honor and integrity poured ice-cold water over his lust. Black, guileless eyes wide, she stared at him with a sort of wonder. That very same look that had pulled him back from so many moments of rage.

Except now it was tinged with sexual need.

Hating himself, because her taste was already implanted in his very cells, he wrenched himself away from her. *Christos*, it wasn't working. Nothing he did to keep her at a distance was working.

"What the hell do you think you're doing?" Every word was gritted out through a tight jaw.

Jas tried not to flinch and failed, hurt and shame diluting the haze of desire in her blood. With shaking fingers, she touched her tingling mouth, wondering if she would ever forget the taste of him.

"I'm offering myself to you. I'm saying—" a balloon could be crushing her lungs "—take what you paid for."

She saw his flinch in the tightening of that concrete jawline, in the slow, almost imperceptible blink of his eyes, as if he was chasing away the shock before it could unsettle him completely. As if nothing he didn't allow himself to feel was to be borne.

He pushed away from her then, and it was that exaggerated, you-are-plague kind of movement that pricked her. "And what would that be, *agapita*? See, to this minute, I'm not sure what made Noah think you were worth that atrocious amount of money. What drove another man to bid for you against me?"

Crackling energy arced into life around them, but she was damned if she backed down now. "Have sex with—"

A flare of warning in his eyes arrested the word on her mouth. Coiled energy seeped from his very pores, as if his usual facade was surface-thin now. "Be careful what you say to me, Jas."

But she couldn't let him intimidate her now or he would do it forever, she realized. It seemed they were engaged in some kind of power play. God knew how, for she had nothing to take him on with, but no way was she going to back down. "Take my virginity. Call my debt done. God, let us walk away from this impossible situation."

"So you're selling yourself to pay off your—"

She slapped her hand over his mouth, a surge of fury washing through her. "Don't say it, or this time I'll drive the knife deeper willingly."

His mouth was a furnace against her palm. Slowly, as if it took him a tremendous amount of willpower, he pushed it back. "Then, what is it you're proposing, *thee mou*?"

She looked away, struggling to marshal her thoughts. His taste still lingered on her lips; her scalp tingled with how hard he had held her.

Had it been a knee-jerk response, then, that kiss? Did men inevitably kiss back with such heat when a woman threw herself at them? Was Dmitri no different from all the other men whose lust was so easily inspired by naked flesh grinding a pole?

The thought made her more than a little sick. But the kiss had felt so personal, as though she was getting a part of Dmitri...

It was tragic how little she knew. Although she had a feeling it wouldn't have come in handy with someone like Dmitri. It had been a week now since he had rescued her and yet she had no measure of him. At all.

"I'll sleep with you once. Just once to get even." Somehow, she held his gaze without betraying herself. "I won't be your mistress, Dmitri."

"You're automatically assuming that you fit the role of my mistress, *thee mou*. You don't. So don't lose sleep over it."

She barely resisted the urge to catch a glimpse of herself in the huge flat-screen monitor as his words ballooned inside her. She knew she was unfit for a lot of things, but this... *"I'm not...fit to be one?"*

"You're not my type."

"I thought anything with a set of boobs was your type."

His gaze dipped to her chest and stayed there, the most unholy light in it. As if he was asking her to give him a peek.

Heat claimed her face, and she folded her arms repressively. She knew what would wipe that look off his face, and for a self-indulgent second, she was so tempted to do it, but...her mouth went dry just at the thought of it.

"How would you know what I prefer, Jasmine?" Nice and pleasant and warm, as if they were discussing the weather.

"The tabloids are full of your manly exploits, as they like to call them. Orgies and parties aboard your yacht, motorbike races, boxing matches with other men who have to thump and pummel each other to prove their stick is bigger than everyone else's—"

His sudden laughter filled the cabin and she stared hard. The man was so unfairly gorgeous…

"Your very lifestyle is providing an economy for some of these magazines."

"And you were spending your hard-earned cash on them?"

She was trapped and they both knew it. "I want to hear about these standards of yours. I want to hear what screening process the most self-indulgent, pleasure-seeking playboy in the world has for the women he—"

"I like my women wanton, willing and experienced. I like them stylish and sophisticated and full of confidence in and out of bed." So basically, everything she was not, she realized. "I like them to want me in bed as if I was air."

Oxygen seemed to be fading fast as he enunciated each word, his gaze full of molten hunger. Her skin tingled; her body ached.

"I like to not wonder if I would find a knife in my back while I'm kissing her or to be wished to hell while I'm moving inside her."

"I would never knife you from the back," she mumbled, her mouth drying at the erotic picture he painted.

His mouth curved into one of those rarely genuine smiles. "That is true. Should I continue?"

"No."

"You're prickly, infuriatingly naive," he said it as if it was the most boring list in the world. "You have a lust/hate thing going on with me and…your virginity means you'll be high maintenance in bed."

"I do not have a lust/hate thing going on for you... What the hell do you mean, high maintenance?"

Damn it, she needed to find a way to stop his words from finding purchase inside her. Or a way to stop her body from wanting him so much...

Because no amount of twisting the truth was going to help her.

She wanted Dmitri with a hunger that knew no reason or rhyme. She wanted him to look at her as if she was the only woman on earth; she wanted him to worship her, look at her as if he couldn't breathe if he didn't have her.

For years, she had lived, cloaking herself in shame, unable to look at any man and not hate herself. It was the only way, clutching that self-disgust, that she had been able to go on.

The only way she had been able to slip into the skin of *Jazmin*, the pole dancer, and still face herself in the mirror come morning.

Now it was as though that shame was beginning to slide off her skin. Now it was as if she could breathe and face herself in the mirror again. For the first time, she could be a woman.

It was as if her sexuality, denied and deprived for so long, was on wings.

"Yes. I'll have to teach you what to do, be gentle so that you're not hurt, and then after the whole thing," he drawled, as if it was the hardest thing to sleep with her, "I'll have to hold you and mop your tears and lie that it was the most beautiful thing ever. Deflowering virgins is highly overrated, Jasmine.

"I like my sex fast, rough and without any accompanying drama, whereas you're an emotional cannon waiting to go off. And as you seem to know very well, I'm incapable of anything but the most insubstantial of emotions."

"I'm not an emotional cannon."

He undid his cuffs and rolled back the sleeves. Plump veins ran over the muscular arm, the sight of coarse hair on that olive skin giving her a warm flush. "In the past week, you have knifed me, sobbed all over me, tried to kiss me and wanted to cuddle as though I was your favorite—"

"Only an utterly ruthless bastard would count those against me in such a way."

"If you think I'm anything else, then you're more foolish than I thought, Jas. Find another way to pay me back."

"So that until then you will tug me along with you as if I was a pet you decided to keep while passing judgment on the choices I have had to make to survive."

"Yes, that's the one upside to this whole thing. I can tell you, repeatedly, what a naive, stubbornly annoying..." He looked away as if his fury couldn't be contained by words.

"You almost sound as if you care."

"And you sound far too desperate to hear that I care. *I don't care*, Jas. My only interest is in keeping you alive. I don't like even a pinprick of guilt, marring my lifestyle. So me looking after you is for purely selfish reasons."

Could he not leave her even a fragment of her pride? But for once, Jasmine had a feeling it wasn't about her, her shame, her nonexistent self-esteem.

Why was he always making sure she didn't form an attachment to him? Why did he insist on reiterating what he didn't feel for her?

What if it wasn't about her?

She looked around the plane, thought of the bike, the hotel he had taken her to. His yacht, his expensive toys, his women... If Dmitri was the playboy he played so well, he wouldn't have come for her like that.

If he hadn't cared, he wouldn't have been so angry

with her, then or tonight when she had suggested a way to pay off her debt.

"Is it so hard to admit that you feel something for me, Dmitri? Even if it was just an echo of our horrible past life together? Everything has to be this sanitized, sterilized version of you?"

His head recoiled back, tension swathing his entire frame. As though she was a danger to him. When he looked at her, his head cocked and eyes narrowed, Jas didn't buy it.

It was as if a storm was brewing in his eyes as he stood up. "That Dmitri was violent and deranged, Jas."

She had shocked him. Into what, she had no idea, but she had. Satisfaction swelled inside her. "At least that Dmitri was real."

"You're like that mutt Andrew saved once, remember? Even after it got better, he wouldn't go away. Kept coming back to him, desperate for another nuzzle."

Instead of the smooth, uncaring tone that he delivered all his insults in, he sounded ragged, on the edge, furious.

And just like that, his insults didn't hurt anymore.

Instead, she felt victorious, as if she had drawn him out finally.

Feeling more out of control of her own fate than her worst working nights had been, she sighed. "You said Stavros was Leah's husband. Are they really getting married again?"

"Stavros married Leah under the worst of circumstances." His voice took on a softer tone when he spoke of Leah. "To make up for it, he is giving her a wedding now."

"He looked so stern and forbidding...but he's doing it for her? That is so romantic. No wonder Leah looks as if she's glowing from the..."

His pointed look told Jasmine clearly what he thought

of her gushing. A burn began to climb up from her chest to her throat.

"Is that what you want, Jas?" he said without scorn or mockery.

"What I want… I've never even had the indulgence to think of what I want from life. It doesn't mean I can't appreciate someone else's happiness. Despite what I've had to do to survive, there's some innocence left inside me, Dmitri."

"Some innocence, Jas?" A light came on in his eyes, rendering Jas still. As if she had gained a little traction with him. Just a little but enough. "Have I been duped in the quality of my purchase? Is there a return tag, then?"

It was an outrageous situation they seemed to be caught in. And it was of their own making, too, Jas realized with a hollowness in her gut. But neither of them, it seemed, would walk away.

And if she didn't laugh, she was afraid she would cry. Or do something equally disastrous, like wanting to prove that she was woman enough for the arrogant rogue in front of her.

Prickly and high maintenance? Oh, how she wanted to do something that broke that smugly satisfied smile. How she wished she could shatter that facade of careless debauchery…

How she wanted him to kiss her, not because she thrust herself at him, not because he thought he should teach her a lesson, but because he wanted to, more than anything in the world.

Nothing more self-destructive in wanting to prove that she had a place in a man's life when he couldn't give a flying fig about it… She had seen her mother do it and had the worn-out child *and* adult T-shirts to wear for it.

"One of these days, you're going to wish you had sent

me on my way, Dmitri," she said, because empty challenges didn't cost anything.

She was far too invested in this strange relationship they had, she realized, fresh panic blooming in her gut.

CHAPTER SEVEN

JASMINE HAD NEVER imagined that she could feel lonely surrounded by at least a hundred guests at the estate where Stavros and Leah were getting married. It seemed as if the entirety of Athens' high fashion society was attending the party that night and would stay for the wedding.

Dmitri had dumped her once again at the estate in the middle of the night and disappeared after he had blurted out, "We'll talk about your future after the wedding."

He had quite literally handed her over to a maid and stormed back into the night.

Clamping her teeth so tight that it hurt, she had forced her mind away from where, and whose bed, he would be going to in the middle of the night.

Having fallen asleep at some strange hour of predawn, she had woken up this morning to the sounds of guests having a lazy, laughing breakfast in the courtyard outside her balcony. Disoriented by the amount of jet-setting she seemed to be doing, she had pulled on a sweater and ventured out to see Stavros and Leah and an assortment of strangers staring up at her.

It was obviously too early and too domestic a setting for Dmitri to be anywhere near.

She had never felt so out of place as that morning.

Yet what was he supposed to do with her, she had asked herself on her walk that afternoon. She was neither a friend for him to voluntarily want to spend time with her, nor was she a girlfriend, which would have been altogether another matter. Nor was she a family member.

She only wished he hadn't brought her to such an intimate occasion. The last thing she wanted to do was to intrude on Leah and Stavros.

She couldn't bear to think about what the couple thought of her. Because, despite everything, she liked them, and in a different life, she would have wanted them to like her.

Granted, she had spent barely any time with them and under such strange circumstances that night, but there had been such a familial bond between Dmitri and the two of them. A bond she had only seen once before, between her brother, Andrew, and Dmitri.

Had she somehow expected the same bond to exist between her and Dmitri, despite his new life and her supposed hatred for him? Was that why it felt as though she was being knocked down by every small thing he did or didn't do?

So she mostly kept herself to her room and walked around the lush acreage whenever she couldn't bear to stare at the elegant furnishings anymore. She had just finished walking through the vineyard and returned to her room when someone knocked on her door.

Leah Sporades stood outside the room. "May I come in?"

"Of course." Jasmine stood back, remembering her manners.

"I'm sorry I haven't been able to spend time with you after you arrived last night. I had so many last-minute details to look over and then of course, Stavros is being his usual arrogant, domineering—"

"Please, Leah, stop." Jasmine was equal parts embarrassed and amazed by Leah's openness. "Don't say another word. I should be the one apologizing for intruding on such a private and important occasion. You're not responsible for unexpected guests who crash in the middle of the night."

"What?" Now the woman looked genuinely baffled. "Jasmine, I insisted that Dmitri bring you. What did he say to you to make you feel as if you were not welcome…" Leah sighed. "He just dropped you here and left, didn't he? In the middle of the night?"

Jasmine decided she would rather die before she betrayed how much that had hurt. *Yet again.* "Yes, but then that's to be expected. It's not as if he's my keeper despite the fact that he… He insists on dragging me along but hates me for it… I don't understand why he won't just leave me to my fate."

The most painfully thick silence followed her outburst.

Jasmine turned away toward the window, mortification burning her face up as if it was a furnace. She had said way too much again.

Sighing, she pressed her forehead against the cool window. "Forget I said that, please. I…I'm usually not so whiny and self-pitying. The past few days, my life's taken the strangest turn after years of…" *And Dmitri was at the center of all the confusion…* "I feel a bit lost and directionless."

Leah joined her at the window and squeezed her hand.

Fighting a gush of warmth at the back of her eyes, Jasmine held on.

Her mom's lifestyle, Andrew's problems and then her own chosen path meant she had never had the chance to have a normal life. Now she realized how many small, simple things, like friendship, she had given up willingly along the way.

She hated him for it, but maybe there was credit to Dmitri's ruthless walking away from the whole lot of them. Cutting away those ties that only added burdens to her very soul. Starting afresh without the past hanging around her neck like a boulder.

He was flourishing, wasn't he? she thought with uncharacteristic envy.

"When Stavros told me what kind of a…situation Dmitri found you in, and how you got yourself out of it, I was amazed." Jasmine raised her gaze and met Leah's, the calm acceptance in her tone going a long way to soothe her. "What stuns me even more is how different and strangely intense Dmitri was around you in just those few minutes. Whatever is going on between you two—"

"Nothing is going on between us, Leah. I'm like that festering sore he wants to close, a dirty stain from his old life he wants to incinerate. In fact, I'm as stunned as you are with each passing hour why he won't just wash his hands of me. He's made it clear enough that this whole thing with me…has disrupted his life."

"But nothing ever disrupts Dmitri. Nothing even touches Dmitri. He has his work and toys. The only lasting relationship he has in his life is with Stavros, and he has that *insane*…lifestyle.

"Whereas with you, it's as if… He doesn't know what to do with himself with you around is what I'm thinking," Leah added, with a twinkle in her eyes that made Jasmine squirm uncomfortably.

Of course, she couldn't tell Leah it was all one-sided.

"You're so much in love," Jasmine said without rancor. "You're seeing rainbows and butterflies and possibility of romance where there is only guilt, Leah. Please don't matchmake."

"Am I that transparent?" Leah said. "All I wanted to say, Jas—I can call you Jas, right?" When Jasmine nodded, she went on, "Is that I know how it feels to not have a friend. And to deal with a man who, at least, *seems* to not like…"

"*Hate* is the word you're looking for," Jasmine pointed out sourly.

"*Hates* the very air you breathe," she said pointedly, and something in her gaze told Jasmine how far Stavros and Leah had to have come. "And turns you inside out. And makes you wish you were anyone but yourself."

Jasmine smiled, something in the other woman's openness catching up to her. "I don't believe Stavros could ever hate you. Even I can see that he worships you."

A blush dusted her cheeks and Leah laughed self-consciously. "But we almost lost each other. The thing is, you have a friend in me. And it has nothing to do with Dmitri."

Jasmine had never known such open acceptance, such genuine warmth. "Thank you."

Walking into the center of the room, Leah looked at her wardrobe. "Now let's talk about something fun. What are you wearing to the party tonight?"

Could one die of an excess of embarrassment? Jasmine wondered for the *n*th time in the past week.

"I…I don't have anything to wear. And I've had a lifetime's quota of being embarrassed and humiliated and whatnot by Dmitri."

Such an effervescent smile dawned on Leah's mouth that Jasmine forgot what she was going to say. "I'm a designer with an entire workroom full of dresses, and I would love to dress you in something that will knock the—"

Jasmine shook her head. "No, not for him," she amended.

What was the harm in borrowing a dress for one night? In opening herself to a friendship? In letting, for once, something good enter her life?

Whether willingly or not, Dmitri had given her her life back. And she was going to live it, for herself, starting tonight. Not her mother, not the pain of the past, not a debt, which somehow she would find a way out of, and definitely not about a man who kept her around because it relieved the little guilt he had about the past.

She faced Leah and smiled.

"I want to look good for myself. I want to have an evening where I forget the past week and don't worry about the future. I would love to borrow your expertise and your dress so that I can enjoy the party and be a part of my new friend's happiness. That sounds good, right?"

Leah beamed, hooked her arm through Jasmine's and said, "That sounds perfect."

Take what you paid for.

Jasmine's outrageous dare kept ringing around in Dmitri's head as he stepped out of his chopper and waved the pilot away.

And her kiss... *Theos*, it had lasted a few seconds too long, because he could still feel her taste on his lips, could still feel the liquid longing flowing through him.

As if she had left something of herself in his very blood.

He turned and stilled, taking in the tableau of the evening spread out from his vantage point atop the roof.

Giannis's estate, the very place that had shielded him and healed him, at least enough to move forward in life, was lit up like a bride. He was glad Leah had decided to have the wedding here. It would have made Giannis ecstatic to see Stavros and Leah begin their new life here.

A huge white marquee had been erected in the vast grounds behind the mansion. Soft, strategically placed ground lights lit up a path from the house to the marquee and all around the gazebo and the pool.

A profusion of stylishly dressed guests flitted in and out of the marquee, and he searched the festivities, only then realizing that he was looking for *her*. That all day, he hadn't been able to get her out of his mind.

Cursing himself, he walked off to shower and dress.

He had dropped off Jasmine past midnight and gone back to the Katrakis offices in Athens, the very force of his need to keep her by his side pushing him to do the opposite.

It had taken every ounce of his willpower, which was not much to begin with when it came to her, to keep rejecting her in the face of her increasingly reckless questions. In the face of her soft mouth flush against his, her breath coating his skin.

Take my virginity. Have sex with me, just once. Call the debt paid.

Something about the casually abhorrent way she had made that offer wouldn't leave him alone even now.

As if she was offering herself up like some sacrifice to circumstances beyond her help and he…he was *unscrupulous and monstrous* enough to want to take it.

It hurt him, he realized, stunned at the new development. It stung that she would think him low enough to take her under those conditions.

Did she think him so completely without morals? Hadn't he done all he could to make her think that?

But the farce he had begun sat like a knife under his ribs now, constantly pinching him. That she thought he was without morals or loyalty or even basic decency grated on him.

Theos mou, the more he tried to insult her and humiliate her and chain her with his words, the more she seemed to sink under his skin, the more she seemed to carve into him.

And the thing that boomed loud inside his head, refusing to be ignored, that had rattled him through the office hours today until he had walked out of a shareholder meeting that he had insisted on, was how tempted he had been to take her up on the disgusting offer.

Tempted to continue kissing her, to swallow her gasps and moans, to tear away the loose shirt and bare her to his gaze, to strip her until all that she worked so hard to hide was revealed to him…

Something desperate and needy inside him was mesmerized by her.

By her daring smile, by her disarming innocence, by her disquieting loyalty to her brother and mother, by her disturbingly sensual mouth that seemed to say the most outrageous things to him…

Having showered and dressed, he made his way back to the grounds, eagerly eating up the space. He spied Leah and Stavros at a distance chatting with a cousin of Giannis's who was an absolute bore, and grinned at the scowl that was beginning to make an appearance on his friend's brow when the younger man kept touching Leah.

Stavros, when it came to Leah, was like a dog with his favorite bone… No one would touch her if it was up to him, no one would even look at her…although for the first time since Dmitri had met Stavros, he began to understand Stavros's possessiveness.

Theos, he wished he didn't but he did.

He took a champagne flute from a passing waiter and downed it in one go, feeling decidedly on edge. Deciding he needed something stronger, he was about to walk toward the bar set up near the house when he heard husky laughter and turned toward the gazebo.

The vividly red curve of a woman's lush mouth met his gaze. Arrested, he stared, realizing slowly that it was none other than Jas.

Jas, as he had never seen or imagined her—exotic, stunning, brimming with a sensuality that had every drop of blood in him pounding south. Possessive desire knocked at him.

You're not my type.

You're prickly, you'll be high maintenance in bed.

Each and every one of his words came back to him as if fate had very neatly and viciously aligned them for him to swallow back.

She stood in the gazebo, a circle of light bathing her from head to toe. He noticed her shoulders first. A strange thing to be noticing about a woman, he instantly thought, the excellent champagne warming his throat.

Bare and delicately rounded, while her long arms had a muscle tone to them. His fingers itched to trace the graceful line of her neck to her collarbone.

Her hair, her glorious hair, finally free of that knot, framed her face in thick, wavy curls, softening that feral look.

A shimmering gold dress, with a neckline that crisscrossed over her breasts, pushed her breasts up and then, right below, flared out into billowing folds. It ended several inches above her knees, baring long, toned legs that literally went on forever.

For days, she had been covered up in the baggiest of clothes.

He had been right, she was far too much on the thin side, all jutting bones and sharp angles. But the shimmering fabric made everything of what there was of her.

She looked like an exotic bird; nothing so pedestrian as the word *beautiful* would suit her. A barely there chain hung over her throat with a glittering diamond pendant nestling in that cleavage.

Desire and possessiveness rolled through him in waves.

It felt like his stamp of possession that she wore a thing he had bought. Even though the simple fact that she was wearing the necklace proved that she clearly didn't know it. She would probably throw it in his face, he thought, grinning.

It had been mere months before Andrew had died,

for her eighteenth birthday. Dmitri had overseen his first million-dollar project and Giannis had made him a stockholder in the company. Two years after Stavros had made it. And had asked him how he wanted to celebrate. Looked at him with such a twinkling light in his eyes when Dmitri had said that he needed to buy a diamond pendant first.

What had he been thinking then? Had he always been waiting for her like this?

No, he told himself, discarding his champagne flute with a flick of his wrist. No, it had been about proving himself. He had wanted to go back to the one innocent in his old life and show her that he had made it. That he was nothing like the man who had raised him.

So he'd had it delivered, uncaring as to how Andrew would explain it. Something inside him roared in delight and he just couldn't silence it anymore.

Nothing ever touched him beyond an ephemeral satisfaction. Nothing ever held his attention for more than a few days.

Except now, with this woman. If her brother had kept him alive, it was as if she breathed new life into his very veins... As if she held the key to making him whole again.

When the man next to her bent too close to her, she tucked away a curl behind her ear in a nervous gesture.

And that hint of vulnerability tugged at Dmitri.

His hair slicked back, his narrow nose seeming all too familiar, the man stood far too close to her. When he turned, the light illuminated his profile, and Dmitri recognized him.

It was the French photographer, Gaspard Devue.

Devue's fingers moved over Jasmine's bare arm, trailed over her shoulder while she froze, her neck holding at an awkward angle, those large eyes of hers too big and trusting.

The bruises, the fear in Anya's eyes when she had come to his hotel in Paris... Gaspard Devue was one of those who preyed on the innocent, defenseless, who needed to use his fists to make himself feel bigger and stronger...

Just as his father had been...

Something detonated inside Dmitri at the thought of Jasmine even breathing the same air. All the sophistication he had acquired slid off him, and he was that fourteen-year-old boy who had finally had enough. Who had finally found enough strength in his lanky arms to defend himself, who had been terrified that one day he wouldn't get up after another blow.

That had been the last day his father had ever been able to touch him. But still, he had been too late to save his mother. Always too late.

Adrenaline punched through his blood, his muscles curling for a fight. It was all he could do to stop himself from marching over there and throwing her over his shoulder, from dragging her back to her room and locking her in...

He couldn't create a scene at Leah's party even if the bastard deserved it...

All he needed was to get Jas away from the man. And then he would lock her up for the next twenty years...

Christos, where was his head?

He didn't understand what was happening to him. He did, however, know what it was he wanted, craved. Sex and passion, he understood. That, for some reason, she trusted him and wanted him.

From the moment Giannis had pulled him away from that life, he had thought of her. He had been with countless women and hadn't felt an iota of what he felt when he just looked at Jas.

He wanted all of her.

* * *

She had known that he was watching her. Not from where or for how long. But the awareness had seeped into her as slowly as the breeze that caressed her bare shoulders, as sinuously as Leah's soft silk dress brushed against her skin, making her feel as if she, too, could be elegant and sophisticated instead of dirty and vulgar.

It was as though there was a chip under her skin that sent out a signal anytime Dmitri was close.

She had been so attuned to those sensations that she had missed half of what the suave Frenchman had said to her.

From the moment she had come down to the party, he had been so polite and attentive that Jasmine had felt flattered despite knowing that he was nothing but a seasoned flirt. Still, he had been telling her about all the photo shoots he had done with models she had only seen in magazines until she realized Dmitri was back and lost focus.

Belatedly, she caught him staring at her mouth and her face with a detached yet somehow intrusive intensity. Caught between embarrassment and hyperawareness, she froze when Gaspard trailed his fingers first over her jaw and then her neck. His strange gaze creeped her out more than the fact that he was touching her.

"So, *mademoiselle*, does my offer interest you?" he croaked out in a husky voice that felt just a little too practiced.

Schooling her face into a vacuous smile, she searched her mind for a way to ask the man what exactly his offer was. Because they had been talking about his studio, the project he took on, and if it was some kind of job or remotely like that, she didn't want to give offense.

And then she heard footsteps behind her—a soft tread like a predator that concealed its very ferociousness from an unsuspecting prey. Refusing to give in to the shiver that began at the base of her spine, she slowly turned, her hand still encased in Gaspard's.

The light from outside the gazebo enveloped him in a halo as he stood at the lower steps. Jasmine couldn't seem to breathe; her lips tingled, remembering, yearning.

A black tuxedo lovingly draped his broad shoulders, the snowy white collar contrasting against his olive skin. His freshly shaved jaw glinted and Jasmine once again felt the shocking awareness of every inch of space that Dmitri occupied.

He fairly breathed sex and masculinity and power, irrevocably out of her reach.

Until their eyes met. And then it was as though the world melted away around them. Every inch of skin that the silk touched felt hot; every muscle curled tight.

She reached out behind her, the wood grain smooth to her touch, hoping it would cool down this…heat inside of her.

He took the steps and a little chill pulsed down her back as his face was finally bathed in light.

Tight lines bracketed his mouth, that cool facade completely gone. His looks. His mood. His cloak of debonair charm. Everything had fallen away. Suddenly, he seemed like the Dmitri she had known once, and it tripped all her alarms.

"Hello, Gaspard."

Pure steel clanged in his voice.

Gaspard turned, blanched and then schooled his expression back to politeness. All in the space of a breath. "Dmitri."

The gazebo, which she had thought lovely seconds ago, suddenly felt like a battleground. Why did Dmitri look like he had seen a ghost?

He took another step, his gaze lingering on Gaspard's

hand over hers. "I see that you're already hovering around Jas like a vulture."

"Jas?" the man said, flicking his gaze between her and Dmitri. His nose flared as if he was a hyena scenting something. "But Ms. Douglas has been regaling me with tales of where she grew up…" He looked at Jasmine again, lingering on her diamond pendant and her dress. His brow cleared. The conclusion he so obviously came to was like a slap to her senses. "Is she one of yours, then?"

"I'm not *anyone's*, Mr. Devue." Jasmine wanted to slap the man and then thump Dmitri. "Really, Dmitri, don't—"

Cutting her off, he clasped her wrist and pulled her roughly to his side.

She resisted, or tried to. As a result, she ended up being slammed against his side.

Her breath left her in a soft gasp, a hundred different sensations swarming at her.

His hip pressed into her belly, the hard ridge of his muscled thigh straddled her legs and his forearm knocked into her breasts. His body was like a hot, hard cage around her shuddering muscles and shivering skin.

Sharp, instantaneous, all-consuming need filled every nook and crevice.

All the while the infuriating man stared at Gaspard, his expression disturbingly menacing. His arm stayed around her waist. "Jas is a childhood friend of mine and is in Athens as my guest." At least he hadn't said she was his possession. "She's not without protection, Gaspard. Do not come anywhere near her."

"Why don't you let the lady decide?"

"Unlike the women you terrify, I have nothing to lose." There was not even a facade of civility in Dmitri now.

Something crawled to the surface in the man's face, Jasmine was sure, before he spoke again. Something that made her uneasy. "Leah has my information, Ms. Douglas, if you would like to see me."

With another dark glance at Dmitri, the man left.

Jasmine felt her face flame as she saw that a few people had noticed the exchange. Saw the tasteless conclusion that they immediately came to.

They thought she was Dmitri's mistress and Gaspard had been poaching.

Bile coated her throat. The entire evening fell apart, instantly became dirty to her in a way that was reminiscent of her old life.

She turned to Dmitri, clutching the fury that threatened to split her from the inside. "What is it with you? Are you so sadistic that not only will you humiliate me but you won't let another man talk to me?"

Instead of the infuriatingly calm expression she usually got, a tic played in his jaw. "You don't know that man. It's got nothing to do with what's going on between you and—"

"Stop, just stop."

She looked around, trying to recall the simple joy she had felt this evening when she had put the dress on, when she had looked at herself…when she had, despite her effort not to, imagined the look in his eyes.

"All I wanted was to spend one evening like a normal person. Just dance, meet a few people who don't know what or where I have come from and have fun. Without you and this whole spectacle between us hanging over my head. Without worrying about the past or tomorrow. Now you have made me into an object of speculation. You made me feel as dirty as I have always believed myself to be."

His silence only lent weight to her accusation.

"I'm going to go over there and apologize to Gaspard. Stay away from me, *please*. The last thing I want is to create a scene at Leah and Stavros's wedding after intruding on it so shamelessly in the first place."

His fingers clamped over her wrist like a vise. "No, you'll not. You don't need to apologize to—"

"No, what I don't need is you in my life, even for another second. What I don't need is you dragging me around and dumping me without a word, leaving me to wonder what I'm going to do the next day. What I don't need is for you to make me feel as though every decision I have ever made is wrong, as if my entire life is one giant mistake.

"*God*, I'm so stupid I kept making excuses for you. I kept thinking…

"No wonder Andrew didn't want anything to do with you. No wonder he told me again and again that we were better off without you."

His skin pulled taut over his bones, his mouth blanching at her reckless words. "You're wrong, about everything."

CHAPTER EIGHT

SHE HAD JUST reached her room when Dmitri barged into the room. The thud of the door as he closed it with his shoulder sank into Jas's bones.

He flung the dinner jacket away, untied the buttons of his shirt. Was he preparing for a fight instead of walking away as usual? she wondered. Even that little bit of attention gathered momentum inside her.

God, she had it bad.

She leaned her forehead against the dark wood paneling of the wardrobe and closed her eyes. "I don't want to look at you…"

"No. I won't let you sneak away. Not until you hear me out."

"That's the problem with you, Dmitri," she said, still stunned at his mutinous tone.

Now he cared what she thought of him, that he had made her angry? That he had hurt her? Why?

"I have made it by myself all these years. Until you… stop treating me as if I'm rubbish you have been forced to rescue by a thin thread of conscience that you can't rid yourself of, I have nothing to say to you. Nor do I wish to listen to anything you might have to say."

They watched each other for an eternity of seconds. How was it that all her self-worth seemed to hinge on what Dmitri thought of her or how he talked to her? Or how he kissed her?

Was it a genetic trait that her mom had passed on to her, this eternal fixation on one man?

And slowly, sinuously, as if it was a snake waiting to strike, that awareness pulsed into life. Jasmine looked away to beat it back. The luxuriously soft red duvet covering the huge antique four-poster bed stared back at her, and the fever in her blood multiplied.

His arm stretched toward his nape, he finally spoke. "I have never thought of you as rubbish."

His deceptively flat statement lay in the space between them. Molten gray eyes challenging her to take it up, and hers surely reflecting her panic...

Her struggle lasted all of two seconds, that *same something* inside her being pulled toward him. As it had always been. "All your actions say otherwise."

"I was so angry that I could have wrung your neck for not coming to me sooner, yes. But I didn't think that of you, not once."

She could see him measuring his words now. What had changed?

Before she could argue, he held up a hand. "I didn't realize that leaving you in the middle of the night could be construed as—"

"Hurtful? Insensitive? It wasn't the point you were exactly trying to make?"

"No. I just couldn't wait to..."

"To go back to whoever was waiting for you, I know." She thought she might be a little sick. "I shouldn't have kissed you like that, not when—"

"No, you shouldn't have. And I don't have a girlfriend."

Something tight relented in her chest and she blew out a breath. Just because she lost the little sense she had when she was near didn't mean Dmitri had to reciprocate. "I only realized this morning how much of your plans I wrecked. I didn't know that Leah insisted that you make me your plus one. I'm absolutely okay with sitting with the guests. Dmitri, are you listening?"

"You have been thinking about this a lot."

She commanded herself to not flush. The traitor that her body was, it continued, as it wanted. "This isn't even your house and you dump me here in the middle of the night, not to mention two nights before the wedding. If Leah hadn't—"

"I knew Leah would look after you. And this is my house," he drawled. "Not that it was still okay," he added when she glared.

Her mouth fell open in an O. "I thought it was Leah's grandfather's estate."

"Giannis was fair to his last breath. According to him, Stavros got Leah and consequently a bigger share in the company, so I got the estate."

"So you got the bad end of the deal, then?" she couldn't help pointing out.

Leaning against the traditional, four-poster bed, he laughed. All Jas could think was that they were in a small room with a huge bed and... "Only you and Stavros think Leah is worth more than a thousand-acre estate."

"You're like a greedy dragon that hoards treasure. How much is enough, Dmitri? Have you really become that shallow?"

"It enabled me to buy you, Jas, didn't it?" he said, and then looked away, as if he had said too much.

And Jas scrambled for something to say, something to fight her body's feverish reaction to him. "I get that you have your own life and that I pushed my way into it. I just... Just don't dump me on someone else. Once we figure out some kind of plan for my future, I won't bother you again."

"I've decided that you're not bothering me anymore," he said, in an arrogant tone that said he had decided a lot more things than that.

What the hell did that even mean?

That was a complete one-eighty, if she'd ever heard one. She didn't dare ask him what had caused this. Because she was terrified he would tell her that he'd moved from mild annoyance to pity, that it was something from his past that had fractured through that facade tonight and not her...that she would realize that when it came to him, she would take anything.

God, she couldn't catch her breath with this man.

"But what you did just now, that was not okay on any level. You humiliated me. It's as though you really think I'm one of your possessions."

"Possession, Jas?" A winter storm blazed in his eyes. "You froze like a deer caught in headlights when he touched you."

"Dmitri, I'm not completely clueless when it comes to men. I know how—"

"Gaspard Devue is the worst kind of man, Jas." He reached her and Jasmine forgot how to breathe. He took her hand in his and looked down at them. Hers, slender and soft, his dark and rough—it was so...simply sexy. "That he gets to roam free like that after everything he keeps doing... I don't think Leah knows what kind of a man he is or she would have never let him step foot here. When I saw his hands on you, bile crawled up my throat.

"He has these toxic relationships with women. He abuses them in ways that I can't even bear to think of. I have seen his handiwork on Anya and—"

"Anya Ivanova, the supermodel? The one you were going to marry?" she piped up. Then wanted to sink through the floor when his mouth tensed.

He stared at her for a long time before he nodded. "He isolated her, beat her and, when she threatened to tell the authorities, he pulled the rug out from under her life by spreading vicious rumors about her work. Terrified to within an inch of her life, she came to me. I offered to stay with her at an Alps resort while she recovered. But however much I reassured her, she refused to press charges."

And the gossip magazines had thought a woman had finally conquered Dmitri Karegas. Dark and light, they had complemented each other perfectly. Jasmine had bought the tabloid, read it through and then ripped it into shreds, and had stood shaken by the depth of her envy for a woman she knew nothing about.

While he had been helping an abused woman recover her life.

Jasmine had a feeling she was seeing a side of Dmitri no one did. Except the unfortunate woman.

"Gaspard was the one who found her in St. Petersburg when she was barely seventeen, gave her her first big break. And through the years, he isolated her, abused her. Until she thought there was nowhere else to go, caught in that relationship."

And Dmitri had got her out of it. "She quit modeling, didn't she?"

"Yes, I helped her get out of some of the contracts." He shrugged.

When there had been no announcement of an engagement coming, the tabloids had gone berserk. Nothing had come out of it except Anya Ivanova, she suddenly remembered breathlessly, had started a retail clothes store in London.

With Dmitri's backing, Jasmine realized, the pieces falling into place. He had helped the woman get on her feet, but she knew he wouldn't mention that.

Just like he wouldn't mention anything that betrayed the man he was beneath the facade. She understood now why he had reacted so violently, saw the shadows of the past fill his eyes.

"I saw that flicker of interest in his eyes when he looked

at you. If he so much as comes anywhere near you again, I will…" The barely restrained violence in him would have scared her if she hadn't known him once.

If he could do so much for an ex, Jas wasn't surprised at what he had done for her. After all, he had admitted that he owed Andrew. For all his playboy persona, Dmitri seemed to have a white-knight complex.

And she had been nothing but a literal damsel.

"Promise me that you will stay away from such men in the future."

"Isn't seeing him a long way from falling into an abusive relationship, Dmitri?"

"It is, but I…"

She gasped as realization sunk in.

He thought she was ripe for picking for a man like Gaspard, that she had no sense of self-preservation at all. Or maybe he thought she was like her mother.

But then, ever since she had come into his life, all she had done was act like a pushover. It didn't help to know that it was only he who made her act so out of character. "You think I'm more prone to it?"

"*Theos*, Jas, I don't want to argue with you. Just give me your word."

"I won't see him," Jasmine said first, wanting more than anything to reassure him. As to what the man's actual offer had been, she had no idea, but she didn't mention that to Dmitri. She sighed. "Believe it or not, I wouldn't have blithely gone off with Gaspard tonight or any other night. You give me far less credit. I made hard, gut-wrenching choices, but I did survive on my own, Dmitri."

"You have no idea how sorry I am about that."

"Why?" She shook her head. "It is not your fault."

And just like that she accepted it wasn't. When she had asked for help, he had come, guns blazing. What more could she ask for?

That they had grown apart was nothing but a circumstance of their lives. That she had held on to the memory of him all these years... It was an affliction she needed to grow out of.

"Partly it is. I...should have taken on your responsibility at Andrew's funeral, should have made some kind of arrangement for your future."

"Stop saying that. I never wanted you to fix my life, Dmitri. I just...needed a friend. Andrew needed a friend."

A growl fell from his mouth, a jagged sound of frustration and regret. "I should have known what Andrew would do. I should have...never trusted him. I should have..."

What did he mean? Fear fisted tight in her gut.

"Tell me to walk away, Jas," he said in that controlled voice that she was beginning to hate. "Tell me to leave the past where it should be. Tell me to hang on to the little honor I have."

He looked so painfully handsome, so achingly real. And she was terrified of asking but equally of not knowing... She felt as though she was standing at a precipice that she had been trying to reach all her life, as though the real Dmitri was finally within her reach.

"What did you mean by that?"

He knelt in front of her and a flutter began in Jasmine's belly. Tilted upward toward her, he reached for her and Jasmine started shivering. Warm, rough hands clasped her bare shoulders. "You're cold?"

"No. It's you," she whispered, knowing that there was nothing to hide from his gaze.

Fragile, she felt so fragile when he touched her like that...

His fingers lifted her pendant off her skin, the tips brushing against the curve of her breast. She closed her eyes, sharp tingles taking over her body. "I should have got the matching earrings, too."

A storm unleashed in her gut as the words fell over her.

Snatching away the pendant from his fingers, she looked up. "Wait...you were the one who had it delivered for my eighteenth birthday? But that's impossible. Why would Andrew say he had ordered it?"

The truth slammed into her from every which way, shaking the very axis of her life.

"Because he lied to you and to me. He told me you were better off without me in your life and I believed him. And I didn't care who you thought it was from as long as you had it."

It was all there in his eyes—the guilt, the pain, the lies he had allowed her to believe. He didn't have to say a word. And in that minute, she saw what she had been too blind to see.

"You came back to see us... Oh, God... When, how?"

He ran a hand through his hair. "That first year, I ran away three times and almost reached London. But Stavros just kept getting better and better at stopping me. Finally, Giannis made a deal with me. If I met every challenge he had for me, he would bring me himself to see Andrew. And I did. I worked round the clock. I begged Stavros to teach me everything he knew. I began to control my temper... And the little money I made in those first couple of years, which was truly nothing, I gave to Andrew."

She didn't care if it might have been nothing. He had been given a new lease on life, a life none of them had ever dreamed of, and he still had come back for them.

"You gave him money..." She slid onto the bench at the foot of the bed soundlessly, the whole picture emerging in front of her. Her gut turned so painfully that she thought she might be sick. "For how long?"

"Years."

Shock shattered her, bringing shards of pain with it.

"When I realized what he'd been doing, when his words

didn't add up anymore, I cut him off instantly. But his addiction to gambling was already in his bones. I should have realized he would somehow find the money, that the burden would fall to you. He had already turned you against me, and after he was gone…there was no point in telling you the truth."

He had protected Andrew even then. *And her from the ugly truth.* For a man who said he had done everything only to alleviate guilt, Dmitri had done so much for them.

More than their own mother.

"The last time he came to see me, I begged him to tell me where you were. And he said he would if I gave him money." He pressed his palms to his eyes. "It was the hardest thing to see him like that…"

"He made me hate you." God, Andrew had not only squandered what Dmitri gave him but borrowed more from Noah… "I'm so sorry…for all the things I said to you. For what he did."

Dmitri crouched in front of her, his long fingers stroking over her bare arms. She shivered, and pressed her forehead in his shoulder. Shame and grief vied for space within her. "Don't, Jas. You've carried his burden long enough."

His hands moved over her shoulders and soon she was in his embrace.

Jasmine wished she could cry and let it all out. But fury had turned into a hard knot and settled deep in her chest. She felt like ice.

Andrew had cheated both her and Dmitri to the very end.

That addiction was in their genes, their blood. And she was just as prone to it as they had been. Did hers come in the form of this man? Was it already too late?

But Jasmine found she couldn't care. She didn't care.

Her brother's betrayal cut too deep. All those years of slaving herself over a debt he had made, of defending him in her own mind, of putting her barely clothed body on display every night—all of it had been for nothing. The grief that she hadn't somehow been enough to get him through it... The crushing weight lifted.

She had paid the price for their weaknesses, their addictions. She would pay no more, not in shame, not in grief, and not by making their weaknesses her own.

The ice cracked just like that, the white-hot flame of her fury, her powerlessness found target in the man in front of her.

She jerked away from him. "Why did you tell me all this today? Why not that first night? Why now?"

Something desperate flashed in his eyes when he spoke. "You wish I hadn't told you?"

"No, I want to know what changed today."

Suddenly, she understood the second layer to his reaction when Gaspard had touched her.

She remembered the carnal promise in that blinding, incinerating moment on the flight when he had devoured her mouth, as if he was drowning. Finally, she understood what Dmitri had been hiding since the first night beneath his lacerating contempt for her...

An avalanche of want and need ripped open inside her as she looked at him with new eyes... He had wanted her all along... Then, why had he pushed her away so efficiently?

"Tell me, Dmitri," she commanded now, fully aware of what she was asking. No longer confused about her own want for him, no longer guilty or ashamed about it.

She'd never been an innocent, except in the most technical sense anyway.

Still, he had given her a choice.

She wanted him; she had known that from the beginning. But tonight, there was no shame or weakness that came with that want. Tonight there was nothing but the two of them.

"Because I realized the inevitability of this thing between us." His soft voice only amplified the spiraling tension in the room. "If not today, tomorrow. If not tomorrow… It's going to consume us both.

"I have never denied myself something I want. I want you. Every time you look at me, all I can think of is being inside you. Every time you lash at me, all I can think of is kissing your mouth… To hell with your debt and my honor, and Andrew… To hell with pretending I'm something I'm not. Nothing in the past decade has made me as hungry or as desperate as you have, Jas. So do you want this for as long as it will last? Do you have the guts to actually take me on, Jas? Because if I touch you, I won't stop."

For a seemingly infinite moment, she looked as though she would tell him to go to the farthest corners of hell. *Theos*, he deserved it just for the way he had treated her this past week. He already had a one-way ticket there for what he was about to do.

He was going to slake his lust and move on… Because that was all he did. That was all he had ever been capable of.

But he was through with being something he was not. He was through with denying himself. And he didn't allow himself to think of the consequences tomorrow. He'd deal with it.

Right now all he wanted was to taste that lush mouth again, remove that hurt from her eyes.

"You were attracted to me all along?" she demanded.

The gold fabric molding her lithe body, she looked like a goddess who had only just realized her power.

His heart threatened to shove past his rib cage. "*Attraction* is such a lukewarm word, *pethi mou*."

Even in that desperate last moment, he had tried for honor, Dmitri told himself. He had sounded nothing like a lover should. *Christos*, he was more tender with women whose name he didn't know, but with her, he sounded like an arrogant, lust-riddled jerk.

But at least he had told her what his terms were. If she didn't want him like that, she could walk away.

He was not seducing her, he told himself.

And then suddenly, she was walking toward him, and he shuddered with relief and tension and anticipation.

Before his next breath, her hands were in his hair and pulling his head down to meet her mouth. They groaned and pressed closer to each other, as if they couldn't get enough already.

He took her mouth with desperation and rough need, swiping at her trembling mouth with his tongue, impatient to possess her. And she…she was draped around him like ivy, her breasts rubbing and pressing his chest, one long leg wrapped around his as she moaned.

And the last flicker of self-restraint he possessed went out.

The taste of her had clung to him for two days, her jagged whimpers etched on his brain. Never had a woman so thoroughly consumed his every thought, never had she felt so out of his reach… He didn't question the possessive fire he felt as he learned her.

He had already decided when it came to Jasmine, he was mad.

Dmitri ran his hands over the taut line of her back to her rounded buttocks, the narrow flare of her hips. There were so many places to touch, so many places to learn. And she sank into his rough caresses, gasping and moaning under his mouth. As if she was as out of control for him as he was for her.

He dipped his hands into her hair and molded her scalp,

bending her to his plundering mouth. Like raw silk, her hair cascaded through his fingers. She smelled of wild-flowers and summer, and he breathed it in, hungry for every texture of her.

The more he touched her and stroked her and tasted her, the smooth forehead, the narrow bridge of her nose, the already red curve of her mouth, the pulse that skittered at her neck, the rim of her dainty ears, the more he thought of someone else's hands on all of it...on all of her...

Of someone, scum like Gaspard or John King or some-one like his father, laying a finger on her, marring skin that was like satin, touching curves that were pure perfec-tion, forever ruining that innocent yet wild spirit inside her, the hotter his anger and desire burned...

He took and took, licked and bit, stroked and tasted, plundered and devoured her mouth until she was panting and moaning, and gasping his name...

"Dmitri..." she whispered against his bristly jaw.

The trailing heat of her mouth against his neck made his throat dry. He pulled her up again, afraid that he would ravage her if she so much as kissed his skin...

Then she said it again, his name.

It fell from her mouth like a warm caress, an entreaty and command all wrapped in one... Hearing his name on her lips did what the little will he had over his body couldn't... It calmed him down, called him down from the edge.

He couldn't take her like every other woman in the world, not because of her innocence, but this was her...

"Keep saying my name like that," he commanded, looking for a hook, or a zipper, something that would re-veal her to him.

Her arms around his nape, her mouth against his, she complied. *"Dmitri."*

Too impatient now to think straight, he caught the crisscrossing strips of the gold silk and pushed it down her shoulders. Not before running the back of his hands over the hard nipples visible through the silk.

She made a sound, like a throaty purr, at the back of her throat, her gaze unabashedly meeting his. The liquid longing he saw there threatened to undo him.

The dress slithered down her breasts and hips with a silky whisper and pooled around her legs.

Dmitri stepped back, the better to see her, his breath knocking about in his throat. And almost lost it then.

It felt as though he had waited forever to see Jasmine like this and hadn't even known it.

He lost all sense of himself and time and space as he took in the glory of her body.

For a woman who'd never been with a man, she didn't slouch or cover her breasts, or bend her knees. Her slender shoulders thrown back, she stared back at him. Only her fluttering lashes and the tremble in her mouth betrayed her struggle.

Something feverish burned in her dark gaze, a gauntlet thrown. As if she was daring him to find fault with her now, to insult her again with his words.

Her breasts were lush and firm, with plump nipples that grew tight under his hungry gaze. His mouth went dry, his breath came in panting gasps as he drank in more and more of her. The flat plane of her stomach, the small tattoo, a rose, just above her bikini line and the shadow of the dark hair covering her sex underneath the sheer skin-colored thong.

Slowly, softly, as if she had done the same thing a million times, as if it was etched into her DNA, she stepped out of the pool of the dress and kicked it with a flick of her foot.

Three-inch stilettos with strings wrapped around her ankles, her long, sleek, toned legs completed the picture.

Somewhere in the past few seconds, his erection went from hard to painful, contained in his boxers. He had never been brought to such arousal just by looking at a woman. If she so much as touched him...

All the while his brain grappled to keep enough blood to form a coherent thought.

Something didn't add up, it said before his libido took over again.

But, drowning in desire, Dmitri found he didn't care.

All he wanted was to bury himself in her so deep that he never had to think again. That she forgot to breathe. "Take off the thong," he ordered, his throat croaking to form the words.

"And the heels?" she threw back, sounding husky and breathless, and he thought he would implode.

It was as if a different woman had emerged when she took off her clothes. No matter, he told himself, pushing himself off his feet.

He would learn every facet there was of Jasmine, every inch of her; every thought that passed her mind would all be his soon.

There would be nothing left of her that he didn't know, touch or taste.

"Keep them on," he said, determined to unravel her just as thoroughly as she had done him from the moment she had come at him with that damned knife.

It was as if with that one strike, she had permanently etched herself into his skin.

CHAPTER NINE

JASMINE WAS FINALLY, incontrovertibly ready to be the woman she wanted to be. She was ready to be just her, devoid of ghosts from the past, ready to own her pleasure, her life.

Clasping her nape with one hand, he caressed her hip with the other. Chest to breasts, hip to hip, thigh to thigh, they stood flush against each other. His erection, a searing brand against her lower belly, lengthened, and the thought of him inside her filled her with a mixture of excitement and anticipation. "It's going to hurt whatever I do," he whispered against her mouth. "I can't change that."

Something more than simple pleasure billowed in her chest that he respected her enough to tell the truth. That he didn't cover it up. That there was finally truth between them, at least in this.

"I don't care." She met his eyes squarely. "I'm not the girl you saved, not the sister of the man you owed a debt to, not the girl you feel sorry for. I'm just me tonight, Dmitri, and I have waited so long to feel like this... And I want the real you. Not tenderness that you have to fabricate, not lies you use to tether me, just you."

"You'll be the end of me."

She smiled, shivering from head to toe. "Then, I hope it's a pleasurable end."

Fisting his hand in her hair, Dmitri took her mouth in a bruising kiss. This kiss was hotter and harder than ever before, his tongue plunging into her mouth mercilessly. She could feel herself getting wet, the chafing of her thong too much to bear.

Her breasts pressed against his, his other hand splayed big and hard over her bare butt. "*Theos*, you're made for this, your body… I've never seen anything sexier."

Jasmine shuddered violently, pleasure shooting across and over her, like molten metal flowing into all the places she had hidden even from herself. Her body had been nothing but an instrument for survival until now, something she had detested, something she had centered her shame on.

Dmitri's words and caresses made her love it as much as he seemed to, freed her from her own shackles.

He pushed her against the wall, his suit-clad thigh jammed between hers, rubbing against her heated core. Pulling her hands above her head, he held them there.

The fiercely possessive heat in his eyes sent her insides swooping as if she was on a downward fall.

He trailed those sexy lips over her cheek, her jaw, licked the rim of her ear and then traced it down to the pulse at her neck. Throwing her head back, she gave in to it. This was what she wanted—Dmitri in all his bad-boy glory.

When his mouth closed over her pulse, Jasmine shuddered, hard. She had been terrified that he would be gentle with her, that he would be that fake, sophisticated version of him. But he was not, and her heart soared at that.

He was in this moment as fully as she had been, as real as he had been to her all those years ago.

Her stomach curled in delicious spasms as he dragged his mouth down, over the valley between her breasts. While one hand still arrested her hands from touching him, he palmed her breast with the other. Lifted the firm weight to his mouth and flicked the tight bud with his wicked tongue. Jasmine arched into him in mindless need.

Sensations sparked all over her, leaving little shivers in their wake.

Holding her hard against the wall with one shoulder while his white-hot gaze consumed her, he took the hard nipple into his mouth and sucked.

She came off the wall like an arrow, pleasure shooting down between her thighs. Her body felt like one pulsing mass of pleasure as he continued the torment with his tongue and, *oh, dear*, his teeth.

At some point, Jasmine stopped fighting and began sobbing and moaning and begging. His name became her mantra as he continued his relentless assault.

She had thought she knew what lust meant, what incited it. Thought it dirty. Despised how willingly one took on such intimacy for a few moments of pleasure, had thought the whole world crazy…

But the intimacy of their heated looks, the shared breaths, the fact his desire for her finally revealed the real Dmitri to her was just as arousing as the pleasure he was drenching her in.

There was not an inch of skin he didn't kiss or taste or suck. An intolerable, insistent ache built in her lower belly.

She sank her hands into his hair as he kissed his way down her abdomen, his willing slave. He was still in the snowy white dress shirt and trousers while she was naked and that, too, felt erotic, that, too, was intended to remind her that he was bending her very body, her will to his.

But she didn't care. All she wanted was to go wherever he took her, revel in whatever he gave her. To be possessed by him in every way that mattered.

And then he was kneeling in front of her, his face pressed to the flimsy triangle of fabric that covered her sex. "*Theos*, I can't wait to taste you, Jas."

She was flushing and panting, and moaning…as he rolled down the thong and lifted her leg.

Jasmine became boneless as he threw one leg over his shoulder, his harsh breath fluttering over the sensitive skin of her inner thighs. Thought she would melt into a puddle on the floor if he didn't hold her up with an arm against her soft belly.

"Oh…" The word floated out of her mouth.

When the first flick of his tongue came over her wet folds, it was as if someone had plunged a knife from her spine to her belly, so sharp and acute was the sensation.

Then he did it again, dipping that wicked tongue into her wet warmth with such expertise that she wanted to die from the onslaught of pleasure.

She shifted and snarled against the wall as he continued licking her, the pressure relentlessly sending her up and up.

"Please, Dmitri…" she pleaded, unable to bear it anymore.

"Look down at me," he commanded in a raw whisper.

Her hands in his hair, Jas looked down. Kneeling in front of her, his mouth tucked against the most intimate part of her, he looked like some pagan god come to wreak havoc, and she his feast.

As she watched, caught in the languorous heat in his eyes, his mouth closed over the swollen, excruciatingly swollen bundle of nerves and pulled ever so gently.

She screamed his name as she shattered into a million shards, her hips bucking against his mouth, her lower belly still spasming violently. He kept on and on until every last drop of pleasure was wrenched from her body.

When her knees buckled, he caught her and lifted her into his arms.

He carried her to the bed, his gaze drinking in her face. She fell in an inelegant heap, her heart still not back to normal after the earth-shattering climax.

Only the moonlight from the veranda illuminated the room, music and voices floating up from the party. Even that intrusion was too much for Jas. She didn't want to share Dmitri for a second.

His gaze stayed on her with the same intense hunger, as if all he wanted to do was to drink in her nakedness. Skin tingling at his perusal, she watched him as he shed his shirt, his trousers and the black boxers. Then he was gloriously naked, all hard angles and masculine power.

His tight shoulders appeared first, and then that muscular chest of his, velvet skin delineated over ropes of muscles, a washboard stomach and then...

"Oh, wow," she whispered at the sight of his turgid shaft.

Color slashed those cheekbones but he didn't smile.

Stretching her arm, which took every ounce of strength she had, she ran a finger from the base all the way to the soft head. So many men had made passes at her, from such an early age, and she had hated them and herself... had tuned out any and all curiosity and interest in men as a rule, first because of her mum and then because of what she had been doing...

"I finally get why so many women go gaga over you," she said huskily, still in a haze from the orgasm. But she didn't want to hide or feel ashamed at what should be natural, didn't want to punish herself for mistakes she hadn't made. "Just looking at you fills me with all kinds of ideas."

"One forbidden indulgence at a time, *glykia mou*." He stepped closer to the bed, and pulled her to him. "And who knows, by tomorrow morning, we might be done with each other."

She was slowly learning him now. When he felt something deeply, which was more often than not despite his facade, that was when he used those cruel words, to better hide behind them. Or to bury what he felt. Or to lash out.

Would he run if he knew how much of herself she was

giving in this moment? How much she wanted her body to please him, how much she wanted to leave a mark on him?

How many of her own shackles he was releasing her from?

She slid closer to him on the soft sheets, came up on her knees and bent. Her hair cascaded around her, giving her a second to overcome the heat tightening her cheeks.

Because more than anything, she wanted to please him.

She brought the rigid shaft to her mouth and licked the length of him. Velvet tightness over steel in her hand, his taste exploded on her tongue.

His breath hissed out of him, his hands sinking into her hair. She did it again and for a few seconds, his fingers fisted in her hair, dug into her scalp and held her there.

That raw glimpse into his need sent power spiraling through her, as if she had been jolted with a burst of it. Wrapping her tingling mouth around the broad head, she closed her mouth around it and sucked on him.

His curse reverberated around the silent room, only fractured by his harsh breaths.

Like an earthquake's aftershock, a tremor went through her lower belly at the taste of him, at the raw-edged need in his guttural groan. Addicted to her own pleasure, she looked up at him and did it again.

When she fisted her hand around that hard length, he pushed her back against the bed, none too gently.

He climbed onto the bed and over her, like a conquering warrior looking at his spoils. Lying on his side, he pulled her trembling body closer to him, one muscular thigh locking her against the bed when she tried to wriggle out of his hold. "Enough playing, *thee mou*. I want to be inside you *now*."

His hands moved down her belly and into her folds, as if he didn't listen to his own rules.

Intrusive and intimate, his fingers parted her. She

twisted the sheets and moaned. But was determined to say her bit. "I want to return the pleasure you gave me," she whispered, desperate to keep the tension out of her voice.

Because now that the flush of her pleasure was fading, anxiety at what was to come ate through her. She wasn't worried about pain; it was a fact of life. But his words still rattled around at the back of her brain.

High maintenance... She would die if he didn't find pleasure with her...

His kiss came like a cinder again, firing off every nerve, just when she thought she would never recover again.

"You think you're not giving me pleasure, Jas *mou*?"

He covered her with his body and Jas lost track of what she was thinking again. "You scream as if you're falling apart, you kiss as if you can't breathe, you sink into every caress, *Theos*... I can't breathe for imagining all the ways, all the places I'm going to take you..."

A gasp exploded out of her mouth when he pushed first one, and then two fingers into her inviting warmth, all the while his thumb pressing against the bundle of nerves at her core.

Through a fog of lust, she heard his pithy curse about protection and stayed his hand. "I've been on the pill since I was sixteen. In that, my mother was the model of a responsible parent. Or maybe she thought I would be just as weak and desperate as her."

She closed her eyes, disgusted that the echo of fear and shame she had held on to for so long still could rattle through her.

He came back to her and kissed her temple with such tenderness that tears knocked at her eyes. "Look at me, Jas."

When she didn't comply, he kissed her eyelids, the tip of her nose and her mouth.

He parted her legs and settled between them, his hip bone digging deliciously into her thigh. "You're nothing like her, *agape mou*. Don't you already know that? Your fire—" he kissed the valley between her breasts "—your reckless courage—" his tongue flicked her navel "—your heat—" her tattoo got his kiss now "—and passion—" long and unbelievably hard, his shaft settled at her sex, teasing her "—and innocence and kindness."

The tip probed the entrance while his mouth closed over her nipple. New sparks of need broke into life and Jas moved under him, restless in her own skin again. Desperate to have him inside her, desperate to be his in that final way...

His hands held her hips with a bruising grip and Jas writhed as the velvet heat of him scorched her already sensitized sex. "You're all the things none of us ever was, Jas, neither me nor Andrew," he whispered against her skin. "You are simply perfection." Drunk on his words, she reached for him just as he thrust into her in one smooth, sure stroke.

A curse ripped from his mouth just as pain cleaved through her pelvis.

Jas became rigid under him, her nails gouging his back, trying to get him to still, trying to breathe through the alien and achy and full feeling of having him inside her.

Dmitri was inside her, the wanton, willing part of her was screaming in her head. Magnificently masculine, he was heat and steel and hard around her and inside her, and there wasn't even a single breath she could take that didn't bring more awareness of him into her. She dug her teeth into his shoulder, tasted salt and sweat and him.

"You're doing beautifully, Jas." Drugged, his words rumbled against her rib cage. "You're... *Thee mou*, you feel like heaven."

Large, rough hands held her shoulders down and then

he thrust again, and he was now as thoroughly lodged inside her as he was lodged under her skin, in her heart.

A gasp tore from her mouth, borne more out of a new fire than discomfort.

His chest rasped against her breasts as he said something in Greek, but the pinch of pain was already receding and Jas was floating because even though she didn't understand what he had muttered, she did know that he was in an agony of pleasure, devoid of his control, shuddering in the wake of it just as she was.

Clasping his jaw, she pulled his head down so that she could look into his eyes. So that he knew it was she as irrevocably as she knew it was him. "Does it feel good, Dmitri?" she asked, determined to know for sure.

A series of curse words fell from his mouth, one filthier than the previous and Jas found herself smiling, her heart stuttering with joy. He pushed back her hair from her damp forehead gently. "That's for me to ask, *agape mou*. How do you feel?"

"As if I will die if you move and die anyway if you don't." A fierce heat began to build up her chest as he played idly with her nipple. The tip puckered at his touch, knotting and sending a pulse of sensation to her pelvis. "Tell me, Dmitri, how does it feel for you?" She dragged at his lower lip with her teeth and he hissed in response. "The truth, if you please."

Softly, slowly, he kissed her shoulder and she felt his damp forehead. She had a feeling that he was cooling himself down, like a wild animal catching a breath, before continuing the hunt. "You're so tight and hot and I'm too aroused and hard…" He rested his dark head between her breasts and expelled a sharp breath, the blade of his shoulders rattling visibly. "Jas, I can't change it and I can't change how good it feels to me while… I've never given anything, true, but I don't want to rain hurt on you, either."

He sounded so unlike himself that Jas smiled. And the man thought he didn't have tenderness in him. "But it doesn't anymore."

She dug her fingers into his taut buttocks and squeezed in closer, anchored herself on his rock-hard thighs. The hair on his thighs rasped against her palms; the leashed power in his body made everything thrum. She couldn't get enough of him, couldn't get enough of what he was doing to her. Couldn't breathe when she imagined all the things he could do to her with that powerful body, couldn't breathe at how fragile and delicate and precious she felt trapped under him. "And I trust you to make it better."

Tangling her hands in his hair, she took his mouth in a soft kiss that soon morphed into something else.

He met her gaze. He was incredibly still, almost crushing her into the mattress but he was gorgeous. "I can't go slow. You're incredibly wet and hot and I…just don't have it in me to be… I'm a selfish man, Jas."

"Selfish man who just made me see the stars and the sky? You're not too bad, Dmitri. And believe me, I won't break."

And to prove it to him, she thrust up experimentally. His hands on her hips holding her down, he withdrew almost all the way and then thrust back in.

Jasmine was in heaven or hell or someplace in between as he moved in and out with slow, measured thrusts that seemed to be for the express purpose of driving her out of her skin. "Faster, please," she said, and when he didn't oblige, she bit his shoulder.

The pace of his thrusts became faster, more desperate, less measured, one hand on her hip and one in her hair, his tight grip adding an edge of pain to the scorching pleasure.

The faster and rougher he got, the hotter and higher she climbed, his swift strokes wrenching arousal from her again.

Just for a second, he paused and sneaked his fingers between them and pressed down. And she fell apart. He took up his rhythm again as she came, his face a study in passion and need.

This time she didn't close her eyes.

She didn't want to miss the intensity of his passion, the gray fire in his eyes, the tightness of every feature, the corded stillness of his shoulder blades, the tiny beads of sweat along his upper lip, the growl that fell from his mouth as he pumped into her one last time and collapsed over her.

Wrapping her hands around him, Jasmine bore his crushing weight willingly.

She was now irrevocably a woman. And she liked all the perks that came with it. And the man who had taken her there with such an all-consuming passion, the man who claimed to possess no tenderness and did no emotions, who took on blame for her brother's sins, who made an art of the mask he showed the world… She was falling fast for him.

But whether it was the postcoital haze or the happy hormones their session of lovemaking filled her with, Jasmine couldn't care.

CHAPTER TEN

DMITRI PULLED JAS with him as he lay back on the bed. The echo of his release still pumped aftershocks through him, a climax that had been as emotional as it had been intense.

Her dares and her questions, the pleasure and pain and joy in her eyes… It wasn't just her body she had shared with him. Just like the little girl she had been, Jasmine gave whatever she had with generosity, felt everything she did with a sharp hunger that was so incredibly beautiful to watch…

For the first time in his life, sex for him hadn't been just about animal release but connection and intimacy, about kisses and sweet promises, about give and take of more than just release.

It was impossible to make love to Jas without taking a part of her.

Without a part of him wrenching away from him whether he willed it or not.

He had never felt this satisfaction, the visceral rightness of what had happened. This…sense of joy at a woman draped over him with such possessive pleasure. It went bone deep and he felt absolutely no inclination to get up and move, even though he usually headed directly to the shower after sex.

Her skin was damp to his touch, her breaths coming in panting pulls against his shoulder. Delicate fingers spread out over his chest, she kept her eyes closed.

She looked and felt perfect against the length of him, her hair spilling over his forearm.

He pulled the duvet up to cover them, his mouth going dry at the sight of her round buttocks, the flare of her hip. Still her breasts were flush against his side, and the thought of rolling those plump nipples on his tongue made him hard again.

"You are fine?" His voice came out gruff and growly.

Without opening her eyes, she nodded. Her hand moved restlessly over his chest, traced the ridges of his abdomen, came to rest on his shaft, over the duvet. He clasped her wrist, but she slapped him away and resumed her position. Heat punched through him as she played with it, a soft smile playing around her lips.

As if it was her right to fondle him. As if there was nothing else she would rather do.

"Jas, if you keep doing that, I will take you again."

Her mouth pressed into his skin. "So who's stopping you?"

Something between a groan and a growl escaped him as she pushed herself upon her elbow and proceeded to lick his nipple. As though she were a cat and he cream. "Your body is unused to this, *to me*. Since you don't seem to possess any good sense, it falls to me. And I'd rather not test my self-control, especially when it comes to you."

"Okay," she agreed, and moved her hand up to his chest but showed no signs of releasing him.

Theos, he hadn't meant to say so much.

Did he have to spell out everything to the infuriating woman? Did she find some perverse pleasure in behaving so outrageously that he inevitably watched over her?

And beneath his increasing fervor to have her again, he found that he liked indulging Jasmine. He wanted to stay there and let her play with him, to see a smile light up her eyes.

Usually, he couldn't wait to get away the moment his release hit. He had tried a couple of times to stay, to wrench some kind of feeling out of himself but all he had felt was coldness, an instant detachment that curdled any pleasure he had found just minutes ago.

An empty hollowness that he couldn't rid himself of.

So he moved on, to the next chase, to the next warm body that would provide that ephemeral release.

And yet, languorous heat pumped through him as she caressed him with more of an artless curiosity rather than skilled strokes designed to arouse. With her vined around him like that, he never wanted to get out of the bed.

Dmitri knew he should feel guilty. Or some other horrible emotion should be coursing through him, remonstrating with him for his lack of tenderness or finesse. Or shame that he had willingly given up that thread of honor Giannis had tried to instill in him.

Stavros would tell him, in that forbiddingly arrogant voice of his, that he should feel guilty about not feeling guilty, at least.

Breathing in the wild scent of Jas and sex combined, feeling her soft curves surround him, he couldn't bring himself to feel anything but the most primal kind of satisfaction.

Sated after the most intense sex of his life, he couldn't hate himself for it.

How could he when he barely ever felt anything this deep? When even the faces of the women he'd slept with the previous night faded by the next morning? When, sometimes, even sex didn't fill the void inside him for a few minutes?

The whole world, including Giannis, even Stavros, who knew him better than anyone else, thought he had no discipline, barely any self-control. That he gave in to every self-indulgence because that was all he cared about—pleasure and wealth and everything superficial.

What they didn't know was his inability to feel anything.

Not after he had cleaved himself in two and removed the guilt of his mother's death and the pain his father's fists had wreaked on him. That if he accessed anything deep, if he stayed too long with any woman or in any relationship, he started to panic.

As if that boy was just waiting to come back to life, bringing with him unbearable agony and pain. So he kept his entire life about casual relationships, transient fun. If not for Giannis first, and then Stavros grounding him, he had a feeling he would have become nothing but an empty shell who fed on transient pleasures and swam through life without meaning.

Until Jas had come into his life.

Her eyelids were drooping, and she still had that silly smile over her face. Then he was smiling because she looked infinitely breathtaking in the utter enthusiasm with which she'd embraced tonight.

And that smile knocked over into his life, kicking everything he had ever believed about himself wide-open, as though she was the domino who started it all. Digging his hands into her hair, he pulled her closer. "Why are you still smiling?"

Finally, she deigned to open her eyes and he found himself falling deeper and deeper into her spell. The openness of her expression made it impossible to be anything but. She looked at him as if he was the most wonderful thing she had ever seen.

It filled him with a strangely exhilarating weight that he had not known in his adult life. It magnified inside him, spreading to his chest, filling every nook and cranny. As if he was now responsible for keeping that smile on her face.

Her fingers found his mouth and traced the seam with

such a possessive touch. Expelling a harsh breath, he forced himself to relax. He never invited the woman he slept with to touch him, never lingered in the moment after seeing to their pleasure and his own. "Because it was *that* good." Her long lashes cast shadows over her cheeks as she struggled to keep her eyes open. "Tomorrow, I swear, Dmitri, you can have whatever you want," she offered magnanimously, as if she was a goddess granting boons.

He wanted to tell her she had already given him something precious—her trust. But he kept the words to himself. "You can, instead, answer my question now," he said, wondering anew at how at ease she had been with her body.

Theos, the woman was like a sensual missile, and thinking that about her made him think of her with other men and right now, he didn't want to go there.

It seemed being in bed with Jas meant every thought he had left him feeling either raw or uncertain or both.

"What?" she said, suddenly tense.

"What did you do all these years at Noah's nightclub, Jas?"

His heart hammered at her continued silence. Propping himself up, he looked at her.

Her shoulders became a rigid line, her gaze not meeting his as she pulled up the duvet to cover herself up.

"Jas, whatever it is—"

"I was a pole dancer in his underground nightclub."

While Dmitri grappled with that, she met his eyes. Full of fake defiance and shadows of shame, her gaze did nothing to abate the rage building inside him. "A pole dancer?" he repeated, disbelief and fury and guilt all rolling into his tone.

"I jumped in only because one of the girls was sick one day and was terrified of losing the spot. I told myself it was just for one night. Apparently, awful as I was that first night, I was still a huge hit. Guess I owe it to my father for his contribution toward making me look *exotic*." Loathing spewed out when she said that word. As if she hated that about her and what it had enabled her to do.

"But the tips, Dmitri, they were ten times what I got waitressing. Suddenly, I could at least dream of leaving that life. I could imagine a different one." Her voice became small; her entire body scrunched into herself.

Shame, Dmitri realized slowly—that emotion in her voice was shame. Was that why she had hidden the truth from him until now? Why she thought she was beneath him?

If only she knew his roots...

"So I practiced until my legs felt as if they would fall off, until the heretofore unused muscles in my thighs and calves burned as though there were knives lodged inside them, put on mere scraps of lace and took to the stage. I tuned out every man who looked at me as if I was a morsel of meat instead of a woman with wants and fears, I loathed myself a thousand times for every night I went up there, but I did it.

"I was an instant super hit."

He blinked to clear the haze of red that covered his vision. "So what did Noah threaten you with that you came to me finally?"

She flinched, her gaze shying away from him again. "In the past year, I went from the side to center stage, and the show went from a huge floor show to an outrageously expensive, custom show.

"Suddenly, the men I'd tuned out all along were too close, their hands pawing me, their comments and their looks getting worse and worse. Noah, unwilling to lose their business, relaxed the security. So in the guise of congratulating me, they kept cornering me everywhere I turned after the show. Even then, I somehow managed.

"Until...he said customers were asking for personal

performances. That they were willing to pay upward of thousands for one dance, that they wanted me to get more familiar with them... Some of the girls told me it wasn't that bad, that they made more money... But all I could see was turning into my mother, hating myself for the rest of my life, falling for one of those men who didn't even know the real me, deluding myself that one of them would actually want me for something more than a quick...

"I couldn't bear to do it. I didn't have the guts to see it through anymore. It just felt as if I would never ever get out of that life if I stayed any longer. There was only so much I was willing to do to repay Andrew's debt."

Men, driven by lust and hunger, leering and pawing at her, because the kind of club that Noah owned wouldn't be anything like the one he had just acquired... The picture her words painted nauseated him. He shot out of the bed, his blood boiling, his emotions raw.

She sat up in the bed, her hair mussed up, her expression so vulnerable that it caught at his chest.

"Dmitri, what is it? Don't, please, look at me like that. As if I..." She didn't finish the words, her throat working conspicuously, her hands fisting the duvet.

But he didn't care what she was feeling. *Theos*, he was drowning in what could have been. "You could have come to me so much sooner. You could have avoided all that. If any of them had gotten his hands on you, if they had forced you into something that you didn't want... *Christos.*" He turned and slammed his fist into the wall.

But even the pain that shafted up his knuckles and arm was not enough to release the fear that crawled through his veins.

"Dmitri, you have to understand—"

"Understand what, Jas? You had a choice. My father was an alcoholic bastard but did you know that my mother was a prostitute?" he said bitterly, giving voice to something he had never shared with another soul. "He drank with her money but hated her for it. It ate through him and he took it out on her and me. Half the time, I couldn't stop him because I was such a runt...until I learned to use my speed and my fists...

"She was saving to leave London, just enough so that she could bring me to Giannis in Athens, who was her uncle. She had to hide the money because he took all of it from her. And then just two days before we were set to leave, he found out. He was in one of his drunken rages and he pushed her.

"She hit her head on the wall and died instantly, before I could even catch her. Then he locked the door outside and he ran." He dropped to the bed, his head in his hands, trembling, shivering, still feeling her cold body in his arms. "I sat there for hours, imagining all the different ways I could have saved her. The silence... I have never been able to bear it since. If Andrew hadn't come to look for me as he always did when he heard from the neighbors that my father was in a drunken rage again, I don't know how long I would have been there.

"You know what I thought when Gaspard touched you today, Jas? Fear that I wouldn't be able to save you. And now to hear you so blithely say that's where you have put yourself willingly for so many years..."

He felt as if he was in that moment today. The pain and the fear that ripped through him... He couldn't breathe.

Turning away from her, he put on his discarded trousers, his chest cold as ice. He couldn't bear to look at her, not all that loveliness, that flush to her skin.

Because if he did, he knew either he would be tempted to wring her neck for her recklessness or he would take her against the wall like an animal, her comfort and soreness be damned, just to rid the shiver in his muscles. Just to feel all of her with his rough hands, just to reassure himself that she was here, safe in his arms, beyond that world's reach now...

And then he would never be able to forgive himself.

He needed to leave until he had a better handle on his emotions, until he understood what was happening to him. He found his hands were shaking.

"Dmitri." Her soft entreaty seared through him and he turned.

The sheet wrapped around her nakedness, she rose from the bed like a goddess, and even drowning in fury, he was drawn to her. "Don't, Jas... I can't bear to look at you."

Her arm fell back against her body. The wariness disappeared from her eyes and something else set in. He was almost at the door.

"I hated you for never looking back," she said then, sounding small and broken.

Her words were like a rope that bound him to the room, to her.

"For years, I imagined that you would come back and somehow rescue Andrew and me from that life. I built you up into...this hope in my head when Andrew got worse, when it felt as if I couldn't take another day." He opened his mouth but she raised her hand. "I know the truth now, I do. But when Andrew told me those lies about you giving up on us, all that hope instantly turned to hate. Because, you see, that hatred was easier to bear than the pain.

"I thought you had abandoned me. Just like the rest of them. Like my father, my mum and even Andrew. At his funeral, you were so distant, so out of my sphere, full of pity for me. You stood there so coldly, offering me money, as if that was all I deserved from you. As if I was a problem you wanted to fix and then forget about."

Pity? He had never pitied her. He had looked at her,

eighteen and innocent and full of such blazing hatred for him, and he'd thought she was better off without him…

He hadn't been able to stomach that he had failed at saving another life… That even with all the wealth he had acquired, he had been of no use… The idea of letting Jasmine back in his life, even if he had been able to persuade her in the first place, the fear of failing had been too much…

It was still too much.

"Andrew always said," she continued in that same, small voice, "pride was my biggest shortcoming. The thought of begging you for help, it made me so angry. I wanted you to look at me and not feel pity… I wanted to prove to you that I could somehow make it without your help… Pathetic, right, that even then, I was so fixated on you."

"*Theos*, Jas…"

"Tonight I told myself I had nothing to be ashamed of. That I wasn't going to hold myself responsible for their mistakes, that I… But I'm in your bed and you are looking at me as if you wish you had never laid a finger on me. Exactly what I had always wanted to avoid."

She didn't give him a chance to negate her; she didn't give him a chance to even process everything she had blurted out in that usual blatantly raw way of hers.

Dragging the red sheet behind her, her shoulders a stiff line, she walked away.

Jasmine didn't know how long she stood under the hot spray of the shower after Dmitri had walked out. But there was such cold in her chest that she felt as though she would never warm up ever again.

Dmitri was disgusted by her illustrious career. She had asked him straight and he hadn't denied her. But even worse than his disgust was the turmoil that churned through her gut.

Because even if he had been able to stomach his disgust, she had betrayed herself, hadn't she? She hadn't known what she had been about to say, had only wanted to make him understand why she hadn't come to him for help. Only wanted to make him see that it had been so hard. Only wanted to take away that anguish in his eyes.

Instead, she had blurted out things even she hadn't fully realized, didn't know what to make of.

She rubbed her head, where an ache was beginning. In reality, she was sore all over, between her thighs especially. Her skin felt extrasensitive to the spray of the complicated jets of the shower. On her hips, where his fingers had dug in so hard and held her down when he had been thrusting into her, her scalp where he had held her for his kiss… He was all over her, inside and out.

Fixated on him, really, had she no self-respect left? Was she going to beg him next to keep her in his bed?

He had made love to her—no, sex. It had been explosive sex, yes, but only that, and here she was, pushing her fears, her fixation for him onto his plate. A long jump for a man who had admitted to just wanting her, under extreme conditions, too, to her dumping her sob story over him.

No wonder he had said he couldn't bear to look at her. No wonder he hadn't been able to even stay in the room another minute.

It felt as if there was a lead weight in her chest that she couldn't push down or breathe out, blocking her very breath.

And knowing what she had learned from him today, she wondered if even his attraction to her was a product of his protective nature, couldn't help but wonder if he would ever really see the real her.

Not his friend's sister, that friend whom he thought he hadn't been able to save, not as a way to satisfy the guilt that obviously had settled inside him as a teenager who had seen his mother's horrific death...

But just her, Jasmine Douglas, ex-virgin pole dancer, penniless and with no prospects of a career, weak when it came to helping abusive family members and desperately falling for the teenage boy she had known once.

But hurting all over, she couldn't summon the energy to be angry with herself. She had decided today to carve her own life, to make her own mistakes if that was what it took, to stop living in the shadow of the past.

Maybe her first mistake was to fall for a man who would never see her, much less want her in his life.

She had a career that reminded him of a past he clearly wanted to forget, she had thrown herself at him, first for help and now for sex, and she had blurted out her obsession over him. Why would a man who had everything in the world want a woman like her?

Dmitri stepped out from the house into the open grounds, the desolation and shame he had heard in Jas's voice running through him in an endless loop.

Theos, he had only realized after he had lost it so thoroughly how she had lived with that shame for so long, how low her self-esteem must have been.

He had thought her merely attracted to him, whereas it went so much deeper. And tonight, by telling her about Andrew's deceit, he had torn down the last barrier.

Her words and the weight of them... He was not ready for them. He was never going to be worthy of them.

He saw another shadow join his in the silence and turned.

His suit jacket gone, Stavros stood with his hand on the stone bench. They had spent many nights sitting on the bench, looking at the stars, each increasingly awed by the generosity of the man who had saved them both from certain hell. And determined to their last breath that they would make him proud of them.

Full of integrity and honor, Stavros had taught him so much. But right now, he was the last man Dmitri wanted to see because he wouldn't lie to spare Dmitri's feelings. He wouldn't spare anyone, especially when it came to doing the right thing.

"You seduced her, didn't you?" Stavros finally said, sounding utterly disgusted.

Gritting his jaw tight, Dmitri strove to calm himself. He would not lose it tonight, not again.

"Before you lose it, your little temper tantrum was witnessed by everyone at the party. Then you followed her and neither of you emerged for the rest of the night. Leah was worried about her." The bastard went on, unperturbed. "The interesting thing is that you're pacing here in the middle of the night. Which means at least you feel some regret."

"She was a pole dancer at that club."

The statement fell into the dark silence like a grenade waiting to be detonated. His gaze stunned, Stavros looked as though he was out of words.

"That's not the worst," Dmitri added. He needed to fix the situation, but for the life of him, he still couldn't hate himself for what had happened.

"What is, then?"

"She…she's full of shame over it, still just as stubborn, however, she's very vulnerable to me, some kind of leftover from our past together—" *God only knew why* "—and now I seduced her, yes. So it's a lot worse. If I had known how much she—"

"*Theos*, Dmitri, don't start lying to yourself now."

Dmitri felt it like a lash, loathing Stavros for being right.

He would have taken Jas come what may. That he had even resisted that long was a miracle in itself.

But he could not simply walk away from her. To do so would mean to torture himself eternally about whether she was safe. About who she was with, if there was another man who had taken over his place in her life, whether that man was worthy of her, if he would treat her well…

Christos!

And the thought of Jasmine with any other man but him, the thought of any man taking that smile, that double-edged innocence, of any man kissing her or learning that sensuous body of hers… It drove him crazy.

He had never ever felt this possessive about a woman, only a cold detachment. At most, sympathy when it had come to Anya.

He knew that Jasmine hadn't given herself to him lightly, and telling her that it was a night of madness for him would only hurt her.

And he couldn't do that. He couldn't hurt Jasmine, not when there had been a hundred people in her life who had only ever done that.

The solution, the only solution to the tangle of mess he had created, came to him slowly, quite simple in its brilliance.

His heart seemed to freeze for a moment, and then stuttered into life, pounding even harder after that pause.

"I know what to do," he said softly, the idea settling into his every pore, every cell, sinking into him deep. Tilting the very axis of his life. But he didn't feel in the slightest bit worried. It was perfect for the situation he had created, the right thing finally.

His austere features bathed in shadows, Stavros, if possible, became even tenser. "And what would that be?"

Dmitri sighed, wishing he could walk away without answering his question, without giving a damn. But try as he might, he had never been able to wrench that detachment for Stavros.

Giannis had done a fine job of making them more than brothers. He had made them each other's conscience. "I'll not hurt her, Stavros."

"There's more than one way of hurting, Dmitri. I stole five years of her life, *five years* that I can never return, from Leah. Don't be so blindly arrogant as I was to decide her fate for Jasmine."

"I'm not forcing her into anything, Stavros."

He would not force Jas. He would only give her what would make her happy, do what he should have done all those years ago. He owed Andrew that much, despite Andrew's mistakes; he owed *her* that much. And it wasn't as if he was making a huge sacrifice, either, when all he did was flit from woman to woman, trying to fill the emptiness he felt.

At least, with Jas, there would be the satisfaction of doing the right thing. At least, with Jas, there would be no emptiness. Not when she looked at him like that.

"Dmitri, I'm—"

Dmitri had had enough. He turned away from Stavros and went back to the house. For the first time in forever, he had found something that made him feel as though he was alive again. Something that helped him look in the mirror and see a worthy man.

Something that he was determined to hold on to.

CHAPTER ELEVEN

TWO DAYS LATER, the most beautiful day dawned, as if the elements had decided to behave in the face of such true, abiding love as Jasmine saw in Leah and Stavros's eyes.

A lone tear slid down her cheek as they posed for a picture under the arch of lilies. With her eyes twinkling and her mouth painted a luscious red, Leah was a perfect contrast to Stavros's severely stunning looks.

She was so glad to have witnessed the wedding, the best part in her mind when Dmitri, looking so breathtakingly gorgeous in a black tuxedo, had walked Leah to Stavros and handed her over.

Something had passed between the two men, a sliver of tension that paused the whole tableau, but then Dmitri had kissed Leah's cheek and gone to stand by Stavros.

If she had thought her life strange before, it was nothing compared to the roller coaster of the past two days.

It had been close to dawn when, after hours of tossing and turning, she had fallen into a fitful sleep that night after he walked out with such anger. While she had refused to cry or pity herself, she had relentlessly wondered where Dmitri had gone. Wondered if he would disappear again.

And then suddenly, he had been there in her bed just as the sun touched everything in the room with a pink glow.

Naked and gloriously, arrogantly masculine, he had been a cocoon of warmth and hardness behind her.

Had she resisted him? Had she even put up a token fight when he had come back to her bed as if he belonged there?

No, all she had felt had been unprecedented joy that he had come back to her, utter relief that he didn't loathe her for what she had told him. She had been weak, yes, but Jasmine didn't know how to be anything else when it came to Dmitri, didn't know how to arrest her heart from jumping into her throat when he looked at her, or how to stop her skin from tingling with one casual touch of his.

At least, the past was all done between them; at least, he still wanted her, she had thought pathetically. When he had given her a breath to think, that was.

Pulling her toward him, he had thrown a muscular, naked leg over her own, his arm a steel band around her waist, his erection already hard and big, nestling against her bottom like it belonged there.

She had moaned and pushed back into him, even as her mind had said she should be doing the opposite. Whispering the wickedest things into her skin, he had sneaked his large hands under her shirt, *his shirt* that she had stolen from his wardrobe at the hotel in London, and found her breasts. Told her he had never been so thoroughly stripped of all good sense, that he had never felt such urgent, devouring need ever before.

There had been such a possessive heat to his words that even now, standing amidst a hundred guests, Jasmine felt the silky slide of those words, as addictive as his knowing touch.

He had stroked her to such a fever pitch that she had forgotten all about how sore she had felt earlier. "Please, Dmitri," she had whispered, apparently the only thing she was capable of saying to him.

Slowly, lazily, he had pushed into her from behind, his teeth digging into her shoulder, his fingers flicking at her sex with that same lazy rhythm. Rocked them both into such a slow climax that had nevertheless left her boneless.

As if all his fury had been pushed out of him, as if he had all the time in the world to enjoy the fire between them. As if he never wanted to leave her side ever again.

Tears had filled her eyes and she had tried to hide them. But he had only turned her to him. "No more tears, *glykia mou*, and no more shame. Whatever you had to do, it's all over, Jas." He had kissed her temple, then her fluttering eyelids, her cheeks, and then had held her with such a tight grip. "Don't judge yourself, don't ever blame yourself for surviving." He had said it so tenderly that she had buried her face in his chest and sobbed, years of grief and loneliness pushing out of her in waves.

And he had soothed her, and hugged her, and fallen asleep next to her.

When she had woken up again, it had been past noon. A single, long-stemmed red rose had been by the pillow along with a note and a velvet case.

Her heart had slammed against her rib cage when she had run a reverent finger against the soft velvet. Sitting up, she had reached for the note first.

"Will be back the afternoon of the wedding day. Have to get something ready. Wear this for me."

Her breath had stuttered out of her at the sight of the delicately wired diamond necklace, along with matching earrings and bracelet. It had looked utterly expensive and somehow he had arranged for it to be delivered in a matter of hours. She had seen a necklace like that once in London at Tiffany & Co. and had blanched from even asking the price.

Something about accepting it right after what they had done hadn't sat well with her. She was already indebted to him, they had the strangest relationship going on and the last thing Jas wanted was to lose the little pride she had left.

And that he had left her that little note meant more to her than anything that he could have gifted her.

She fingered the diamond pendant that she had worn instead, hoping he would understand.

Every inch of her thrummed as she waited for the ceremony to be over so that she could tell him all her news. More than anything, she couldn't wait to just hold him again.

The crowd of guests erupted into laughter then, and she turned to see Stavros pick up Leah in his arms and head for the house. She found herself smiling again.

Corded arms wrapped around her from behind. She let out a breathless little gasp as his powerful thighs straddled her, his arousal evoking that powerfully intoxicating need freely in her veins.

She felt the press of his soft lips against her neck and trembled. Long fingers instantly laced with hers, anchoring her. He felt so good and warm around her that her heart took a little tumble in her chest.

"You smell divine, *moro mou*. I can't wait to taste you all over again."

She half turned, trying to speak with a dry mouth. "Dmitri, I have something—"

"You wanted to dance the other night, didn't you?"

Without waiting for her answer, not that she would have refused, he tugged her to the dance floor that had been erected to the side. The grounds looked like they were straight out of a fairy tale as little Moroccan lanterns illuminated the path and cast beautiful shadows everywhere. A sweet smell wafted over from the orange groves.

Dusk wasn't far away and the party was in full swing. A little signal from Dmitri and the band instantly shifted to a slow tune instead of the peppy Greek number. In such a short time, the world suddenly seemed like a wonderful place, and she didn't doubt that it was because of the man who seemed to entrench himself more and more in her heart.

His hands went around her and Jasmine found herself looking straight into his eyes.

Dancing with Dmitri was like eating the most deliciously decadent chocolate, except the sensations were everywhere instead of just in her mouth. His movements effortlessly elegant; he maneuvered them around the floor with a fluid grace that was far from the boy who had used his fists for survival.

Feeling light-headed even though she hadn't touched a drop of alcohol, she put her cheek on his shoulder and looked around.

Leah's wedding list was a who's-who of the fashion world, ranging from models to designers to fashion magazine editors. Wherever she looked on the dance floor and elsewhere, there were stunning beauties, each one more gorgeous and sophisticated than the next. But it was the list of their accomplishments that stung.

What is he doing with me? an insidious voice whispered in her mind, and she tried to tune it out.

She could feel more than one woman's gaze slide to Dmitri surreptitiously, had seen more than one woman come on to him in the guise of polite chitchat.

Because if there was one thing she knew, it was that kind of lust, the one that only wanted the package without knowing what was beneath.

All they saw was a spectacularly gorgeous man with wealth, power and raw sexuality. *I know him like none of you ever will*, she thought with a fierceness she had never known before.

Her hands tightened over his shoulders before she even

realized. *Mine*, she wanted to say in an utterly possessive way.

One muscled thigh grazing hers, Dmitri tipped her chin
up. "You're tense. Is something wrong?"

"No," she replied, determined to not let her stupid insecurities ruin what was the most wonderful evening of her
life. She would make something of herself, she promised
herself. She would make him proud of her even if it took
her the rest of her life.

Bolstered by it, she leaned her head on his shoulder and
let his body guide her into the soft rhythm.

For a few moments, they said nothing, sinking into the
sensuous silence that was filled with languorous promises. Every move reminded her of how he had moved inside her, every glance he sent her way a promise of the
night to come.

"You dance like a dream," she whispered.

Their relationship had begun in a strange place, a bed
of all places, and even after two days, she couldn't seem
to look at him and not remember the erotic intimacy of
what they had done.

If she looked at his mouth, her lower belly clenched as
if it remembered the havoc he had wreaked on it. If she
looked at his hands, her hips remembered how he had held
her down for him.

"Giannis, if you can believe it, made us take classes.
He was determined to transform Stavros and me from
the little thugs we were." She shivered as he pulled her
closer. "But I'm not at all surprised that you move like
every man's fantasy."

Her gaze flew to his, but it was only full of a wicked
light. There was no judgment in his tone, implied or otherwise. It was her own shame that ricocheted through her,
that led her to drop her gaze.

He tipped her chin up. "You dance beautifully, Jas,"

he said so tenderly that she couldn't help but smile in return, warmed to the farthest corners of her heart by the depth of his perception.

Stepping back, he looked at her from her hair in an elegant knot to the pendant and the elegant knee-length beige silk dress that Leah had chosen for her, all the way to her feet tucked in nude-colored pumps.

Tingling at his leisurely perusal, she reached for his hand when he frowned.

"You're not wearing the diamond necklace. Why?"

He had spoken softly, yet the displeasure in his tone was clear. "I…"

"Let's get out of here."

He didn't wait for her answer. Clasping her fingers, he tugged her off the dance floor and through the throng of guests, to a path that went away from the crowd.

After another couple of minutes, they arrived at a side door to the house, and then they were in a study that was utterly masculine from the dark brown leather sofas to a huge mahogany table to the scent of cigars that permeated it.

When voices filtered through an open window, Dmitri closed it with a firm click.

"Now." Turning to her, he lifted her over the table, pushed her legs apart as far as the dress allowed, which was indecent enough for her, and stood between them until she was straddling him. "All I have been able to think about is this…"

He claimed her mouth with a hunger that buckled her knees. Instantly, Jasmine was lost in a sea of spiraling sensations.

With a hand on his chest, she pushed at him, and his mouth released hers and slid lower to her neck.

"Please, Dmitri, wait. I want to talk."

"I'm not used to being denied what I want, *pethi mou*,"

he breathed against the pulse in her neck, while his thigh lodged square against her aching sex. "And I want you, need you more than I need air."

With that, he moved his leg and tremors spread through her lower belly. Her hands on his shoulders, Jasmine moved, needing that pressure to push her to the edge.

An arrogant, utterly masculine smile on his face, he obliged. And the satisfaction in that male gaze told Jasmine how easily and effortlessly she was playing into his arms. If she didn't hold her own even a little now, she never would be able to in the future, she realized. However murky the future was right now.

She dug her teeth into his lower lip and pulled, until he looked up with a guttural groan. "I want to talk, so hands off, Dmitri."

He ran a long finger over his lower lip, his eyes threatening retribution. Jasmine held her breath, knowing that she wouldn't last a minute if he didn't back off.

"Please." She pouted, lowering her voice. "If you let me talk first, then I'll do whatever you want tonight."

He turned his neck this way and that, and his broad chest rose and fell. It was like watching a predator take a step back from his prey. "So talk. And tell me why you're not wearing the diamond set I ordered for you?"

In the face of his ruthlessly direct question, she floundered. God, had she ever thought this man frivolous and uncaring? The intensity of his looks, his touch, even his questions spun her head. She lifted the diamond with not-so-steady fingers. "You already gave me a diamond."

"That's all I could afford then. Now I can—"

"It was far too expensive." She injected some steel into her words, and when he scowled, she added hurriedly, "Really, where am I going to wear it to, Dmitri? I have no need for such—"

"You'll have lots of occasions." Masculine satisfaction

dripped from every word. "Tomorrow morning, there will be a stylist here. Order yourself a new wardrobe, everything you want."

"You're just angry that I steal your shirts, aren't you?" she quipped, trying to hide her anxiety.

He kissed her then, just a quick touch of their mouths. "I don't think I've ever seen anything sexier than you wearing my shirt, *matia mou*. But I—"

"I have some really exciting news," she said, interrupting what she sensed was another argument she wouldn't win right now. A thread of unease began to permeate her mood, like the charge that built in the air long before the storm burst.

"What is it?"

"You remember Gaspard." She covered his mouth when his frown turned into a scowl. "Anyway, he referred me to a modeling agency. The head of the agency, this superstylish, sophisticated woman, she was here this afternoon. She said Gaspard had excellent taste when it came to faces, asked Leah about me, and Leah introduced us. Dmitri, she wants me to come in for a screen test in Athens as soon as I can manage it.

"It's true I'm older than the models they sign on but she said I had a different kind of face, whatever that means. Isn't that just great?" Her tone trailed off at the end there as Dmitri's expression remained the same. "Dmitri?"

"It sounds great, *pethi mou*," he said finally, his brow clearing, "but a career in modeling, this is what you want?" His accent suddenly became more pronounced than she had ever heard it.

Her shoulders slumping, Jasmine struggled to keep her voice upbeat. "I've no idea what I want, but it's not as if I have a degree or experience in a worthwhile field, is it? And I'm broke. I thought, why not give this a chance? Eventually, I have to start making a living again and then there's that gazillion pounds that I owe you." The last bit she had added with a smile, because her skin cooled as if there was a chill in the room.

The look in Dmitri's eyes was near lethal. "That debt means nothing between us after what happened two nights ago. As for making a living, I'll take care of you, Jasmine."

She tilted her chin. "And I told you that I won't be your mistress. You can't just come to me at midnight and send me gifts in the morning. That's not what I want, *now or ever*."

"No, I don't like that option, either."

As if he were a magician, he pulled out a small box from somewhere. Her heart slammed so hard that Jasmine gasped. A diamond ring, a princess cut with tiny ones set around it, glittered and winked at her. His gaze remained shadowed as he looked at her. "Marry me, *thee mou*, and we'll never talk of debts and mistresses ever again."

Every inch of her froze as he slid the ring onto her boneless finger and the damning, breath-stealing, soul-wrenching thing was that the ring fit her so perfectly. The cold weight of it felt unfamiliar against her skin, her breath ballooning up in her lungs.

Jasmine looked at the ring for several seconds. Shock and joy roped together in her veins, and beneath all of it, fear pulsed.

She looked up and tried to smile, but it wouldn't come. Her hands on his chest, she expelled a long breath. "I don't know what to say, Dmitri. Wow, I just… This is… I…"

Clasping her cheeks, he took her mouth in a long kiss that stole all the air from her lungs again. "Say yes, Jas." His hands moved to her back and pulled her closer to him, until all she knew was Dmitri and his broad shoulders, and his corded strength and his thrilling words. She felt as if she was floating on a different plane, far removed from reality.

"I have the license ready and we can marry here to-morrow evening. Once we tell them, Leah and Stavros will stay on. Leah undoubtedly will have a dress that's as gorgeous as you are in her wedding collection, and everything else has already been taken care of."

Burying her face in his chest, Jasmine willed her racing pulse to slow down, to give her a chance to breathe. And the moment her heart settled to normal, something else followed. "Tomorrow?" Only the one word escaped her.

Stroking her lip with his tongue, he breathed his answer into her mouth. "Yes. I want us to marry as soon as possible. That way...you don't have to worry about making a living, don't have to jump into something that you're not sure about.

"Take a couple of courses at the university if you like. Just take it easy, *matia mou*. Or if you decide all you want to be is Mrs. Karegas, that's perfectly fine, too."

Her head spinning, Jasmine pushed away from him and slid off the desk. "You don't want me to work?"

He shrugged, his hands in his trouser pockets. "I don't ever want you to worry, Jas, about anything. Everything I have is yours."

"Wow, Dmitri. I...I'm drowning here," she said, feeling dizzy with the number of emotions claiming her.

"All you have to say is yes, Jas. And tomorrow night, we can set off on our honeymoon to wherever you want to go."

Impulsively, she hugged him, the scent of him pushing the word *yes* to her lips.

And yet something held her back; something punctured the utter joy of the moment. Panic fueling her movements, she jerked away. "Wait, Dmitri, let me breathe, won't you?"

He smiled and nodded, his gaze moving hungrily over her.

Rings and diamond sets, dresses and wardrobes, it

seemed there was nothing Dmitri couldn't wait to lavish upon her. But love... There was nothing of love in his
words. That was it.

Because she loved him with all her heart, she thought
in a daze. Somewhere between knifing him and kissing
him, she had irrevocably fallen in love with him, had
moved from a childhood obsession to feeling as though
she would never have enough of him.

It had been that moment when he had told her about
Andrew's deception. Or maybe the moment when he had
called her perfection. Or when he had held her so tenderly
as she had sobbed her heart out.

Everything in her life was shifting and uncertain, but
how she felt about Dmitri... There was no doubt about
that.

Shaking at the realization, utterly terrified now, she
looked at him.

He had removed his jacket, and the white shirt hugged
the breadth of his shoulders, a perfect contrast to the olive
skin. He looked so utterly gorgeous and he wanted to
marry her.

He could have any woman in the world. Why did he
want her?

Did he love her?

Did he know how she felt about him? She had never really tried to hide her feelings from him, had she?

Questions burned through her head in an endless loop,
slowly but surely siphoning off the warmth from her.

But suddenly now she wanted to hide away from him,
wished she could give herself time to let the truth sink in.

Why else would he want to marry you? the hopeful
part of her, the part that had forever loved everything
about him, said.

Her thoughts still scrambled, she turned to him and
said the first thing she could think of. "You'll give up your

playboy status? You'll give up all those women? Because marriage is nothing without fidelity and respect, Dmitri."

He didn't seem in the least bit offended by her questions. On the contrary, a smile cut grooves in his cheek as though he wanted nothing but to allay her fears. "I will be the most faithful husband in the world, *pethi mou*. I'll give even Stavros a run for it, yes?"

Reaching her, he put his hands on her hips, kissed her temple. And standing in his arms, soaking in his words, Jasmine desperately wanted to say yes.

"I'll do everything in my power to make you happy, Jas, to take care of you. You'll want for nothing, you'll see."

Just like that, Jas felt her answer float away from her lips. Her happiness, her well-being, all Dmitri talked about was her. As though she was one of his possessions—a well-oiled bike, a smoothly run nightclub, a well-maintained portfolio that only kept on giving.

What about him?

What did he feel for her?

What had shifted that he wanted to marry her?

Still grappling with how deep her feelings ran, how much weight each word of his carried with her, Jas felt his words like a rope binding her to him. "What about love, Dmitri?" she said finally. Her chest was so tight, her fingers chillingly cold as if she had dunked them in ice.

He became absolutely still, but something uncoiled in those gray eyes. "What about love, Jas?"

So he was going to torture this out of her. "Do you love me, Dmitri?"

"No, but then I don't believe I'm capable of it, Jas. I feel a certain affection for Leah, loyalty for Stavros, but that's about the breadth of my emotional range. And you—" her breath hung in her throat "—you'll have my fidelity and my friendship."

Her hopes fell away, his words shattering her heart into

a thousand pieces inside her chest. She slumped against the table, her limbs shaking uncontrollably.

He reached her instantly and caught her. "*Theos*, Jas, I thought you would be happy. I thought this was what you wanted."

And there it was…the final proof in his own words.

Cradled against him, Jas felt herself tearing into two halves, one gleefully, treacherously ecstatic that this strong, powerful, honorable man would be hers, and the other, warning away from a fate that could leech away every ounce of joy from her life.

If she married him because he made her feel safe and because he was offering friendship and because of the wild heat between them, if she willingly went into this knowing that he would never even open himself to the possibility of love, knowing that his vows were born out of guilt and a protective instinct that was a mile wide while she, bound to him irrevocably, would wait for him to open his heart, while she crucified herself wondering if it was something within herself…

The fear that she had been holding at bay for so many days, *years actually*, twisted and swelled inside her…until she saw herself turning into her worst nightmare. Her mother had waited and wasted away her entire life for a man who had never looked back.

Would that be her fate, too, if she weakened in this minute? Was her choice to smash her heart into pieces now or wait for it to fall apart piece by piece over years?

"I never wanted you to marry me, Dmitri. I would have settled for…" Her words seemed to dissolve on her lips when he pinned her with his gaze.

Because then, she could hope for a better future than the one he had so thoroughly mapped out for her. Because then, she had foolishly thought, she would make herself worthy of him, that she would somehow make him proud of her.

A stillness seemed to creep up into his face while his gaze, that gaze that had never been able to lie to her, burned with a ferocity that he had kept leashed until now. "I offered marriage because you deserve better, Jas."

Her throat was so thick with ache that she thought she might be sick.

God, if he talked about her one more time as if she were something to be cosseted and protected, she was going to scream. And then crumple into a heap. "Have you offered marriage to every woman you have ever slept with? Or is it a special offer reserved for virgins?"

"*Theos*, you're different from the numerous other women I screwed. There, is that enough?"

"How? How am I different?"

"You're Andrew's sister." Jas wanted to cover her ears and scream. "And you're the most annoyingly stubborn woman I've ever met."

Before she knew, he was clasping her to him and plundering her mouth with his.

It was a kiss meant to possess, to captivate, to lay claim. And still, Jas lost herself to it. Lost herself in the erotic strokes of his wicked tongue, lost herself in the heat he so easily stroked into life, lost herself in the hard body.

Lost herself in the man who promised her so much except the one thing she really needed.

One hand cupped her breast reverently while the other pulled her snug against him to feel his rigid shaft. Her breath left her in a soft flutter, tears she couldn't fight anymore spilling onto her cheeks.

"I promise you, Jas, I have never known anything like this fire between us… You would walk away from this?"

She caressed his jaw with her mouth, breathing in the scent of him. "I have to."

How could something that felt so good eventually turn out to be bad for her? Her body, pulsing with need, seemed to find it impossible to grasp.

Steeling her spine, she pushed away from him for the last time. "I can't marry you, Dmitri. I have barely found myself after years of living buried under others' mistakes, others' addictions. I can't do that to myself again." *Not even for you.*

"I'm promising you a life that will lack for nothing. How is it not—"

"But this is about guilt, *your guilt.* I'm your project for all the things you failed at. For not being able to save your mother all those years ago, for your supposed failure with Andrew, for not *saving* me from my tasteless past soon enough.

"All of this—" her voice broke, a deluge of tears knocking at her eyes "—is only because you want to feel better about yourself."

"I know how you feel about me." His control slipped then, his anger spewing into his words. As if she was the one hurting him, as if somehow this was all her fault. As if she had somehow damaged him. "I know what that night meant to you. How does it matter when I'm offering everything I can of myself?"

Was this how it felt when one's heart broke? Did the world keep on turning? "It's because I feel so much that I can't accept this. I can't let my love for you break me, Dmitri.

"Because I do love you. I love you so much that there's this voice inside that's *screaming* that I'm stupid to walk away from this, that I should grab it with both hands. That I should take what little I can get of you." She grabbed her head, as if she could silence it. "And it won't stop. I don't think it will ever stop."

"Then, listen to it. For once, *thee mou*, do what is good for you. Don't walk away, Jas."

Grasping the door handle, Jas looked at him. The thing that hurt the most was that he didn't understand. He didn't see how painful it was for her to walk away, how hard it would be for her to accept the little he gave of himself when she wanted everything.

When he walked toward her, she shook her head. "No. Don't touch me and don't come to my room. Don't…do anything more for me, Dmitri, please."

CHAPTER TWELVE

DMITRI DIDN'T KNOW how he had made it through the night.

He remembered pacing the study like a caged animal. It was how he had felt in that first year when Giannis had brought him to this very house. He had once called it house-training a wild animal.

He had, through will hanging by a thread, kept himself in the study. Every cell in him wanted to convince her the only way he knew but then he told himself she deserved better.

So he paced and drank and paced some more, trying to think of ways to stop her. It was now morning and he was no closer to a solution.

Except the renewed resolve to keep her in his life. And the panic that flared at the thought that he might fail, that he had somehow lost Jas irrevocably, and that it was nothing compared to all the losses he had lived through…

For a man who had floated through most of his adult life loathing his inability to feel anything, loathing the fact that his father had stolen more than his mother from him, it was like drowning after being parched for years.

He needed dark, blistering coffee to ground himself, to make sure he didn't do anything that he would regret later. His shirt half undone, his hair in disarray, he reached the breakfast room.

The scent of sweet pastries and coffee filled the room, the house blissfully silent after last night.

Dressed in a long-sleeved sweater and slacks, his hair still wet from the shower, Stavros looked like the very picture of matrimonial bliss. Their gazes met and held.

Stavros poured some of the thick, dark coffee and pushed a cup toward Dmitri. "You look terrible."

"Why aren't you in bed with your wife, Stavros? Or better yet, why aren't you gone yet? This is my estate now."

A brow raised, Stavros stared at him. "I was waiting for you."

Dmitri took a long sip and felt marginally human again. He ran a hand over his jaw and felt the bristle. *Theos*, he must look like the savage he felt like. He would have to shower and shave before he went up to see her. He still didn't know what he was going to say.

Do you love me, Dmitri?

He had offered her everything and she had asked for the one thing he didn't know how to do.

Fear and confusion like he had never known before gripped his insides.

It felt as though overnight he had lost something, something precious he hadn't even known he had. Not for a moment had he thought she would say no.

If she loved him, wouldn't she want to spend her life with him?

He finished his coffee and turned toward the door. To hell with civilizing himself.

She was the one person in the world who knew what he was beneath the mask he showed the world. She hadn't even relented until he had showed himself to her. Had goaded him, challenged him…had made him feel so much again.

There was no way he was just letting her walk away from this.

He had almost reached the door when Stavros spoke. "She's not here, Dmitri."

The words hit Dmitri as if they were fists he couldn't evade. His breath knocked out of him. He didn't think, even for an infinitesimal second, that Stavros might be talking about Leah; he couldn't delude himself even for a second that his entire world hadn't just cracked under his very feet.

And fury came to his aid, filling the hollowness in his gut. "What do you mean she left?"

"Leah said Jasmine was waiting for her when she came down. That she begged her to help her leave. That she couldn't stay another minute here. So I had the jet readied and she left."

His gut dropped. "You let her go back to that pit that she calls home?"

"Jasmine said she never wanted to go back there, asked Leah if she had a job for her, even carrying coffee back and forth at her factory. Since she has the screen test in two days, Leah insisted that she stay at her old flat in Athens for a little while. She went with her because Jasmine looked as if she was barely keeping it together."

Dmitri exhaled a relieved breath, once again eternally glad that Leah and Stavros had such generous hearts.

And the relief was followed by a cavern of longing ripping open in his gut.

He slid into the chair and buried his head in his hands. He should be glad she was gone, shouldn't he? If she was safe, why didn't the weight on his chest lift?

When had wanting to keep her safe changed to missing her as if he had lost a vital part of himself?

If this was what it felt like to lose Jasmine after a mere matter of weeks, what would it feel like after a month, a year or a decade of the marriage he had proposed? What would it feel like to lose her forever, to become the man who had pushed her into losing herself?

And suddenly, he understood her panic. He understood how hard he had made it for her, how strong she was to have walked away.

He realized the truth in her words. It had not been about protecting her at all, just as she had said.

It had all been about him. About pacifying his guilt, about his selfish needs, about keeping her in his life, about taking everything she gave without reserve but giving nothing of himself.

Was that what he had always done? Had the gut-wrenching pain of his mother's death made him a self-fulfilling prophecy, a man who only chose the shallowest of relationships, the most ephemeral of things to fill his life?

Could he reach for more now? Could he risk that pain, knowing that he might have lost his chance with Jasmine? Wouldn't that pain still be better than this emptiness?

He felt Stavros's arm on his shoulder, feeling as though nothing would ever touch him again. "I thought you would be angry with me for interfering," Stavros said softly, as if he knew how raw Dmitri felt inside. "I thought you would come at me with your fists."

But then, nothing in the world had ever laid him this low.

Breathing through a throat rough with emotion, Dmitri shook his head. "Because you did what I was unable to do and cared enough about what she wants? I was determined to not let the past matter, Stavros. I was determined that it wouldn't leave a mark on me. And yet…"

"It is a part of you, Dmitri."

"I hurt her and I don't know how to fix it now. I don't know how to tell her that I need her in my life, and not for all the reasons I made her believe.

"*Theos*, everything we have built, everything I told myself I needed to fill my life, they mean nothing to me if she's not there."

Stavros squeezed his shoulder and left without another word. As if he understood, for once, that there was nothing he could do to help Dmitri.

Long after noon gave way to dusk, Dmitri sat there in that vast kitchen in that house that Giannis had given to him, where he had learned to be civilized, where he had learned that he didn't have to live with pain, where he had learned that not all men were alcoholic, out-of-control cowards like his father. Where he had learned that he could be more than the product of his genes and his father's abuse.

But more than anything else, Giannis had tried so hard to give Dmitri back his self-worth. Suddenly, Dmitri was filled with purpose, hope and a yearning.

If he had to spend the rest of his life waiting for Jasmine, proving to Jasmine that he needed her in his life, that he absolutely couldn't breathe for knowing that she was somewhere in the world and not his…

He would do it. He would show her his heart; he would show her that his life was empty without her.

Fashion photographers, Jasmine discovered to her utter shock over the next few weeks, were apparently a whole other species who thought they didn't have to follow the dictates of polite society.

One week into her new career and she felt as though she had been steamrolled, turned inside out for everyone to see.

Maybe it was that she had gotten used to seeing the very obvious appreciation and lust in her customers' eyes when she had taken the stage at the nightclub, even though she'd hated it at that time. Or maybe because, apparently, she was the twenty-three-year-old village idiot, who knew nothing about how the fashion industry worked, amidst models, both men and women, younger and more experienced than her.

That first week after she had left Dmitri—because her whole life was now clearly demarcated by that one event, before Dmitri and after Dmitri, as if nothing else could even come close to holding significance in her life—had been a seamless blur of outward activity, more than she had seen in the past five years of her life, and a growing sense of stillness within.

She found herself asking the same question during the strangest moments during the day.

Had she thrown away her only chance at life with the man she adored in the name of weakness? Had she traded the happiness of at least a few days for the emptiness in her gut?

The agency had loved her after the screen test, calling her their next big find. With help from Stavros's lawyer, without whom she would have signed away her entire life, she signed a very tight, time-limited exclusive contract with the agency.

Sick of moping around the flat while she waited, she had made a habit of visiting Leah every day at her factory after a rigorous workout at the gym next door to keep in shape, and really, to keep the ever-gnawing void in her stomach at bay.

There wasn't a minute that she didn't think about Dmitri, a day where she felt like she would ever be normal again.

It had been a month of torture, as she started calling it.

Because while she had been crying herself to sleep every night, Dmitri, it seemed, was taking the media and the world by storm.

It had begun when she had heard that the huge charity event organized by Anya Ivanova, the model he had helped, had sported his custom-designed Bugatti bike.

The next week had been an expose about his yacht, which apparently was currently being bought by a Russian oil billionaire. And the most shocking thing of all was when a courier had arrived at her doorstep one evening, following a call from Dmitri's executive assistant, to pick up the diamond set he had gifted her and she had never worn.

Then came another lengthy phone call with his lawyer about setting up steps for her to pay off her debt to him. Something she had insisted on.

What was he doing? she wondered, going half-mad. Was he moving? Desperate to understand what he was up to, she spent countless hours trawling luxury real estate websites to see if he had put Giannis's beautiful estate also up for sale.

But not once had she heard anything from him, even indirectly through Leah, whom she saw regularly.

Had he decided that he had had an easy escape?

Then came her first client, a lifesaver in so many ways.

In the first week of the photo shoot as the new face of a small Italian shoe company, she had learned what a stressful, hardworking slog it was. Especially if it was something you fell into as an escape from throwing yourself at the man who didn't love you.

Her first shoot with the photographer, apparently a Spanish genius called Eduardo de Cervantes, had been the worst. Eduardo possessed no polish like Gaspard had, whatever monster he was in his personal life, kept losing his temper when she couldn't get a pose or expression right, and at the end of the longest three hours of her life, had called the whole shoot utterly useless and walked away, spewing curses in Spanish.

If she had been the type to burst into tears, that moment had been it. But somehow, or maybe because her heart felt as if it was already encased in ice, she had made it through it without turning into a puddle.

They had finally had a breakthrough on the third day when he had once again snarled at her about not having a sensuous bone in her body and she, smarting about the one thing she was good at, had grabbed his hand, marched him over to the next floor where she had heard they had been shooting a firemen-themed calendar, had then proceeded to show her particular talent with a pole.

It had been quite the glorious thing to see Eduardo's jaw hit his chest. And the transformation in his demeanor and her response to it had been thrilling. Suddenly, it was as if he knew what to say to her, how to tease her into a pose, how to make her pout, and she'd eased into the rapport they'd suddenly had going, put her trust in him.

She wasn't exactly an overnight sensation but still her success had given her a new kind of confidence.

After those first two weeks, November passed in a haze as her initial contract with the shoe company got extended to cover Europe and North American markets, and then a fashion magazine invited her to do their Christmas runway show.

She didn't miss the irony of the fact that, once again, it was her genes that had enabled her entry into the fashion world. Not that it was without hard work.

The money began to flow in. Not huge chunks, not enough to cover her humongous debt to Dmitri, but enough to give her a new insight into life, enough to make her appreciate life and all the exciting opportunities it held. Enough to tell her that her heart wasn't in modeling and that it was only a way to give herself a cushion, and that she didn't want to live this life he had given her back doing something she didn't absolutely, gloriously enjoy.

Which in turn brought her back to Dmitri and how much she enjoyed doing anything with him.

Somehow she had thought she would feel better once she was self-sufficient. Maybe even hoped that the magic of being in love with him would dim with distance and independence.

If so, she was apparently as foolish as Andrew.

Some days, all she could manage was to come home to the flat, wash her makeup and the day's shoot off herself, drink her smoothie and fall into bed. As if waiting to strike her at a weak moment, the grief and pain came then.

She thought of laughing, smiling Andrew who had loved her so much and yet given in to his weakness, of how she had made excuses for him because she had thought he had never had a break. She thought of her mother, who had had two loving, affectionate children, and yet had chosen to lose herself in drink.

But Dmitri, who had suffered so much worse, had not only made it, but had also looked out for them. It didn't matter that he'd had help in the form of Giannis and Stavros. It was he who had made something of himself, made himself more than the product of his father's abuse and violence.

So why couldn't she?

But you have already, an arrogant voice sounding quite like Dmitri said.

And it was as if the entire world remained the same chaotic, sometimes utterly soul-crushing, sometimes gorgeously life-giving mystery that it was, but it was how she looked at it, how she looked at herself that underwent a seismic shift.

Even through the darkest, coldest, most depressing night of her life in the past decade, she had never once accepted defeat, had never once surrendered herself to things beyond her control; she had never once let herself drown.

It would have been so easy to give in. She had had all the temptation. And with Dmitri, *God*, she'd had more than temptation.

But she had walked away. It had torn her in two but she had walked away, hadn't she? And she had kept on walking.

She had stared her weakness in the eye and not only emerged from it unscathed, but she had made something out of herself. She had stood without flinching in the face of a cruel, unfamiliar world that seemed to be even more mercurial than her mother's moods and stayed the course.

Despite the results to the contrary, why did she keep measuring herself by Andrew's and her mother's sins?

She was not them. She was Jasmine Douglas, former pole dancer, maybe model and something fiercer in the future.

She was stronger and she deserved any happiness she could get. And her happiness, oh, her very heart was with Dmitri. It would always be.

Everything changed as if floodgates had been opened.

She didn't care that he wanted her because he thought she needed protection, that he did it out of guilt.

So what if he wasn't willing to call it love? So what if he thought he was incapable of it?

He had protected her, cared for her, helped her emerge from her own shame; he had counted her worthy even before she had counted herself. If that wasn't love... Every second she was with Dmitri, she lived and loved more than she had the rest of her life.

She had never given up before, even when the odds had been stacked high against her. Not on her brother, not on her mother, and now, she wouldn't give up on the most important thing in her life—she wouldn't give up on Dmitri.

She would prove to him how much he already loved her, even if it took her the rest of her life.

CHAPTER THIRTEEN

ONCE SHE HAD made up her mind, Jasmine couldn't bear to wait another minute before she went to see Dmitri. Even worse was the fact that he was in the same city yet so far away from her.

It took her another week to finish her current photo shoot and find a free day, so close to Christmas. Another day then to drum up enough guts to ask Stavros, when she saw him, about Dmitri's whereabouts.

He was in London, Stavros had said pithily. When she had probed as to why, he had muttered, "Personal business." Jasmine had a feeling Stavros hadn't wanted to give out any information at all.

When she had asked him, tethering her desperation just by the skin of her teeth, when he would return, he had said today. When Leah had glared at him, he had added that he would return to his Athens flat because they had a superimportant deal he was finalizing to talk about.

Jasmine had barely held her curiosity in check, because she wanted to know what deal was so important two days before Christmas and what Dmitri's personal business was, because it was sure as hell not about her, and not with Leah or Stavros because they had both been in Athens the past week.

Acknowledging that nothing was going to make what she had to do easier, she showered that afternoon and dressed in black pencil jeans and a royal blue sleeveless silk shirt that highlighted her physique without hugging. She paired the blouse with a sleekly cut white jacket. Black pumps and her hair in a French braid and she was ready to go.

Wouldn't you have a better chance if you were dressed to attract his attention? a devilish voice inside whispered, but she shushed it.

She wanted them to talk rationally. She wanted to tell him everything she had thought of, and dressing demurely would help.

Dmitri's flat turned out to be a penthouse on a pedestrian street in the city center of Athens, only a short walk from an art gallery and a lively café where she had spent more than a few hours gathering courage and drinking far too much of the dark, thick Greek coffee.

Wired and anxious was not a good combination, her stomach decided, going on a downward dive while the lift took her to the seventh floor.

A landscaped atrium was across the entrance, revealing breathtaking views of the Acropolis and Lycabettus Hill on either side. Early-afternoon sunlight amplified the open plan.

Jasmine stood awestruck, taking in the warm appeal of the soaring ceilings and the refined wood finish. She walked through the atrium and noted that the penthouse expanded on either side, and ahead was a large heated pool overlooking the spectacular Athens skyline.

Hadn't Leah mentioned to her that Dmitri's flat was all chrome and steel and utterly soulless?

A small sitting area was by the side of the pool. Her heart hammering against her rib cage now that she was here, Jasmine stood by the pool, not wanting to check each room, and there seemed to be a lot, for him.

She was wondering if she should have called him first when she heard footsteps behind her. Each and every one of her senses tingled as if someone had sent a spark through her body.

Bracing herself, Jasmine turned.

Black sweatpants hanging low on his hips, his torso naked, there was Dmitri, standing only a foot away from her. Jet-black hair cut to enhance that narrow, angular face, olive skin gleaming like the finest velvet while beads of sweat clung to the ridges of muscle, he looked like he had done after he had made love to her that next morning.

He leaned against the wall, as if he was not at all surprised that she was here.

Jas fought to control her instantly volatile reaction—tingling skin, racing pulse, the sudden and insistent tug in her lower belly—and failed. Heat flashed over her as she realized he had blocked her path purposely. Behind her was the narrow stretch of pool and then the skyline of Athens, and before her Dmitri, looking at her as if he couldn't wait to devour her.

That brought on images of his dark head between her legs and the way he had devoured her, and she pressed her legs instinctively together, the denim rasping against her inner thighs, and then their eyes met and she knew he was remembering it, too, because there was such an intense hunger in his gaze...

Her breath rushed out of her in a shuddering exhale.

She might as well have walked in in her underwear for all the time she had spent carefully choosing her outfit.

"That would have been nice after the torture of the past few weeks," he said, pushing off the wall, and Jasmine realized she had said it out loud.

It was as if she was standing in a bubble of sensual haze and didn't have her usual faculties.

She wet her lips, searching for how to start what she wanted to say. "You've been busy the past few weeks," she finally managed to say.

"As have you, *pethi mou*" came the soft drawl.

"What's going on, Dmitri? Why so many changes?"

"I decided that I needed to remove all the empty, meaningless things I have filled my life with. All the things that I believed made it better. All the things that I used to hide from the truth." He ran his knuckles over her cheek as if he couldn't help himself.

"When Stavros told me you had asked about me…" He swallowed and looked away for a second. When he spoke again, his voice was almost steady. "Tell me, Jas, what are you doing here?"

"I'm traveling to New York for a shoot in January. And I didn't want to leave without… I came by to tell you that I want a compromise between us."

He was closer and the masculine scent of him drenched her pores. She inhaled a long breath as if she were a junkie getting her fix.

He was her drug, she realized. But unlike her mother's and brother's choice of poison, he made her stronger, bolder, more *her* than anything she had ever been.

His gaze lingered over her mouth. "What sort of compromise?"

Oh, how tempted she was to taste that mouth of his again… "I want to be with you. I want us to give our relationship a try. But you can't ask me to marry you again. Not like that. At least, not until we decide together that it is a step we want to take, until we decide it is what we want."

He flinched. She knew he did because she was standing so close, breathing in every nuance in his face. Slowly, he took a step back and studied her. "But you want this?"

Her heart racing again, she nodded. There was a bittersweet pang in her gut but she ignored it for now. One day, he would admit to her that he loved her. One day, she would prove to him that he was the most honorable man she had ever met.

She stepped forward, eating up the distance between them. Pressing her hands into his shoulders, she pulled herself up and kissed his mouth.

Those large hands of his snaked around her and slammed her against that chest. Powerful frame shuddering around her, he kissed her forehead. "I'm so sorry I hurt you with that arrogant proposal. I have become such a stranger to emotions or love that I didn't even realize what I was doing until you told me. You were right. You deserve so much more than I offered."

Hot liquid filled her eyes. Jas blinked, trying to keep the tears away. "Dmitri, are you listening? I'm not afraid anymore." She clasped his jaw, willing him to understand. "I won't break like I thought. Loving you makes me stronger, not weaker. All I want is to be with you."

"And if I do ask you to marry me again, not to protect you, but because I love you?"

"You're not playing another game with me, are you?"

"No, *pethi mou*. I've been counting the days, waiting to show you how much I need you… I thought I would show you that you've changed me already. Irrevocably."

"Wait, that's what you've been doing? Selling your bike and yacht?"

"For years, I filled myself with expensive toys that gave nothing but fleeting pleasure, with women who made me feel nothing but an echo. But with you… You have made me see that I never forgave myself. That I never thought myself worthy of anything meaningful, even though Giannis tried his hardest to tell me that it wasn't my fault that she had died."

Her chest aching for the boy he had been, Jasmine embraced him with everything she had. "It wasn't your fault, Dmitri. Just as it wasn't my duty to sacrifice my life over

Andrew's and my mother's mistakes. I want to live this life for me and I want to live it with you."

"I will wait as long as it takes. I will spend my entire life showing you that I love you." He kissed her so softly then tenderly, as if he was determined to fill all the lonely places inside her with his love. "I love you, *matia mou*. I love you so much that the world itself feels colorless without you.

"Marry me, Jas. Marry me because I want you to be mine eternally. Marry me because I need you. I need you to make me laugh, to make me feel, because I need you to love me every day for the rest of our lives."

Her heart overflowing, Jas buried her face in his chest. Fear still pulsed through her, but it was a soft echo rather than the raging growl it had been when she had come in. They would make this work; they loved each other too much for it to fail. "I love you, too, Dmitri. I want to wake up with you. I want you to help me figure out what the hell I'm going to do with my life. I want to grow old with you. I want to be a part of the family you have with Leah and Stavros. I want to spend forever with you."

"Then, you will," he said before crushing her mouth. "I promise, Jas. I will never treat you as if you were something to be protected. I will never shower you with gifts and riches instead of my heart."

"Your kisses, those are all I want," she moaned, air already an alien concept.

"Those you will have, in abundance, and in every imaginable place. Remember how you promised you would give me anything I wanted?"

Her reckless offer pulsed in the air around them, turning his eyes into a stormy sky.

"Would you dance for me one night? Just once, Jas," he said softly, but it didn't hide the guttural quality of his voice.

She braced herself, but instead of that usual wash of shame that had always flooded her, something else filled her.

Anticipation, joy, even a sense of power. Wrapping her arms around his nape, she pressed herself into his chest wantonly, reveling in the thunderstorm she could unleash in his eyes. "For the man I love? I would do anything, Dmitri."

With a smile that set her nerves on fire, Dmitri picked her up and walked over to the sitting area. And while Athens burned bright around them, he made love to her so tenderly, so softly that Jas fell in love all over again.

EPILOGUE

JASMINE WOKE UP with a huge smile on her face and then realized it was Christmas morning. Her first Christmas with Dmitri and a happy one after a long time, she thought, lazily soaking up the warmth of the Egyptian cotton sheets.

Her smile turned into a frown as she remembered her upcoming three-week trip to New York in January.

If truth be told, she had been more excited about seeing New York than her photo shoot. And now, even the attractions of the city that never slept paled in the face of not seeing Dmitri for so long.

Would Dmitri come to New York if she asked him?

Imagining all the ways she could try to convince him, she quickly showered in the en suite and dressed in a red-and-white sleeveless knee-length collared dress. She quickly braided her wet hair, applied some lip gloss and went in search of Dmitri.

The atrium gleamed in the morning sunlight, the sound of voices drawing her to the cozily contemporary kitchen.

There was no fire in the fireplace, but a four-foot Christmas tree, complete with ornaments and lights, stood near it.

Tears filled her eyes as Jas looked at it. She had spent so many Christmases trying to convince first her mother and then Andrew that they had more than most people in the world had—each other. But nothing had ever made a difference. Lost to their own weaknesses, she had never made a difference to them.

And after Andrew had been gone, she had been so lonely that even thinking of Christmas had been painful.

Strong arms encircled her from behind.

"Merry Christmas, *yineka mou*," he whispered, before turning her around and kissing her with a tender warmth that chased away some of the pain.

Wrapping her arms around his neck, Jas sank into his kiss. She nibbled at his lower lip, dueled with her tongue, poured every bit of herself into it.

And he returned everything, his hands roaming around her back, whispering promises of forever.

Holding her at arm's length, he stared at her for a long time and caught one of the tears that had escaped. "I'm so sorry about him, Jas. I wish I had saved him for you."

Jasmine shook her head, knowing that it was a habit that she had to cure Dmitri of slowly. That protective instinct was in his genes. "I wish he had saved himself, Dmitri. But no, I don't want to ruin Christmas morning with—"

"Merry Christmas, Jasmine," Leah said from behind her, a beaming smile on her lips.

Tears coming to her eyes again, this time happy ones, Jasmine returned Leah's fierce hug. And then Stavros's.

They all chattered at once and then Dmitri tugged her toward him. "Is it okay that I invited them over? I knew how happy they would be for us."

Jasmine kissed him again. She couldn't seem to stop. "Absolutely. Dmitri, I have a trip to—"

"New York, I know. If you agree, I will fly out the week after your shoot and we can see the city together. You will adore New York."

"I love you, Dmitri."

"I love you, Jas. Come, I have something for you."

While a smiling Stavros and a grinning Leah watched, he opened a small velvet box, went down on one knee and said, "Jasmine, will you marry me?"

Crying again, Jasmine nodded, absolutely incapable of speaking. Dmitri slipped the ring on her finger, a single princess-cut diamond on a plain white-gold band, his heart in his eyes.

Then he took her in his arms again and kissed her. "We'll take as long as we want, *ne*? I'm starting an inner-city program for young adults who come from broken homes and with a background of abuse and neglect. Stavros and I have already found an old building to renovate here in Athens and then we will start hiring staff.

"If, at some point in time," he stated matter-of-factly, "you have had enough of modeling and want to work on something like that, you would be more than welcome. I'm trying to cut down on my interests so that I can give it some time instead of just throwing money at it. Give a chance to someone like Giannis did for us."

Stunned into speechlessness, Jas could only stare at him.

"Jas, there is absolutely no pressure. If modeling is where your heart is, then that's what you should do. You have my support in any career you want to pursue and I will follow you around the world."

Her heart bursting to full, Jas finally spoke. "I would love to work on such a project. Dmitri, do you still have that license?"

Shock flaring in his gaze, he nodded slowly. "Jas—"

"I want to do it today, Dmitri. With Stavros and Leah as witnesses. I want to go to New York as your wife. I don't want to wait. Not when I love you so much."

When he still looked doubtful, she took his hands in hers and kissed the rough palms. "I have never wanted a big wedding or a white dress, Dmitri. I only wanted my knight. And you're it."

Dmitri lifted her off the floor in a bear hug that crushed her lungs. And then yelled the news at a stunned Leah and Stavros.

Their smiles and the way they instantly decided on their tasks made Jasmine as if like she had family again.

Breaking into supereffective mode, Leah called her assistant to have wedding gowns that she had ready delivered while Stavros made a few more arrangements.

That afternoon, they feasted on turkey, which had been ordered for her, honey-glazed ham for Leah and roast pork for Dmitri and Stavros with a variety of side delicacies. They ate delicious cinnamon-and-clove cookies drenched in honey and drank ouzo and coffee. And toasted to their new family.

When four o'clock came and a priest appeared, Jasmine felt as though she was floating on the clouds. The ivory gown Leah had chosen for her had a beaded bodice and wide skirt, and Jasmine thought it was the most beautiful she had ever looked.

Looking dashing in a black suit, Stavros walked her the little distance from her bedroom to the atrium which was filled with a golden glow.

And then there was Dmitri in a black tuxedo.

Drowning in the love that filled his gray gaze, Jasmine thought her heart would burst out of her chest. Reaching him, she smiled at him as the priest began the simple ceremony.

Jasmine was his wife. The thought repeated in his head in circles as Dmitri stood near the pool and stared at the Athens skyline. He turned the platinum band on his finger round and round, wondering if one could shatter out of joy.

Stavros joined him on silent feet and handed him a wine flute. Raising it, he said, "To Giannis."

Dmitri raised his flute and said, "To Giannis."

They remained silent, thanking the man who had made today's happiness possible in their lives.

* * * * *